Rise of the Dwarven Empire

I0658702

William
Zackery
VanderHorst

Book 2 of
The Guardians of Nalawren Series

Cover Art by Zackery VanderHorst

Published by

LAUREL
Mountain
PRESS

PO Box 1973, Clayton, Georgia
www.laurelbooks.com
email: myfantasyworldwide@gmail.com

Dedicated to:

My wife,
Kimberly Ann VanderHorst,
who gave me the
inspiration to start writing,
and to my children,
William Nathaniel VanderHorst
and
Benjamin Travis VanderHorst,
both of whom give me
the desire to keep creating
my worlds.

The Lands of Nalawren

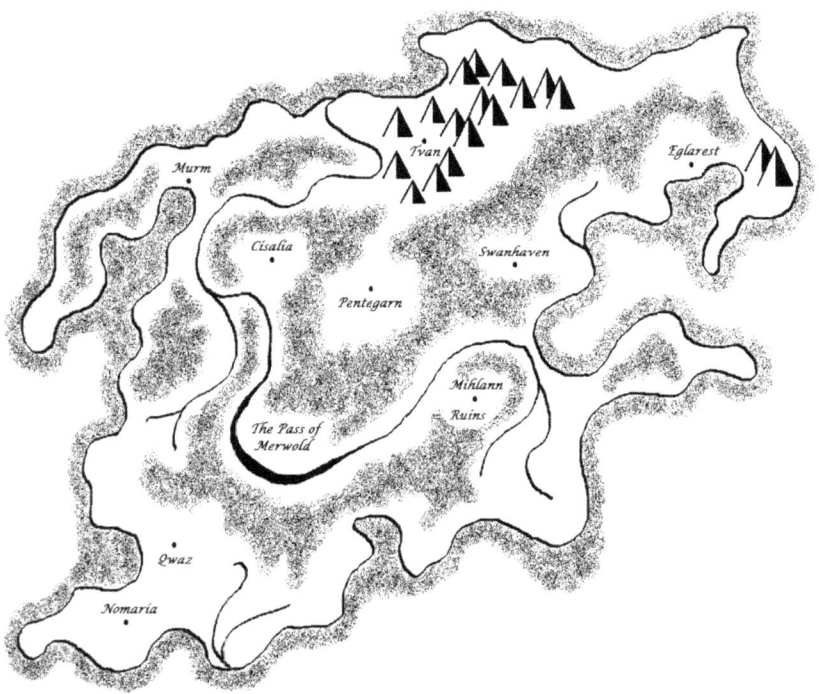

The Lands of Nalawren
Dwarven Kingdom

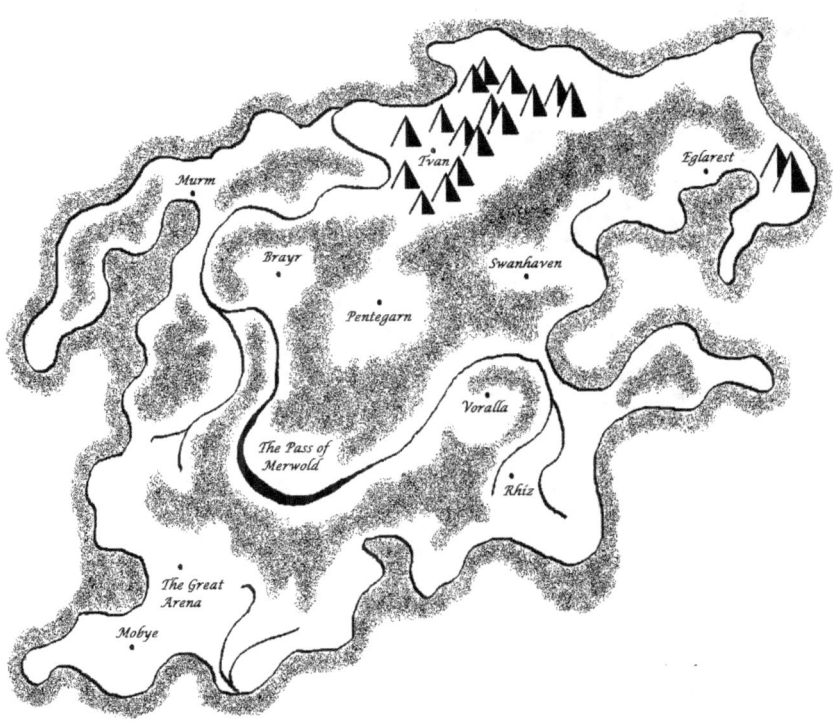

Murm

Tvan

Eglarest

Brayr

Swanhaven

Pentegarn

Voralla

The Pass of
Merwold

Rhiz

The Great
Arena

Mobye

The Rape of Nalawren

*T*he wars that had spread across Nalawren left the lands in disarray and the races that inhabited them struggling to pull their lives back together. The armies of Goblins had arrived on the southern shores and soon after ravaged the Human lands. The wars in the south destroyed not only the Human fortress, but forever scarred the lands around it. The forests that were once beautiful and lush were now twisted and gnarled, having no beauty at all. The lush fields that had covered the south were now cracked and dried wastelands without a sign of life to speak of. The wars had forced the Humans north to hide in the forests above the Elves, their people barely surviving as they worked to construct a new home that would be known as Cisalia.

With the Humans driven from their homes the Goblins and their armies had taken over Qwaz for themselves. The city darkened and soon it too looked as rough and fallen as the lands around it. While Cisalia was being built in the north, the leader of the southern armies began constructing his own fortress even further south. By pulling all of the minor races to him, Valsera managed to construct a city so vast and impenetrable that it soon became a beacon for the armies in the south known as Nomaria. Marching into battle knowing that the entirety of Nomaria was behind them was the boost they needed to continue to push north.

The southern forces moved north, breaking the Elves at the line that had long been the barrier between the north and the south in one massive battle. The Elves were pushed back over and over until they finally turned and retreated, giving the border to the Goblin armies. Instead of turning and chasing the Elven armies as would be expected, the Goblins turned to the east and laid siege to the fortress city of Mihlann, the heart of the border between the north and south. What had been thought to be a quick siege turned out to last days and days as the Goblins threw entire armies at the walls. Like the waves of the ocean the forces rose and fell on the stone walls. But the fortress stood.

Days later the first of the siege weapons appeared and the Elves of Mihlann felt a shockwave of fear. Massive stones and logs rained down on the city as the Elves strengthened their defenses with whatever they could find. But it was not to be as the gates cracked and the Goblins flooded in, raiding the city and burning it to the ground. No matter where the armies of Goblins and Ogres went, destruction was sure to follow. The wake they left behind them was completely void of life.

When the armies of the south began to move north again, they received an interesting surprise in the form of several thousand Elves and Gnomes massed at the Pass of Merwold, determined to hold the pass against the evils from the south. For the first time, the Goblins stopped their progress and waited, seeing the masses of well disciplined soldiers waiting to engage them in battle. A day or two passed, and still the armies waited. The Goblins and Ogres stood on the southern shores of the river and watched as an entire Human Knighthood arrived to reinforce the armies on the northern shores. The new soldiers were a threat, but it was apparent that the southen army was not intimidated in the least. If anything they were happy to see them, and soon it became apparent why.

Hours after the massive force of Human Knights arrived, a horrible attack took place. The Humans suddenly rode into the lines of Elves, cutting them down in the sudden wave of shock that the betrayal brought with it. The Humans worked across the northern beaches killing all that they could as the Goblins and Ogres rushed into the confusion to help the traitors from the north.

The massacre at the pass gave the armies of the south momentum. They became more brazen, believing their forces could sweep the northern lands in one massive push north. The armies spent the next day crossing the pass and filling the fields and forests between the Pass of Merwold and Pentegarn. With the black horde spreading across the fields and forests, the ravaging and rape of the lands pushed further and further north.

The city of Qwaz still smoldered from the massive battle that had battered the city all through the night. Plumes of smoke from the fires on the battlements and across the city filled the air. Goblins fought the fires all through the night and in the rays of the morning light they managed to extinguish the flames. But the damage was done. The entire southern wall was burned black and crumbling to the ground. The most damage to the city was centered on the top wall near the base of the towers. Charred and smoldering bodies covered the walls and the Goblins began moving around the fortress trying to manage repairs.

Bodies were tossed from the walls to the dead fields below and carted away to clear the battlements. With the defenses cleaned free of dead bodies the rest of the damages were realized. Anything wooden had been scorched to ash and even the stone had cracked in several places. The front gate was blackened from top to bottom, but it remained standing. From the air the city looked like a mound of ants scurrying to repair the damages to their mound. Despite the damage the city had received in the powerful attacks from the Dragons and their allies, it was in surprisingly good shape.

The attack had pressed the large army that still remained at the city to begin spreading through the surrounding lands, searching for those who had been shot from the sky. Hundreds of Goblins spread through the forests in search of any sign of the enemies that had brought war to them the night before, but none were successful in locating any of their attackers. On the far southeast edge of the forest a large patrol of Goblins was suddenly attacked and demolished by a party of Lizardmen set on revenge. The creatures came from the swamplands quickly, surrounding and slaughtering every last Goblin before dropping back into the fogs and marshes from which they came.

The assault the night before that had left the city in ruins was a pressing matter for Qwaz, but receiving word that the Lizardmen had decided to stand up and fight back was a completely new problem. Though their numbers were not great, the Lizardmen were strong and mysterious when faced on their own ground. It was apparent that if they were going to battle the reptiles, they would have to venture into the fogs of the swamps.

Infus stood just inside the doorway, looking at the frozen form of Valsera in the hardened crystal. The sorcerer did not move, his expression forever frozen. The Demon slowly approached the crystal prison and ran its clawed gauntlets across the cold stone. Drawing back, it slammed its fist on the crystal with all its might but the stone was secure. The Demon let out a low growl and walked past the crystal to the balcony where it had been bested the night before. To the left the Demon found its sword but as it searched across the entire balcony, the handle containing the magic whip was nowhere to be found. Infus stopped at the spot where the Dragon had landed, staring at the deep gashes in the marble floor where her talons had caught the stone.

The expressionless darkness behind the hood was void of emotion but anger was swelling within the creature. It balled its fist and turned to the north, knowing that the Elf it had battled now possessed its most powerful weapon. With the whip in his possession, the Elf would be immensely more powerful even if he did not know exactly how to use it. The Demon knew that in time the Elf would learn how to wield the weapon.

Infus walked back into the room and stood next to the remains of the throne, staring at the prisoner of the crystal that had once been the most feared leader in the southlands. Even though the Demon was arguably more powerful than Valsera, Infus was reluctant to take control of the armies. The door to the right opened and a mass of Slayers walked in, forming a semicircle around their master. Infus stared at each one and then returned the sword to the sheath inside its robes.

"We have lost more than a leader this night. The Elf has taken from me a weapon very unique, the most powerful weapon to surface in these lands. With it they pose a real threat," Infus told the Slayers angrily.

The soldiers did not move as the Demon walked in amongst them, staring at each one before moving on.

"Also, in the possession of one of their group is an item which shares a sort of life force with the prison holding our leader Valsera. I want it back. Together we will travel north in search of the Dragons and the one Elf with them who carries the weapon, and the key to freeing our master. Now go, prepare!"

The Slayers all turned at once, marching towards the door and filing out one at a time. Infus watched until the soldiers were gone, turning back to the block of crystal and then to the floor. The Demon cocked its head sideways as it noticed a piece of wood splintered at the edge of the crystal. It stooped and picked up the two pieces of the staff and looked at them. At the top of the second piece was another splintered piece. Infus suddenly realized that the top of the staff was missing. It was finally apparent that the key to freeing the sorcerer was hidden in the top of the staff. Infus turned and hurried to the door, knowing that if they could get their hands on the top of the staff, they could free the sorcerer and bring a hellish revenge to those responsible. And in the Demon's mind there was something else, another reason to find the head of the staff.

The Demon swooped down the stairs like a great black shadow, pushing Goblins out of its way as it walked. Infus crossed the open courtyard where charred bodies had been piled and walked out of the battered gate and into the open fields outside of the city. Infus stood in the open, staring to the north where its weapon and the head of the staff had fled. Suddenly the lands around the city, and every soldier inside of the fortress could hear a mighty scream of anger from the robed Demon.

Calyn sat on his horse and watched the thousands of soldiers crossing the river at the Pass of Merwold. The numbers of Goblins and Ogres filing across the river were more amazing than anything the Human King had ever seen. He had at one time despised the creatures that he now sided himself and his people with, but it was certain that the southern armies would wash across the Elven lands and take it for their own. His mass of Knights had formed behind him and though they followed the King, it was obvious that some of them were not happy about the turn of events.

The line of Goblins and Ogres stretched from the plains on the other side of the forest to the wastelands behind the southern forests. It would take more than the next day to move the entire army through the pass. The Elven bodies were piled high on the edge of the pass and left stripped of their weapons and armor.

The King rode out to the edge as a large soldier stepped out of the ranks and waited for Calyn to approach. The soldier was strange compared to the Goblins and the rest of the soldiers. Calyn reined his horse in next to the soldier who gave a short nod.

"Can I help you soldier?" the King asked, looking at the creature.

"I am in charge of this army, Human. If you are here to lead an army, lead your own."

Calyn urged the horse forward a bit and looked at the

creature. The Human felt a certain bit of resentment towards the ugly soldier, especially after slaughtering his own allies to help the southern armies to victory.

The creature brought its open palm up to the Human, showing a brand resembling the standard for Valsera's armies. Calyn leaned back a little, repulsed by the sight of the scarred hand.

"I am Uljic, and these armies are mine. Consider yourself lucky we do not put you and your traitorous kind in your place here and now."

"Oh you wouldn't want to do that my ugly friend."

The statement was a slap to the face of the creature but at the same time it was now intrigued as to why the Humans were of any value at all. It crossed its muscular arms and stared at the man with hollow eyes, waiting for an explanation. Calyn dropped from his horse to the ground and sized the odd creature up and then down. After a brief standoff between the two, the Human King nodded.

"A very interesting plan I have, and since you seem to think you deserve to know, I will humor you. The Elven army at Pentegarn under the rule of Elendil will not be broken by your mass of Ogres and Goblins. There is not a chance in the least that the city will fall. So instead, my Knights and I will return to Pentegarn with a tale of horrible slaughter that befell our forces here at the pass. With the King caught off guard, it will be easy to deal him a deadly blow. Then, the city will have less of a chance of withstanding your siege."

Uljic stood rigid, wondering whether or not to believe the Human.

"Why would I trust you when you betray your own people? What keeps you from doing it to us and what makes you think you can simply leave once you kill the King of the Elves in his own city?" Uljic asked with a gruff voice.

"Personally, I would rather cut off your filthy, insolent head than have to look at you another minute, but I do have a task to complete. Perhaps later I will teach you the respect that your kind is obviously lacking. As for escaping after my duty is done, I will do my best. If I do not make it out at least Elendill will no longer lead his armies."

"Sacrificing yourself for our cause are you?"

"I am not dead yet," Calyn noted sternly.

"Quite a pity, Human."

Uljic turned away from the Human King, rejoining his forces that continued to march north. The Goblins and Ogres in the ranks of the southern army stared down the Humans as they marched past, remembering a time when the King and his forces had been their enemies. Trusting them now was seemingly out of the question, but those in charge ordered the alliance to be made. It was an odd feeling as the Lizardmen that had once been allies were now enemies and the Humans that had been enemies were now standing beside the Goblins and Ogres.

The Knights watched the forces trudge by, marching in rhythm with their faces forward to the Elven lands they were set to invade. The southern armies would now have renewed resources to use for their armies. The further they pushed, the more they could take to fuel their army. Thick forests, fresh rivers, and plenty of food gave the army new life and energy. Soon the lands that were lush and beautiful would become barren and stripped like the wastelands around Qwaz and Nomaria.

The Human King turned his horse back to the Knights behind him and raised his hand for silence. "We will ride to Pentegarn ahead of the armies and do our duty to cripple the Elven defenses before the siege. We will not take our entire Knighthood, only between fifteen and twenty soldiers to show a heavier loss than we actually received. This has to be convincing. We only get one chance."

The Knights agreed in a loud chorus, their swords and spears raised into the air in unison. Calyn turned his Knights to the left and moved alongside the Goblin soldiers as the mass moved north. The Knights pushed ahead faster than the rest of the units as they moved towards their task. The betrayal at the Pass of Merwold was horrible and some of the Knights seemed to disapprove of the situation. Now they were to move on the largest of the Elven cities and somehow make an effort to kill one of the greatest rulers in the lands. The worst looking of the soldiers were the ones chosen to enter the city, the ones with wounds and damage to their armor. It had to be convincing.

The worst of the southern armies was moving onto the edge of the Elven lands, threatening to strip the beauty from it without the Elves even knowing it was coming. Elven scouts made trips through the southern forests on a regular basis but if discovered, they could never make it back to the city to alert the King.

The plan was to move in around the city in the forests, surrounding the city on three sides and revealing their positions all at once. The plan was to shock the Elves and catch them off guard after the King had been slain.

If the Elves had the slightest clue that the siege was coming they would be able to mass their armies and create a strong force. Even though the Elves were greatly outnumbered by almost four to one, the Goblins would be faced with an almost unbreakable wall. The mass of soldiers looked like a giant carpet spreading throughout the plains and forests, dotted with massive weapons for siege and destruction. Never before in the history of the wars of Nalawren had a force so massive marched across the lands. It was an army bred for a single purpose, to strip the lands of the northern races and enslave them for good.

With the masses of creatures marching like a shadow through the lands, even the weather seemed to fall into gloom. Storm clouds began to form on the horizon and the sky grew as dark as the shadows beneath the soldiers. Drops of rain began to fall onto the army and a soft rumble of thunder echoed in the distance. The army marched with their faces down, their duties very clear. They would bring the strongest of the nations crumbling to the ground and leave them smoldering in a pile of rumble. It would be the first of the cities to fall to the army, making it clear to the rest of the races. There was no escape.

Stranded South of Hell

The fog was thick in the lands south of Qwaz. Thorgrim ran his hand across his face, shaking mud from his armor. He leaned against a fallen tree, running his other hand across his belt and looking at the empty slots and loops. During the plummet after the Dragon had been struck from the air, the Dwarves had been pulled in against its chest. When they met the ground the two Dwarves were flung through the air. The weapons that had once lined his belt had been thrown in every direction. The only exception was his war hammer which he clutched to his chest. He left the tree and trudged through the muck of the swamp, looking continuously through the marshes for any sign of his weaponry.

Nimir stood next to the Dragon with a hand on its face. The beast was deathly still, having not taken a breath in quite some time. The younger Dwarf had been right beside the great beast the moment it had died and refused to leave its side still. He patted its head gently as if to calm it even though he knew there was no life left. Nimir dropped his head and sighed.

Thorgrim reached down into the mud, feeling around for anything that remotely felt like one of his weapons. After a few minutes he gave up and flung the mud from his arm in disgust. He slid the war hammer into his belt and turned around in the mud. He trudged toward Nimir and stopped a few feet short, looking down at where his feet were hidden in the mud. He reached down into the muck and wrapped his fingers around something firm. From the swamp he pulled the muck covered form of a dagger.

"One down," the Dwarf grunted, slinging the mud from his arm and the weapon in his hand.

"Is that all you care about… your lost weapons?" Nimir asked, looking the older Dwarf in the face.

"What am I supposed to do Nimir? I can't bring that Dragon back to life. I don't know where we are, I don't know how to get out of here, and I am not going to sit here and wait to be found. Get your head straight boy. No one is going to get us out of this so we'd best get moving."

Thorgrim ignored the fact that he only managed to find one weapon in the swamp, knowing they did not have the time to spend looking for the rest. They had to get as far away from where the Dragon had gone down as they could before creatures from Qwaz stumbled upon them. He stood with a hand on his belt as he watched the younger Dwarf give the body of the Dragon one last pat. Nimir checked the sword sheathed over his shoulder, making sure that it was still secure as he walked carefully through the swamp.

The two Dwarves looked back at the Dragon for one last moment before Thorgrim put a hand on Nimir's shoulder and turned him back in the direction he believed was east. A hike north would mean a greater chance of capture by the forces around Qwaz and the same thing would happen if they tried to move south. East would take them deeper into the swamplands inhabited by the elusive Lizardmen. The danger from an encounter with them was just as great as facing the rest of the southern forces. The two Dwarves walked side by side through the mud, their spirits dampened but their cause very clear. They had to keep moving or risk being captured by the enemy.

The further they walked, the denser the fog seemed to get and the thicker the swamps became. Solid ground was becoming less and less visible as they struggled to keep their footing. The trees were growing thinner and shorter as they had less ground to support them. Nimir reached out and grabbed the gnarled tree next to him as the mud caused him to slip and almost fall face first into the swamp. Thorgrim watched and then continued on once the younger Dwarf had managed to get his footing.

Nimir looked down at the stagnant water around him and ran a hand through his hair. "This just is not right."

"What is it?" Thorgrim asked without turning around to face the Dwarf.

"Being this thirsty when none of the water is drinkable... how is that fair?"

"The world is never fair Nimir. We just have to keep

moving. Maybe we will find water somewhere else."

Nimir stared at the swamplands around him and shook his head sourly. "How can those Lizardmen live like this? There is nothing here to survive off of. No food, no water, nothing…"

"Nimir, part of getting out of this mess would be keeping quiet while we hike through these enemy lands. The louder your voice… the more likely they will hear you. Shut it!" Thorgrim growled, his hand resting on the top of the war hammer.

Thorgrim moved further through the fog and marsh with Nimir only half heartedly keeping up. The marshes grew thicker but from time to time there were sections of solid ground and the water was clearer. They looked through the fog, finding it thinning slightly as they continued further east. An hour of walking did little to get them clear of the dangers they were facing but it was successfully leaving them exhausted. Thorgrim knocked mud from his pants and boots as he leaned against the tree at the edge of the marsh.

They looked through the marsh slowly, wondering if the creatures in the swamps were all around them without them even knowing it. Thorgrim kept his head up, staring into the fog and wondering the exact same thing as the younger Dwarf. If they were being followed, if the enemies knew they were there, nothing would protect them now. They were on their own.

The Dragon dropped low above the swamplands, its wingtips cutting through the fog as the pair kept their eyes peeled for any sign of the fallen Dragon and the two Dwarves. The sun did little to penetrate the fog but they did not give up. Ectle held onto the Dragon as it made a strong left bank and cut further across the lands to the north. They had no idea where the Dragon carrying the Dwarves had fallen but he was determined to find them. The wizard cut through the sky back and forth, keeping a keen eye on the area below them as they continued flying. The Dragon made another bank and flew back south.

Ectle reached up and patted the Dragon on the side of the neck as it dropped lower towards the fog. The Dragon turned its head and looked back at the wizard.

"You do not have to keep flying. As soon as there is a clearing you can drop me and go back north. I will be fine."

The Dragon nodded, flapping its wings and taking a higher vantage point as they scanned back and forth. Ectle looked down into the swamps and suddenly pointed to the west a little, seeing a small area where the fog was not as thick. The trees were sparse and as the Dragon dropped lower, the fog was pushed back. Ectle held tight as the Dragon finally made it to the ground and lowered its wings. The pair scanned around for any sign of enemies.

Ectle dropped to the ground and lowered his staff, muttering softly and slowly bringing on a steady wind from behind him. The wind pushed the fog back away from the two and the wizard raised the staff, looking at the much clearer area around them. The swamp stretched in every direction as far as they could see but still there was no sign of either Dwarves or the fallen Dragon. The wizard turned and faced his companion.

"By all means, if you want to leave you have my permission. You do not have to be here, this is not your fight."

"How will you escape if you find them?" the Dragon asked, cocking its head to the side.

Ectle looked to the ground and pondered the question. "I do not know…"

The Dragon turned and looked back through the swamp. The area made the beast very uneasy and Ectle knew it. He reached out and touched it on the side and the Dragon turned and faced him.

"Go… there is nothing left for you to do here. All I asked was that you bring me here and you have done that. I will be fine."

The Dragon waited for the wizard to step back and then leapt into the air, beating its wings fiercely as it slowly rose higher, disappearing into the clouds. Ectle gripped his staff with both hands and took the first step into the swamp. He watched as the fog slowly crept back towards him. He walked slowly, step by step through the swamp looking around in every direction. The further he walked, the harder it was to find solid ground. He used his staff for support as he trudged through the marsh, his robes dragging in the mud. He looked down at the bottom of his robe and sighed, seeing the dark mud stains all across his clothing.

A soft rain slowly began to fall and combined with the fog and mud, the wizard felt a very cold chill run up his body. It was almost like torture trudging through the swamps, fighting the sinking marshes and the falling rain. He pulled the hood of his cloak over his head and huddled over a little, fighting the rain as it grew stronger. He found a clump of trees ahead and stomped up to them, taking shelter from the rain. It only took a few minutes for the rain to blow over and stop and the fog took back its hold on the swamp.

He tossed the hood back off of his head and ran his fingers across the top of the staff, creating a beam of light that stretched twenty feet through the fog. The beam cut the fog away and gave him a better chance of finding the lost Dwarves. He took one deep breath and lowered the head of the staff in front of him. The fog seemed to fall back away from the beam of light, giving the wizard a clear view in front of him. The next step he took saw the mud sink all the way up past his knee and he spent the next few minutes fighting the muck to pull free. There was a terrible feeling inside of him that even if the Dwarves had not been found by the enemy they could still be lost forever in the swamps, swallowed up by the depths of the mud.

Ectle pushed forward a little harder as the thought of losing them to the swamps was out of the question. He had come back to save them and that was exactly what he planned on doing. He kicked his legs to free his clothes of the thick mud and continued on, determined to find them.

The two Dwarves followed the clearer water through the swamp, finding with it came ground that was much firmer and the vegetation was beginning to return to the land. Thorgrim walked in front, keeping his eyes set on the fog as it had begun to thin somewhat but continued to hinder their vision. The rain had stopped but the humidity had become almost unbearable. Sweat poured down Thorgrim's face and collected in his beard. He wiped his brow and shook his head angrily as the two pushed on. The thought of getting clear of the swamps and into the lush forests that awaited them was what kept the two going. A sudden commotion up ahead caught their attention.

The sounds of battle filled the foggy air, the clash of swords and the cries of pain and fury. Thorgrim and Nimir drew their weapons and stopped, straining their ears to hear what was happening ahead of them. They crept through the scraggly trees and fog, getting closer to the sounds of battle. Stopping behind a fallen tree they peered through the fog as the wind finally cleared it enough to make out some of the scene.

Nothing was clear in front of them but they were able to vaguely make out shapes battling back and forth. From the fog came a body, thrown backwards toward them and they ducked as the body struck the other side of the downed tree. Thorgrim peeked over the edge of the tree, seeing the dead form of a Goblin crumpled on the ground. It had a horrible gash from the top of its head to the middle of its chest and the sight pushed the Dwarf back down.

Confused, he turned to Nimir and whispered. "Goblins."

"Who are they fighting?" Nimir asked, his voice shaky as he dared to peek over the edge of the tree.

"I don't know."

The two looked and their blood turned cold as they found themselves staring at a large Lizardman. It looked towards them and the Dwarves ducked back down, hoping they had not been seen. Thorgrim gripped the war hammer with both hands and held his breath, praying the creature would turn and leave. They heard the large beast approach and stop only feet from the tree. Nimir turned to his right and looked through the limbs at the monstrous creature as it bent and picked up the body of the Goblin. It looked at the Goblin body and then flung it across the swamp, turning and moving back into the fog where the battle was beginning to quiet down.

One last scream pierced the fog and then everything was silent. They could hear the heavy footsteps of the Lizardmen on the ground and through the mud and they pressed their backs against the tree, praying they would not be seen. Footsteps grew louder and the two waited. After several grueling minutes the Lizardmen dispersed into the fog and everything became silent again. Thorgrim slowly stood and took a step over the tree with Nimir timidly following him. He drew his sword from over his shoulder and though it gave him a small form of bravery, he still feared what was hiding in the fog. The pair took their steps slowly, their ears stabbing at the fog for any sign of the enemy.

Thorgrim stepped into the clearing and found bodies all around his feet. The Goblins were all killed in the battle but there was not a single body of a Lizardman to be seen. All together they counted a total of fifteen Goblins killed in the skirmish and the mud around them was now dark red from the blood. Nimir turned his sword around and poked at several of the bodies, finding them all void of life.

"Lizardmen did this... why?"

"I... uh... have no idea. Maybe it was a mistake with the fog and all."

Nimir heard a noise behind him and turned, lowered the blade of his sword, aiming into the fog where the noises had come from. Thorgrim looked over his shoulder and followed the younger Dwarf's gaze. "What is it?"

"I heard something."

Thorgrim turned too and raised his war hammer, following the gaze of Nimir until a form appeared low in the fog. They watched as a Goblin appeared, crawling towards them slowly. It stopped and collapsed on the ground at their feet, blood flowing freely from a deep gash across the neck. Nimir reached out and pushed the body with his foot, finding that it was dead.

The two Dwarves looked at one another and then around them, wondering what direction was the safest to retreat away from the carnage. They took a step back in the direction they came and turned. As soon as they turned they stopped in their tracks, finding a mass of Lizardmen standing in the fog. The Lizardmen were silent, their long spears pointed down at the two Dwarves. Thorgrim drew the war hammer back and as he did, the mass of creatures took a fast step forward, the spears inches from the two.

"Put it down," Nimir whispered as he dropped his sword, staring at the head of the spear closest to his face.

Thorgrim slowly lowered the weapon as one of the Lizardmen reached out and ripped it from his grasp. They took a step back but from the scene behind them came more of the elusive creatures, their weapons ready as they surrounded the two Dwarves. Nimir and Thorgrim looked around at the enemy that had moved in around them silently. At the points of the spears the Dwarves were marched away from the area where the Goblins had been slain.

The rain returned to the swamps, driving the fog back and revealing more of the marshlands. Rain was common in the southern swamps, making it very tricky to navigate the marshes and even harder to find solid ground. The thickest parts of the swamps were isolated in the immediate south but they extended north, moving in with the more forested areas. Most of the northern races had never ventured into the swamps as the Lizardmen had established their hold in the southern marshes.

The rain did not stop for hours, soaking everything in the fog until nothing could possibly remain dry, Thorgrim and Nimir walked with their heads down, exhausted and disheartened from the capture. The Lizardmen led them out of the thickest part of the swamps and further east where the land was less marshy. Thorgrim looked up as he found himself now on firmer ground and the fog disappearing. In front of them was a group of Lizardmen and the same behind them. Up ahead the gnarled trees parted and in a large clearing they found another mass of the reptilian creatures. Their numbers were far greater than Thorgrim had expected.

The creatures leading them moved away and the Dwarves now stood in front of a massive line of Lizardmen. The two stared at the mass of creatures with a mix of confusion and fear. The two Lizardmen tossed the weapons they had taken from the Dwarves to the ground, almost tempting the two to try and fight back. Wisely, the two Dwarves did not move from where they were standing. One of the Lizardmen approached, staring down at the weapons on the ground.

It was different from the rest of the Lizardmen in the clearing. It looked older, worn from time and battle with scars on its face and chest. It walked leaning on a tall staff with bones tied along the head. Instead of the leather and sections of chain armor that the other creatures wore, this one was dressed with bones as a form of armor. It stretched its long neck out and stared at the two Dwarves.

"Thorgrim… is there a plan?"

The Lizardman cocked its head to the side and its mouth parted, an evil sounding hiss cutting through the air. "Plansss… no plansss."

Both Dwarves looked at the creature, shocked to hear it speak so clearly to them. They had thought it a barbaric creature of no intelligence. Thorgrim glanced down at the weapons at his feet and then quickly back up to the creature standing before them.

"You... can talk?" Nimir asked quietly, immediately hoping what he had said had not insulted the creature.

The creature turned its head to the younger Dwarf and stared deeply at him. "Yesss... why wouldn't I?"

"Uh... I don't know."

"You think we are... animalsss?"

"No... animals can be useful. You and your kind are slime," Thorgrim noted bravely, staring at the creature angrily.

The creature took a quick step towards the Dwarf and stood with its face only inches from Thorgrim's. He could smell its foul breath and leaned back a little, trying not to show any fear. The creature's small eyes darted across his face, looking him over completely before finally taking a step back.

For the first time during the whole ordeal, Thorgrim noticed the crude huts and defenses around the clearing. This was more than just an army of Lizardmen, this was their entire encampment. The more he looked around the area, the more the Dwarf saw. Dozens and dozens of huts and buildings, crude yet very impressive. The fog had cleared back away from the encampment and more was there to be seen. Dozens of Lizardmen appeared from the forest at the back of the clearing. If the situation had been different, the sight might have been impressive. The two Dwarves were grabbed from behind and pulled to a pair of large posts in the center of the encampment where the head Lizardman now stood waiting. Rope was brought and they were each tied to a post, their weapons and gear stripped from them and tossed into a pile at the side of the posts.

Thorgrim struggled briefly but it was futile. Escaping would only mean finding themselves fighting against the entire encampment, greatly outnumbered and overpowered. The elder Lizardman approached slowly, staring at the two Dwarves for a long time before anyone spoke.

"What are you going to gain by keeping us here?" Nimir asked, feeling the ropes tight around his chest.

"We... are going to learn all we can. Now... why are you here?"

Thorgrim looked away and ignored the question even though it was directed to Nimir. The younger Dwarf looked at the creature and then to the right, wondering whether or not their predicament should be revealed to the creatures. The Lizardman stretched its head to the right further and stared at the Dwarf in the eyes again. Nimir sighed briefly.

"We're stuck here... and not by choice."

The creature leaned back a little, looking at the Dwarf to the left and then to the right, its eyes scanning them each very slowly. At first it struggled to decided whether or not there was truth in the Dwarf's words. The other Lizardmen in the area seemed to lose interest with the Dwarves and moved back into the swamps and the surrounding crude buildings. The old creature reached out and clenched the Dwarf by the chin with its clawed fingers.

It looked up as a pair of smaller creatures approached and gave a long nod.

"Yesss?"

"Goblinsss... in the north swamp."

The three exchanged silent glances and the head Lizardman waved its clawed hand to the north. "Kill them all."

Nimir and Thorgrim looked at one another and then back at the Lizardman. It had turned to leave when Thorgrim spoke openly for the first time.

"Why? Why did you kill your allies?"

The creature stopped and turned its head back to the two, pondering the question. More than just the thought, it wondered why the Dwarf even cared. After several minutes of standing completely still and looking at the two, the Lizardman turned and approached once more.

"They are our enemiesss... not our alliesss."

"You fought alongside them for years, since when have you become enemies?"

"They killed my kind... we follow them no more."

With those last words the creature disappeared back through the trees, leaving the two Dwarves tied in the clearing. The rest of the Lizardmen darted around, preparing to move north against the Goblins. The last skirmish in the fog had left an entire clan dead in the swamp. The Lizardmen had the terrain and their thirst for revenge on their side, and it would be more than enough to defeat the Goblins once more.

Nimir and Thorgrim looked at one another, wondering what was going to take place in the swamps around them. Being tied to a stake with no way of defending themselves was a nightmare that they could not shake. Now, that nightmare was a reality. The rain came and went as the creatures scurried around the camp, preparing to move back out into the swamps where the Goblins were rumored to be seen. The elder approached the two Dwarves once more, looking from one to the other. Its eyes pierced through them, prodding them for information. It didn't speak and turned after a few minutes, disappearing into one of the huts. Thorgrim and Nimir exchanged a glance, neither sure what to expect next.

A Twisted Tale of Woe

The storm clouds were visible to the south from the walls of Pentegarn but the lands around the Elves remained clear and sunny. A soft breeze kissed the tall grass in the fields outside of the city, making them dance like the waves in the ocean. Soldiers maintained regular patrols around the city and throughout the lands day and night. The gates were wide open as traders and carts of goods rolled in and out of the city, continuing the day to day life that the Elves had grown accustomed to.

The southern tower holding several Elven archers was alert when a small group on horseback appeared at the most distant edge of the field. The Elves caught sight of them instantly, picking them out amongst the waves of grass and the sway of the trees behind them. The first of the Elves pointed them out to the rest and the news spread across the walls. It only took minutes for the news of riders approaching to spread all the way to the inner keep where Elendil sat upon his throne.

"Ten riders coming from the south my Lord," the archer pointed out as the King arrived.

"It looks like… yes, the standard is Cisalia. Humans returning from the Pass of Merwold. News at last," Elendil said hopefully, taking the stairs down to the inner courtyard.

He walked to the gate and watched as the group drew closer to the city. The archers on the walls kept their eyes narrowed on the group as they finally reached the gates of the city and stopped in front of the King. Elendil stared at them as the rider in the front slowly dismounted and pulled his helmet from his head. Elendil crossed his arms and stared at the Human, confused as to why the man was arriving at Pentegarn. Elendil took a step forward, noticing a section of the King's armor stained with dried blood. The soldiers behind Calyn also appeared to have sustained wounds from an apparent battle.

"What happened to you and your soldiers?" Elendil asked, looking at the Humans one at a time.

"We need to speak with you Elendil, there is no time to waste. We should go inside while we can."

Elendil looked at the King and lowered his brow, uncertain if he had heard Calyn correctly. He stared at the Humans and then nodded, watching as the rest of the soldiers dismounted and joined their King. The Elven soldiers joined their King and the group walked back to the keep, the Humans following close behind. They crossed into the second courtyard in front of the castle and then finally into the fortress. The walk seemed to take forever for the Humans, taking each bend in the hall and stairway with a nervous breath. They came to a stop in front of the large throne room doors and waited as the Elves pushed them open.

Elendil led the group inside, offering them chairs around the table and taking a seat on his throne. He slowly took his seat and stared out at the Humans. Calyn stood and walked to the end of the table where he leaned against it, staring back at the Elf. Elendil took a deep breath and nodded to the Human.

"What has happened to you and your soldiers Calyn?"

The Human tapped the hilt of his sword and looked at his soldiers behind him. "Elendil, it is over…"

"What are you talking about?"

"The Pass of Merwold… it fell. The forces that we faced were too strong for our combined armies. They are flooding across the river as we speak, probably all throughout the forests to the south. I am sorry, there was nothing we could do."

"Nothing… really? How is it that your forces are all that remain? Why is it that the Elves I sent to the pass are nowhere to be seen yet you and your forces managed to survive? How is that?"

Calyn shifted to the side as the Elf flooded him with questions. He looked down and then back up at the Elf. "The attack swarmed across the river but also it came from the side. A force flanked us from the east and overtook most of the formations. The ones that were left retreated back away from the pass but when we saw forces pursuing us, the Elves combined with many of my own turned and fought to give us a chance to escape."

The story sounded honorable and it was something that

the Elves would do to ensure the King escaped with his life. Elendil swelled with pride inside at the thought of his soldiers giving their lives to allow the Human King a chance to escape. He knew that the forces lost at the pass were great, but at the same time, the thought was pressed from his mind. All Elendil could focus on was Calyn standing before him.

"Are you wounded Calyn?" the Elf asked, pointing to the armor where the blood stained the metal.

"No... I am fine, it is not my blood. Might I ask what your plan of action would be in dealing with the incoming threat. Obviously with the pace the enemy is setting, there will be very little time before the southern armies arrive."

Elendil looked up to the Elves in the room and raised his hand, catching their attention and drawing them closer. The Elves stepped in around the Humans and waited as Elendil pondered his orders.

"See that the guard on the wall is doubled and bring all food and provisions inside. If the army is as close as Calyn fears, there will be no time to flee the city. They will surely catch us off guard if we try. Have all available soldiers and reserves brought up and armed at once."

"Yes my King, at once."

The Elves turned and left the room and Calyn took a seat at the end of the table away from his soldiers. He seemed misplaced, as if only his body was in the room while his thoughts were clearly elsewhere. Calyn looked around the room and found that other than the King a mere four Elves remained. His plan was starting to take shape. Having the Elves leave was the worst possible mistake that Elendil could have made. The only thing against him now, was time.

"What is wrong Calyn?" the Elf King asked, staring at the man.

The Elf's words snapped the Human back to reality, catching him off guard for just a moment. "What? Oh, nothing Elendil... I was pondering what will happen once the armies reach these lands."

"Were you... I can assure you that this city will not fall to their horde. We are well supplied for a siege lasting as long as months, and prepared with a surplus of soldiers willing to give their lives to protect their home."

Elendil looked again at the dried blood on the Human's chest and then up to his face, his eyes slanted oddly as he rolled over the thoughts in his head. Calyn looked down and then to the King.

"What is it Elendil?"

"You were not wounded... yet you have blood on you from the battle. Who's was it?"

"I have no idea. It was hectic in the fray of battle. There is no telling."

"How about this, do you even know what race you bled in the battle? Perhaps you were simply stabbing at anyone and anything that moved. That would make more sense to me."

Calyn gave a hollow stare and pursed his lips. "What are you talking about Elendil?"

"Let me explain. The blood on your armor is obviously not yours which would mean if your story were true, it should belong to one who you killed in battle. However, it is clear that the blood is not that of a Goblin and not even that of an Ogre. Their blood is almost black, much darker than that dried on your armor Calyn. That means you've killed either an Elf, a Gnome, or a fellow Human."

The Human stared at Elendil, disbelief washing over his face. He didn't have time to think about what he was supposed to do. All he could do was stand with his eyes fixed on the Elf as Elendil continued.

"That makes sense as to why it was so easy for you to escape. When everyone is dead, there is no one to stop you from riding here to tell me the battle at the pass was lost. If I am wrong, by all means, correct me."

"Wh... where are you getting such awful information Elendil? What makes you think something like that would ever have happened?" Calyn asked.

Elendil nodded as the corners of his lips turned up in a very slight smile. He raised his head to the Elves who remained in the room. To their right the door opened and a large group of Elven soldiers entered. They spread out behind the Humans and in the middle of the group of Elves was a Gnome. He stood, fearful of the sight of the Humans but he had done what he had set out to do.

"Wha... what are you thinking El... Elendil?" Calyn

stammered.

"For someone who proclaims his innocence so loudly, why do you reach for your weapon? Seems like you are quite surprised to see a Gnome here Calyn, why is that?"

Calyn did not answer.

"Do you remember when I told you to choose a side, to make a choice? Today I see the choice you have made and now I will punish you for that."

The Humans at the table pushed the chairs back and drew their weapons along with their King, but found themselves surrounded. Calyn's plan never even had a chance to begin with. The Human King drew his sword and faced Elendil. The loyalties of his alliance melted away and he was shown for what he truly was, a traitor. Elendil followed the move and drew his own sword, prepared to face the Human.

To the right on the balcony Elven archers appeared, their bows drawn and arrows sighted in on each of the Humans. The Human caught sight of the archers, the tips of an arrow trained on his head. Calyn grit his teeth and slowly lowered his sword, not breaking his stare with the Elf. There was nothing the Human could do.

Behind the King the Human soldiers suddenly broke away from the table, their intentions to keep the Elven soldiers at bay long enough for Calyn to strike down the King. Calyn looked at his sword and then to Elendil, afraid to move from the spot now that the truth was out. Archers sighted the Humans in and loosed their volley into the group from the side, bringing them to the floor. Calyn looked over his shoulder as the last of his Humans collapsed, and his heart sank. The tip of his sword slowly dropped, meeting the stone floor silently. He could see the tip of an arrow only feet away out of the corner of his eye and with one last sigh Calyn dropped the sword.

The metal of the sword struck the stone and Elendil took a step down, lifting the tip of his sword up under Calyn's chin. The cold metal stopped before it could penetrate his skin and the Human held his breath, waiting for the strike that would end his life. The thrust did not come, but instead he felt hands grab him from behind and he was pulled from the room.

"Are you alright my Lord?" one Elf asked, sheathing his sword.

"Yes, I am fine. Dispose of the bodies and prepare the defenses at once. Double the wall guard and bring all provisions inside the walls. With the betrayal at the pass the southern armies will have been moving north this entire time. I need scouts sent out at once."

"At once my Lord!" the soldier replied, leaving as the rest of the soldiers worked to remove the fallen Humans from the floor.

Elendil saw the Gnome standing off to the side looking at the damage caused and approached him, sheathing his sword in the process. The Gnome looked to the side at the King and immediately dropped to the floor on his knees before him.

"Please, stand up. I owe you everything. What is your name?"

"Thank you good King, my name is Lenn. I only wanted to keep them from doing here what they did at the Pass of Merwold."

"You have done just that my friend. I take it the pass was a complete loss. There is no chance anyone other than yourself has survived?"

"I do not know. I left the moment the Human killed the Elf commander. The battle I left behind was so intense that I doubt anyone else made it out alive. I could hear it as I ran. I suppose it is possible that someone could have escaped the fray."

Elendil reached low and patted the Gnome on the shoulder, thankful to have received the information that the Gnome had revealed. Amazingly, the Gnome on foot had made it to the city ahead of the Humans on horseback. The news had appeared impossible when Elendil first heard it but acting on it had saved his own life. Somewhere inside he felt that he always knew the Humans would not stay true to the alliance.

"You have a room Lenn and you are free to stay as long as you wish. You are my guest. If you will excuse me, I am going to find where they have taken the Human King."

Elendil left the Gnome in the throne room and traversed the halls slowly, still reeling from the events that had just unfolded in his own city. He shook his head to himself as the list of allies was growing shorter. The Gnomes had been eradicated and the Humans were now enemies. The Wood Elves were still an ally, but as they had fallen back to the northern fortress, they could not reinforce the High Elves in their time of need. He turned to the left and followed the small hallway down into the belly of the fortress where the dungeon was located.

Guards at the door pushed it open the moment they saw the King approaching, saluting as Elendil moved past. He entered and right away he noticed a mass of soldiers in the dungeon with the remaining Humans. Out of the fray, two of the Human soldiers survived along with the King and now they had been chained and confined in their own cells.

"As you were. You soldiers return to your posts and alert me the moment anyone or anything comes into view of the wall."

The bulk of the Elven soldiers left the dungeon and returned to the walls and towers from which they had been pulled. The King noted the few soldiers remaining and moved past, staring into the sunken face of Calyn.

"How were you planning to escape Calyn? I mean, I know you came to kill me, but what were you going to do afterwards? Give your life for the Goblins? I just do not understand why. If I had not sheltered you and your people in the Chaos Wars there would be nothing of your race left."

"I don't know…"

"You don't know? So that is it? You betray us and all you can say is you don't know?"

Calyn stared at the floor, his arms stretched above him by the chains. The plan had rolled through his head over and over. He was supposed to strike down the Elven King before he died, but now his plan was worthless.

Elendil turned and left the dungeon. He was on the edge of rage but kept walking, staring straight ahead. It would only be a matter of time before he let the anger swelling inside him explode. At the moment, all he could think about was getting away from Calyn before he took out a measure of revenge on his own. He walked out into the sun and stared up at the clouds. Rays of sunlight pierced them and created funnels of light that stretched down to the land below. It was an amazing sight.

Archers on the walls above covered the battlements, each staring out at the fields and forests. Rumors had passed through the forces in Pentegarn of a massive army moving towards them. An army that had yet to be stopped.

Two days had passed since the attempted betrayal in the throne room. Elendil maintained his distance from the dungeon, the urge to strike the Humans down still flowing through him. Though the army was on high alert, there was still no sign of the enemy forces claimed to have been marching north. It was an uneasy thought, knowing a massive army was coming but having no idea where it actually was. Restlessness began to show in the Elves of Pentegarn and though he stood by his decision, Elendil wondered if he should have moved north to avoid the siege.

Elendil paced slowly on the inner wall, watching as the soldiers below continued patrols on a regular basis. The Elven army looked a lot like ants as they moved along the walls and through the city in every direction. The King leaned against the stone defenses, wondering what it was going to take to break the army rumored to be closing in on them. The sun had traveled across the sky and was just beginning to start back down from its highest point.

It was after midday when the King made his way through the city and out onto the outer walls. Soldiers passed, saluting as they moved through their routine. He stopped near the outer gate and slowly walked up the wide stairs that led to the battlements above. His steps were slow and methodical, showing no emotion to the world around him as he continued up to the top of the wall. Even with everything happening in the lands around him, Elendil was in a different world. The King arrived on the outer battlements and was greeted by each of the passing patrols. He ignored them.

The air was beginning to grow colder with each passing day and for some reason it was especially cold that day. The Elf noticed his breath in the air and looked down to the fields that stretched out to the forest. He squeezed his hands together tightly and watched the seemingly endless blades of grass in the field dance with the wind. That was until a disturbance caught his attention.

The guards pointed and shouted, the alarm in their voices was troublesome. Some turned in fear while others crowded closer to see if what they had heard was true. Elendil was ripped from his state of mental solitude as the shouts reached his ears. Out of it all he understood only one word, *Dragons*.

Elendil turned to the southeast and as the rest of the soldiers had claimed, he witnessed the spectacle for himself. In the air above the forests he spotted a large, winged beast headed towards the city with several smaller following close behind. His heart was pounding as he turned and ran down the stairs to the courtyard below. He was not sure what was driving him at the moment, fear or amazement, but whatever it was he kept moving until he was standing at the gate. As Elendil watched, the monstrous Dragon began to drop lower, circling back across the field as it prepared to land.

The Accused and the Vengeful

Elendil stared at the creature as the Blue Dragon dropped into the tall grass, its eyes tracing up the city walls with interest. Behind it came smaller creatures that landed in the rear. The Elves on the walls had their bows fitted with arrows, not sure whether to fear the beast or welcome it. The King took a step out of the city and then another, watching a figure drop from the Dragon and stop next to it, looking up.

"Erzel... are you sure this will not end similar to the last stop?" Alora asked, recounting the events that had taken place at Eglarest.

"This is my city Alora. I led these armies for countless years and they will remain loyal to me. Relax a little."

Erzel walked slowly towards the gates, wondering what the Elves on the walls were thinking. The sight of a Dragon surely had them all on edge. He saw the figure at the gate and the two approached one another. Erzel stared straight ahead and seconds later realized he was walking towards the King. Three more steps and he instinctively dropped to one knee.

Elendil stopped a few feet away, half looking at Erzel and half at the Dragon. He got a good look at the Elf bowing before him and was just as stunned. "Erzel... is that you?"

"Yes my King, it is. Forgive my unannounced approach. There was no time to warn of the method of our travel. I know it is a shock..."

"A shock indeed! Where did you manage to find a... Dragon?" the King asked, looking at the strong creature.

"That is indeed a very long story my King. With your permission, may we retire to the keep so I may tell you what has taken place?"

The King nodded and watched as several others approached from the smaller birds. They too gave a courteous bow and Elendil recognized Kail right away. The other woman he had no knowledge of who or what she was. She turned and waved to the group of creatures behind her, watching as they all immediately took flight and disappeared into the sky to await being summoned once more.

Elendil turned and led the group towards Pentegarn, still half watching the Dragon as it circled back over the city and disappeared to the north. He turned to the right and looked at Erzel inquisitively.

"I take it this is going to be a very interesting story indeed. Where are Ectle, Rathe, and Thorgrim?"

"This should probably wait until we are inside my King. This has not been a very easy journey for us. We have lost many comrades trying to get back here."

Elendil swept ahead of the group, ordering the guards back as they continued through to the inner city and finally the keep. Erzel, Kail, and Lavian stayed close behind as the King led them up to the throne room. The guards pushed the door open and hesitated as the armed group followed the King in. As Elendil entered he ordered the room emptied and the doors closed and waited for the orders to be completed. As the doors closed, the King looked up at the three guests.

"I find introductions appropriate," he noted, looking at the woman in plated armor.

"Of course. This is Lavian, acting head of the Celestial Knights and native to the Dragon Isles. Lavian, this is King Elendil of the High Elves and ruler of Pentegarn. I take it you wish to know everything we have been faced with?"

The King gave him an obvious glare and Erzel nodded to his own question. The Elf took a seat at the end of the table and began his tale. He described the circumstances that led his group to leave Tvan and then the voyage there. He told of the island and how it actually seemed to float with the water, making it nearly impossible to chart. When he finished the battle on the island, Elendil held up a hand to stop him.

"Yes my King?"

"A Slayer? What exactly is a Slayer?"

"A Slayer, good King, is a creature summoned to serve the Demon Infus and the sorcerer Valsera. They are more of an empty shell, acting only on the orders of their master and having no real drive or desire of their own. They are strong, and tend to be difficult to destroy in battle," Lavian answered from beside Erzel.

"Thank you... continue Erzel."

"After leaving the island we forced the Princess to remain at Eglarest with her parents and we flew south to Qwaz where Yanosh believed we would find Valsera. He was correct. In the battle we lost more than half of our forces and some are still missing, but Yanosh managed to imprison Valsera in solid crystal. Sadly, his rule has not been broken and the Demon will now take over."

Elendil stared at the Elf for a solid ten minutes before finally speaking again. "So, by taking Valsera out of the equation, we have effectively made things worse. From what you say, Infus is invincible."

"Not entirely. The Dragon Alora managed to knock the Demon off the balcony with a bolt of lightning. The Demon is not completely invincible."

The words seemed so easy to say, but Erzel knew inside that the only thing that managed to damage the Demon was the blast of lightning. His attacks had done nothing to slow the creature down during the battle and the creature's strengths seemed to make it much stronger than normal. The creature's endurance and discipline were admirable, if only it had not been an enemy.

"So... now it is believed that to break the armies in the south we must destroy a Demon with limited vulnerabilities? Am I correct so far?"

Erzel looked up with an uncertain glance. "Honestly, there is no guarantee that destroying the Demon will break the armies marching towards us. This would be the time to send to the Dwarves and call for aid."

The room was quiet for a few minutes as the two Elves looked at one another, the information setting in at last. Elendil looked at the group as he he too had something to share with them. The events that had taken place at the city were just as disturbing as what he had heard, with the added twist of betrayal. The King stood from his throne and walked to the edge of the table where the three were seated.

"There is more that you do not know Erzel... much

more."

Erzel looked at the King with a raised eyebrow, the suspicion welling in the back of his mind. He knew that the lands around Pentegarn and to the south were alive with battle, but now there was something else to add to his worry.

"What happened Elendil?"

"We sent an army led by your head Knight Aric to the Pass of Merwold. They were joined by a small force of Gnomes that had decided to do what they could to help fight off Valsera's onslaught. They met the incoming horde at the pass, and as they prepared for battle, were betrayed by the Human army thought to be arriving to reinforce them. Calyn has turned against us."

Erzel stared at the Elf King in disbelief, his eyes scanning over Elendil's face. He looked at Kail and then back to the King. "What has become of the matter?"

"Our forces at the pass were annihilated completely. Only one survived to our knowledge, a young Gnome who arrived in time to warn of the impending attack. Not even a full day after he arrived, Calyn and a force of Knights rode into the city, warning of the loses at the pass and those marching north towards Pentegarn. Thanks to the Gnome, we knew ahead of time that he would lie and he sought to further his betrayal."

"Where is Calyn?" Erzel asked angrily, his temper rising as the news sank in.

"Restrained in the dungeon. He and a pair of his soldiers were captured, but the others were killed on the spot. We will get what we need out of him and then he will be put to death."

The four in the room were silent, knowing that the Humans had finally shown their true intentions. Erzel remembered the hostility in the throne room after Rhen had been abducted and how the King showed little concern for the matter. Calyn had plotted against them all along.

Elendil took a deep breath and looked to each of the soldiers at the table one by one. He bit his lip and nodded to himself. "I suppose there is nothing more to speak of. We shall continue to the dungeon where the Humans are held. I want to know all that I can before their lives are taken. Lavian my dear, you are free to retire to one of the available rooms. This is a private matter now."

Lavian looked to Erzel who nodded to show it was the

best choice at the moment. She gave a quick bow and left the room. Elendil walked slowly with Erzel and Kail following. They took their time getting to the dungeon as they were still reeling from the reality of the matter. Both had shared bad news and neither had anything to show as a sign of hope.

The doors opened and the three entered, their eyes all stopping instantly on the Human King chained in his cell. Calyn raised his head and stared at them hollowly. Elendil ordered the door open and the jailor did so at once, stepping back as the cell door swung inward.

"We are going to have a talk Calyn, and depending on how you answer my questions, you may come back to this cell feeling a little better. On the other hand, if we do not hear what we want, there is a good chance you will not have the ability to walk back under your own power. I hope this is clear to you."

The Human did not respond but dropped his stare to the ground at the King's feet, the reality of what was about to happen sinking in. The guards unfastened his manacles and he fell to his knees on the stone floor at their feet. They grabbed him and pulled him to his feet, walking him to a room and sitting him in a chair at the table. Erzel and Kail followed the King in and the guards closed the door behind them as they left.

Erzel approached the table and stared at the man, his eyes probing him for whatever emotion there might be hiding in the Human. Erzel turned his head to the two behind him and drew his arm back. With his fist balled he viciously struck the Human across the jaw, knocking him from his seat. Calyn fell from the chair, sprawled out on the floor with Erzel on top of him still swinging. Kail rushed forward and grabbed the enraged Elf from behind, pulling him away from Calyn as the blows continued to rain down on the Human. With Erzel pulled back away from the man, Elendil drew his sword and ordered the Human back into the chair.

Calyn slowly took the seat as he was ordered, staring at the Elf as a trickle of blood appeared from his nose. Elendil pulled a second chair up close to the table and sheathed his sword, taking a seat and staring at the Human. The room was silent as Kail and Erzel approached, standing on either side of the King. Knowing his fate, Calyn hung his head and waited.

"Did you honestly think you would get away with this

Calyn?" Elendil asked bluntly.

The Human chose not to respond, staring at the table in front of him. The Elf waited a minute and then turned to Erzel, giving a nod. The Elf took a step to the right of the table and swung one time, catching the Human in the temple and sending him to the floor again. They waited as Kail forced the man back to the chair and the interrogation started again.

"Perhaps a different question this time... what did Valsera promise you? Hmm, gold, land, protection? Was it worth it Calyn?"

"No sane man chooses to stand with the side of the slaughter when there is a choice. No matter what you do, there will be no victory for you and your kind."

The aggressive response surprised the three and Elendil narrowed his eyes. "Well, I will live long enough to see your death I assure you. There is much you have no knowledge of and for that you have paid a heavy price. Even with their superior numbers, we have much on our side to balance the odds."

"Like what?"

"For one, Valsera no longer leads his own armies," Erzel noted boldly, taking a step forward. "The sorcerer is frozen in crystal and now his general has taken up command. Thankfully, we have our ways of disposing of the new threat."

"You lie!"

Erzel reached down and grabbed the man by the collar, jerking him up from chair. "I wish you would live long enough to see the south fall. I really do... more than that I wish I was the one to take your life. Lucky for you that the King has more he needs out of you. Valsera is gone, and his armies will crumble when we are done."

Calyn narrowed his stare with the Elf, a smile forming on his face. "You would have made a better jester than a Knight. You expect me to believe the strongest sorcerer in all the lands is now a prisoner, trapped in crystal? This is pathetic."

Rage surged through the Elf as the Human's attitude infuriated him further. He took a step back and brought his foot up from the floor, thrusting it forward. The heel of his boot smashed the Human's jaw and Kail grabbed him once more, watching as the Human crawled away from the Elf with his face bleeding heavily. With the Knight subdued, Elendil approached and shoved the man back against the wall, his foot on the Human's chest.

"Believe it or not Calyn, he is not quite as angry as I am. This is the last time I am going to ask you. After this, you will be punished for your crimes, and for your silence. Now, tell me of their forces, numbers, races, weapons. Tell me while you can."

Calyn looked up at the King with his chin split and bleeding heavily. He thought of what the punishment for his silence would be and at the same time, the price he would pay for what little information he had. It wasn't hardly worth it.

"Goblins, Ogres, the usual forces. I imagine my Knights that remained behind will serve amongst them in my absence..."

"What else?"

"Their forces disassembled the siege weapons that your Elves brought to the Pass of Merwold and are moving them north in the army. They plan to use them here."

"How very interesting. What more can you tell us?" Elendil asked, running his fingers across his chin.

Calyn looked from Elendil to Kail and Erzel, wondering what more needed to be said. He had answered what had been asked of him but now they were pressing for more information. Nothing else he knew would be relevant.

"Nothing more? Very well, you will return to your cell where you will await your death. As it stands, you have supplied us with very little. Guards!"

The door opened and the Elves grabbed up the Human, taking a second look at the damage to the man's face that had not been there before. As they locked him into the manacles, the King ordered the other two Humans to be brought into the same room. The guards forced the two former Knights into the room and stayed, watching as the two men fell back to the corners of the room. Erzel and Kail closed on the one on the right as the guards and King turned to the one in the left corner.

"You might as well kill us, we're not saying a word!" the soldier in the right corner shouted as the two closed in on him.

Hearing the taunt, Erzel kicked the man in the stomach and pulled his dagger from its sheath. As the Human fell to his knees, Kail grabbed him from behind and restrained him as the Elf pressed the blade in against his throat. Looking up he found the King staring at them and they waited for an order.

"Wait just one moment Erzel, just in case he changes his mind."

Sheathing the dagger he gave the King a disheartened look. "As you wish sir."

The three turned back to their prisoner, their hollowed stares probing him for emotion. "Though I may have stopped him for now, your fate is certain unless you are able to tell me something I need to know. Your King, Calyn, will be executed for his crimes. Now, as you are the only two remaining from his attempted betrayal, perhaps one of you would like to share with me information. If not, you will be sentenced and executed here on the spot."

The two Humans exchanged nervous glances and looked back at the Elf. "What do you want to know?"

"Ah, very good. How many are there moving north? How many in the southern armies?"

The Human swallowed. "At the pass... I am not sure, twelve thousand, maybe more. Goblins, Ogres, and Humans."

"Impossible..." Erzel snapped, looking at the man. "It would take days to cross the pass with that kind of army. Calyn claimed they would be here in the next eve if not sooner."

"They began crossing a day before we arrived."

Realizing that there had been close to four days now between the losses at the pass and the current day, the claim that there were that many soldiers was suddenly possible. What if they were still crossing the pass? Elendil looked at Erzel and then to the Human.

"Erzel, the group that arrived with you on the... birds. Could they be sent out to scout and see if there is any truth in the man's statement? Sending out a mounted rider would just prove if there were soldiers, but not how many we are facing."

The Elf nodded. I am sure that can be arranged, sir. I will speak with Lavian immediately and have her send out scouts."

Sweat began to drip on the Human's forehead as the Elves began debating what to do now. He wondered what gave them the ability to scout from the air.

"Guards, restrain them in their cells. Erzel, Kail, come with me. Send word to the others that arrived with you to join us in the royal courtroom. We will debate our next move accordingly."

"Yes my King," the Elf replied.

Erzel and Kail left the dungeon immediately, walking back down to the gates and outer walls where all but Lavian continued to wait for their arrival. Alora took a long step forward and stopped next to the Elf as Erzel approached.

"What news Erzel?"

The Elf sighed. "Much has changed since the last time I was here. The Humans have betrayed our alliance and taken up swords with Valsera's soldiers. On that matter however, Calyn, the King of the Humans, is currently held prisoner in the dungeon. He will be executed soon. I have a task for you and some of the others if you do not mind."

"Of course, how can we be of service?"

"We know that there is a massive army moving north towards Pentegarn, the largest army we have ever faced. One of the prisoners claimed it no less than ten thousand strong. I need to know if he bluffs, or if these numbers are true. If so, Pentegarn will surely be in for a horrible siege."

"At once. I will inform the other Celestial Knights. We will return with the information you and your soldiers require," the Blue Dragon replied, turning and lumbering back out into the fields where the rest of the Warbirds and Celestial Knights waited.

Seeing that the scouting was going to be taken care of, Erzel and Kail turned and made their way back into the city. They walked slowly, the events that had been unveiled to them still swimming in their heads. Knowing their forces would receive no help from the Humans in the least when the Goblin armies attacked disturbed him. A thought crossed his mind and he held a hand out to stop Kail.

"I wonder... what will Elendil do with Cisalia now that we know the Humans are traitors? Surely he does not plan on simply ignoring the fact that there are still Human forces in the city that could cause further distress."

Kail shook his head. "I do not know, but perhaps we should bring that up when we meet with him later. Possibly the King had not thought of that as a pressing matter."

"Perhaps..."

Together they navigated the many corridors that led towards the center of the castle. Nearing the courtroom, Erzel stopped, knocking on one of the rooms where soldiers would normally stay if visiting from another city. No answer. He continued further down the hallway and found similar results at each door he came to.

"What are you doing Erzel?" Kail asked, following and watching curiously.

"I thought perhaps we should inform Lavian of the meeting in the royal courtroom but apparently I do not know what room she was given. How are we going to find her now?"

"Find who?" came a voice behind them.

"They turned and standing in the doorway two rooms back was Lavian, her face worn and tired but seemingly brighter than before.

"We were looking for you. There is a meeting with our forces in the royal courtroom set to take place shortly. It would be a good idea for you to join us for this," Erzel replied, nodding in the direction of the room they were headed.

"Of course."

The three finished the trek through the castle and found themselves at the doors leading into the large room. With the doors opened, they found King Elendil sitting alone at the head of the table, his brow troubled as he battled the worries in his head. He scarcely took notice of the three entering until Erzel cleared his throat and addressed him.

"My King, we are here to discuss the matters mentioned earlier... as well as some not thought of previously."

Elendil looked up from the table and sighed. "More troubles to address? I think we already have enough facing us as it is Erzel, but by all means, everyone have a seat and let us work to come up with a solution."

They walked to the far end of the table where Elendil was seated, taking seats around him and waiting patently for the meeting to begin. Erzel looked up to Elendil and bit his lip, nodding to himself to assure that it was right to proceed.

"What of Cisalia my Lord? Will you destroy the city for the crimes of Calyn and his soldiers?"

Elendil stared straight ahead not blinking. "I honestly had not though of Cisalia. In all this commotion I had forgotten that Calyn still had forces waiting in the city to do his bidding."

"Shall we strike them before they have a chance to come

after us here?"

Elendil did not answer, unsure of how to proceed at the moment. On the one hand, it was Calyn and his Humans who had betrayed them but on the other, there was no guarantee that everyone in the city of Cisalia was guilty of the crimes committed by their King. If they destroyed the city of Cisalia and its people, the Elves could end up being just as bad as the Goblins and Ogres moving north towards them.

"No... not yet. We can not destroy the city yet. If there is a chance that some of their kind are innocent, no matter how unlikely the odds, we must give those a chance to live. Not all of the Humans would have gone along with such a plan, I am sure of it."

The King made sense but at the same time, it added yet another challenge to the already seemingly impossible situation. If there were Humans in the city of Cisalia that still supported the Elves and the alliance then they would have to be given the chance to evacuate the city before the armies closed on them. How would the Elves know who followed Calyn still and who remained loyal to the old alliance? Every question brought with it a new challenge, not all of which seemed to have an obvious answer.

"How do you suggest we separate those loyal to Calyn and those loyal to the alliance?" Erzel asked, interrupting the King's thoughts.

"I have not the slightest idea, Erzel. For now, we will not bother ourselves with the Humans in Cisalia. We shall instead turn our attention to the armies advancing on this city and what we plan to do to stop them. Have you any suggestions there Erzel?"

"None other than what was noted earlier, sir. Sending word to the Dwarves to try and raise their armies and bring them south is the only step we can take to face the forces coming towards us. Twelve thousand... Pentegarn has never faced a force that strong directly."

"Twelve thousand strong?" Lavian asked suddenly. "How did they manage to muster numbers so strong with the continuous wars and battles that have been dotting the south?"

"Before he was frozen in crystal by Yanosh, Valsera had almost unlimited resources and no race was strong nor brave enough to defy him until now. No matter how many of their kind we manage to kill, he has more to send in to replace those lost. Think of them like locusts," Erzel explained.

Elendil stood from the table and leaned across it, placing both hands on the surface. "If I send you and your party to Tvan to raise their armies, will you go in the same means that you arrived?"

"Yes, it will be much faster if the Dragon and Warbirds assist us instead of traversing the forests, rivers, and mountains. I sent Alora and the Warbirds out to scout and inform us of the enemy's true numbers. When will you have us leave my King?"

"I will let your group rest when they return and depending on how things have changed between now and the time they arrive, I will send you north no later than the morning after tomorrow."

"A thought, if I may?" Kail spoke for the first time.

"Go ahead Kail."

"Have you set a date for the execution of the prisoners?"

Elendil shook his head. "Not as of this moment, no. We will discuss the matter further tomorrow morning in a formal trial. Though guilty, it is in our best interest to keep to our ways. Calyn will be given a trial, sentenced, and executed at a later date. I will send for you in the morning prior to the trial."

"Thank you my King. If you have further need of us, just let us know," Erzel added, standing with the rest of the group as they turned to leave.

Elendil nodded and after a brief bow from the three, followed them to the door. The guards closed the door behind them and waited as Elendil paced through the courtroom, wondering what would become of the city once the armies arrived. All of Nalawren knew that Pentegarn was the strongest and most heavily defended of all cities, but as it had been stated earlier, the city had never gone up against numbers so great.

Even knowing what his people were up against, Elendil was optimistic. He knew inside that the city would hold against the greatest of odds and that the Dwarves would come to push the armies back into the southlands. This time though, Elendil didn't plan on stopping. They would push the Goblins and Ogres back till there was nowhere else to go, and then destroy them.

Erzel sat on the edge of his bed later that night, rolling the handle of the weapon he had taken from the balcony in his hands. He had seen the whip of fire emerge like a serpent when Infus had attacked him but he could not understand how the Demon had activated the weapon. There was no switch, no button, nothing to bring the whip to life. He set it back on the table next to the bed and stood, walking to the window and staring out at the city below. Torches dotted the walls and towers, illuminating the streets throughout the city. Like ants the Elves scurried all through the night, keeping watch in every direction.

A knock at the door turned the Elf and he wiped his eyes. "Enter."

The door opened and he found Kail standing in the doorway. "I take it you were not asleep Erzel?"

"No, watching the night outside. Something is keeping me awake tonight. Have you not been able to sleep yourself?"

"No… I worry about what the scouts will say when they return. I know the Human claimed the numbers as high as he did but for some reason I am worried that the estimate was low. What happens if there are more?"

Erzel pondered the thought for a moment. "You know there are more don't you Kail? When you served Valsera you saw the might of his forces."

Kail lowered his gaze and hung his head silently, remembering what had happened in the throne room after the truth had been exposed. "You trusted me enough to come back for me. I fled Valsera the first chance I had, coming north and fitting myself in with the people north of Swanhaven, the drifters that roamed from town to town with no purpose. I believed that Valsera would never find me that far north and for a while I was right."

"What changed?"

"The Goblins began arriving in the lands between Swanhaven and Eglarest, searching for people who had fled the service of the sorcerer. Many were caught in the wilderness and killed for their treason. By fleeing to Pentegarn I managed to escape the punishment awaiting me. It wasn't until we were in Qwaz that I even remembered what I had done in the service of Valsera. I am glad to be free."

Erzel knew the torment the man was feeling was horrible, betraying the strongest sorcerer ever to scar the earth to hide amongst those he was warring with. Then to have to go back and face the truth. Maybe that was why he had not exposed to any of the others the truth of what had been said in the throne room that night.

"Kail, what happened that night… what was said… it needn't be spoken of again. You fought against those who fought against us. Your past may have been filled with confusion and you may have at one time served Valsera, but no longer. Put this behind you my friend."

Kail nodded and turned to leave, stopping only briefly in the doorway. "What do you think will happen Erzel?"

The Elf paused, thinking the question over carefully. He honestly had no idea how to answer. "I think we are in for an interesting turn of events. I do not know what will happen, or when, but I do know that this is going to be bloody. I just hope the city can withstand what is coming until the Dwarves arrive."

"Me too."

Kail slowly pulled the door closed behind him, leaving the Elf standing in the center of the room. Erzel turned back to the window and continued to stare out at the city. He knew there would be no sleep tonight.

Erzel had been lying in the bed for almost an hour when a knock at the door woke him once more. He stood and walked to the door, pulling it open and peering out into the hall to find a soldier waiting for him.

"Sir, you have been summoned to the courtyard at once. It is urgent."

"Yes… give me one moment."

Erzel dressed quickly and followed the soldier down to the courtyard. In the torchlight he could see the large form of Alora, her wings tucked into her sides as she scanned the walls and towers around her. The Elf stopped a few feet away, looking at the Dragon with a little surprise.

"I didn't expect you and the others back so quickly. Were you successful?"

"Yes Erzel. We scouted from Pentegarn back across the Pass of Merwold and further into the southlands. We found quite a surprise."

"The Human claimed there were some twelve thousand soldiers making their way towards the city. I am hoping this was a bluff on his part."

"The Human was wrong Erzel. There was not a force of twelve thousand soldiers moving north towards Pentegarn."

"Then that is excellent news."

"Not quite my friend. The force crossing the pass and moving into the Elven lands makes up the twelve thousand the Human spoke of. A day's march behind them at least three times that number is coming from Qwez. At least forty thousand soldiers will be closing on Pentegarn within the week.

Trials of the Troubled

*E*rzel was sitting in the courtroom when Elendil arrived first thing the following morning. The King stepped through the doors and stopped, staring at the Elf sitting at the table. Erzel had not bothered trying to go back to sleep after hearing the news from Alora, knowing that he would never be able to close his eyes. Erzel looked up at the King and stood from the table.

"Erzel... what are you doing here so early?"

"My King, I received word early this morning from the scouts that were sent out in search of Valsera's forces. The estimates were not what I expected."

Elendil nodded, knowing that there was a good chance he was not going to enjoy the conversation as it progressed. "So... the prisoners were not accurate?"

"Alora informed me that their initial estimate of the forces moving across the Pass of Merwold, some ten to twelve thousand strong was indeed accurate. It was the force behind them following from Qwaz that has changed everything. Some thirty thousand more reinforcing their initial push."

Elendil stood with his face stricken in disbelief. "Forty thousand? That is not possible. We could possibly hold the initial attack but another thirty thousand after that would surely break Pentegarn."

The two Elves took seats at the long table and began thinking to themselves about what they were up against. It would still be a few hours till daylight and the city was already full of life. The armies moving north would decimate any economy that Pentegarn once possessed, forcing the Elves to focus only on war. Elendil tapped the table impatiently, forcing his brain through every possible scenario that presented itself. Only one thing came to mind.

"We only have one choice Erzel. We must send to the Dwarves of Tvan, tell them of what is set to take place here. Otherwise, I fear the worst."

Realizing that Elendil was no longer sure of the strength of the Elves made worried Erzel. Even if there were forty thousand soldiers marching north, they were about to encounter the most impenetrable city ever built. The walls stretched higher than any other and the fortress at the center appeared as broad and vast as a mountain. Even if the enemy managed to break through the gate, there was another even stronger wall waiting. Erzel was not so quick to give up hope.

"My King, I agree to the fullest in calling for the Dwarves but we should not abandon hope so easily here in Pentegarn. You know as well as I that this city, this castle, has stood the tests of time and has never fallen. This city will never belong to the horde of Valsera."

"The walls are not the problem I feel we face Erzel, nor the castle itself. If these numbers are correct, we are greatly outnumbered. We've little time to call for reinforcements before their forces arrive and we have no guarantee that the Dwarves will come at all."

Erzel sat straight abruptly. "They will send help, or they may find Valsera's armies on their doorstep with no one to help them."

It was the truth, but at the same time Tvan would probably be able to hold against the armies. The mountains that held the city served as a natural wall against outsiders. Pentegarn was in the open, vulnerable and a clear target for the armies of Valsera. Tvan was nearly invisible except to those familiar to the lands in the mountains. With everything the Elves stood to lose, surely the Dwarves would extend their help.

From the doorway appeared Lavian, Kail, and a handful of royals and soldiers all ready for the trial of the accused Humans. Elendil and Erzel left the table and joined the group that had arrived, greeting them and informing them of what was to come. Finally the King took his seat at the throne with Erzel on his right and the head of the royal guard named Naomi to his left. They waited as the rest of the groups found their seats before Elendil stood and addressed the room.

"Citizens of Pentegarn, royals, soldiers, and guests we find ourselves here after a great wrong has been done to us. Earlier this week forces from Cisalia led by King Calyn himself made their way to the Pass of Merwold where they attacked and decimated the Elven forces. After this attack, the King and a small force of Knights arrived here in Pentegarn spinning a tale of deceit and lies, warning of an attack to soon fall on Pentegarn."

Elendil stopped briefly to take a long look around the room at the people within it. So far, it appeared that everyone was clear on the points being made. He looked to Erzel and then back up to the room, continuing to lay out the events that had recently unfolded.

"It was the intent of the Human soldiers to penetrate and kill the leaders of Pentegarn, sending the city into disarray and aiding in the impending seige. This plot was however thwarted as a single Gnome had arrived a day earlier and warned of the betrayal. Caught off guard, those responsible were killed and three were captured. These three, including the King himself are to be held accountable for the betrayal at the pass and the attempted assassination of myself. Are there questions thus far?"

The room was silent but in the back a single hand raised from the group.

"Yes?"

"The forces at the pass were all destroyed?" the Elf asked as he heard the news for the very first time.

"Sadly, every soldier sent to defend the pass has to my knowledge been killed. Also, the entirety of the Gnomes who agreed to help were killed with the exception of one, the one responsible for warning us of the attack."

Silence took over the room again and Elendil waited patiently as he looked from face to face. Feeling satisfied that they had nothing to add, Elendil nodded to the guards at the doorway.

"Alright, see the prisoners in at once. We are ready to begin."

The room turned in their seats and watched as the guards opened the doors and waited, holding them open as more of the royal guard entered with the three Humans led in chains. They had all been stripped to only pants, degrading them further. Calyn was led in last, his hands bound and a chain from the manacles attached to the soldier in front of him. In the center of the room the soldiers stopped and waited for the King's orders. They dropped the chains to the floor and locked the prisoners to restraints. After receiving the nod from the King they took steps back out of the way. Elendil looked down at the three prisoners, shaking his head slowly.

"The three of you are here to be sentenced for your crimes against the Elves and their allies. Though it means little in relation to your final sentence, this court will now hear any statements that you have. Have you anything to say?"

The three prisoners stood in the center of the room with the eyes of the court surrounding them. There was nothing to say that would right the wrongs they had committed, but could there be something to lessen the severity of their sentence? Calyn knew that no matter what, they would be sentenced to death. By what means still waiting to be revealed.

"I have something to say," Calyn muttered, half biting his tongue.

"Go on."

The Human rattled his chains and looked up at the King. "You have no idea the weapons that Valsera possesses. Goblins, Ogres, Lizardmen, they are mere pawns when compared to the real strength he hides in Qwaz and Nomaria. Creatures that are just short of invincible. No army will ever stand against the might of his forces once he unleashes his secret on the lands of Nalawren."

"I beg to differ!" Erzel announced, standing from his seat. "The creature you speak of is a Demon known as Infus. It serves Valsera even with the sorcerer no longer able to give orders. I watched its invincibility myself, seeing my weapon pass through it with no effect. However, I also watched the same creature lose its strength when faced with the might of a Blue Dragon. The lightning the Dragon breathes is his weakness."

Calyn was obviously caught off guard by the sudden outburst. Not only did the Elf know the creature the Human spoke of, but at the same time he claimed to have found a weakness in the Demon. The Human wracked his brain trying to find something to say in return but nothing was coming to him.

"Infus is the might of Valsera's army, the true heart of his forces. When the Demon arrives there will be nothing left standing here in Pentegarn. Its only purpose is to enslave all of

Nalawren in the name of Valsera. Nothing you can do will…"

"If the prisoners have nothing to say relevant to their sentencing then we will proceed," Elendil interrupted, looking past the Humans to the guards at the rear of the room.

"Just get it over with Elendil… none of this will matter soon."

The Human's disregard for his own life disturbed Elendil. The Elf realized that Calyn knew he was going to die and it did not matter what the Elf did to him now. Even the thoughts of torture did not seem to shake the Human in the least.

"Very well, on the eve of tomorrow you and your two remaining Human soldiers will receive your punishments. I hereby sentence the three of you to death. Your Knights will be hung from the outer city wall by the neck until dead."

The two Humans looked at one another and were grabbed from behind, unchained, and drug back to their cells to be held until their execution. Calyn looked up at Elendil, waiting for his sentence from the Elven King. Elendil leaned back in his throne and took a deep breath, pondering what sentence would seem fitting for the King of the Humans.

"Calyn, to be hung for your crimes is too simple a punishment. I hereby decree that you shall be publicly executed by beheading. Your crimes dictate a punishment even more severe but as I have a small measure of respect for royalty, your execution will be swift. Now, lead the prisoner back to his cell."

One of the remaining guards grabbed the Human as the other unhooked the chains. They led the prisoner back to the dungeon by the length of chains binding his hands. Calyn walked with his head down, not daring to look up at the Elves surrounding him in the room. Nothing would save him now and he knew it. He silently accepted his fate.

"Erzel, with your Dragon and those Warbirds back from their scouting, how soon can you be ready to leave for Tvan?" the King asked.

The Elf thought for only a second or two before turning to the King. "Before nightfall."

"Excellent! Spread word through those following you and prepare to leave at once. The sooner the Dwarves get word of what is taking place here at Pentegarn, the sooner they can get their armies mobilized. Time is of the essence."

"Of course my Lord. Though I think it may be better if it is just Kail, Lavian, and myself that go north to seek aid. We will leave what remains of the Celestial Knights and their Warbirds here at Pentegarn to help if the Dwarves do not arrive in time."

Elendil nodded. "Very well. Please hurry Erzel. Between the two of us, I do not know for sure if Pentegarn can stand against the might of thirty thousand soldiers. We will do everything we can."

Erzel nodded to Kail and Lavian and the three left the room in search of the rest of the Celestial Knights. He knew the trip to Tvan would take no time at all compared to the last trip when the Princess was in with them. The Dragons and Warbirds would not have to worry about the terrain and it would be a straight shot from Pentegarn to Tvan. It would be easier this time around.

Thorgrim fought the rope that bound him against the stake for what seemed like the thousandth time, thinking that maybe it would loosen, but after several minutes of struggling he gave up. Thorgrim and Nimir had been forced to stand tied to the stakes in the rain, day and night since they had arrived and were only fed what the Lizardmen discarded. It was a new kind of torture for the two Dwarves. Nimir looked over at the Dwarf next to him, seeing the once strong Thorgrim now hunched and weak, nothing like his former self.

The Lizardmen moved throughout the camp quickly, the threat of a massive Goblin force closing in on them. Even though they were strong enough to deal with the weaker enemies, the Lizardmen were greatly outnumbered. The two Dwarves watched as the one that had spoken with them earlier approached.

"Still alive I see…"

Neither Dwarf spoke, keeping their eyes on the ground as the creature looked from one to the other.

The Lizardman started to take another step towards them, but a large commotion to the right in the fog caught its attention. He chose to turn and investigate the matter instead. Lizardmen were coming from every direction to see what the noises were, leaving the two Dwarves alone once more. Nimir could hear footsteps approaching behind them but neither he nor Thorgrim could turn to see who or what was coming their way. Sweat ran down Nimir's forehead as panic started to set in. Suddenly the ropes holding the Dwarf against the pole slackened and fell to the ground, followed by Thorgrim's. The two Dwarves turned quickly, finding a tall Lizardman standing behind them.

"What the hell is going on?" Thorgrim asked, looking at the beast.

The Lizardman didn't move from the spot and Nimir quickly turned, finding their weapons and gear and carrying it back to Thorgrim.

"Thorgrim, come on... we have to hurry," he said impatiently, strapping the sword across his back.

"Why did one of them set us free?"

"Thorgrim!"

The Dwarf leaned down and retrieved his weapons, not taking his eyes off of the creature that still stood rigid as a stone statue. As soon as the two had their things the Lizardman suddenly turned and started off away from the camp, hesitating as if waiting for the Dwarves to follow.

"We need to follow it," Nimir whispered, starting off after the creature.

"Are you insane?" Thorgrim asked, grabbing the Dwarf by the sleeve and jerking him back a step. "I don't care if it did set us free, I am not about to follow it through a swamp filled with its kind."

Noises to the right reminded them that the other Lizardmen were close by and Thorgrim took a deep breath, regretting his decision even before making it. He let go of Nimir's sleeve and fell in close behind the Dwarf as they caught up to the waiting Lizardman. They followed it slowly, their eyes scanning every inch of the fog around them.

"Why are you helping us? Where are you taking us?" Nimir asked quietly.

The Lizardman did not reply but instead continued on its course through the fog. After walking for some ten minutes the Lizardman led them to the right into a thicker stand of trees and just inside it stopped and stood completely still. Following slowly, Nimir was suddenly filled with excitement when the wizard Ectle appeared from behind the trees. He beckoned them to join him.

"Ectle! What are you doing here?" Thorgrim asked,

amazed that the wizard was standing in the swamp with them.

"I came in after we escaped Qwaz. I saw the Dragon carrying you go down in the swamps and I was not about to leave you behind if there was a chance you two were alive. I've been walking for two days now and finally I found you."

"What is going on? A Lizardman released us. Would you happen to know why?"

Ectle looked at the creature standing still just inside the trees and it took a few steps forward, stopping next to the Dwarf. He looked at the creature and smiled.

"It has no idea what it is doing right now. It only does what I tell it to do. I was coming through the swamp earlier and it attacked me without warning. I was able to gain the upper hand and easily put it under a mind control spell. It was the only way I could think to get you out of the encampment without being seen myself."

"What about the noises and the commotion at the camp that drove all the Lizardmen into the swamps to investigate? Was that you too?" Thorgrim asked as he suddenly remembered how they had been freed.

"Not exactly. I did manage to lead a pursuing party of Goblins in on the camp. After that I have no idea what happened. I take it the Goblins and Lizardmen are no longer on the best of terms. Either way, we have to get out of here before they send their scouts out looking for us."

"What about this Lizardman? What will happen to it now?"

Ectle looked at the creature. "I will keep it here and eventually we will be far enough away that my mind control will wear off. It will not remember anything it saw or did while under my control. Come on, let's get moving."

The Dwarves and wizard quickly moved out of the trees into the swamp once more, pushing their way through the mud and filth that made up the land. They kept moving further and further until Nimir finally collapsed on a fallen tree, his muscles burning.

"Are you alright Nimir?" Ectle asked, sitting on the tree next to the Dwarf.

"Yes... just so tired. We were tied to those stakes for what seemed like days. I couldn't sleep at all. Just exhausted that's all."

"I am quite surprised that the Lizardmen didn't eat you. They have only been known to take prisoners when they planned to use them to feed the camp. I thought for sure when I realized that they had the two of you that I would find your bodies."

"One of the Lizardmen was set on learning all about us. It asked us all about our people, why we were here, what we were doing... all sorts of things that seemed useless for a creature to care about."

"I do not know... I can not begin to understand what their kind does and why. Whenever you are ready Nimir, we need to keep going."

"Ok, just one more minute..."

"Do you know how to get us out of here Ectle?" Thorgrim asked, looking around the swamps.

"Not exactly. I think it would be best if we keep moving east, away from Qwaz and Nomaria until we reach the ocean. Once we are out of the swamps we can move up the coast and eventually we will find Swanhaven. I know it is a very long hike, but it is the only thing I can think of right now."

The two Dwarves looked at the wizard and then at one another, the thought of hiking for days on end in the swamps and over the coast to reach the Elven lands was insane. To make it worse they had no food, water, shelter, or gear of any sort. There was no way they would be able to make that journey in their current state.

"Ectle, that will never work. We're never going to make that kind of trek without supplies. Surely you have another idea," Thorgrim replied with disbelief.

Ectle hung his head and took a deep breath. "I'll think of something."

Rhen sat on the edge of the balcony at Eglarest, looking out across the land with a face of sorrow. The events of the past week had thrown her into a world of stress she had not imagined before. She'd learned of her condition and though there was a reason for her sickness, it did not seem to lessen. She fought off being sick on a regular basis as she dealt with the worry of the armies in the south and the one person in all of Nalawren she cared so deeply for. Erzel and his soldiers had been sure that if they successfully defeated Valsera on his own ground that the armies under his control would stop. So far, the attacks kept coming. She sighed to herself, wondering if they had been successful or if they had fallen against the sorcerer.

"Princess… are you alright?"

Rhen turned and looked behind her as one of the servants approached. The young lady carried with her a basket of sheets for the bed. She sat down her basket just inside the room, walking out to join the Princess.

"I suppose. This just does not feel right to me. He should be here. He has no idea what is going on here and I know… I know that I will not be able to do this without him. What if they didn't make it?"

"Dear Princess, you must not think such things. I am sure that they still live. Everything you have said about him, there is no way this Erzel is not still alive. He faced Dragons, the armies in the south, those… Demon creatures… he is still alive."

"What if we are wrong? What if the south is still pushing north and I am forced to bring a child into this world with no one here to help protect it?"

"Please do not think such things. You have to think positively Princess. No matter what, you can not let yourself believe you have lost him. If nothing else, hold onto the belief that you will see him again."

The servant held out her hand and the Princess took it, getting down from the edge of the balcony. The servant quickly moved about the room cleaning and changing the bed as the Princess left the room and walked silently through the castle. She could remember how her father had reacted when he realized Erzel had taken her to the Dragon Isles. Oddly, finding out that his daughter was carrying Erzel's child did not anger the King of the Wood Elves in the way Rhen had thought.

He spent three days confined in the throne room not speaking to a single Elf in the castle until he finally exploded one morning, yelling at himself until he had blown off his pent up anger. When he finally came around he simply hugged his daughter, showing her everything was alright. He didn't need to say anything. His embrace was all the reassurance she needed.

She stopped outside of the throne room and waited, trying to decide what she was going to say. She wanted to talk to her mother, to have someone understand her pain. Taking one last deep breath she pushed the door open and walked inside. Tanis sat at the head of the table with the Queen at his side. Also she found several soldiers sitting at the table. They all wore a serious look, and she almost wished she had waited a little longer.

The King looked up as she entered and the room fell quiet as Rhen approached the table. "Yes my dear?" Tanis asked.

"I uh… I don't know. I am sorry I interrupted you and your meeting father. I will go."

"No," Tanis said abruptly, standing from the table. "Have a seat. We were just about to discuss your future."

Rhen silently took a seat and looked around the table at the many faces looking back at her. She tapped the tabletop and met her father's gaze. "What about me are we going to discuss?"

"Things are getting rough around Eglarest again. We have suffered no losses here but how soon will it be before that changes? I have no answer to that. For your safety…"

"Hold it one second…"

"Rhen, do not interrupt me. The circumstances have changed. You are not well. You have more to think about than where you want to be and who you want to be there with. You will go to Tvan once again and this time you will stay there until we are able to ensure that the armies in the south have stopped pushing north. You will be joined by your mother and the guard and you will remain there."

Rhen didn't reply right away, taking in the fact that her father could very well be right. She could no longer think about just herself. There was more than one life at stake now and she nodded in agreement.

"I am sorry Rhen. I know how you feel about being separated from us and from… Erzel… but this is for your own good I assure you."

"I know father, I agree. I just… I don't belong underground. It does not feel right to be hidden from the sunlight day and night. No wonder the Dwarves never leave the caves… they can no longer handle the sunlight. They've been without it for far too long."

The Elves around the table agreed unanimously that the Princess should be moved deep into the mountains of Tvan where the armies of Goblins and Ogres would never reach her. Even if they managed to siege all of Tvan, it would take an unthinkable amount of time to flood the caverns and chambers running through all of the mountains. It was a sound decision.

"I know you do not like the idea Rhen, neither do I. For now though, this is the only thing that will guarantee your safety. I have a group ready to take you tomorrow afternoon, assuming my scouts do not turn up any unfriendly forces in the area."

"What will happen when I leave?" Rhen asked her father.

"I plan to leave Eglarest with the rest of our armies and we will move back south to do what we can to help Elendil and his forces at Pentegarn. I have felt nothing but guilt for pulling our forces from the southlands and leaving the High Elves to deal with the threat. We return to do our part in this war."

Rhen was somewhat shocked to hear that the Wood Elves would leave their fortress in the north to face the armies in the south on their own battlefield. She and her mother would be safe in Tvan while the rest of their people fought and died to defend the lands in the middle of Nalawren. Rhen stood slowly from the table and turned to leave the room, the new information weighing heavily on her mind. She started towards the door when her father's voice stopped her once more.

"Rhen... this is difficult but I need you ready to leave tomorrow night at the latest. We will use our archers and the cover of night to move you and your mother out of the city," he said, receiving a halfhearted nod.

Moments of Silence

"What is that Erzel?" Kail asked as he arrived on the outer balcony.

The Elf held in his hand the long handle that he had picked up on the balcony at Qwaz. Somehow the Demon had used it to produce a magic whip that was beyond any weapon the Elf had ever seen. Erzel held it up and studied it closely before turning to greet Kail.

"The Demon Infus dropped this on the balcony when Alora attacked with her bolt of lightning. I am not sure how to activate it, but from the handle appeared a bright green flame, like a whip. I imagine if the Demon had it in its possession it is powerful."

"That makes sense. No switch, button, or trigger of any sort?"

"Nothing," Erzel replied, running his fingertip up and down the handle. "I ask only out of curiosity, but while serving Valsera did you ever see anything like this?"

"No... never have I seen a weapon like it. As of now it doesn't really seem like a weapon though."

Erzel shrugged and continued to examine the handle. It did not have characteristics of any race he knew, but at the same time the Elf knew very little about the world outside of Nalawren. If it came from a land of Demons, he would know nothing about the weapon. Thinking over every possible way to activate the weapon he flung his wrist forward and then sharply to the side, trying to force the magic to the head of the handle. Still nothing happened.

"Maybe you have to be a Demon to wield the weapon Erzel, did you think of that?"

He nodded. The thought had in fact crossed his mind.

"Surely we can find its secret and use it against the Demon though. Imagine facing Infus again, but this time fighting it with its own weapon. I would love to see the look on its face when the flames appeared from the handle, if it had a face"

The statement made Kail chuckle softly even though Erzel had not meant it in a comical fashion. Erzel whirled it around again and shook his head in defeat. He could think of nothing more to activate the magic hidden within the handle of the weapon. Turning it in his hands however a minor detail in the craftsmanship suddenly caught his attention. It was small enough to overlook and probably impossible to feel with the palm of the hand. Erzel brought the weapon closer and studied it.

The handle was wrapped tightly in black leather and hollow in the center from the top but just above the highest wrap of the leather Erzel noticed a small glyph etched into the metal. He turned the handle over completely in his hand and stopped on the same glyph once more, studying it closely. He had never seen a marking like it in his life. He waved Kail over, not looking up from his discovery.

"What did you find now, Erzel?"

"Tell me what you think. I have never seen anything like it before. Is it a Demon language?"

Kail looked at the etching closely and shrugged. "I have no idea. I have never seen anything like it either."

Erzel raised his thumb and pressed it down over the glyph, watching as nothing happened. He flung his wrist around and watched with the etching out of sight but still the weapon remained lifeless. He stopped and regrouped his thoughts. An idea swam through his head and he raised an eyebrow. He slid his fingernail into the uppermost part of the etching and slowly began tracing it through, feeling more and more excited as he neared the end of the etching.

The moment his fingernail finished with the emblem in the handle the Elf felt a surge of power flow through his hand and out of the top of the whip. Just like when Infus had wielded the weapon the green flame appeared and snaked its way out of the whip. It dropped down and coiled on the ground, ready and waiting for a chance to strike. Kail and Erzel marveled at the intense light radiating from the flames, wondering of the power the weapon was sure to have.

"Amazing Erzel, the glyph activates the weapon. Do you feel anything?"

"No… no heat, nothing. I wonder how powerful this really is," the Elf replied, turning and setting his sights on the shaft of a torch hanging on the wall.

Erzel snapped the whip back and forth, watching as the curl of the flames arched through the air and then caught the wooden handle of the torch. It took only a second for the flames to wrap around and cut through the torch. As the flames of the whip fell to the floor once again Erzel ran his thumb across the glyph and the weapon quickly slid back into the handle.

"Remarkable. This could turn the tide against the Demon. With the whip we may actually have something for Infus to fear. If the Demon is now the head of the armies, killing it would solve everything."

Erzel shook his head as Kail finished. "That may be the problem. Now that I have a weapon with the strength to fight the Demon, it may do everything in its power to get it back. I may have inadvertently invoked the wrath of the creature."

It was true. If there was a weapon powerful enough to destroy Infus then logically the Demon would stop at nothing to ensure no one else had control over the item. Erzel wondered how far the creature would go to get the whip back and if they were even safe inside the walls of Pentegarn. If not, where would they be safe?

"Kail, this is as much a gift as it is a curse. It holds within it power I have yet to see rivaled, but at the same time it is the one thing Infus will never stay parted with long. How can we even be sure that the whip will effect the Demon? It may simply pass through him the way every other weapon has in the past."

Kail shrugged. "I guess we will see when the time comes, huh?"

It was not the answer he had hoped to hear but it was the truth. They did not know if the whip would damage the creature or not but when it came time, Erzel would not hesitate to find out.

Erzel, Kail, and Lavian stood next to Alora in the field just outside of the city of Pentegarn. Elendil waited as the two Warbirds that would carry Kail and Lavian to Tvan landed. They glided in and landed softly in the grass on either side of the Dragon and stood proudly, waiting for the riders to mount. The Elf gave another long look at the creatures, still with a measure of disbelief even though he was seeing them with his own eyes.

"You may have some time persuading the Dwarves to rally to our cause, Erzel. They lost so many during the Chaos Wars that I fear they have drawn away from the thoughts of battle. I do not know how to open their eyes but then again until recently I had never believed a Dragon to exist."

"They stay in their mountains seeking wealth and hiding away from the problems of the rest of the world. Even so, I am sure that I will be able to convince them that if they do not help us now, there may not be another chance. I will have them on the field of battle once more, whether they like it or not."

Elendil nodded to himself. "No race wishes to go to war other than these creatures we face. I do believe though that the Dwarves are not like our former allies. They will keep our alliances strong. The Humans were weak, and it shall be their undoing."

"We will not return until the Dwarven armies are on the march against the Goblins. Don't let Pentegarn fall my King."

Erzel, Kail, and Lavian turned and prepared their mounts. As Kail and Lavian mounted, Erzel stopped in front of Alora. The Dragon lowered her head as if waiting for the Elf to tell some sort of secret.

"Yes young one?"

"Are you ready for this Alora? Not that we are in any danger... I mean I guess I do not know that for sure. There is no telling..."

"Yes Erzel, I am ready. You do not need to worry yourself so. Everything will be fine."

Erzel wondered if he should tell the Dragon of the whip and why he believed the Demon would be chasing after them. At the moment it was only he and Kail that knew of the situation, and he figured it might be better if it remained that way. He took a deep breath and pulled up onto the back of the Dragon. He looked down as the King approached to the left side of the Dragon.

"Come back in one piece Erzel. I will need you here when this begins."

"Yes my King."

The two Warbirds took off suddenly leaving the Dragon and Elf behind. They watched as the birds disappeared over the castle before taking off to join them. Erzel felt the air running across him again and greeted it with a smile, remembering the feeling of flight, a freedom few could experience. As they topped out at the clouds Erzel looked back at the city, taking in the beauty one last time before it was scarred by the siege.

"Everything is happening so fast Alora. It is almost impossible to keep up with this now," Erzel shouted over the wind rushing past them.

Alora cocked her head to the side to catch sight of the Elf on her back. "You know this is only the beginning of something bigger. Take a deep breath and hold on tight."

The Dragon pulled her wings in tight and dove down towards the earth, spreading them as she neared the tops of the trees. She skirted the tops of the forests as Erzel stared down at the ground. Even though they were mere feet above the green treetops, Erzel pictured them charred black and smoldering. There was no guarantee that the lands below them would hold their beauty after this war ended.

Rhen stared at the carriage sitting just outside the main gate of Eglarest. She remembered the horrors that had changed her life during the last carriage ride. It made perfect sense that she was not ready to get in another if she could help it. The soldiers outside the wall had stretched their numbers all throughout the field and to the tree line as the group prepared to leave Eglarest.

"Rhen, are you ready?" Tanis asked as he approached from the castle gate.

Rhen shook her head in response.

"No? What's wrong? Is something the matter?"

"Father, to me this war started when they abducted me from my last carriage. I am in no hurry to get back in another. I would rather have my own horse if it is not too much trouble."

"I do not want you riding out in the open. The countryside is crawling with forces looking to take our city and it would be too easy if they found the Princess of the Wood Elves riding out in the open, vulnerable. No, please ride in the carriage this time, daughter."

From where she was standing she could see the peaks of Tvan and the dusting of snow that had begun to cover them. The air had become noticeably colder over the past week and Rhen drew in a deep breath, feeling the sting from the chill. She knew the land well and knew that it would be covered in snow in a matter of weeks. If they did not get to Tvan soon, they might be trapped by the heavy snow.

"If I must then."

"That's better. I am sending more soldiers with you this time and there is very little distance you have to travel. I will not let you fall into their hands again, I swear it. Now please, hurry and gather whatever you will need. I will send help at once."

Tanis turned and left, leaving the Princess standing in the open field with the archers and soldiers scattered all throughout. Somewhere out there she knew Erzel was still alive and coming back for her. No matter what he was faced with, she knew he was going to come back for her. The thought of the Elf arriving in Eglarest and finding neither her nor the rest of the wood Elves troubled the Princess, but Erzel was clever and surely he would know how to find her.

The Many Wounds of War

*E*ctle walked a few feet ahead of the two Dwarves, keeping a vigilant eye on the swamp around them. Nothing moved other than the three of them, but he knew that by now the Lizardmen were aware that the Dwarves had escaped and were more than likely combing every inch of the swamp in search of them. The creatures had the upper hand, considering they lived in the swamps every day while Ectle, Thorgrim, and Nimir had never before set foot there. The wizard stopped and threw a hand up to catch their attention and stop them, listening to the sounds around them. Silence gripped the area.

"What did he hear?" Nimir whispered to Thorgrim, scanning their surroundings.

"Not the slightest idea. I don't hear anything. Come on," the older Dwarf replied, stepping up next to the wizard silently. "What is it Ectle?"

The wizard shook his head. Closing his eyes he scarcely breathed. "The Lizardmen are on the move. They have our trail."

"How can you be sure?" Nimir asked.

Ectle turned and stared at the Dwarf silently as if the answer to the question should be obvious. Nimir lowered his eyes a little and realized the wizard surely had means of telling whether or not they were being pursued.

"How far behind us Ectle?" Thorgrim asked, gripping his weapon to brace for a fight.

"It is hard to say... hour, maybe two at the most. They are closing on us fast."

"That close... what do we do? How many are there?"

"Too many to tell at the moment. I think it best if we keep moving. We need to try to get as much distance between us and them as we can. With any luck we may reach the cliffs and shores to the east and be able to move north where they will not follow."

Their new pace was plagued by the thick muck of the swamp, causing them all to loose their footing repeatedly. As he scrambled through the mud Ectle had time to wonder how the Lizardmen were able to move so swiftly through the same environment. Every time he thought of the creatures they had moved closer still and he realized that they would not reach the cliffs to the east in time.

Ectle pondered his options, knowing if they stood their ground against a swamp full of the creatures they would surely be taken captive or worse, killed. If they ran there would be little or no chance of escaping the faster moving creatures. It felt like a stalemate. The wizard shook his head and turned back to the east, starting off once again.

"Ectle... what are we doing?" Thorgrim asked as he and Nimir watched the wizard leaving the area.

"Getting as far as we can before they catch up with us. We're not going to make it to the cliffs and out of the swamp but we have got to try. We will be better off trying to get there than standing and fighting."

"Just a thought Ectle," Nimir asked as he started after the wizard. "If the Lizardmen fought with Valsera's armies, what would stop them from chasing us up the shoreline and across the cliffs?"

Ectle didn't stop walking. He had hardly thought of the fact that the Lizardmen were willing to leave the swamps to fight throughout the forests and at Qwaz. If the creatures were leaving the swamps before then what would stop them from doing it again to chase the three? The wizard kept going regardless as their hopes for survival diminished. The swamp had begun to thin a great deal compared to the area around the camp of the Lizardmen and it made the trek easier. Even though the three were exhausted and struggling to stay on their feet they kept going.

After another hour or so of hiking through the swamps the wizard stopped once more and closed his eyes, slowing his breathing enough to focus on the party of creatures closing in on them. Something didn't feel the same and he held up a hand to stop the two Dwarves. As Thorgrim and Nimir came to a stop behind the wizard he focused his energy on the Lizardmen pursuing them. Not far behind them he could sense the Lizardmen in a smaller number than before. They were less than an hour behind and closing fast.

As the wizard spread his reach further he probed the swamp, trying to find why the mass of Lizardmen had suddenly lost so many of their numbers. The group he could sense was half the size he had originally detected. Ectle spread his mind further than the group behind them, stretching across the swamp and opened his eyes quite suddenly.

"Get ready you two!"

"What's wrong Ectle? What is it?" the Dwarves asked together.

The group of Lizardmen behind them was closing fast but during their flight through the swamps a smaller group had broken away from the rest and taken a wider approach to get ahead of the wizard and Dwarves. Ectle looked to the east and shook his head.

"Somehow a group got in front of us and is closing at the same rate as the one that is approaching from the rear. They are coming at us from two directions. We will never make it to the cliffs in the east now."

"How can you be sure? Why can't we move to the north away from them?" Thorgrim asked angrily as he refused to give up.

"I didn't say it was over yet. Get your backs all together here in the clearing. Face away from one another. That way we can not be taken from behind. We kill anything that comes through the fog. Get ready!"

The Dwarves hurried to the wizard and pressed their backs together against Ectle, their eyes probing the fog for any sign of life. They stood with their backs pressed together for a full ten minutes before any of them had any sighting of the enemy. It happened slowly but in one fluid motion. In every direction from the fog arrived the Lizardmen, approaching together and completely surrounding the three. The wizard kept the head of his staff pointed out in front of him, aiming it back and forth at the ten plus creatures approaching his position. Sadly, the numbers against the two Dwarves were similar.

"This is not possible... ridiculous... this is..."

"Nimir, no matter what it seems like, it is happening. Get ready and don't hold back."

The Lizardmen all moved into view and stopped, their forces staring at the three intruders in their swamps. Time had slowed to a crawl as the creatures eyed the Dwarves and wizard angrily. Ectle took a deep breath and looked from enemy to enemy, each one just as fierce and dangerous as the next. Soon, the area was completely silent. Thorgrim held the war hammer ready even though for the first time in a long time he felt afraid. Nimir did the same with his sword but fear had torn through him completely.

"What now Ectle?" Thorgrim asked in a whisper.

The wizard didn't answer, staring at the creatures nervously. He had an arsenal of spells, uncountable ways to dispatch the enemy but they were greatly outnumbered. He feared that if they moved the entire mass of creatures would attack all at once from different directions. He dropped his hand down by his side, hiding it from sight in the event he decided to go on the offensive.

"Ectle?"

"Stay still. I don't know why they've stopped… I don't want to find out. Get ready and when I tell you, hit them with everything you've got. It's all we can hope for right now."

"… to survive?"

"Perhaps we can do enough damage to send them into disarray and maybe we can slip through and keep moving. I don't know what else to do."

Ectle curled his fingers and muttered softly to himself, diving through the list of spells suitable for their situation. Nothing would completely rid them of the Lizardmen but he had plenty to use that would be destructive enough to drive them away. A wave of energy rolled through his fingers, growing quickly and taking form in his hand. He twirled his fingers and waited, looking for the opportune moment. The Lizardman directly across from the wizard took a step forward and Ectle attacked.

Mere seconds passed between the step the Lizardman took and the spell being released. Ectle flung his hand forward, watching as the ball of light shot out toward the creatures. The Lizardman brought its arms up to cover itself from the attack but the moment the ball of light struck the enemy an explosion rocked the clearing, sending several of the creatures flying back-ward through the air. Ectle followed with a second attack with similar results.

"Here they come!" Thorgrim shouted as the Lizardmen facing him broke and charged at the Dwarves.

The creatures leapt from their positions into the air, land-ing in full stride towards the group. Thorgrim grit his teeth and stepped away from the group, charging at the opposition with a yell of fury so sudden it caught the creatures by surprise. It was enough to slow their advance and Thorgrim charged headlong into the group, his war hammer ricocheting back and forth off of the enemies.

"Thorgrim!"

Nimir watched helplessly until he finally found courage somewhere inside him. He hefted his sword and followed the Dwarf, his yell as loud and just as angry. Fear was pulling him back towards the wizard but he ignored it. The closest enemy was unaware of the charging Dwarf and Nimir brought his sword around with all his might, the splatter of blood hitting his face. The warm blood gave him a boost of courage and he no longer felt the same fear. He continued attacking over and over, chop-ping his way towards Thorgrim.

Ectle did not bother watching the two as he cast spell af-ter spell, hardly managing to keep the charging Lizardmen at bay. Another fell to the side, its body completely engulfed in flames as he turned to the next. For a brief moment, it looked like things were going their way. Thorgrim retreated back towards the wiz-ard with Nimir under one arm. The young Dwarf still carried his sword but his left arm was marred with gashes from his wrist to his shoulder. A spear flew through the air and Ectle moved just in time, avoiding the sharp tip.

"Ectle, Nimir's hurt bad. What do we do?" Thorgrim asked, knocking an attacking Lizardman back off his feet with one swing of his war hammer.

Ectle dodged an attack and delivered a powerful blast to the Lizardman, looking back at the two briefly. There was noth-ing he could do for the Dwarf while so heavily engaged in battle. He started to reply but a kick to the chest sent him sprawling back to the Dwarves, hitting the ground hard.

He raised his head and watched as what was left of the

Lizardmen rallied together and moved to attack. There were no more than ten remaining but from the fog to the rear of the clearing came another group, fresh and ready to taste blood. Ectle pushed himself up to his feet, watching as the new force joined with those remaining from the first. Together they boasted numbers close to the initial attack and the wizard knew they would not be able to stand another attack with Nimir wounded.

"Thorgrim, protect Nimir as long as we can. There are just far too many of them."

"It was a pleasure fighting with you Ectle... and thank you for getting us out of that camp. I wish we would have made it out of this swamp though."

"Me too."

The Lizardmen spread out in a half circle, advancing slowly on the two as they prepared for what looked to be their last stand. Ectle could feel sweat on his brow and took a deep breath, a fireball building in his right hand. The flames swirled and twisted through his fingers as he waited for the right moment to release the spell. A soft breeze rolled through the area, cooling the wizard briefly as he narrowed his eyes on the opposition. The Lizardmen continued until the breeze became a soft wind, strengthening and getting the attention of everyone in the clearing.

"Ectle, what are you doing?" Thorgrim asked nervously.

"It's not me Thorgrim..."

The wind grew stronger and the fog was suddenly forced back away from the group. Ectle and the Dwarves looked to their right as a massive thud echoed through the air. Just when the wind stopped a new noise filled the air, one that sounded more like a hiss. It was almost familiar and Ectle quickly pushed the two Dwarves to the ground.

"Stay down!"

The hiss changed to an explosion that was accompanied by a massive wall of fire rushing towards the Lizardmen. The fog was melted away as the raging torrent of flames met its target and all of the Lizardmen were sent into a panic. Some retreated away from the fire while others never had the chance and now lay torched and smoldering on the ground. Ectle looked up and watched as the massive form of the Dragon that had brought him to the swamps appeared from the right. The wizard stared in disbelief. Minutes earlier he had given up all hope and now they were saved. He grabbed Thorgrim by the collar of his armor and pulled him to his feet, shoving him towards the Dragon.

"Go! Get as close as you can. I'll take Nimir."

Dragging the unconscious Dwarf was more laborious than he had expected but Ectle managed to pull him in beside the Dragon as the last of the Lizardmen disappeared into the deeper regions of the swamp. Ectle waited until the Dragon had finished with its attack and stood from the Dwarves, looking into its eyes.

"You came back? How did you even find us in this swamp?"

The Dragon turned its head down to the wizard. "I had given up and was headed back north when I saw the flashes of your spells and the sounds of battle below. I knew it was you. I did not want to leave you behind if I could help it."

Ectle smiled thankfully. "I thank you for that my friend. The younger Dwarf is gravely wounded. I will do what I can to heal him now but I am afraid his wounds are far worse than my skills."

"Do as you must. I will stand watch while you heal him."

Ectle turned to the Dwarf lying unconscious on the ground. He was covered in blood from the gashes running up the full length of his arm. Ectle reached into the pouch on his belt and retrieved a small vial only half full of a silvery liquid. He sighed to himself sadly. There was not enough of the liquid to fully heal the wounds. He pulled the cork and gently sprinkled the liquid across the wounds, watching as they slowly began to draw themselves closed. He closed his eyes when the wounds stopped just shy of becoming fully healed, mere slivers remaining where the deep gashes once were.

"Will it not do?" Thorgrim asked, looking at the wounds over Ectle's shoulder.

"For now, until we can get him somewhere to better treat them. They will continue to bleed, though not nearly as profusely. This will have to do."

Ectle took the dagger from Thorgrim's belt and cut the sleeve of his robes, quickly tying off the pieces on the wounds in the hopes that it would keep them from bleeding during the flight. The wizard, with the help of Thorgrim, picked the wounded Dwarf up off the ground and readied him on the Dragon's back.

"Can you carry three?" Ectle asked again, looking around the clearing.

"Not for very long. I will be able to get us clear of here before I must stop to rest. The Dragon who went down in the swamps with the Dwarves was much stronger than I am. I will do my best."

Ectle helped Thorgrim up in front of Nimir and then he climbed up behind the Dwarf, steadying him as the Dragon stretched its wings and started off into the air. The bodies of the Lizardmen still smoldered below them, but Ectle ignored the sight, his attention set squarely on the Dwarf in front of him. The Dragon flew higher and then started off towards what Ectle assumed was the north. He looked to the east and sighed deeply, seeing the cliffs and ocean less than a mile away.

Elendil stood on the royal balcony overlooking all of Pentegarn, his eyes focused on the sun as it climbed into the sky. It was the day he had both waited for and dreaded. The tree line in the distance had no sign of enemies in the least but he knew that the Dragon had not been wrong in its scouting. If the armies were not there yet, they would be soon and all of Pentegarn would be swallowed in war. The King scanned every inch of the trees, expecting to see the first scouts from the southern armies but saw nothing. He let his thoughts wander, thinking back to the times when war did not exist in the lands of Nalawren, back when the races coexisted peacefully. He wondered if times would ever be that way again.

The lands had changed almost overnight when the armies arrived in the southlands. The Elves had mobilized their armies in a matter of days and from that moment, they had been on guard, battling the hordes as they pressed north. The losses that spanned from the beginning of the war till now were uncountable. The King looked out across the lands again, seeing the lush, green forests in every direction. Would they too become gnarled and hideous like the forests to the south? It was impossible to tell.

The doors in the room behind him opened and a group of servants along with the head of the guard entered. They carried with them the ceremonial armor for the King and his sword to match the occasion. Elendil left the balcony and took a slow stride into the room, approaching the group. The soldier nodded and extended his hand to the armor at his left.

"We have brought your armor my King. This is a public affair now and it would be good if you looked your best, sir."

Elendil nodded in agreement. "Yes, this is an important matter though an unsettling one all the same."

The King waited as the servants helped strap on the armor piece by piece. They fastened the breastplate onto the King and pulled it tight, finishing the suit with a long cape fastened at the shoulders. The weight was hardly noticeable to the King who had worn the armor all his life throughout peace and war. Now he would dawn it for battle once more. The soldier held the sword at the base of the blade, kneeling and offering it to the King who took it and held it aloft. The sword felt comfortable in his hand, like an old friend he had found once more.

"Magnificent my Lord, this blade completes you. It has desired your hand for some time now, I can see it."

"I do not wish for battle. This is a necessary battle though and I will do everything within my power to defend the Elves of these lands. I will not allow them to lose faith in our might or fear the enemy which seeks to destroy us. We will meet them in battle all the same and we will be victorious. I swear it."

The soldier nodded in agreement, forcing himself to agree even though he was not sure of what the King said. If they were to meet the some thirty thousand soldiers in battle they would surely need a miracle to survive. The possibility of survival seemed slim, if any.

Elendil sheathed the sword at his hip and turned to the doorway, exiting and heading for the courtyard inside the second wall. Through the day and night the Elves had worked to build the platform required for the execution that was set for later in the day. The wooden platform was centered in the square with a set of stands on either side for the soldiers and royals and the throne at the front for the King. It was to be the first ordered execution ever within the walls of Pentegarn and the Elves were filled with mixed emotions about the event. Elendil walked out the stone archway into the clearing and looked on the builders still working to finish their tasks. He took the steps slowly and walked to the center of the platform where the King of the Humans would be executed.

"Is this right?" he asked himself.

"Excuse me, good King."

Elendil turned and looked behind him. At the foot of the steps he found one of the Celestial Knights. The soldier took a knee, waiting to be addressed. Elendil turned and walked to the steps. The rays of sun glinted off the armor and he raised a hand to shield his eyes.

"Yes, how may I help you?"

The Celestial Knight stood and took the steps one at a time until he was standing beside the King.

"I am Odimous, acting commander of the Celestial Knights while Lavian is away. I know you have set to execute the Human prisoner responsible for the betrayal today, and I am here to speak on behalf of our remaining Celestial Knights. We will not be in attendance during this event."

"I understand your decision Odimous. This would be against your beliefs?"

"Correct. Though we are not against death, we find that a prisoner, even one responsible for a crime as horrid as that the Human King is being executed for, should be allowed a chance to fight. If sentenced to death, our soldiers would prefer one to be given the chance to fight to his death."

"I respect your decision, and know that an execution has never taken place inside the walls on Pentegarn until this day. I do not feel that this the right nor the wrong choice to the issue at hand, but in the manner that we were betrayed, I do not feel the prisoner deserves his honor. You are allowed to do as you see fit for you and your people."

The Celestial Knight gave another nod and turned to leave the King to think about the words he had spoken. It was an obvious decision that he would not give the Human the chance to defend the actions he had committed, but at the same time, there was no honor in killing an unarmed man. Would his people understand if he executed Calyn without a second thought? He did not know.

The builders had finished and disappeared from the clearing, leaving only the King and the occasional round of soldiers checking the defenses. As the sun climbed higher into the sky Elendil knew it would soon be time to punish the Human for his crimes. He took a seat at the throne and looked out at the courtyard in the city, waiting for the rest of the Elves to arrive.

"My King there is no reason for us to sway from our decision to execute the Humans in response to the crimes they have committed. They should not be given the chance to defend their actions. Please, do not entertain this notion," the royal advisor pleaded with the King as he heard the Elf out in full.

"It is obvious that the Humans will not be allowed to leave here alive, but is there honor in killing them without a chance to defend their lives?"

"My King, how will your people see things when you allow the Human who has tried to take your life and who has aided in killing our forces at the Pass of Merwold a chance to fight for his decision? He should be taught that the choice he has made is unforgivable and the punishment should be swift and merciless. Sir, will you reconsider this decision before it is too late."

King Elendil stared straight ahead at the stands of Knights and royals that had gathered for the execution as well as the hundreds massed in the massive courtyard itself. He had never thought to allow the Humans a chance to fight for their lives but as he had always been honorable, Elendil wondered how it would affect his conscious if he did not give the men one last chance for their honor.

"No… I will allow those who have congregated here to see the execution they choose. If those in my court decide that the Humans deserve one last chance to defend their life for their own honor than I shall permit it. If not, then they will be executed as we had originally planned. This is my decision."

"As you wish, my King," the advisor replied, choosing not to pursue the matter any further. The King had made up his mind.

With the courtyard filled with the Elves that had decided to attend, Elendil took a deep breath and nodded to the executioner at the edge of the platform. The Elf was dressed from head to toe in plated armor with a visor closed on his helmet, hiding his identity from the rest of those in attendance. The Elf stopped and waited at the center of the platform where he was expected to carry out the sentence when the accused arrived. With everything in place Elendil stood and addressed the soldiers at the entrance of the castle.

"You may now bring the prisoners forward."

The entire congregation fell silent and turned toward the castle, watching as the Elves moved out into the sunlight, the three Human prisoners locked in chains led toward their deaths. They walked slowly, giving every Elf in attendance the chance to see those responsible for breaking the old alliance. No one uttered a sound. Calyn and his two soldiers walked with their heads down, their eyes not daring to leave the ground. It was the longest walk of Calyn's life and it would be his last, each step bringing him closer to his last breath.

The Humans were led one at a time up the stairs and then to the center of the platform where the executioner waited patiently. As they stopped Calyn took a step forward from the other two and raised his eyes for the first time to where Elendil sat on the throne. The two shared a silent thought before Elendil cleared his throat and stood to address everyone. Every Elf in attendance knelt as the King stood, waiting for him to speak before rising.

"My fellow Elves, we've been brought here today to punish those who have wronged us in recent days. As many of you know, the forces sent to the Pass of Merwold were slaughtered by the traitorous Humans of Cisalia whose King stands here before you today. Not only is he now being held responsible for the actions at the pass, but also he will be punished for the attempted murder of myself in the throne room of Pentegarn only days after his soldiers killed ours. I have come to a decision on this…"

All of Pentegarn waited as the King paused on that thought, waiting as he pieced together what he wanted to say. Did he really want to allow the King one last measure of honor after the betrayal that had cost Gnomes and Elves their lives? Was it worth the consequences?

Elendil nodded. "I will ask of you my subjects for your opinions as to how these three traitors shall be punished. I have recently come to the realization that there is no honor in a simple beheading while the prisoners are bound and forced to their knees. Killing an unarmed, defenseless person for their crimes makes me feel as guilty as those who killed our Elves at the pass. For this I ask, should we allow them one last chance to regain their honor before they are punished with death?"

Hushed whispers fell upon the crowd as they conversed amongst themselves for what seemed like forever. The soldiers did not need as much time to decide as honor and dignity were amongst the highest values to an Elven Knight. It made sense that the Humans should be allowed a chance to die with honor. Elendil waited as the subjects in the lower areas finally came to a decision.

"My King…"

Elendil turned to one of the soldiers waiting at the edge of the platform. "Yes sir Knight?"

"The soldiers here in your presence have unanimously decided that for our own conscious the three should be allowed one last chance to reclaim their lost honor. As for the remainder of your subjects in attendance, we follow your decision without question."

Elendil took a deep breath, surprised that the decision had been so unanimously in favor of allowing the Humans one last chance. The King stood from the throne and slowly descended the stairs that led to the platform floor. He stopped in front of the three prisoners with the executioner at his side. Staring at Calyn he made his decision.

"The three Human prisoners will be allowed to face the executioner in battle with the chance of earning their freedom as the reward for their success. If they are able to kill our Elven executioner, they will be allowed to leave the city and make for Cisalia. Soldiers, arm them."

Disbelief rushed through the crowd as the King's words echoed in their ears. How could he even consider allowing the Humans a chance at freedom if they had committed a crime against the crown? As the Knight had said though, not a single Elf argued the decision of the King. Soldiers from the edge of the platform approached, cutting the restraints from each prisoner and tossing a short sword at the feet of each of the Humans. The two Knights immediately picked their weapons up from the floor, but Calyn neglected his.

Elendil turned to the executioner and stared into the slits in the visor. "Make it interesting. They are not going anywhere."

With the last words the King walked back up the stairs to the throne and took his seat, watching as the two Human soldiers took a nervous step towards the Elf. Even with the promise of freedom Calyn still had not moved. The executioner looked up at the two and drew his sword from its sheath, brandishing the long blade at the two Humans. It was unlike any sword the Elves carried, two handed with the blade curving very gradually as it reached its tip. Though silent at first, a low cheer for the Elf started from the crowd and soon everyone in attendance found themselves watching anxiously.

The Elf moved to the left, watching as the two Humans moved into position, circling him slowly like animals set for a kill. The man to the right made his move quicker than his comrade and the Elf deflected the swing of the sword with ease, shoving the man to the side and preparing for the next to come. Just as he had expected the second attacker was on top of him instantly and the Elf dodged again, staying one move ahead of his opponents. Blows continued to rain down on the Elf who managed them with ease, delivering a powerful punch across the face of one of the attackers. The Human rolled across the platform and climbed to his feet slowly.

Elendil knew the Elf was a match against the three Humans all by himself and he was showing it now. Even though Calyn had neglected the offer and still had not moved from where he had stood the Elf never seemed to be in danger. The King watched as the executioner ducked another sword stroke and returned with his own to the chest of the attacker, halting the man in his steps. The second prisoner moved quickly to catch the Elf off guard but expecting the attack gave the Elf the upper hand. In one swift move he pulled his sword from the chest of the Human and whirled around quickly, the blade of his sword cutting the Human's throat with ease.

As the two Humans crumbled to the floor the Elf rounded on the third prisoner, eyeing the sword that remained on the platform at his feet. Calyn had not made a move to join his Knights during the battle but would very soon fall with them. The Elf approached and with one last look at the man he kicked the sword to the side and off the platform. The blade hit the ground below and the Elf turned to Elendil, awaiting the order to finish. The King stood from the throne.

"Calyn, you have been deemed a traitor to the Elves and to the entire alliance of old. Your crimes have given you a penalty of death and this is to be carried out today. You were offered a chance to redeem your honor and you refused. As of now, I hereby sentence you to death by beheading. Have you anything to say before your sentence is carried out?"

Calyn looked up at the King and met his gaze for the first time since the attempted betrayal in the throne room. The Human's face was expressionless and Elendil waited patiently, giving him one last chance to speak his mind. "I will not apologize for the wrongs I have ordered my soldiers to commit. I will not admit that I was wrong in what I have done. I was only looking out for the future of my people. What else is there to say?"

Elendil heard what the Human had to say but whether it meant anything to him would never be known. The Elf turned to the executioner and gave a slow nod. The Elf in plated armor slowly approached the Human and extended the sword in his left hand. In his right he held a flask of purified water and he carefully poured the liquid down the length of the sword, cleaning and purifying the blade for the task at hand. The water trickled to the floor at the Human's feet and the Elf shook the weapon to rid it of any excess.

"Kneel," the executioner ordered shortly, staring at the Human through the slit in the visor.

Calyn continued to stare straight ahead as he slowly dropped to one knee and then to the other, his hands resting lifelessly at his side. He waited for the inevitable swing from the Elf without the slightest hint of emotion on his face. Everyone in the area waited silently as the executioner stood poised, waiting for the order to attack. Elendil took one last look at the Human and looked to the back at the executioner, nodding to the Elf.

The executioner returned the nod and stepped around to the left side of the kneeling prisoner, his eyes never leaving Calyn. He stopped and drew the sword back to strike, hesitating briefly to allow the Human one last breath. Calyn raised his eyes to the sky above and locked them on a passing cloud, marveling at the careless freedom it possessed. He exhaled. The Elf planted his front foot and swung the sword down onto the Human's neck, feeling the blade meet the skin and continue through cleanly. As the sword left the body time seemed to move in slow motion. Calyn slumped forward and fell to the platform floor, his head rolling to the side as the body bounced softly. Silence gripped the area and the Elf stood from the attack he had just carried out, looking up to the King at the throne.

A nod ensured that the Human was no longer living.

Elendil watched the expressions of the entire courtyard, seeing a lot of relief on the faces of the Elves. He took a deep breath and stood from the throne, slowly descending the stairs to the platform below. He walked to where the Human's body lay in large pool of blood. The King stopped and turned in a slow circle to the Elves.

"All here today have witnessed the punishment for any who dare betray us the way the Human King did. There will be no escape from our wrath. Let the word go out to all those involved that from this day forth they will be hunted to the death."

Elendil looked down at the body of the King as the soldiers approached the platform to remove Calyn's remains. He nodded to them as he passed and stopped next to the executioner. The Elf gave a low nod and turned towards the body.

"You have done what was expected of you my friend. You are relieved of your duties and I expect you will take what time you need for the next day or so."

"Thank you my Lord."

The Elf poured what remained in the flask over the blade once more, washing the blood from the sword. Once clean, he slid it down into the sheath and turned, leaving the platform and disappearing into the castle. The crowd began to disperse back into the city and within the hour the entire square had been cleared. The bodies had been removed from the platform and the body and head of Calyn were staked in the fields outside of the city walls as a warning to those who stood against the Elves.

Elendil stood on the battlements of the outer walls, staring out at all that he could see. In every direction he could see empty fields leading up to the forest edge. There still was no sign of any enemy forces that had been claimed to be moving in against the city of Pentegarn which gave the King an uncomfortable feeling in the back on his mind. The Dragon had told of some forty thousand soldiers moving north but there had yet to be the slightest sign of their presence. Questions began to arise in the King's head.

What if the armies in the south bypassed them completely and moved on the weaker lands above them? What if the armies had already passed the lands surrounding Pentegarn and were pillaging Swanhaven and the northern Elven settlements? The southern armies could be destroying everything between

Pentegarn and Tvan and the High Elves were doing nothing to help them.

The thoughts bothered him but he knew as the King of the High Elves and the ruler of Pentegarn that he could not send his forces through the northlands on a whim. Every Elf would be needed at the city if the Elves hoped to last through the siege. The Celestial Knight Odimous approached and cleared his throat, taking a quick bow before Elendil. The King nodded and the Knight stood from the ground.

"I must say I was surprised to see that you allowed the prisoners the option to fight for their honor. I was impressed. You truly are a just King, even when faced with the turmoil that is plaguing these lands."

"Thank you for your kind words Odimous."

"I have yet another thought if I may sir?"

"Of course, go ahead."

"If I have been informed correctly, this Calyn was the King of the Human city to the north. What will become of his people in the aftermath of his betrayal?"

The King nodded slowly to himself as these thoughts had crossed his mind recently after the execution of the Human. He had not come to an answer that comforted his thoughts.

"I have thought on this matter for a while now and I am ashamed to say that I do not have the slightest idea what should become of them. I ask myself, should they be punished for the actions of the King? Whenever I decide that they should be punished, I then wonder if the people had any knowledge of their king's actions. One thing I will not do is chastise the innocent for the actions of one."

"Very honorable. There are sure to be innocent mixed in with the guilty and segregating them may be near impossible once they learn their King has been slain. I must admit I do not know the nature of the races here in these lands, but I do know that the death of their King may push them to stand against you in full now. No matter what the outcome, if Lavian says we stay, we stay. For what it is worth, you have our allegiance."

"That is comforting to know Odimous. There are few of you, but your strength and desire for what is right is as powerful as what I find in my own Knights."

The words gave the Celestial Knight pride in his fellow

soldiers. Another race they had never before found themselves with had seen their strength even with their fewer numbers. Added to the fact the compliment came from a King. It was a day he would remember for a long time to come.

Reunited Amongst the Dwarves

*T*he peaks of Tvan were all covered with snow as the colder months began to stretch across the northern lands. The carriage followed the road up into the mountains as the soldiers stretched in front and behind keeping a close eye on the forest around them. The road steepened and in several spots the carriage had trouble in the snow. The road soon became impassable and the Elven caravan came to a halt. The soldiers all pulled back to the carriage and set up a perimeter through the trees and on the road. Rhen looked out of the door at the soldiers moving through the snow.

"What do you see Rhen?" her mother asked, leaning forward to catch a glimpse as well.

"I don't know. They are walking around the carriage and moving out into the trees. It has been a long time since I have seen this much snow. I want a better look," Rhen said as she pushed the door open.

"Rhen, stay in the carriage!" her mother scolded.

Rhen stepped out into the snow, pulling the heavy cloak around her shoulders to keep her warm. The snow made a soft crunch under her feet as she walked towards the front of the carriage. She stopped as one of the Knights approached her.

"Princess, you should not be out. Please return to the carriage at once."

"I just wanted to see the snow. Why did we stop?" she asked, avoiding the order from Knight.

The soldier looked up the road. "The horses are having trouble pulling the carriage in the snow. They lost their footing in the snow and with the road getting steeper in the next few hundred yards we have a dilemma. I will speak with the Queen."

The Knight walked past the Princess and stopped at the

door of the carriage, speaking quietly with the Queen just out of earshot of Rhen.

Rhen turned and walked a little further up the road in the snow, looking out at the snowy mountains around them. Tvan had been different when she had come with Erzel and the others. Now it was like visiting a completely different land. She could see her breath in the breeze and pulled her cloak a little tighter. Tvan was much different this time.

When she turned to walk back towards the carriage she saw her mother step out into the snow as well. The soldiers were beginning to pull back towards the main group and it was evident that they would try to get started again. Most of the baggage and gear had been removed from the carriage and the Elves carried it as the driver snapped the reins and got the horses moving again. They struggled at first but finally were able to gain their footing and the carriage moved forward up the hill.

Rhen watched the horses as they passed and waited as the group of archers and Knights moved up around her. She fell in beside her mother as they walked slowly up the hill. The road finally began to level off a ways up the hill and the carriage was waiting for them. The Queen and Princess stopped next to it and admired the view. They had been traveling uphill for a long while and had reached a point where the rest of the world was below them.

"It is amazing…" Rhen whispered into the wind.

"Very. Come, let us get back in the carriage where it is a little warmer. The soldier said it is only a short way to reach the entrance to the mountains. Once we are safe inside the halls of Tvan we can relax."

"Ok mother," Rhen replied reluctantly, taking one last look at the lands below the mountains. The blanket of snow stretched down to the foothills and beyond that only a very light dusting was present. She reached up and gripped the handle on the side of the carriage and pulled herself up the steps one at a time.

Rhen took the seat across from her mother and felt her breath catch as the carriage suddenly leapt back into motion. They arrived at the entrance of Tvan in twenty minutes, just as the soldiers had estimated. They dropped into formation as one of the Knights opened the door for the Princess and Queen of

Swanhaven. The Elven soldiers dropped to a knee as the Queen exited and even the Dwarves managed a bow in respect. Narissa stopped and looked around the clearing where the two massive towers marked the entrance of the city.

"This is Tvan... how very inconspicuous," she muttered sarcastically at the sight of the towers in the middle the forest.

Rhen remembered the other entrance that she had seen when she had arrived with Erzel and the others. It was very similar to the one she was standing in front of now but today there was a heavier presence of soldiers. A group appeared and the force of Elves stopped in front of them.

"Greetings Queen of Swanhaven, welcome to the mountains of Tvan. We are prepared to accompany you inside whenever you are ready."

The Queen nodded and the Elves followed the Dwarven soldiers inside as they all lit torches and spread through the tunnel ahead. Narissa, Rhen, and a handful of Knights headed into the passage with the Dwarves. They walked for what seemed like forever, following the passage down deep into the earth where the Dwarves lived. They passed countless Dwarves of all types; miners, soldiers, and merchants. They soon noticed that the air in the passages was much warmer than outside, giving the Elves reason to shed their heavier cloaks and take in their new surroundings.

Even though they were deep in the earth the torches gave off ample light to keep their eyes from straining too much. The passage finally opened into the massive world under the mountains. They stopped at the gate that led to the city and Narissa marveled at the sight.

"An entire defensive structure underground? This is very impressive I must say," the Queen whispered, seeing the outer wall of Tvan for the first time.

"This is small compared to what the inner city houses, mother. It is like all of Pentegarn doubled. Not to mention the mines that stretch through the mountains, the city itself houses merchants, traders, and metalworkers that can fashion nearly anything you can think of, and the fortress, a mountain all its own..."

"I take it you've learned quite a lot while you stayed here then. I am impressed."

"... and the lake. There is a lake within the mountain.

This is the most amazing world that the sunlight never touches. As much as I love it, I can not stand it for long though. Sooner or later the lack of sun makes you feel strange."

The gate to the wall guarding the city was opened slowly and the Dwarves led the group in. The Elven Knights followed the last few Dwarves deeper into the heart of the city until they came upon the massive fortress at the heart of Tvan. The steep walls of the castle stretched up into the cavern, ending at the broad battlements where the Dwarven archers kept a close eye on the torch lit city below. The group stopped at the front of the castle as the gates were opened to allow them in.

With the castle being well lit they no longer needed the mass of torches to find their way through the halls. One lone Dwarven soldier led the Knights, Princess, and Queen up through the castle to the great hall where the Elders would be expecting them. They finally arrived at the two great doors and the Dwarves guarding the room pushed them open, announcing the visitors.

"Elders of Tvan, we present the Queen of Swanhaven, Narissa. Joining her is her daughter Rhen, the Princess of Swanhaven."

The Elders sitting at the long table stood together as the two Elves and their escorts entered the room. They stopped on the opposite side of the table and waited to be addressed further. Rhen looked at the Elders, remembering them from her first stay in Tvan.

"Mother, starting from the left we have Velex, the Elder of diplomatic affairs. Then we have Odar, Elder of the defenses underground and next to him Ardis, Elder of the defenses above ground. Lastly is Divos who... um... I don't remember what he is in charge of. I am sorry."

The Dwarf stood from the table to address the Queen and Princess. He was larger than the other three but it was evident that age had played a part on him. "Yes, my name is Divos, and I am in charge of all the mining communities here within the mountains as well as what is done with the gems and ores that are mined from the earth. It is unexpected to see you return Princess, especially having not known you had left the city without any sort of word or warning."

"I apologize, both for not remembering you and as well

for leaving as I did. I had no other choice," Rhen replied quietly.

"You could have... no, you should have stayed here. You were supposed to stay here where you would be safe. You promised us that you..."

"I know! I know I promised," Rhen interrupted. "I just did not want to be left here while someone I cared about went off without me. He saved my life mother, more than once."

Narissa looked from her daughter to the four Elder Dwarves at the table. Her head was blank as she fumbled to address their reasoning for their stay in Tvan.

"Please, sit down," Velex offered, showing them seats directly across from the Dwarves. Rhen and Narissa pulled the chairs out and took the seats that had been offered to them.

"I thank all four of you for allowing us refuge here in the mountains. The dangers that existed when my daughter was sent have grown in strength and in number. As we speak the Wood Elves are returning to the southlands to do what they can to help. I fear that this will not be enough."

The Dwarves looked at one another and then back to the Queen. "We have already received news of the trouble in the south. Earlier this morning a group arrived from Pentegarn, exhausted and starved they were immediately sent to recover. Apparently they fought day and night to get here without stopping once."

The question on Rhen's lips was who, but she found that it was not even necessary to ask. The doors opened behind the two and Rhen snuck a peak over her shoulder. Standing in the doorway and just as shocked as she was appeared Erzel, followed by Kail and Lavian. Rhen's mouth was agape as Erzel and the others crossed the room and waited to be addressed. Velex nodded and noted the chairs waiting for them at the table.

"This is quite a surprise. I never would have dreamed of seeing you here in Tvan, Rhen."

Rhen did not respond. She stood from the table, pushed her chair out of the way, and crossed the space them in three hurried steps. She flung her arms around the Elf with enough force to knock him over but Erzel managed to stay on his feet. They were silent for nearly a minute before Rhen finally pulled her face out of his chest.

"I... I didn't think you'd survived. The armies keep coming… surely Valsera was defeated if you are here."

Erzel took a deep breath. "Let us sit down. There is much to discuss with everyone here."

The two Elves joined the rest of the group at the long table as Erzel prepared to tell of what had happened at Qwaz. His eyes slowly moved around the table and he finally settled himself enough to continue. "It is an odd thing to have happened. We arrived at Qwaz and a massive battle erupted all across the city and through the air. We managed to infiltrate the throne room and found Valsera. He was stronger than Kail, Yanosh, and myself combined. Though he had help from the Demon that serves him, Valsera easily bested us one by one."

Odar stopped with a raised hand. "Through the air?"

"Yes… when my group left this city we went in search of the Dragons. Though everyone thought them to be only rumors and myth, we managed to locate the island and they agreed to help us. We lost members on their island during an attack from the Demon's soldiers. Yanosh, the head of the Celestial Knights sacrificed himself to fully encase Valsera in a prison of crystal. It remains intact even now."

"A prison of crystal? How can you be certain that his soldiers have not found a way to free him by now?" Odar asked quietly.

Erzel looked to Lavian and waited as the Celestial Knight produced the top of the staff and the crystals that continued to pulse as they had when Erzel first found them. She held it up for the Elders and Queen to see, watching as it continued to pulse softly.

"This is the top of the staff carried by a powerful wizard named Yanosh. He managed to imprison Valsera by sacrificing himself. As the crystals here continue to pulse, the crystal prison remains intact," Lavian explained, returning it to her belt.

"Then why have his forces continued to move north? Why did they not break and disperse when their leader was defeated?" Narissa asked sourly.

"There are two possibilities to that. One, because Valsera is not dead and only imprisoned, his soldiers continue to feel his power and fight all the same. Two, Infus has taken charge of the armies and now leads them in the place of the sorcerer."

"Which do you lean towards master Elf?" Velex asked.

"Honestly... both. Valsera is as good as defeated but even so the armies have not faltered a single step. In fact, they have grown in strength lately. Calyn of Cisalia and his Knights aided the southern armies at the Pass of Merwold. They completely annihilated our entire presence there. Now there is nothing stopping them from completely invading the Elven lands."

"Now I see why you have come to us Erzel. Is there no way to hold the armies without our intervention?" Velex asked, knowing that furthering the conversation would eventually lead to war.

Erzel turned to Lavian who looked to the Dwarf. "With all do respect sir, I have seen these armies and the damage they cause first hand. We Celestial Knights lived as the Elves did until Valsera's armies descended on our lands. It was like a plague sweeping across our world. If you do nothing to help, Valsera's armies will be on your doorstep in no time. What will you do when there is no one to come to your calls for help?"

The four Dwarves looked at one another as the reality of what the woman had said sank in. If they waited too long, there would be no one to help. The Dwarves had managed to avoid the wars in the south for quite a long time now and none of the Elders was ready to send their race into the fray of battle. Erzel caught a glimpse of Rhen out of the corner of his eye. He knew she was staring at him and it was obvious that the fear of never seeing one another again had taken a very heavy toll on her.

Velex looked up at the group. "Erzel, did you know that the Wood Elves have left Eglarest and are returning to the Elven lands near Swanhaven?"

The High Elf looked from the Queen to the Dwarves. "I mean no disrespect my Lady, but the Wood Elves will be of very little help against the mass that is approaching. More than forty thousand soldiers are marching on Pentegarn as we speak, perhaps having already arrived. We need more than the Elves. We need your Dwarves."

Narissa, who had been mostly silent during the entire conversation stood from the table and looked at the group. "The Humans have betrayed us and the armies of Qwaz and Nomaria still march. This argument will do nothing to slow them down. There has to be action if there is any form of hope for the alliance now. My husband, the King of the Wood Elves personally leads his forces south to face them no matter what their numbers. You have twenty times the number of soldiers. What are you waiting for?"

The Queen stood rigid as she stared at the Dwarves who remained silent. She could not understand why they would do nothing to help when they had armies that could more than likely overrun what was left in the southlands. The Dwarves remained speechless a she finally took a deep breath and lowered her gaze to the table.

"Will you please show me to the room where I will be staying?"

Odar looked to the doorway and snapped his fingers. The guard left the door and approached, stopping beside the Queen. "Yes Elders?"

"Show Queen Narissa to her room at once," he told the Dwarf, turning back to the Queen. "I hope you will find our room accommodating. You are free to explore all of Tvan."

The Queen did not bother to thank them as she turned and followed the Dwarf out of the room. They watched her shadow in the torchlight until she rounded the corner and Erzel turned back to his group. He, Lavian, Kail, and Rhen remained at the table and he found himself struggling to control his own flaring temper. How could they not send any form of help to the south? Without the Dwarves the Elves would surely lose Pentegarn. He shook his head, knowing he should have more faith in the city and its defenders.

"I don't get it…" Erzel started, still digging through his head for the right words.

"I am sorry master Elf, what don't you get?" Ardis asked, folding his hands on the table in front of him.

"The Elven races are on the verge of being completely annihilated and no one is willing to help them. The Humans have betrayed us, the Gnomes were slaughtered, and now the Dwarves have decided to ignore us. Can one of you four explain that to me?"

"The Humans have always been a bit…"

"I am not talking about the Humans. I am talking about you Dwarves!" Erzel interrupted angrily. "I already know that the Humans have betrayed us, that will not change now. I want to know why you and the Dwarves hide in your mountains."

"Erzel, you need to calm down," Velex ordered sternly, standing from the table.

Erzel stared at the Dwarves in bewilderment, anger continuing to surge through him. He could not understand why the Dwarves would not commit to the defenses of Nalawren as they had in the past. He raised his hands and shrugged, disbelief obviously working through him.

"Calm down? This is ridiculous. We're going back to Pentegarn with or without your help. We are not afraid to fight and die for our freedoms so let me know when you decide to follow suit," Erzel replied bitterly, turning away from the table.

Lavian and Kail stood to follow the Elf as the Dwarves stood to stop them. They watched the group walk to the door and stop as Erzel turned back to the Princess. "Rhen, will you come with us?"

Rhen stood at the table and looked from the Dwarves to the Elf, wondering what was going to happen. The Dwarves didn't seem to care what happened to the Elves and their people so long as they were safe in the mountains. She too was angry, but at the same time was not as eager to show it as Erzel had been. She took a deep breath and crossed the room to join them. Erzel took her hand and led the group towards their rooms.

"Why won't they help us Erzel? Are they going to let Valsera's armies take our lands without a fight?" Rhen asked with a sunken expression.

"The armies no longer belong to Valsera. Infus has taken control of everything and will stop at nothing to cover all our lands in an endless darkness. The Dwarves are afraid."

"There is no way the southern armies, whoever commands them, would win against the Dwarves combined with the Elves."

"Only if we had their help, Rhen. Right now, I don't know if this is going to go the way we want. Right now Pentegarn is being marched on by the combined armies of Qwaz and Nomaria. There is not much time."

Rhen walked beside Erzel wondering if it was a good time to tell him the news she had discovered. She could tell he was quite stressed about the lack of allegiance the Dwarves were showing but at the same time she was unbelievably excited. He should know, but not until the time was right. She walked beside the Elf, amazed that he was that close to her again. It was like a dream.

Erzel let Rhen take the lead as Kail and Lavian arrived at their rooms and disappeared inside. He was only a step behind her, catching every scent from her hair to her skin. It was a feeling he had not felt in a long time and took him back to the time they spent on the island with the Dragons. If they were both going to be together in Tvan, even for a night, Rhen wanted to make the most of it. She waited a moment and Erzel stepped in beside her. She caught his hand in hers and they walked together down the hallway. She stopped once they were clear of anyone in the hall and turned to face him.

"Did you ever think we would see one another again? I knew the moment you left Eglarest that was the last I would see of you but here you are. I can't believe it," Rhen exclaimed with a cheerful expression.

"I didn't know what to expect to be honest. I knew going up against the most powerful enemy in all of Nalawren was very risky. I did not expect to come out alive but I did. Sadly, not everyone escaped unscathed."

"What happened?"

"Come, let us retire to a room. I will tell you everything in private," Erzel replied, leading the Princess further down the hall.

They arrived at her room in the fortress and Erzel opened the door, quickly checking inside before letting the Princess in. He closed the door behind her and she walked to the bed and took a seat, waiting to hear all that the Elf had to say. At the same time, she could hardly wait to tell him everything she had discovered. Erzel pulled a chair up next to the bed and took a seat, leaning back and taking a deep breath.

"We assaulted Qwaz just as we had planned. Some of us hit the north tower while the Dragons and Celestial Knights on their Warbirds provided what cover they could offer from the air. In the end, Kail, Yanosh, and myself found ourselves face to face with the sorcerer and his servant Infus. The battle was intense. Infus was much stronger I, but Alora managed to save my life just when things were at their worst."

"Infus?"

Erzel remembered the way his sword passed through the

opponent without a hint of resistance. "A Demon summoned to serve Valsera. It is very powerful and seemingly invincible. We shall see. Yanosh fought Valsera and in the end sacrificed himself to imprison the sorcerer in crystal. The forces in the south did not break as we thought. The Demon apparently has control over them now and it leads while Valsera is unable."

Rhen did not know what to say. The plan had been to kill Valsera and the armies would break. They would not have strength or will to continue fighting with their master dead. She realized however that Valsera was not dead and obviously the solders were willing to follow the next in command.

"Who else did not make it?" she asked, remembering how the wizard had treated her with the utmost respect even when they had not been welcome in the lands of the Dragons.

"Most of the Celestial Knights and their Warbirds fell in the battle. All but Alora and another Gold Dragon fell. As for our group, everyone but Nimir and Thorgrim are accounted for. The two Dwarves were rescued from the walls by a Dragon only to be shot from the sky and plummet into the swamps to the east. I do not know what has become of them."

"Thorgrim... Nimir... maybe they... could they have lived?"

"Doubtful, and if they had they would be deep in enemy territory. Ectle returned to find them, but I never heard from him again. There is no way of knowing now. Our sole purpose was to rally the Dwarves to fight alongside us when the armies arrived at Pentegarn but now it does not seem that it will happen. We have failed," the Elf said bitterly, picturing his home smoldering in ruins.

"Erzel... there is something you need to know. Something... wonderful," Rhen said suddenly, no longer able to hold in her excitement.

"What is it?"

"I uh... I... I'm not quite sure how to say this now," Rhen stammered, her stomach whirling in excitement and fear.

"Just tell me. Rhen, there is nothing you can say that will make me look on you any differently."

"Ok... you... Erzel, you have to come back to us safe and sound."

"Us? Rhen I am going to do everything in my power to

make sure I am with you after this ends. We will be together."

"No Erzel... us... I do not know if you will have a son or daughter waiting for you, but we will be waiting for you. Us."

"Are you saying..."

Erzel trailed off. He sat in the chair staring at the Princess with the same look of disbelief that Rhen had worn in the mirror the day she found out. He swallowed and found himself staring at her stomach, not knowing what to say. Pentegarn, his soldiers, the enemies marching north, all of it seemed to disappear. Now, the only thing he was focused on was her.

"Are you sure? How do you know?"

"I fell ill while at Eglarest. My father brought a healer to see me and he realized what I told you. That night on the Dragon Isles gave us more than an unforgettable memory. Erzel, are you angry with me?" Rhen asked timidly, finding his silence a little intimidating.

Erzel looked up to the Princess's face. "Angry with you? Of course not. I am not angry at all. I am happy, but very much worried. Rhen, these lands are falling apart all around us. Surely now you will stay here where it is safe until the south has finally fallen?"

"Yes... of course I will. Erzel... I will be a mother before the next summer."

He could hear every word, but he sat in a state of shock. His thoughts danced back to the brief time he had spent at the graves of his parents. He remembered the way his mother had looked at him, the way she had passed her hand over her own waist, as if caring for a child of her own. He had seen the truth for himself and never realized it. He reached up and took her hands, trying to think of the right thing to say.

"Your father will surely have me hung. I take it he was quite displeased."

"Somewhat, but we will not worry about what others think, Erzel. So long as we have one another everything will be perfect. No matter what, you have to come back to Tvan. I will not leave so long as you promise you will come back for me."

Erzel knew what he could not guarantee. There was no way to know what would happen when he met the enemy on the field of battle again, but to settle her he decided to agree, nodding his head quietly.

"I need to hear you say it Erzel."

"I will come back for you... I promise."

She squeezed his hands, happy to hear that he would come back for her. He knew in the back of his head that there was a chance he may never come back but he was not about to tell her. He wanted to make sure she was happy. Erzel leaned up to her, kissing her on the cheek as he wrapped his arms around her shoulders. As he let her go to leave Rhen stood from the bed.

"Erzel... will you stay a little longer please?"

The Elf stopped in the middle of the room and turned, looking at the Princess.. She was just as perfect as she had been the last time he had seen her at Eglarest. He nodded and walked back to the bed and sat down next to her. There was time to spare for her and he was happy to spend it with her.

A new day arrived at Tvan even though the whole world beneath the mountains had no idea that the sun had risen again. The Elves and Erzel's group were forced to rely on their senses to judge the time of day as the light never changed. Erzel found himself sitting before the Elders of Tvan as he desperately pleaded his case. He was not sure how to make them see how bad things had gotten in the south.

"Erzel, we heard your case yesterday and yet we are still no more willing to go to war than we were the first time. By all means though, if you feel you must explain once more, we will listen," Odar said with a touch of impatience in his voice.

"This is true, I may have already explained the situation at Pentegarn and south of the city but it is apparent that you do not fully understand how serious this matter is. If nothing is done there may not be a Pentegarn for us to return to. This is my home we are on the verge of losing..."

"Pardon me Erzel, but how sure are you that the Elves at Pentegarn will fall against the armies? To my knowledge Pentegarn has a history much like that of Tvan, impenetrable."

Erzel took a deep breath and continued. "Be that as it may, Pentegarn has never been forced to defend itself against more than forty thousand soldiers at once. Has Tvan?"

"Do not mock us Erzel," Odar stated firmly.

"I was not mocking you, but this is a matter you obviously do not see as clearly as we who are set to face this opponent. I remember when our Elves numbered in the hundreds of thousands... possibly even millions. Now, after decades of war with the Goblins and their master we have been reduced to a fraction of those numbers. The same can be said for the Wood Elves, and though through this time we have managed to inflict great damage to their numbers as well, we are facing oblivion. The Dwarves number like the stars in the sky, why do you not help us to put an end to this nightmare?"

The Dwarves looked to one another and Divos, who had hardly uttered a word throughout the discussions tapped on the table. "How eager are you to send one of your High Elven brothers into battle to die? I take it this emotion is somewhat depressing for you?"

"At times, yes."

"Then surely you understand we do not want our brethren to die in a war we can avoid."

"You can not avoid this war Elders! If we are defeated, if the High Elves and the Wood Elves are finished, then there will be nothing to stop them from sweeping up to the foothills of Tvan and into the tunnels themselves. My Elven brothers know the risk they take when they draw their swords and bows and are willing to lay their lives down knowing that they protect their families and loved ones. Those who have lost their lives against the enemy have gained something we have not."

"And what might that be Erzel?"

"They will forever be remembered by those who remain as the ones who made our freedom possible. Their lives may have been taken, but their memories will be immortal."

The Dwarves looked around at one another again, all four with the same ideas. If they did send their soldiers into war and they were successful in defeating Valsera's soldiers, they would never be forgotten. The Elves had always been the buffer between the north and the south. Perhaps it was time for the Dwarves to step in.

"The last time our soldiers met Valsera's in battle were the early days of his invasion. Since then, we have left the protection of these lands up to you and your Elves. I suppose it is time for us to return to the surface once more. Are we in agreement?" Ardis asked, looking around the table.

The three other Elders talked amongst themselves in a

hushed whisper and looked at the forth, all nodding together in agreement. They had hidden in the mountains for too long. Though comfortable beneath the surface, it was time for them to join their allies once more.

"Thank you... now we have a chance. I only hope it is not too late. We will need to leave as soon as your soldiers are ready to meet the armies at Pentegarn. They may have already come under attack."

"We will begin assembling our army at once and the first battalion can leave as early as tomorrow. Send word to the other two you arrived with and be ready to move. Somehow, you managed to show us that this war is necessary."

Erzel thanked them a second time and left the room, hurrying up the halls to find Kail and Lavian. Both were in the great hall at one of the tables, finishing whatever meal it was time for. They looked up as the Elf slid in next to them at the table.

"That's quite a smile Erzel, what have you done?" Kail asked, wiping his hands.

"The Dwarves are sending their army out. We leave with the first battalion tomorrow. We're going back to Pentegarn!"

The two looked at the Elf in a state of awe, amazed that he had managed to sway the Dwarves from their decision to stay out of the war. The four Elders had been so set on remaining in the mountains that it seemed impossible for anyone to change their minds.

"I have not the slightest idea how you managed to change their minds but I am very impressed. We should prepare. Pentegarn is waiting," Kail said as the three stood from the table.

"I will go speak with Rhen. This is what we came here for and it is now time for us to go. She will understand, I know it."

Rhen stood on the balcony of her room, looking out at the millions of torches that lit the city. Though they were deep underground, the torches almost managed to give the impression of sunlight as it bounced off the cavern walls and buildings. Erzel stood in the doorway, looking out at the Princess in the dancing light of the torches. He finally walked out of the room to the balcony and stopped behind her, clearing his throat. Rhen turned and looked at the Elf.

"Erzel... what are you doing back?"

"I managed to convince the Elders to send their armies after all. We will be moving out with the first group of soldiers tomorrow and more will follow behind us. Perhaps now we have a chance to end this once and for all."

"So this is your last night here with me then?" Rhen asked glumly.

"Yes... this will be it. I promised to come back for you Rhen and I meant it. I will be back in Tvan the moment Valsera's armies have been defeated. Nothing will keep me from you."

Rhen crossed the floor between them and threw her arms around his waist, burying her face in his chest. She wanted to cry but she was happy to hear that the Dwarves would not abandon them. One day, things would be back to normal.

"We have a little time if you would like to go for a walk, one last time before I have to leave."

Rhen took his hand and together they walked back through the room and out into the hallway. They slowly dropped through the levels of the castle and out into the city, taking their time and marveling at every detail of the buildings and statues the city had to offer, making their last walk together one to remember.

A New Kind of War

The trees were growing thinner as Tanis and his army marched on towards Pentegarn. By his estimates the King assumed they would be arriving within a few hours. The Elves marched with their heads high even though they knew that before them was the army that threatened to destroy the northlands. As they moved through the forests silently Tanis took the lead, scouting with hopes of seeing good news. Then again at the moment, no news was good news.

"My King, we are nearing the city. Should we rest in case the city is under attack and we are forced into battle the moment we arrive?" one Knight asked, stopping in next to Tanis.

The King pondered for a moment and turned back to them. "Hold the soldiers here, fifteen minutes rest, quick rations and water. We will need our strength in the coming days. I need a volunteer to scout ahead."

A soldier approached, finishing his water. "I will go my King, I have plenty of energy."

"Good then, move ahead of us and see if there is anything of concern in our path. Return as soon as you have news."

"Yes my King," the scout replied, securing his bow and starting off through the trees to carry out his orders.

The King turned back and watched the soldiers gather in groups around their packs and supplies, taking the time to rest up for what was sure to come soon. He leaned against a fallen tree and stretched, his thoughts turning to the war that was spreading towards them as fast as they were moving towards it. There was no telling what they would be faced with in the upcoming days.

One of the soldiers approached and leaned against the same tree, offering the King a skin of water.

"Thank you soldier. Are you nervous?"

The soldier looked up through the trees and then back around at the Elves in the clearing. "Honestly... yes. Quite a bit. I know what this army has done to the south and I am in no hurry to face it. On the other hand, if everyone lets their fear rule them we will not stand a chance. I will keep my head even when I am afraid."

"That is admirable. Get your rest while you can. We will be moving again very soon."

The soldier nodded and left, leaving the King to his thoughts. Tanis found that it was a bittersweet moment. He preferred the solitude while he was deep in thought but at the same time, his mind was prone to wander wildly when there was nothing to keep him distracted. Soon he began to wonder about the size and strength of the southern army.

The Elves began pulling their packs together, loading everything onto their horses and carts and preparing to begin moving once more. Tanis walked to his horse and took the reins, gently rubbing the shoulder of the large animal to keep it calm. Its deep breaths shook the muscles in its chest and the King could feel it through his armor. He reached up and pulled himself into the saddle. The horse pawed the ground and the King looked back to the soldiers.

"Alright everyone, let's get moving. We have only a few hours left and we should be there."

The King snapped the reins and the horse slowly started forward with the Elves falling in line behind him. They had walked no more than ten minutes when up ahead the scout returned from around a bend in the path. He moved at a brisk pace and stopped in front of the King's horse, taking the reins to steady the animal as he caught his breath.

"Have you news soldier?" Tanis asked, looking at the red face Elf.

"A very strange sight indeed my Lord. The Humans of Cisalia are moving south. A decent sized army marching parallel to ours in the same direction. They look to be going into battle as well."

Tanis looked at the soldier. "Alright then, let us find out where they are headed. I will ride out to them at once. Perhaps they march to help Pentegarn as well."

The King spurred his horse ahead of his army with a handful of his Knights and the flag bearer riding with him. They followed the scout through the trees to the point where he had seen the Human army moving south. Just as the scout had claimed, the Humans were on the move. Their infantry stretched back out of sight and the Elves saw groups of archers in their ranks. If there were any mounted Knights they were either still in the rear or had already passed.

Tanis looked through the soldiers and took a deep breath, moving out of the trees in search of their commander. The Knights followed and the group crossed the clearing together. The Humans marched on, seemingly oblivious to the Elves coming towards them. It was a small group of archers that first spotted the Wood Elves crossing the open area between them and the trees. Tanis and the Knights slowed their horses and watched.

The archers quickly alerted the soldiers and took positions to guard their forces from an attack. The Elves came to a complete stop and stared as the Humans appeared to be on the offensive.

"What are they doing my King? Do they mean to attack us?" one soldier asked, pulling the reins of his horse to turn it.

The King watched silently, seeing the archers readying their bows "Fools, what are they doing? Surely they do not think us enemies?"

The Humans released the arrows and a small wave spread across through the air between the two. Tanis pulled the reins of his horse as well and started to turn it, watching incredulously as the arrows dove at them. The sound of the sharp heads finding targets filled the air as they fell all across the clearing on the Elves. One struck the King's horse in the neck and the animal reared violently, throwing Tanis backward to the ground. The Elf struck the ground hard and for a minute he was deaf, a strong ringing overtaking his hearing. He struggled to focus on the world around him as double vision plagued him.

"My King!"

Tanis rolled and staggered to his feet, the ringing in his ears disorientating him as he tried to get back his senses. He felt a strong hand on his back as a Knight grabbed and forced him into the saddle of a horse.

"Take my mount my King. Ride back at once!" the Knight ordered, slapping the horse on the hindquarters, sending it into a strong gallop.

Tanis gripped the reins tightly, his legs clinging fiercely to the animal as it bolted into the cover of the trees and through the forest. He finally managed to slow it down and turned in the saddle to see back into the clearing. The trees were thick enough to completely block his view and he was forced to imagine what the clearing looked like now. One thought was pounding in his head. Why had they attacked his Elves?

The soldiers in the clearing retrieved their arrows as the Humans pulled their forces back to the clearing in full. They slowly began moving out through the trees in search of the one lone Elf that had managed to escape. They closed in on those who had been struck by the arrows and found them all either dead or dying. In any case, the Humans did not waste any time in making sure there were no survivors in their swift but deadly attack. The swordsmen drew their weapons and in long lines they moved into the forest.

"Filthy Elves. How dare they come north after what they did to our people. Our King, slaughtered at the hands of a race that was supposed to be civilized. I want them all dead, no excuses."

"Sir, the soldiers here in the clearing are all dead. One escaped back into the forest. We are looking for him now. What orders have you?"

The man looked around at his small but able body of soldiers and felt a swell of pride. After word of Calyn's execution had reached the Humans in Cisalia, the royal advisor to the King had taken charge of the city, vowing that the Elves responsible for it would pay for their bloodthirsty decisions. Even knowledge that the King of Cisalia had plotted with the enemies in the south did not seem to mean anything to the advisor as he set out to war only days after hearing of the incidents.

"I want that Elf's blood. It is as simple as that. Our King was worth a hundred of them. The first hundred Elves are revenge for our fallen King. The rest are revenge for his people. We may be small in number, but we will not be overlooked. All soldiers push forward into the forest. We will comb every inch until we reach Pentegarn."

"Yes sir."

The archers and footmen moved into the forests in waves as the mounted Knights brought up the rear with the advisor and now leader of the armies of Cisalia in the center of the mass. He was bound and determined to punish the Elves for the loss of their King no matter what the cost. If it meant the life of every last soldier, so be it.

The horse stopped as the soldier reached out and took the reins, helping the King down to the ground. His head had nearly stopped ringing but he was still quite beside himself at the events that had taken place. Humans had attacked Elves for no apparent reason. There was no chance of mistaken identity. It was obvious that the Humans would have seen the banners. How could they have mistaken the Elves for the enemy?

Soldiers crowded around. "My King, what happened? Where are the others that were with you?"

Tanis looked up at the soldiers who all wore concerned looks on their faces. Not fifteen minutes earlier the King had moved ahead with a company of Knights and the scout and then returned alone, fatigued and very disorientated. The King of the Wood Elves rubbed his eyes and took a deep breath, gathering his senses.

"I am not quite sure how to place this... give me a moment," the King responded quietly. He knew it would not be long before the Humans came through the forest and found them. "It seems that we have come under attack. Curious though as it was not by Goblins or Ogres, but instead by Humans from Cisalia marching south."

Hushed whispers moved through the soldiers as they turned back and forth to one another, fighting to grasp whether this could possibly be true. Tanis raised a hand to quiet them and turned to look behind him.

"There is a good chance they will be moving through the woods after me. I escaped and I am sure that if they were so eager to kill us they will want to finish what they started. I am asking something of you I had not before thought I would ask."

The soldiers crowded around their King, eager to hear what orders he had to give them. He thought back to the Knight that had lifted him into the saddle and given his life to see that the King made it out alive. His jaw tightened and he looked up.

"Leave none of them standing."

The Elves stared, some in disbelief, some angered by the loss of their fellow Elves. One of the Elves took a step forward and cautiously questioned the King's orders.

"Sir, is it possible that this was just a misunderstanding? Should we not at least try to find out why this happened before we rush to attack the Humans?"

The Elves surrounding the soldier did not nod in agreement, nor did they show any dissatisfaction in his words. It made sense not to be hasty with the decision of rushing into battle. At the same time though, Elves lay fallen on the other side of the forest by the hands of the Humans. Before Tanis could reply, his and every other Elf in the forest had their minds made for them. From the trees behind them came the cry of the enemy.

"There they are! Kill them all!"

The Elves fell into their formations, the front row of archers dropping to one knee as the second remained standing. They drew their arrows back and sighted down the shafts toward the first signs of Humans appearing through the trees. Tanis drew his sword and looked at the ones responsible for the deaths of his soldiers not twenty minutes earlier, the thought of a diplomatic solution not even an option.

The soldier looked to the King and drew his own sword, still apprehensive at the lack of thought in the ordeal. "I hope you're sure about this my King. At this rate, we may never see Pentegarn."

Tanis ignored him and watched the Humans start to build up in the trees, their shields locked tightly together and slowly moving forward. It was set to be a battle of two different kinds of soldiers. The archers and swordsmen of Swanhaven against the footmen and mounted Knights of Cisalia. Each side had its strengths as their numbers were very similar. Tanis hardly wanted to face an enemy this far from the reinforcements of Pentegarn but now he had no choice. They were going to clash whether he was ready or not.

"Archers to the ready!" the King ordered, watching as the Elves drew their bowstrings back and waited.

The Humans stopped their advance and pushed the broad shields tightly together, forming a nearly impenetrable wall stretching through the forest. The archers held their fire, waiting for an opening. There was nothing for them to aim for. The shield wall had stopped and suddenly sections broke open, allowing the Human archers a chance to fire off a volley and quickly fall back the moment their arrow had left the bow. The targets fell to the ground as a number of Elves tried to pick off the enemy archers only to have their arrows strike the reformed wall sections.

Tanis looked around as the Elves fell to the ground and felt his face flushed with anger. He noticed the shield wall's weakness and turned to the soldiers around him. "Get archers up in the trees. Fire down on the Humans!"

Elves began climbing the trees into the higher branches, looking down on the wall and its only weakness. There was nothing protecting them from an attack from above. The moment the Elves reached a position where they could see their targets they began releasing arrows as fast as they could. The arrows rained down on the Humans and gaps began forming in the seamless shield wall. By the time the Human archers realized where the Elves were, countless soldiers had been slain.

The wall pulled tighter together and slowly began moving back. The Elves continued to fire until the soldiers left the trees, regrouping and waiting in the clearing with a newly formed shield wall, bigger and stronger. The soldiers held shields over the front line at an angle, creating a defensive line against the Elves in the trees. They stood in the field, waiting for sign of the Elves.

"My King, they've fallen back to the field! Orders sir?"

"Do not pursue them. We are the stronger here in the forests. If they want to continue this then let them come to us."

The Elves kept the positions well defended, their arrows still trained on the gaps in the trees for the first sign of an enemy. The Elves that had fallen in the attack were quickly pulled back into the ranks away from the frontlines. The Elven swordsmen moved forward, a disciplined line that stopped just short of the clearing. They looked out at the force of Humans no more than two hundred yards away and waited, wondering what they were waiting for. Having seen enough they returned.

"My King, they seem to wait for us in the clearing."

"Yes, of course they do," Tanis replied skeptically. "They will not engage us in our own surroundings again. They lost three times the soldiers in that quick skirmish by underestimating our ability to adapt. We will hold our positions here until they either come back to face us or give in and leave. Hold here!"

The leader of the Humans paced angrily up and down the lines yelling at the soldiers for their embarrassing defeat. Their only purpose for leaving Cisalia was to punish the Elves for the torture and execution of their King and now they had been forced to retreat away from the first contact with the enemy. To say he was angry was an understatement.

"What are you all, scared? You run from a bunch of tree loving Elves and their wooden bows? You are the Knights and soldiers of Cisalia and you have shamed your people horribly. Why not march into the forests and surrender next time? I refuse to lead an army that does not have the spine to fight when the fight arrives!"

"Sir, if we had not fallen back you would not have an army to lead. You were not there, you did not see the soldiers falling around us as we tried to hold the shields and push on. Maybe you would like to offer your shield to the front line?"

The advisor rounded on the soldier with a bloodthirsty rage surging through him. His swing caught the man in the temple and sent him staggering only to receive countless more blows to the head and face. As the soldier fell to the ground the two closest Knights grabbed the advisor and restrained him, allowing the man on the ground a chance to get back to his feet. Blood flowed from his nose and he struggled to keep his footing.

"Have you any ideas sir?"

The Human turned to the Knights and narrowed his gaze, the taste of blood in his mouth. "Burn it all to the ground. We'll run them out or burn them alive one."

The Elves slowly pulled a little tighter together and fell back away from the clearing, finding themselves further in the depths of the forest. They pulled out of the trees and moved together as they began a very slow retreat. Soon, an overpowering smell began to fill the air and the Elves stopped.

"My King, what is that smell? Is it… smoke?" one solder asked, looking into the treetops.

Tanis looked around and took a deep breath. "Yes…

they're burning the trees. They're trying to flush us out by burning the forest. We've got to get moving."

"To where my King?"

"To Pentegarn. Retreat out of the forest and fall back to the city. We are close enough that if we get ahead of them now they will not have a chance to stop us before we reach the city. Send the order, we make for Pentegarn."

The soldiers began pulling back into their formations and started moving back away from the fires that the Humans started. The Elves marched angrily, feeling the pain in the trees as the fires rolled through the underbrush, scorching everything it touched. They wanted nothing more than to punish those responsible for the pain to the forests. Their army moved on as the fires roared behind them. Tanis looked ahead to Pentegarn, knowing that they would get their revenge when the Humans arrived at the city.

The Elves marched until the smell of the smoke started to disappear, becoming fainter as they continued moving. In the hours that they marched they managed to finally break the edge of the forest. The army marched out into the clearing, looking out at the massive city of Pentegarn.

Between Tvan and Pentegarn

*E*rzel sat at the edge of the wide lake deep in the mountains of Tvan. The torches around the long dock illuminated the dark waters slightly. He tossed one of the stones beside him in and watched the ripples spread across the surface. The Dwarves had spent the better part of the day preparing to march with Erzel and his group. He tossed another rock and laid back on the dock, looking up towards the roof of the massive cavern. Even the flickers of the torchlight did not manage to cast a glare on the stone so high above the ground.

The past day had been spent in deep thought, pondering what would happen when the forces from Tvan met with those from Qwaz and Nomaria. The rumored forty thousand soldiers moving north were a formidable force but the armies in Tvan were greater. There were more Dwarves, but they were not nearly as strong as the Ogres that moved alongside the Goblins. The size could be an obstacle for the shorter Dwarves. Even so, they had strength in numbers.

The soldiers of Tvan had been massing all through the day, preparing for the march to the south. Erzel had planned to leave the day the first of the army was ready and by the looks of things it would be sooner than expected. Though they had initially been reluctant to join the Elves in the war the Dwarves were wasting no time. The majority of the soldiers preparing to march were the veterans of the army, those who had seen the Goblins before in the Chaos Wars. They knew how to fight them and were eager to draw blood again.

"Erzel... what are you doing?"

The Elf brought his head back and looked up the dock, finding Rhen standing at the edge of the wooden planks. She stepped down and walked towards him.

"Just thinking about what is about to happen," he replied, sitting up and waiting as Rhen took a seat next to him on the dock. "I worry. The Southern armies are vast and strong but the Dwarves outnumber them. I am getting tired of the bloodshed. One day I hope things will be calm again."

"What will you do after the wars end?"

Erzel thought about the question. He knew inside that there was a chance the wars may never end but he would not tell Rhen that. "I do not know. I will always serve Elendil and the High Elves. Perhaps I can do so with a family as well."

"I hope so."

Rhen leaned to the side against Erzel's shoulder. He tossed another stone into the water and together they watched the ripples spread across the surface. Rhen picked up the last rock and threw it out near where Erzel's had landed, watching the splash and remembering the way the water had felt on the Dragon Isles. It was cool and inviting. Rhen slid to the edge of the dock and pulled her shoes off, dropping her legs over the edge to the water. The Princess let her feet sink into the water and quickly brought them back out. The water was colder than freezing and was nothing like what she had felt when she had been on the Dragon Isles.

"Too cold?" Erzel asked, looking over the edge as she curled her feet back under her.

"Yes, this is nothing like the water on the islands. It was warm and inviting. This is… cold."

"It never sees the sun so likely it will never be as warm as the springs that ran across the Dragon Isles. Down here it is lucky that the air stays as warm as it does. Most would assume that this deep in the mountains there would be no warmth at all."

Rhen rubbed her toes as she sat back on the dock next to Erzel who was starting to get to his feet. He reached down and took her hand to help her to her feet and they started toward the shore.

"Where are we going Erzel?" Rhen asked.

"I have to find Kail and Lavian and then meet with the Elders. The army is massing and we are to be ready to move with them. We will take the first battalion south to defend Pentegarn and the rest of the army will follow shortly thereafter."

"How soon?"

Erzel stepped up off the dock and helped Rhen to the shore as well. "I am not sure, less than a day. They are moving quite swiftly for a race not hardly willing to commit to war."

Rhen and Erzel walked hand and hand back to the city and to the castle where the meeting was to take place. He stopped outside of the throne room and turned to the Princess, placing his hands on her shoulders. He kissed her on the cheek and turned back to the door.

"I will find you after the meeting. I promise I will not leave without seeing you one last time."

"Ok... bye..." she whispered as he walked through the doors without her.

Erzel walked through the room to the long table where his group and the Elders had met the first time. All four of the Dwarves sat on one side waiting for the Elf and his soldiers. Erzel found that neither Lavian nor Kail were in the room.

"Greetings Erzel, I am glad you've made it. Please, sit down," Velex said with a gesture to one of the chairs.

"Thank you, is there any word from Kail or Lavian? I thought they would be here before me."

No sooner had the question left Erzel's mouth did the doors to the throne room open and the two walked in. They took seats on either side of the Elf and the meeting got underway.

"Alright then, let us get started. You are aware that the first battalion is nearly mobilized. It will be tonight before they are ready to start south. In the meantime, we have come to a decision about something."

"What is that?" Erzel asked intently.

"One of the Elders will be with the first battalion moving south as well as you and your soldiers. Since Ardis is in charge of the defenses above ground, he is the most qualified to lead the soldiers south. The rest of us are not quite accustom to the sunlight just yet."

Erzel was understandably surprised. The Dwarves were suddenly making quite a stance. "Very well. Ardis, I take it you are ready for what you will find at Pentegarn. There is no guarantee we will receive a friendly welcome. More likely we will walk into a full fledge siege the moment we leave the forests."

"If you are questioning my military knowledge and abilities, I assure you that is a mistake. I am very capable in combat."

"Far from it sir. I merely wonder if you will be so sure of those abilities once the strength of the southern lands has been unleashed on you and your soldiers. I have seen firsthand some of its most elite creatures and even the most seasoned of soldiers would falter in their presence."

The Elders sat in silence. Ardis finally cleared his throat and addressed the concerns of the Elves. "I take it these forces are still unknown to our race. Stronger than the Goblins, Ogres, and Lizardmen that we have heard make up their armies?"

"Far stronger than those you have named. The Demon that now leads the armies has forces far stronger under its control. I do not know whether we are set to face them at Pentegarn but it is a guarantee that eventually they will reach the battlefield."

"And these creatures are called?"

"Slayers. They are well armored and dangerously armed. They fight with a ferocity that catches many off guard. You'll know when you have defeated one though. No sooner do you strike it down does the armor and body crack apart and burn. It is truly a strange sight.."

Lavian suddenly looked up. "They are very susceptible to brighter lights and this tends to be a great way to weaken them long enough for a soldier to deal a deadly blow. They tend to use weapons that are either poisoned or cursed to deal massive damage to any caught in their path."

"They can be killed?" Divos asked, speaking up for the first time.

"They can. We have done so already and we will do so again. They may be the terror of the southern army, but we will face them all the same."

The four Elders sat quietly, pondering the opponent that none of them had ever before seen. Granted, they remained in their mountains where no such monster could reach them but now they were thrust upon the world and all that plagued it. They wanted to know everything about the creatures that they could.

"What do you think Ardis? Will your soldiers manage well against this unknown foe?" Velex asked.

"Do you mean to insult our abilities or was that just an oversight on your part? We will meet them in battle and we will run them over with no more than a thought. I am saddened that you question the abilities of our Dwarven brothers."

"I question not their abilities. I do however see the potential for disaster if they meet these Slayers in battle and are not prepared for the strength and resilience that they have been claimed to have. We must not falter, not a step."

Erzel looked to Lavian and Kail and waited as the two Dwarves argued over the smallest of details concerning the courage of the army. It was obvious that with Velex being in charge of diplomatic affairs that he was not comfortable with the confrontation of war.

"Velex, I promise you that the soldiers of Tvan will be a strong match against the Slayers. We will lead your soldiers into battle and clear through to the other side of it. We should stop worrying about whether or not the Dwarven soldiers are going to run when they see the southern armies and start worrying about getting to Pentegarn before it is too late. I have no doubt that the enemies in the south have started to move on the Elven lands by now," Erzel interrupted, seeing that the argument could continue for quite some time at the pace the Elders were taking it.

"Very well Erzel. I can see your hurry to get moving. We will end this discussion and when Ardis and the rest of the soldiers are ready to move, we will call for you."

Erzel and the others stood from the table and gave a quick bow, heading for the door quickly as they did not want to be swallowed into another debate. Lavian turned and headed for her room while Kail and Erzel took a slow stroll through the hallways away from the throne room.

"They are still in there arguing. It makes no sense. They have already agreed to join the war and send their soldiers into battle. What do they need to debate now?"

"I don't know, Kail," Erzel replied, rubbing the back of his neck. "I wonder that myself. Perhaps this is their custom, their way of doing things. Even after coming to an agreement they look for the reasons as to why they decided the way they have."

"It is a waste of time."

"I know. Like they said though, the moment Ardis is prepared the army will move out. Once we are out of Tvan with the army marching behind us there will be no need for the arguments and discussions. Once we are on the move, we will not stop."

"What will you do until they call for us?" Kail asked,

looking down the passage that led to the dining hall.

Erzel looked down the hall to his left and then back at Kail. "I suppose I will spend what time we have left with Rhen. I suppose this could be the last time I ever see her again. Who knows what will happen when we march against Valsera again. I will meet up with you later on."

The two parted paths and Erzel followed the winding halls that led higher into the castle. He had never been afraid of battle or leading an army into one, but now the thought of being a father was weighing heavily on him. He knew he was leaving behind the only family he had in the world and there was no guarantee he would ever see them again. The Elf came to a stop a few doors away from the Princess's room and waited, regaining his composure. He wanted his last moments with Rhen to be happy and memorable. With a forced smile he started off again, ready to say his goodbyes.

The gates of Pentegarn stood strong when the Wood Elves broke the forests and marched towards the city. With the traitorous Humans driving them they moved swiftly through the fields. Tanis rode out in front, breaking from the group and stopping in front of the gate. He waited and from the walls above came the order to open the gates. He moved quickly up through the courtyards as the High Elves stopped their daily duties to witness the Wood Elf army marching through the city gates. Tanis reached the inner wall and stopped as the second set of gates opened and Elendil walked out to greet the Elves.

The two Kings stood in front of one another for a few minutes, neither one speaking as they took their time with their words. Elendil approached and placed a hand on the shoulder of the Wood Elf, a thin smile forming on his lips.

"I had not expected you to return Tanis. This is truly a very well appreciated surprise, and of the greatest timing."

"I take it things are becoming quite a mess in the southlands?"

"Very much so. The armies surrounding Qwaz are moving north, already passing through the Pass of Merwold. It will only be a matter of days before the fields are overrun with them."

"You seem to be well prepared for them. There is more though. Please, may we move inside?"

"Of course. Follow me."

Elendil led the King of the Wood Elves into the massive castle of Pentegarn, taking his time up the stairs that led to the throne room. He waited as the guards opened the doors and together the two Kings walked in, each taking a seat at the long table in the center of the room. Tanis looked at the throne and then to Elendil sitting across from him.

"Much has happened since your departure for Eglarest. We sent an entire battalion of Elves to the Pass of Merwold to hold against the armies moving north. They were joined by the Gnomes of Domari. There…"

"The Gnomes joined with the Elves? They have never been a warring race. What drove them to fight?" Tanis asked, surprised to hear a race so peaceful would turn to fight against the strongest enemy Nalawren had ever seen.

"The settlement they had here in Nalawren was destroyed by Valsera's armies. Even a peaceful race has its limits. Valsera found a way to break our defenses at the pass and are now massing no more than a day south of Pentegarn. Things are not looking so good my old friend."

Tanis looked at the Elf incredulously. "How? How did they break the Pass of Merwold?"

"The Humans. A Gnome escaped the fray and returned to tell us. A massive force of Knights and the King of Cisalia himself arrived at the pass to reinforce the Elves only to betray them when the moment presented itself. Our army at the pass was destroyed in the blink of an eye."

The news of the Humans having already betrayed the Elves once surprised Tanis as he himself had witnessed their traitorous nature himself. He recalled the volley of arrows that had brought down his forces in the forests and the skirmish that had given proof that the Humans were indeed set to fight against the Elves. He looked up at Tanis and nodded.

"I too have found myself faced with their betrayal. Not a day north of Pentegarn my army came across a force marching south. Thinking they were moving to help Pentegarn we rode out to them. They fired on us the moment we left the trees and then again we fought them in the forests. They knew we were Elves. They knew and still they attacked us."

"They are surely coming to take revenge on us here at

Pentegarn."

The Wood Elf turned his head back to Elendil quickly. "Revenge? They betray you at the Pass of Merwold and you claim they are here to seek revenge? If nothing else you should have burned down all of Cisalia in return for their actions."

"No… they come for revenge for their King. Calyn arrived here days after the betrayal at the pass with a story of horrible losses at the hands of the southern armies, all the while plotting to kill me and send Pentegarn into disarray. His plan did not have the effects he had hoped."

"What has become of Calyn?" Tanis asked, almost hoping for the chance to punish the King himself for his actions.

"As I said, they come for revenge. Calyn was executed only days ago by the blade of a sword. Word travels fast and I am sure they come to fight for their fallen King. It will not matter though, they do not stand a chance once the city has been locked down. We will blanket them with arrows for days on end. They will never reach the walls." Elendil said proudly, knowing the Humans were not half as well trained as his Elves.

"The King of Cisalia… dead? Much has changed since my Elves left Swanhaven. I am surprised he was brazen enough to try and assassinate you here in your own throne room. That is simply… incredible."

"Incredibly foolish. All the same, we have the upper hand. We have the greatest soldiers to ever set foot in these lands and the strongest city as well. They may one day break our outer walls, but never the inner and certainly never reach the castle."

The two Elves sat at the table for a while, thinking about what they were faced with in the coming days. Elendil felt a wave of relief knowing that the Wood Elves had returned to stand with them instead of staying in Eglarest where they would be safe from the hordes of the south. Tanis stood from the table and stretched, the thought of war only being days away giving him a shiver.

"Alright Tanis?" Elendil asked as he watched the Elf shake his head clear of the feeling.

"Yes, of course. The memories of the last time Valsera marched on our lands are still fresh in my mind. This feels different. He has managed to infect the Humans with his false promises of glory and freedom. He has stretched his armies deep into our lands and threatens to besiege all of Pentegarn with several different armies. I fear this will be much different this time."

Elendil stood from the table and joined the Wood Elf, walking towards the doorway. "Come, let us get things ready for them. You look like you are in need of a good meal and your soldiers could probably use a long rest before it starts."

"That sounds great Elendil, lead the way."

Erzel leaned against the railing looking back into the room where Rhen stayed in Tvan. She walked across the balcony and stopped next to him, turning and following his gaze. After a few minutes she turned back to him and tried to look into his eyes, finding it difficult as he was taller. She rubbed his arm and Erzel fell out of the apparent trance.

"What are you looking at Erzel?" she asked, glancing up into the room.

"I uh... I don't know, just in deep thought I suppose. Forgive me, I did not mean to ignore you."

"It's ok Erzel, I thought something might have been wrong. Are you worried about going south again with the army soon?"

Erzel hesitated, wondering if admitting he was indeed worried was a bad idea. He did not want to place unnecessary stress on the Princess. "Honestly... yes, I am a little worried about leading the armies south to Pentegarn."

"Why? You've fought in battles all your life. You've faced the Goblins and Ogres before. Talk to me Erzel. What has you in such a worrisome mood?" Rhen asked, rubbing her hand up his back softly.

Erzel took a deep breath. "It is not the Goblins nor the Ogres that worry me Rhen. There is another beast serving Valsera that has already proven its strength. When we attacked Qwaz we found ourselves in the throne room. There, Yanosh, Kail, and I squared off against Valsera and Infus, the Demon serving the sorcerer. It was stronger than anything I ever could have imagined facing."

Rhen took a step closer and wrapped her arm around his back, urging him to keep going. "What made it so strong?"

"I am not sure," Erzel replied. "I don't know how it managed, but my sword would pass through its body every time I attacked. No matter what I did, I could not harm the Demon. It was Alora who finally knocked Infus from the balcony of the fortress and saved my life. She has been the only one able to bring any harm to the Demon."

"What will you do? If you can not hurt the Demon, how will you defeat it and stop the armies marching on Pentegarn?"

Erzel reached to his belt and pulled from it the handle to the whip Infus had lost in the fray of battle. He held it out in front of him so Rhen could see.

"What is that?"

"This is a weapon the Demon attempted to use on the balcony. I found it just before we retreated back from the fortress. If Infus wields it then it must have some sort of special power. I will use this against the Demon and maybe it will be the key to evening the fight some."

Erzel quickly traced his finger across the etching in the handle he and Kail had found earlier and just as before the whip came to life, the green flames licking the air around them. Rhen marveled at the weapon, never before seeing anything like it. The bright green glow from the flames illuminated the balcony in an eerie glow. He gave a quick snap of his wrist and the whip lashed out, leaving a deep gash in the stone railing. Rhen ran her finger down the spot on the railing and turned back to the Elf.

"That was solid stone Erzel."

"I know. Surely something with this kind of power will be what I need to best the Demon the next time we meet. It is like nothing I have ever held in my hands before."

Rhen looked at the glowing green flames. "Erzel, if the Demon wielded this weapon… it would be just as evil as the Demon. Is it a good idea to use it against the creature?"

"It is all we have Rhen. If I don't try, the next fight will turn out the same as the last time I faced Infus. This war will not end until the Demon has been destroyed."

Erzel snapped the whip again and then quickly deactivated it, watching as the flames slid back into the long handle. As the weapon returned to its quiet state, Rhen left Erzel and walked into the room. The Elf followed her and stopped in the doorway behind her.

"It will not be long now Rhen. The army is getting ready to move and we are to lead them out."

Rhen looked at him but did not leave the table just inside the room. "Will you come back?"

"Rhen... you know I can't say for..."

Rhen looked at him sternly. "Just say it Erzel."

He looked at her strangely as she cut him off in mid sentence. He looked down at the floor and then back up at her. He did not want to lie to her. He did not want to tell her he was coming back if he didn't know it for sure."

"Erzel!" she snapped, taking a step towards him. "I told you to tell me you are coming back. I know you may never come back. I know you are marching into a hopeless fight and I do not care! Just tell me you are coming back."

The Elf looked at her and nodded. "I will come back for you Rhen, I promise."

She walked the rest of the distance between them and wrapped her arms around his waist. She hugged him and took his hand, walking toward the door to the room.

"Where are you going?" he asked, walking by her side, her hand in his own.

"I am going to see you off. I can not go, but I will make sure I am with you every possible second before you leave"

Erzel started towards the door but stopped before they reached it, grabbing the Princess from behind and turning her back to him. He caught her hands and leaned down, kissing her lips slowly. Rhen was taken by surprise but wrapped her arms around his neck, kissing him back. The world around them blurred and for the moment their lips were together, nothing else mattered. He ran his hands down her sides, spreading them across her hips as their lips finally parted.

Erzel reached up and drew a finger down her cheek, their eyes inches apart as the moment continued. The Elf leaned in again and kissed her quickly, hoping it would not be the last time he felt her lips. As they parted Erzel turned and started out the door, Rhen's hand still clasped in his.

The two Elves walked through the halls hand and hand as he led her down to the massive courtyard outside the castle. There they found Kail and Lavian waiting with the Queen Narissa. As they approached, Erzel felt he should release Rhen's hand but the Princess held him tightly. The two stopped and Erzel gave a quick bow to the Queen.

"Hello Erzel. I take it you are prepared to leave?" the Queen asked as she glanced up the tunnel that led to the surface.

"Yes, as ready as we are going to be. No matter how long you prepare, no soldier is ever truly ready for a war."

"Very true. Rhen, I will accompany you and these soldiers to the surface to say our goodbyes. It is customary for one to accompany her loved one out before they leave for battle. I believe your soldiers will fair well, but I fear these armies are stronger than expected. It will be horrible if you never see your child after this war ends. Having said that, have you thought of a name?"

Lavian and Kail stopped in their tracks and turned as the words from the Queen reached their ears. The two stared at Erzel and the Elf felt as if their eyes were cutting through him. Kail raised an eyebrow and looked the Elf in the eyes.

"What are you two looking at?" Erzel snapped, his secret now reaching others.

"Correct me if I am wrong Erzel, but the Queen is speaking of your child? A child that you don't have?"

Erzel tightened his jaw and cut his eyes at Kail. "Yes, you heard her correctly Kail. I have no children... yet."

He turned and looked at Rhen, his eyes dropping down her body to her stomach. He reached down and touched her, looking up at the group. "I have not thought about a name. There has been so much going on I have not been able to think clearly. I apologize."

There was a moment of silence among the group as Erzel was given a few minutes to think. He took a deep breath and looked up the tunnel to the surface. "We should get moving to the surface. The Dwarves are ready to move and the armies serving Valsera will not wait for us to get to Pentegarn. They will attack whether we are there to fight or not."

Kail and Lavian started up the tunnel with Rhen, Narissa, and Erzel following them. The walk was silent as the sound of their footsteps was the only thing that could be heard. Erzel had not meant to be so defensive when the Queen revealed the child that was growing within her daughter. He lowered his eyes to the ground as they walked. Soon the wave of sunlight engulfed the tunnel, blinding them as they moved out into the open.

It took a few minutes for their eyes to adjust but once

they had, Erzel looked out into a clearing filled with heavily armored Dwarves ready to march. He stared out across the massive formations of Dwarves, their numbers all standing in disciplined lines awaiting their orders. The Queen wrapped her cloak around her as the chill of the mountain air rolled across the clearing.

Erzel stepped out into the snow, greeted by the soft crunch under his feet. To his right he caught sight of Alora standing alone, her eyes probing the massive number of Dwarves outside of Tvan.

"Alora!" Rhen shouted, scrambling up the hill to the Blue Dragon. "It is wonderful to see you!"

The Dragon lowered her head to the young Elf. "You as well. I am glad to see you well. I take it you are very safe here in the mountains?"

"Very safe. We have been here since my father marched the Elves from Eglarest back to Pentegarn to help," she replied. She noticed the gash on the Dragon's cheek. "What happened Alora?"

The Dragon stared back at the Princess. "An arrow in the assault. It was a small price to pay to deal the blow to Valsera."

Rhen reached up and touched just below the wound, sad to see the Dragon injured.

"We are nearly ready to move out Alora. Kail, Lavian, and I will be taking horses with the main part of the army. I would appreciate it if you and the two Warbirds would take to the air and keep an eye on the lands ahead of us."

The Dragon gave a distinct nod. "Of course Erzel. I will wait for your armies to move out before I leave."

The Elf turned back to the Queen and Princess, walking slowly through the snow. He stopped in front of Rhen and gave a courteous nod to the Princess. He leaned in and kissed her on the cheek one last time. As he pulled away the Princess caught him by the collar of his armor and pulled him back to her, their lips meeting and locking for what felt like a full minute. When she released him he then turned to the Queen and gave a low bow, his face flushed from being caught off guard by Rhen.

"I promise, I will do everything I can to ensure that your husband returns to you safe and sound. We will not let their armies move any further, I promise."

Narissa nodded and reached out to him, placing her hand

on his shoulder. "Thank you Erzel. Come back to my daughter. She will need you. The child will need you both in the years to come. You are her love and as such, you have my love. Move swift, and never give up while you still draw a breath."

Ardis appeared from the right and nodded to Erzel, waving his hand out to the large gathering of Dwarven soldiers. "Are they not marvelous?"

"Yes Ardis, quite a battalion of soldiers they are. However, I see that you are not prepared to leave. Why is that?" Erzel asked, noting the Dwarf neither wore armor nor carried a weapon.

"Ah, straight to the point. I like that in another. Very well, Odar and I have decided that we shall follow this first battalion with the main army in the next few days, when it has been fully mobilized. I trust you are a very capable leader and my soldiers will follow your orders without a hint of hesitation. A safe journey to you all."

Erzel nodded and turned, Lavian and Kail following him to their mounts. Lavian stopped next to the horse and looked back to her Warbird. She took a deep breath and looked to Erzel. The Elf noticed her hesitation and stopped, an inquisitive look on his face.

"Lavian, what is it?"

"Erzel, I mean not to insult your expertise in these lands but I would prefer to stay with my mount. I have seldom traveled if not on its back and I think I will stay with the Warbird."

Erzel gave an understanding nod. "As you wish Lavian. I am not in charge of you nor your Knights so I will allow you to choose as you see fit."

"Thank you."

The Celestial Knight rubbed the horse down gently and turned to her Warbird. She stopped and turned back to Erzel. Reaching to her waist she pulled the head of Yanosh's staff from her belt. "Erzel, I think it best if you keep this for now."

The Elf looked at the item and raised an eyebrow. "Why? It belonged to your master... should you not keep it?"

Lavian shook her head. "No, if I am to be on my Warbird, it will only be the two of us. You however, have all of the Dwarves and Kail here with you and it will be much safer for you to keep. We can not allow anything to happen to it."

Erzel reached out and took the top of the staff. "Nothing will happen to it. I will keep it safe."

The Celestial Knight reached out and gripped the saddle on the Warbird, pulling herself up and snapping the reins. It shot into the air, followed by the riderless Warbird and it was apparent that they were ready to move out. Alora hesitated a moment before she too took flight. Erzel secured the cluster of crystals in the pouch on his belt and climbed into the saddle. He and Kail turned and started down the trail that led to the foothills of Tvan. He looked back over his shoulder at the Princess, praying silently that he would see her again.

The formations of Dwarves stretched down the mountains with Kail and Erzel somewhere in the middle. They bounced softly in the saddles, looking around them at the army that finally agreed to help them. All of the Dwarves carried with them some form of melee weapon and a large round shield in their opposite hand. The shields were gold in color without any form of decoration. In the rear came a large mass of Dwarves carrying with them curved war bows. They were not accomplished archers but they did their best all the same. With the armies finally on the move Erzel could only hope Pentegarn was not beyond saving.

When the Horde Arrives

*T*he city of Pentegarn had been on high alert from the moment Tanis and his Wood Elves had arrived with news of the Human armies on the move. Elendil knew all of Qwaz and Nomaria was bearing down on them but had not expected to find himself surrounded with Cisalia moving down from the north. The King also knew the armies marching from Cisalia were nowhere near the size of the ones moving from the south. Though the Humans had a measure of ferocity on their side and a hunger for revenge, they alone were no match for the Elves.

Elendil and Tanis stood together on the battlements of the inner wall, looking back at the massive castle at the center of the city. Elendil felt hardly any fear of the coming war, no worry that his soldiers would be able to defend their homes. Instead, he wondered to himself just how far the armies serving Valsera would reach. Tanis turned and looked back out at the outer wall and gates.

"What troubles you Elendil?" the Wood Elf asked.

"I wonder just how well we will hold their siege," the High Elf replied. "It is no longer a question as to whether or not we will face them, but instead a question of how well we will defend against them until our reinforcements arrive."

"Do you truly believe Tvan will send its armies? They've had nothing to do with the defending of the lands since the end of the Chaos Wars. I would not rely on them, Elendil."

The two Elves looked out across the city wondering if they would indeed see the armies of Tvan lend their numbers to the Elves. If there were no reinforcements, if the Dwarves did not arrive, the siege might end up a success.

Even if the armies breached the first wall, they would face

a second, taller, thicker, and stronger than the first. The inner wall was twice that of the outer, the battlements wider to support twice as many soldiers when the need came. Elven soldiers covered the walls, towers, and courtyards, waiting for the enemies to arrive.

"If we are not to receive any help from the Dwarves, it will be much more difficult to break them here. They have countless battalions at their disposal. If reinforcements do not arrive, Valsera's armies will simply replenish their numbers and return."

"I know. Forgive me for placing any doubt in our soldiers here today. You realize the force we face. From what you have said, there has never been an army this large march against the northern lands in the history of Nalawren."

"I know, Tanis," Elendil whispered, looking up as a dot in the sky caught his attention. "I wonder."

The Wood Elf followed the gaze of the King and searched the sky until he too caught sight of the dot, growing larger as it came closer. Elendil seemed hardly concerned at the sight as if he expected company. Elendil started towards the stairs and looked back over his shoulder at the Wood Elf.

"Come Tanis, let us see what to make of this," Elendil said with a nod, continuing down the stairs.

The two Elven Kings followed the stairs into the lower courtyards and then to the gate at the outer wall. The soldiers pulled the mighty gates open and once the light had filtered through to the soldiers inside, Elendil and Tanis started out into the fields. The massive shadow crossed their path and the two Elves watched as a monstrous Gold Dragon descended to the fields outside of Pentegarn. Tanis hesitated, remembering his last encounter with the winged creature.

Elendil waited until the Dragon had landed in the field before approaching. As they got closer, the two Elves watched two figures drop from the Dragon's back, a third falling limply to the ground with them. The King picked up the pace, rushing towards them as he realized the figures were Ectle and Thorgrim. The wizard grabbed the figure from the ground and began dragging it towards the city.

"Ectle! What happened? What's wrong?" the King asked, seeing the wizard and Thorgrim dragging the second Dwarf.

Ectle stopped as soldiers from the city arrived behind the

King, taking the Dwarf from the two and helping get him to the city. The wizard fell to one knee in front of the King, gripping the staff and taking long, deep breaths. His head was pounding as he slowly stood, looking Elendil in the eyes.

"My King... after the assault in the south, Thorgrim and Nimir were lost in the swamps, the Dragon carrying them shot from the sky. I went back for them and found the two Dwarves had been taken prisoner by Lizardmen. Nimir was injured horribly in our escape. The Dragon came back for us. I need to help Nimir, he is fading quickly."

Elendil turned and nodded to the castle. "Of course, at once. We have to get inside at once. Valsera's armies are closing in fast."

The group moved out of the fields as the Dragon took to the sky once more, disappearing behind the clouds. As the Elves moved into the outer edges of the city the gates were pushed closed behind them. The large doors closed with a thunderous boom, the Elves setting the locks and bracing the gate once more.

The soldiers carried the wounded Dwarf into the castle, finding an empty room and setting him on the table. Nimir appeared lifeless. His head rolled to the right, his eyes were closed, and his breathing shallow. Ectle waved everyone out of the way and stooped to the table, pressing his ear close to the Dwarf's chest. His heartbeat was faint.

"How did this happen?" Tanis asked, seeing the blood and open wound on Nimir's arm.

"Lizardmen in the swamps took them captive. I freed the two, but the beasts pursued us and we were forced to fight. Nimir was injured in the encounter," Ectle replied, taking bandages from a basket at the side of table. "I did what I could to heal him in the swamps, but there was only so much I could do. This wound may be beyond me now. There is little I can do for him. At best, we can wrap it and keep salve applied."

"Ectle, things are getting bad around here very quickly. It turns out that the armies of Cisalia are moving south to join with those of Valsera, looking for revenge. Valsera's armies have crossed the Pass of Merwold and look to besiege Pentegarn. Truth be told, I am glad to have your power here with these armies on our doorstep."

"Of course my Lord, I would be honored to stand here

with your armies," Ectle said, a hand on Nimir's unconscious shoulder. "Why is Cisalia marching against us my Lord?"

"While you were gone, Calyn led his Knights to the pass and betrayed our forces, slaughtering them all in one swift battle. He then led them here with the plan of assassinating me, but I received warning prior to his arrival. Shortly after Calyn was executed. They surely march to revenge their fallen King."

"Much did happen while I was gone. How long before their armies arrive here at Pentegarn?" Ectle asked as he left the Dwarf's side.

"Any day now. They've been massing to the south for the past day or so."

"How strong are their numbers?"

"Somewhere between forty and forty-five thousand."

Ectle stared at the King with obvious shock on his face. He wasn't sure if he had heard Elendil correctly. "Forty… five… thousand?"

"I am afraid so. I know what you are thinking Ectle…"

"My King, no army has ever massed those numbers against us. Forty-five thousand soldiers? Is there any way Pentegarn will stand against this kind of force?"

Tanis took a step towards the wizard, shaking his head slowly. "Forty-five thousand not counting the force marching from Cisalia. If my calculations are correct, that would mean close to sixty thousand enemy soldiers are on the move."

The wizard took a deep breath. "This is not possible."

"Perhaps not. Erzel and the remainder of his group have departed for Tvan. He was certain he would return with the armies of the Dwarves behind him. If Tvan sends their armies south, we may very well hold our lands after all."

Tanis gave a nod and left the room, leaving Ectle, Thorgrim, and Elendil alone to talk. The King closed the door behind the Wood Elf. Ectle took a deep breath and approached the King once more. The wizard knew Pentegarn was the strongest of all the cities and it would be an incredible feat to break its defenses. Then again, he had no idea what chance they had against forty thousand of Valsera's soldiers.

"Ectle, we have to get ready. We don't have the extra time to spend with Nimir at the moment. You've done all that you can but we have to get ready. We can not afford to wait."

Ectle nodded and gave a wave to Thorgrim. "Ok, lead the way. He is stable for now. If we do nothing to stop Valsera's armies he will die for sure. Thorgrim, if you would stay with him while the King and I continue this conversation I would be grateful."

The Dwarf gave a nod and together the King and Ectle started out into the halls of Pentegarn. They continued out onto the inner wall where Elendil had been when the Dragon arrived. Ectle looked out into the courtyards between the inner wall and outer wall, watching massive forces of Elves make their rounds through the city. One particular battalion crossing in front of them caught the wizard's attention. They were all archers and dressed differently from the rest of the High Elves.

"Wood Elves... Tanis brought quite a few archers with him I see," the wizard noted, watching the soldiers headed for the northern walls behind the castle.

"Yes, nearly all of his army arrived a day ago. They will surely be more than enough to hold off the Humans if they try to attack the northern walls. That leaves our High Elves to maintain the rest of the walls and towers."

"How do you feel about this my Lord?"

"Pentegarn is the most heavily defended city of all the Elven lands. Even so, I do not know what to expect. I believe the Dwarves will come. Somewhere inside I know they will not leave us to face this army alone."

"Erzel is very persuasive. Perhaps he will be able to convince the Elders of Tvan to at least consider coming back out of the mountains."

The air around the castle was calm and quiet, interrupted briefly by a slight breeze that brought a chill. The King felt the kiss of the cool air on his face and closed his eyes, taking a deep breath. In that moment he was more at peace than at any other time in the last few months.

The silence in the air was suddenly shattered by a deep rumble that echoed across the plains. Ectle and Elendil turned to face one another, a look of confusion on Elendil's face.

"What was that Ectle?"

The wizard tapped his staff and looked out across the plains. "Ogre horn, they're on the move. Usually the horns are accompanied by...war drums..."

The moment he mentioned the drums, the deep thuds of drums being beaten joined the horns. The Elves all turned their attention out across the plains, listening to the thunderous sound of forty thousand Goblins and Ogres marching toward Pentegarn. It had been years since Elendil heard the sound of a massive army on the move and it gave him a chill. It was the first time the Elves had any evidence of the armies hiding in the forests to the south. Elendil and Ectle exchanged a long glance as the Ogre horn sounded again in the distance.

The King nodded and watched as a full patrol of spearmen moved past, headed down to the outer wall defenses as the war drums were joined by several more horns. It was very clear that the armies were on the move. Ectle reached up and placed a reassuring hand on the King's shoulder.

"It is starting my Lord. We'd better get the city ready. I will head for the outer wall while you tend to the inner wall and the castle. Should they get through the outer defenses you will need to be well prepared."

"You are right. You have full command over the outer defenses without question. Do whatever you need to ensure the walls stand."

"Yes my Lord."

Ectle turned and started down the stairs, the soldiers rushing past him on their way to the outer wall and defenses. He moved slowly, taking his thoughts one by one as the forces of Pentegarn hurried about. The wizard moved to the side as a large group of archers moved out to the walls. He found himself at the stairs to the wall and took them slowly, taking a deep breath as he came to the top of the battlements. He looked to the fields to his left, expecting to see the start of the enemy armies. Instead the fields remained empty.

One of the archers approached from the edge of the wall. "Sir, can I help you? This area needs to be clear of civilians at once."

"I am Ectle. I was sent from the castle by King Elendil to manage the outer defenses. Pull your archers together and get ready, Valsera's armies are on the move as we speak. This is the fight you have all been waiting for."

Ectle moved past the soldier and stepped up to the edge of the battlements and stared out across the field, wondering how long it would be before the land between the city walls and forests were filled with the hordes of the south. As the Elves filled the spaces on the battlements, Ectle cracked his knuckles and got ready for the long nights to come.

Elendil found Tanis as the Wood Elf was leaving the throne room deep inside Pentegarn. They stopped and the look on the High Elf's face caused Tanis concern. He pushed the door to the throne room open and together they walked inside, the door booming behind them as it swung closed. Elendil stopped at the archway that led out onto the massive balcony, staring out into space.

"What is wrong Elendil? You look quite lost."

"Didn't you hear them Tanis? The drums, the horns?"

Tanis looked from the King to the balcony, wondering what had happened to push the High Elf so far off his normal demeanor.

"Hear what? No, I apologize, I was in here since you and Ectle left for the city walls. What happened Elendil?"

The King held up a hand and motioned the Wood Elf closer to the balcony. The two Elves stood half in the room and half on the balcony, waiting in silence until a long blast from an Ogre horn filled the air, followed again by the steady beat from the war drums. Elendil turned and his eyes met Tanis's, together hearing the sound of the opposing armies closing in.

"Are those..."

"Yes Tanis, Valsera's armies are on the move. This is what we have been preparing for. Take your archers to the northern wall of Pentegarn and hold there in case the Human army from Cisalia attacks. I know you are eager for revenge after their attack in the forests."

"Of course. My soldiers and I will ensure no Human steps foot inside the walls of Pentegarn, I promise."

The Wood Elf clapped Elendil on the shoulder before turning and leaving the balcony. He hurried through the halls, finding himself in the lower courtyards in a matter of minutes. He pushed past the Knights and archers of the High Elves on his way to the walls to the north. In the back courtyard he found his entire force of Elves all waiting for their orders. Tanis approached the group, his hand resting on the hilt of his sword, ready to be drawn to spill blood.

"Listen up! Cisalia is marching in against Pentegarn as we speak and Elendil has charged us with defending the northern walls so the rest of the High Elves can move back to the southern gates. The odds that Valsera's forces will be larger than those from Cisalia is a guarantee. They need every Elf they can get to stand against the hordes of Qwaz and Nomaria."

"We're with you my King. Give us an order and we will follow."

"Good, relieve Elendil's soldiers on the battlements at once and keep an eye on the forests for any sign of the Humans. They will be here soon."

Tanis waited in the courtyard as his archers began filing onto the battlements above and the High Elves began leaving. The Wood Elves were masters with a bow and there was no doubt they would be able to blanket the enemies with arrows the entire time they made an assault on the city walls. With Elendil's soldiers on their way to the main gate to the south Tanis felt the first wave of worry. He and his soldiers were all that kept the Humans from flooding into the city.

The Wood Elves covered the walls of Pentegarn as if it was their own city they were defending, their bows and spears ready for the first sign of their enemies. One of the soldiers handed Tanis his bow and a quiver of arrows, helping the King fasten them over his shoulder. He stepped to the edge of the wall and waited, his forces prepared.

Elendil walked from the castle down through the courtyards, making his way up the stairs to the inner wall and its battlements. The drums and horns were getting louder, the telltale sign that the enemy was getting closer. The King watched intently and after a full ten minutes of waiting he caught the first glimpse of the enemy moving out into the fields to the south.

The lines of Goblins stretched out of the forests in an endless stream, grouping together and forming large massed formations lacking any form of discipline. The masses soon began forming rows and the armies of Goblins spread further to the north, their numbers starting to wrap around the castle in a large half moon formation. From the King's position it looked like thousands and thousands of ants swarming out of a hill after an attacker. Soon the forests coughed forth the larger forms of Ogres, appearing far more menacing than their smaller comrades. The drums continued as the armies flooded the fields, stopping out of range of the Elves as their allies continued to mass behind them.

The Elves on the walls watched, amazed at the sight of the some forty thousand soldiers marching into the fields for the first time. Elendil stood rooted to the spot where he was standing, fear gripping him for the first time in the history of the wars. He watched intently, seeing their forces more like a plague of insects swarming toward their prey. The fields were starting to turn black as the numbers of Goblins and Ogres kept moving from the trees.

"My King... how are we to fight this?" one Elf asked, watching in the same awe as Elendil.

Elendil did not answer. He watched the nightmare that was Valsera continue flooding the lands around Pentegarn until there was no escape. With it came countless catapults far larger than that of the Elves, as well as the siege weapons taken at the Pass of Merwold. The sight of their own siege machinery being used against them was depressing, making Elendil bite his lip, his assurance that the Elves were fully capable of holding the city starting to leave his head.

"My King, orders sir?" another soldier asked, his shield and spear in hand.

"I uh... take another full battalion of spearmen and swordsmen to the outer wall at once. We are going to need everything we have to hold the defenses."

The spearman looked at the King and gave a bow. "My Lord, we should consider arming the villagers as well. Even an amateur with a bow can be deadly firing into that mass of soldiers. How could they miss?"

A light appeared in Elendil's eyes. "That is a good idea. We can station them here at the castle and inner wall and move our hardened soldiers to the outer wall where we will need their skills. Continue to the wall with the two battalions and I will see that every able bodied Elf is armed and prepared to fight for their homes."

"Yes my King, at once."

The combined force of Elves marched through the inner

gate, headed for the outer defenses. Elendil turned and stopped a group of swordsmen before they were able to move out with the rest of the forces, leading them back towards the castle. Elendil was not keen on the idea of having common citizens fighting against the creatures of the mangled southlands. He stopped outside of the main entrance to the castle and turned to the swordsmen.

"Listen up. I need the ten of you to move through the city and castle, finding any Elf able to wield a bow, spear, or sword and send them to the armory at once. If we are going to hold this siege back until help can arrive we will need everyone able to fight for their city."

"Yes my King."

Elendil could see the worried faces of women and children hurrying to the center of the city, struggling to get away from the walls. Amongst them were the common citizens that tended the everyday businesses and shops throughout Pentegarn. Blacksmiths, carpenters, potters, and more, none ever having had the need to wield a weapon in their lives. Even so, there was a need and Elendil could think of no other way to fill it.

Another blast of an Ogre's horn snapped Elendil back to the horde outside the walls of Pentegarn and he turned to follow the soldiers to the outer wall. The walk from the castle to the outer wall only took a few minutes but each step he took felt weighted and difficult, as if his feet were locked in stone. He took the stairs one at a time, dreading the sight once he reached the top of them.

The soldiers at the top of the battlements moved out of the way as the King approached, giving Elendil a clear view of the battlefield. Standing on the outer wall made their numbers seem even larger, their ranks pressed together tightly as more filled into any available gaps.

"My King, look there, just outside of their ranks to the south. What is that?"

Elendil followed the glare of the soldiers and found one soldier much different from the rest accompanied by six large Ogres approaching the city. They walked half the distance between the city and forest and stopped, apparently waiting for the King of Pentegarn to do the same.

"What do they want my King?" one Knight asked, looking at the creatures in the clearing.

"They are waiting for us to come down to them. Certainly they do not think we will negotiate with them. They've invaded our lands, there is no way we will lay down our arms and give up without a fight. Ectle! Where are you?"

The wizard appeared from a mass of soldiers to the right of the King. "Here my Lord, what brought you down to the outer defenses?"

"They are waiting for us. No matter the hate we share for them, we will honor this gesture. Come with me."

The large gates of the outer wall creaked and swung inward, revealing the King and a small mass of soldiers behind him. The King walked slowly out of the city with the wizard by his side and a small group of the royal guard behind him. The King's battle standard flapped in the wind as they approached and with a mere fifteen steps between the two forces the King stopped. Ectle paused beside the King and waited, staring at the massive Ogres and the strange creature in front of them.

After a few minutes of silence Elendil spoke. "If you've come to ask for a surrender, you are wasting your breath."

"Surrender... what makes you Elves think I would let you surrender? Uljic never accepts a surrender," the creature bragged, looking from Elf to Elf.

"This is a waste of time Elendil, let us go back into Pentegarn. They will never get into the city, no matter how big their army is or how strong Uljic thinks...."

"Quiet fool! We shall see about that... wizard."

Ectle looked up at the creature, finding it as ugly as it was offensive. He cut his eyes at it and then a subtle smirk appeared on its face. "I think it is time for you to leave, before I wipe your face off your head."

"Wouldn't that be... wipe that smirk off your face?" the creature corrected, staring at the wizard with hollow eyes.

Ectle stared at the creature, his temple throbbing softly. "Take another step and I'll show you exactly what I mean."

Elendil held up a hand to stop the wizard, taking a deep breath. "This is getting us no where. Get this clear, I will not leave Pentegarn. No matter how many of your soldiers you throw at the city, you will never take it from us, I promise you that!" Elendil shouted, his temper flaring wildly.

"What if I cut that tongue out... maybe then you will be a little more careful about what you say," Uljic replied, reaching for a dagger sheathed in his belt.

Ectle gripped his staff and lowered the top of it, a flash of light causing the Ogres to take a step back. The crystal at the top of the staff was emitting a dull glow and the creatures all sulked away. All that is except for Uljic. The creature looked at the head of the staff with a curious stare, not the least bit afraid of the wizard. The creature straightened and stared past the King and wizard as another group appeared from behind the Knights.

Elendil and Ectle turned, finding Odimous and the remaining handful of Celestial Knights approaching. The group stopped behind the King and wizard, staring at the creature and Ogres. The moment was tense and silence gripped the clearing. Odimous took a step forward, his eyes still set on Uljic.

The creature let out a dissatisfied growl. "Strange to find your kind here. I thought we had killed off your Celestial rabble."

Odimous lowered his eyebrows and stared back at the creature. "Not even close. You may have destroyed our homes and run us from our lands, but we are here and I promise you this time we will destroy you."

"Cute... we'll see," Uljic growled, a crooked grin on his face.

"Come, back to the city," Ectle said as he turned, looking out the corner of his eye at the creature, half expecting it to attack when he turned his back. The creature did not move from its spot.

The King walked with the wizard and the Celestial Knights by his side, wondering how they would hold off the armies. After seeing them from the bottom of the fields Elendil realized just how massive the force he was facing. A deep sigh of relief came as he crossed through the gate back into the city of Pentegarn, knowing there was now thick stone between him and the armies outside. Elendil turned to Odimous and the rest of the Celestial Knights gathered at the gate.

"Forgive me, I had forgotten you and your forces were still here Odimous. Thank you for your support. Apparently your soldiers and the creature in the field have some sort of history I was not aware of."

Odimous looked up at the King. "Uljic served Valsera

when their forces invaded our homelands long ago. It is not a normal creature. Uljic was created by Valsera, through a combination of creatures and the darkest of magic."

"Combination of creatures? Like what?"

"A troll gives it its strength and regenerative properties, a Goblin added its swiftness and agility, a demonic spirit of the underworlds gave it life and intelligence. All and all, the breed is not one you will likely ever see again. Uljic is the only one of its kind. It feeds off of pain, fear, and hatred, growing stronger with each bloody victory."

An Ogre horn blasted through the air and Elendil raised his eyes to the sky. "How is it you know so much about the creature Odimous?"

The Celestial Knight shook his head and looked to the ground, recounting the horrors in the past. "Because we have fought it numerous times, almost killed it even. Every time we thought we'd found ourselves victorious the creature would rise up again, snatching victory from the jaws of defeat. Uljic single-handedly slaughtered an entire force of our Knights in one bloody battle. Now it has its sights set on your city. We will do what we can, good King."

Elendil nodded and the Celestial Knights turned to leave, pushing their way through the mass of soldiers to their Warbirds at the rear of the city. A handful remained, and against insurmountable odds they would take to the sky and do what they could to defend the Elves. The King turned back to the wizard and looked to the walls again, his eyes darting from soldier to soldier.

"Go back to the inner wall my King. Defend the inner wall and the castle. I will remain here and should they break our defenses, you and your forces will then have to hold them. Go, before it is too late."

Elendil hesitated, feeling guilty for asking the wizard to defend the outer walls of a city he hardly had any ties to. The King knew he should be the one on the wall, leading his soldiers against the enemy. It was his duty. With a quick nod he turned and headed back towards the castle, the royal guard following behind him. As he passed through the city between the inner and outer walls he watched Elves readying catapults and arming ballista.

Closer to the outer wall were several larger catapults, the head of the weapon modified so that a large barrel of oil could be used in the place of the stone or other debris. In several spots on the barrel torches were attached and just before firing they would be lit so the barrels would create a massive explosion when they reached their target in the fields.

Ectle made his way back up the stairs to the battlements of the outer wall, looking out at the open field between Pentegarn and armies of Valsera. A cold breeze rolled across the top of the wall, bringing with it the realization that winter had arrived in the lower lands. A light shiver made Ectle rub his arms as he continued to stare at the enemies in the fields. The archers to his left and right all drew arrows from their quivers and notched them, waiting for the order to fire.

The armies in the fields did the same, the Goblin archers pulling arrows and readying their bows, waiting for the Elves to make the foolish first move. Uljic stared around at his soldiers, leaning against the long shaft of a spear. They would charge when he said charge, fight when he ordered them to fight, and die when he wanted them to die. It was the life of a soldier serving Valsera. They were expendable, like the leaves on the trees.

Ectle raised a hand and stared out at the enemy ranks. "Ready yourselves Elves!"

The archers drew the bowstrings back and sighted down the shafts, the Goblins and Ogres so thick no shot would miss a target. Ectle looked down the lines of archers atop the battlements for as far as he could see, their disciplined ranks an impressive sight for anyone to behold. The wizard took a deep breath and looked back out at the countless enemies.

"And so it begins."

Word of the enemies' arrival had spread to the northern reaches of the outer wall where Tanis and his Wood Elves were now stationed. The King of the Wood Elves seemed restless as the sound of the Ogre horns signaled the attack on the southern gates. He felt that was where his archers should be.

"My King, are you feeling well?" an archer asked, seeing the King's pale face and obvious dissatisfaction with the turn of events.

"I will be fine. This is the largest meeting of armies since the end of the Chaos Wars."

"True, soon all of Nalawren will be at war. We only wait for the Dwarves."

The Wood Elves were obviously nervous, their smaller numbers having less to contribute than the forces of Pentegarn. The High Elves were stronger and there were more of them, defending the city they called home. The Wood Elves felt more like refugees doing what they could to help their stronger brethren.

"My King, look!" an archer exclaimed, pointing down onto the fields. At the edge of the forests the beginning of the Human army appeared, their shields locked together to form a wall the same way they had when the Elves met them in the woods. Their entire army appeared and their wall grew, an impenetrable mass of shields. Tanis drew an arrow from his quiver and the rest of the Wood Elves did the same, sighting in the Humans in the fields.

"Aim for their weakest points, the shields have small gaps. We can not afford to fail."

"These are the Humans responsible for the death of our soldiers back when we encountered them in the woods on our way to Pentegarn. Our brothers deserve revenge for the actions of these traitors," one archer noted, drawing his bowstring back and sighting in a spot on the wall of shields.

"We will kill them, all of them," the King replied, a fire within him suddenly erupting. He had not known hate but the death of his kin was enough to drive the usually calm King mad.

Tanis drew the bowstring back and sighted in a spot where the shields were locked together, waiting for them to part. A single snowflake drifted into his line of sight and then disappeared out of view. He exhaled and released the arrow, watching as it arched down towards the mass of shields. It met its target, greeted with a loud clash as the tip struck the steel shield. Tanis lowered the bow and stared into the clearing with a face of disgust. He had missed.

The arrow striking the shield seemed to breath new life into the army of Humans and they took a few steps towards the city walls in unison. The wall of shields appeared impenetrable and it would take far more than arrows to break it. Tanis turned and looked back towards the city, seeing the unarmed catapult and a pair of ballista. He turned to the closest soldiers and ordered them to the siege weapons. If the Wood Elves were to keep the Humans from breaking down the gates and flooding the northern reaches of the city they would have to act now.

The air around the city of Pentegarn grew silent, but then, like a wave in the ocean, the arrows were released. The Goblins watched, waiting for their orders and then as one massive force returned fire, the arrows crossing paths in the air. The glimmering tips of the Elven arrows reached their peak and curved downward, mimicked by the dull and rusty arrows from the Goblins. The two sides waited, almost welcoming the attacks as the arrows made their descent. After days of waiting, the siege to break the midlands had begun.

An Unexpected Horror

R hen rolled onto her side, looking out at the lake from the dock. She had spent what felt like hours at the lake under the Tvan Mountains, marveling at the darkness that she was beginning to adjust to. The air inside the mountains was cool, but thankfully not nearly as cold as the weather outside of them. She reached up and rubbed her shoulder, the cool air starting to give her goose bumps. It was difficult now. She had seen Erzel only briefly before he was gone again, leaving her with a bittersweet feeling in the pit of her stomach.

"Daughter, are you alright?"

Rhen turned her head back, finding her mother standing at the edge of the dock behind her. She rolled and pushed herself up into a sitting position, rubbing her arms with her open palms. "Yes mother, I am fine. I was just... thinking."

The Queen took a step down onto the dock and then another. "Well, would you be opposed to me joining you for a while? We've not talked much lately."

The Princess shook her head and moved over a little, giving her mother plenty of room to sit down next to her. The Queen folded her dress behind her knees and knelt to the wooden dock beside her daughter. She pulled her cloak around her shoulders a little tighter and took a deep breath, wondering where to start. There were several things concerning her at the moment, but all were very touchy.

Narissa reached over and touched her daughter's hand, a soft smile on her face as she slid a little closer. "Rhen, why is it you feel so strongly for this Erzel? What is it about him that you can not forget?"

Rhen did not look at her mother and instead stared out at the water. She could hear the slight movement in the water as the current from the river running through the mountains emptied into the lake before continuing on deeper into the mountains. She finally did look back at her mother.

"I love him."

Narissa leaned her head to the side and looked at her daughter incredulously, a sort of curious smile forming on her lips. "I know that Rhen, I wanted to know why it is you love him so deeply. It is not that you have known him your entire life. He's just recently had an impact on your life."

"Yes, exactly. He was the first person I saw while prisoner in that horrid dungeon. He didn't even have to come for me. He chose to on his own. Because of Erzel I went from being a prisoner to free again…"

Narissa nodded to the statement. "I understand that. It makes sense that you should have feelings for someone who has given you another chance at life…"

"… and not just that!" Rhen interrupted, staring at her mother intently. "Erzel never left my side. After saving my life he was there every day, the journey to Murm and then on to Tvan. The trip to the Dragon Isles and through the battle waged on the island. It wasn't until we arrived back in Nalawren at Eglarest that he left me and that was only to try to end this war. He did so reluctantly."

"I never truly realized how passionate you were towards him. I am very impressed Rhen."

"Really? Impressed?" the Princess asked, not sure she had heard her mother correctly.

Narissa nodded. "Yes, really. I know how it feels to be in love. I know you have been following your heart. No woman can be wrong if she truly follows her heart. It will lead you where you belong."

"Mother, is love supposed to hurt like this?" Rhen asked, rubbing her stomach where her child was growing.

"What do you mean?"

"I feel so lost. I grew so accustomed to having Erzel there beside me all the time when we were traveling across Nalawren and the Dragon Isles. He left me at Eglarest and rushed off to face Valsera. Then, he and what is left of his soldiers arrive here in Tvan and I am able to see him for maybe two days before he disappears again. I feel the love when he is here and then the pain when he is not."

The Queen laughed quietly to herself. "Alas, you are in love. Yes, it is going to hurt Rhen. You are young and you do not know the misery of having to wait for the one you love to return, the thought that he may not always tugging at your heart. I can not remember how many times I was forced to endure while your father marched to protect our lands. Like now."

She reached down by her thigh and picked up a pebble, rolling it between her fingers before tossing it out into the darkness. The Queen heard the stone meet the water with a soft splash. She found another and it met the water as the first had. Narissa reached up and put a hand on her daughter's shoulder.

"There is something else bothering you. What is it Rhen?"

Rhen breathed softly, thinking her words over carefully. "Well, what happens if Valsera's armies are not stopped? What happens if the Dwarves that were sent south fail and Pentegarn falls and the armies of the south keep spreading north? How will we live?"

"Rhen, we will survive. No matter what happens in the south we will survive and rebuild."

"What if there is nothing to rebuild. If all of the lands we call home are stripped and destroyed then how will we rebuild? I can not live underground forever and I can not imagine forcing my child to do the same."

"Rhen, I know you can not see things getting better. You just have to believe. Believe that our armies will break Valsera's at Pentegarn and continue south. Believe that they will burn all of Qwaz and Nomaria to the ground when they get there."

Rhen slid away and pushed herself up onto her feet, extending a hand to her mother and helping her to her feet. Rhen looked out across the surface of the water and then back to her mother.

"I don't understand how you do this so calmly when I am an emotional wreck."

Narissa smiled and turned Rhen away from the water, leading her back towards the city of Tvan. "I've had a lot of practice dear. For years I have watched your father lead soldiers out of Swanhaven into battle while I remained at the city. I hope you do not have to know what it is like to always wait for the one you love to return, and never knowing whether or not he will."

Rhen walked beside her mother, the torches giving off just enough light to make their way back towards the city. They were quiet as they walked, each with her own thoughts. Rhen was stressed and on one hand wanted to be left alone, but her mother understood the pain she was going through. It was difficult to manage alone.

"Come on Rhen, we should get you back into the city. The air is rather cold and you have another to think of. Surely there is a fire we can find to sit in front of and warm ourselves."

The Princess nodded and the two continued up the path to the rows of shops that filled the monstrous cavern under the mountains. They passed through the city and then on to the castle, taking their time as the long staircases wound upwards. Narissa and Rhen moved through the castle and found their way to their room. Inside they found the fireplace already alive and warm, giving a beautiful glow to the room.

Rhen stood at the edge of the large fireplace, the flickers of the flames bringing warmth to the room. The chill was leaving her body as she rubbed her arms, ridding herself of the numbing cold. Her mother was standing at the mouth of the balcony and drew the curtain to keep more of the cold out. The Princess stared down into the heart of the fire, the orange and red glows mesmerizing. Finally, something to take her mind off of her stressful worries.

Erzel and Kail rode out in front of the Dwarves, keeping an eye out on the forests around them. Their progress was slowed by the enormous army following behind them but the Elf kept his emotions in check. Inside he was angry that they had not gotten further in a day of marching. They were still a ways from Cisalia but their constant march moved them closer. Erzel looked back at the line of Dwarves still maintaining their disciplined lines through the forest.

The Elf took another look back at the Dwarves and then to Kail. "This is taking a lot longer than I thought. There has to be some way of speeding things up."

Kail nodded. "Perhaps, if we take the army further west we can bypass the thickest parts of the forests and use the fields and thinner woods to gain some ground between us and Pentegarn."

Erzel shook his head. "That would take us much too close to Cisalia."

"Yes, that is true," Kail replied, his opinion not wavering. "I agree, we would be a little closer to our enemies but at the same time we would double our pace through the fields north of Pentegarn and possibly get past the Human city without them ever realizing we were there. Of course, this is up to you."

Erzel let his horse move up the trail at its own pace as he pondered what had been offered as a solution to the current problem. Erzel knew that every hour they spent in the woods was another hour that the forces of Pentegarn had to defend without reinforcements. If they were going to help defend the lands around Pentegarn they needed to get there as quickly as they could. Kail's logic was sound.

"Very well. We do need to get to Pentegarn as soon as we can and at our current rate the Goblins and Ogres will have destroyed the outer wall and its forces by the time we get there."

"Indeed," Kail replied, moving his horse in next to the Elf. "I think that if we move to the west now we could probably cut a full day out of our travel by using the fields and I would not worry about Cisalia. With this force of Dwarves behind us they will not dare attack."

The Elf hesitated, giving a slight nod. "Yes, Cisalia has turned against the Elves. Their King Calyn was executed in Pentegarn after attempting to assassinate the King. I expect there will be some sort of revenge in the future to come from them."

"Then should we be moving so close to the city?" another Dwarf asked, continuing with the concerns of the first.

"That is the fastest route to Pentegarn and with the size of your numbers and the speed we will be moving I do not see the Humans brave enough to attack us. Just as well, we will not be in sight of the city," Erzel replied firmly, staring at the mass of soldiers. "Are there any who object?"

The Dwarves looked around among themselves, finding no one who was willing to defy the orders of the Elf. Even if reluctantly, they all agreed to follow Erzel's orders and the mass replied with silent nods. Erzel looked to Kail who immediately turned off in the new direction of their route. It was only a mile or so through the woods before they would reach the open fields that led south to the forests around Pentegarn but the trek was through the thickest part of the woods.

The Dwarves were forced to abandon their disciplined formations and weave their numbers in and out of the forests, struggling to get the entire army through with any sort of timing. Erzel and Kail found the forest a challenge as well and were forced to dismount and walk their horses through the trees. Suddenly in the back of Erzel's head came the realization that he had no way of letting Alora and Lavian know that they had shifted their course.

"Kail, there is one minor problem to this idea," the Elf noted, ducking a low branch.

"What is that Erzel?"

"Well, how will we let Alora and Lavian know that we are not taking the same route we had planned out initially? They are our eyes above and if there is something we need to know about ahead of us they will not be there to scout it."

"Perhaps they are keeping an eye on us and will see the army move out of the trees to their west. At least I hope so."

"Alora is clever, surely she will notice the lack of an army beneath her at some point."

Erzel and Kail finally broke the line of trees and moved out into the grassy field to be sure and secure it before the rest of the army appeared. From what they could tell they were the only ones in sight. Kail turned and gave a loud whistle, signaling to the Dwarves to begin moving out into the fields. Rows of short soldiers began appearing, filing through the grasses and forming large block formations. Erzel and Kail waited patiently as the last of the Dwarves appeared and took their places.

"Alright, let's move out. Pentegarn is waiting for us and we will answer the call for help. Move out and keep up!"

Erzel's orders echoed through the lines of Dwarves as they started marching, following the two horses out in front. There were no songs of glory, no chants, no talking of any sort. The Dwarves marched in silence, their minds brewing with the thoughts of battle and bloodshed to come.

Erzel turned to Kail, a random question taking hold in his head. He tried to force it down but as he did, the desire to know the truth rose again. "Kail, can I ask you something?"

"Of course Erzel, why wouldn't you be able to?" Kail asked, noticing the sound of concern in the Elf's voice.

Erzel found the nerve and looked at the soldier. "I want to ask you about when you served with... Valsera."

The Elf took a second before asking, making sure the Dwarves were far enough behind that they would not overhear the conversation. Kail did not look up, neither surprised by the subject nor enthused to be reminded of his past. He took a deep breath and turned his head to Erzel.

"That is ok... what is it you want to know?"

"Several things actually. Knowing now that Valsera was responsible for the assaults on the homelands of the Dragons and the Celestial Knights, I wondered... I mean, I was curious... were you a part of that?"

Kail shook his head. "No, I was not."

Erzel breathed a sigh of relief. He raised his head again and continued. "Well, in serving Valsera, are you aware of anything stronger than the Goblins, Ogres, Lizardmen, and Slayers under his control? What else does he have in his arsenal of creatures that we have yet to see?"

Kail looked up and stared out into space, recalling his time serving under the darkest of leaders. The sorcerer had an uncanny ability of pulling all sorts of evil creatures into his service. The creatures Erzel had mentioned were only those Valsera had invaded Nalawren with. All across the west their were other islands and nations that had been conquered by the sorcerer, the native races enslaved to serve or suffer under the wrath of Valsera.

"Erzel, there are countless other races that Valsera has destroyed and enslaved, forcing them to serve his armies in other far off lands. The Goblins, Ogres, and Slayers are those that he used to invade Nalawren."

"What other sorts of races has Valsera to call against us?"

Kail shook his head. "None. They are so far away that it would take weeks for word to reach them. In the west he has conquered everything. Goblins, Ogres, Trolls, Humans, Hobgoblins, and in the farthest reaches to the west he enslaved a race of Giants. Like I said though, there are no reinforcements coming for the sorcerer. Not that he needs them.

Kail had not served Valsera when the sorcerer destroyed

the homelands of the Dragons and Celestial Knights but he remembered the other minor races and how fast they had fallen. The Humans and their kind had been far more primitive in the western lands and it took a week to break their defenses and enslave them. The Goblins, Ogres, and Hobgoblins never even dared stand against the sorcerer even though they outnumbered him and his Slayers an unbelievable hundred to one. They had all pulled to his armies and created the single largest force in existence. That was, until they arrived in Nalawren and faced the combined armies of Dwarves, Humans, and Elves.

"There is more though, something only heard through rumor of the other soldiers in his army."

"Yes?" Erzel asked, his curiosity peaking as he realized there was even more they may be faced with soon.

"Valsera was beginning to dabble in necromantic magic. The sorcerer was obsessed with the ability of raising the dead to serve him. Like an endless supply of soldiers at his fingertips."

"Was he ever successful?" Erzel asked, a hint of fear in his voice.

"I do not know. As I said, it was only rumored. Though with the power Valsera possessed I would not put it out of his reach."

The Elf breathed a sigh of relief. "It is wonderful that he remains imprisoned in the crystal. He will not be able to summon reinforcements from his other lands or from the dead either. We have a chance."

A large shadow crossed their paths and Erzel watched the Warbird float to the ground in front of them, finding Lavian waiting, a concerned look on her face. She dismounted and briskly walked up to the two on horseback.

"Why have you deviated from the path we were on?" she asked, seeing the Dwarves marching in behind them and stopping.

"Things were moving much too slowly. At this rate we will shave an entire day off our journey and that could be the difference in saving Pentegarn and watching it burn. Forgive me, I was not able to warn you and Alora."

"Very well. I was concerned that something had driven you and your forces out of the forests. I will keep an eye out," the Celestial Knight replied, remounting her Warbird and taking off, the grass in the field swaying away from the powerful beating of the wings of the Warbird.

Erzel and Kail exchanged a look, neither one too surprised that the Celestial Knight had noticed they were no longer on the same route as those in the air. They pushed on through the fields as the sun started to take its downward plunge to allow night into the sky. Erzel noticed the chill in the air for the first time in the trip, realizing that in the fields there was nothing to protect them from the cold sting of the wind. In the forest they had the trees and the wind never managed to reached deep between the thick trunks.

He looked back over his shoulder at the Dwarves, their pace not faltering in the least even with the added cold of the wind. He did not show it but he was rather impressed with their spirit. They kept going no matter what weather they faced. The Elf turned back around and gave a weak smile, hiding his face as a particularly strong gust of wind numbed his ears and nose.

The two crossed the crest of a hill and started down towards the lower edge of the field where the trees began to appear once more. The forests were sparse in the beginning but would eventually thicken before they reached the outskirts of Pentegarn. Erzel caught movement out of the corner of his eye and turned quickly, staring for a minute before dismissing it as his imagination. He turned back to the front and looked ahead.

Something in the back of his head was twitching, like a nerve sending a warning to his brain yet he ignored the feeling. Nothing seemed out of place in the land around them and the two soldiers kept moving forward. From above came a rush of wind and they looked up, watching a Warbird land in front of them with Lavian gripping the harness and waiting for the large beast to settle before climbing down.

Erzel gave an inquisitive look as the Celestial Knight's arrival was not expected in the least. "Is something wrong Lavian?"

"Erzel, there was something in the trees. I only saw it briefly, like a flash and then it was gone. You should get the Dwarves ready."

"I too thought I saw something briefly not minutes before you landed," Erzel claimed, remembering the movement out the corner of his eye. "I do not know, what would you expect to find against us up here Kail?"

Kail shook his head. "I don't have a clue Erzel. We are close to Pentegarn and with Valsera's armies pushing north to Pentegarn there could be all manner of creatures moving about. I will assemble the troops."

Kail turned his horse and started back towards the Dwarves who had just started crossing the crest of the hill. Out of the corner of Erzel's eye he saw movement again and turned, this time finding figures exiting the trees all around them. The Elf saw the bows armed and ready, waiting for their targets. He turned to Kail as a pair of arrows left the bows. The arrows flew straight and both hit the horse carrying Kail, one in the neck and one in the shoulder. The horse reared violently, slinging Kail to the ground.

"Slayers!" Erzel yelled, drawing his sword and turning his own horse towards the enemy. They were now coming from three different directions, using the trees as cover.

Lavian brought her crossbow to her shoulder and aimed down the sights when a sudden blow from behind knocked her to the ground, her weapon landing out of her reach. Two Slayers grabbed her from behind and pulled her to her knees, the tips of their swords inches from a deathly blow. To his left Erzel watched a similar fate befall Kail as one of the Slayers shoved its boot onto his back and pressed the head of a spear against the back of his neck.

The Dwarves rushed forward but Erzel turned his horse and raised his hands, beckoning them to stop. "No! Stay where you are!"

"Very smart, for an Elf." came a hiss from behind Erzel.

He turned, finding Infus surrounded by Slayers standing just inside the clearing. In all there were twelve, maybe fifteen of the sinister creatures, and they had the upper hand. They had Erzel's friends. The Elf dropped from his saddle to the ground, drawing his sword and watching every move the Demon made. Infus stopped next to Kail, kneeling and raking its clawed gauntlet across the back of his head.

"It looks like we have quite an issue here, don't we?"

Erzel stood rooted to the spot, his mind blank. He fumbled for words. "If you... what is it that you want Demon?"

The question was foolish. Erzel knew why the Demon was there. Secured at his belt were the crystals that held its master imprisoned. It was the only conceivable reason for the Demon to make an attack in such a wide open area. The Dwarves scattered as the Blue Dragon glided down behind Erzel, her landing loud and her anger growing at the sight of the Slayers.

The Dragon took a step forward, her roar shaking the Dwarves and Slayers alike. Only Infus and Erzel were unafraid. The Elf remembered Lavian and Kail and quickly turned, locking eyes with Alora.

"No, you can not attack Alora. They will kill Kail and Lavian."

The Dragon looked to either side, seeing the soldier and the Celestial Knight captive with the weapons of the Slayers mere inches from their skin. Alora brought her head back around, locking her glare of hate on Infus as she slowly took a step back. For the moment, the two enemies waited, neither one making a move against the other.

Infus finally took a step back away from Kail towards the center of the clearing between Erzel and the forest behind the Demon. "Perhaps I can interest you in a trade Elf?"

Erzel allowed the tip of his sword to drop ever so slightly, curious at the Demon's offer. "A trade? You attack us and you want to trade? Let me tell you what you can do with your…"

"Careful fool!" Infus snapped, the hiss making the Dwarves pull away in fright. "I would be very careful how you respond. It would take seconds to finish your two friends. Now, you were saying?"

"What have you to trade?" Erzel asked through gritted teeth.

"Why, how about the lives of your friends. Surely you do not want to see their blood spilled because of your inability to negotiate."

"In exchange for what?" he asked. The conversation with the Demon was tearing Erzel apart inside. He knew the creature did not care for the two prisoners at all. They were already as good as dead in its hands.

Infus took a step towards the Elf and then another, stopping close enough for the Elf to get off an attack with the sword. Erzel did not though. He knew it was pointless and he would never have enough time to reach the whip and activate it. Reluctantly he looked to Kail and then Lavian, waiting for the Demon's response. On either side he saw the bows of the Slayers trained on him and the Dwarves.

Infus stopped and looked the Elf up and down, as if deciding where to plant its dagger. "What could you possibly have to trade? A very interesting question. I wonder what would be worth the lives of two soldiers? Of course, one of ours."

Erzel's heart hardened as he knew what the Demon had implied.

"Where is it Elf?" Infus asked angrily, staring Erzel down with its hollow darkness beneath the hood.

Erzel looked down slowly, his eyes landing on the leather pouch at his hip where he had stored the crystals. He could feel the weight of the stones in his pouch, pulling at him. He looked back up to the Demon and lowered his sword, reaching down with his free hand and revealing the cluster of crystals. The Demon's hooded face followed the crystals from Erzel's hip to his hand and then higher as the Elf brought them up into view. The Elf looked to the side at Lavian, her face disheartened at the realization of what was about to take place.

"I will not give you the ability to free Valsera. You'll have to kill us all first," the Elf said bravely, fearing for the wellbeing of Kail and Lavian.

"Oh? Well what if I just kill one of you?" the creature replied, waving a hand behind him.

From the trees appeared another Slayer. It pulled with it the form of another person, the face shrouded in a sack. The creature grabbed the sack and ripped it off, revealing the form of a young Elf. Erzel nearly fell to his knees when he realized the Elf was Rhen.

"Im... impossible," Erzel stammered.

"Well Elf, what is it going to be?" Infus asked, drawing its sword and pointing it towards the young Elf.

The Elf was in shock, not daring to believe what was taking place in front of him. He gripped the cluster of crystals and stared at the young Elf, having no idea how the Demon had gotten its claws on the Princess. Infus thrust the sword closer to her and Erzel cried out loudly.

"Very nice. So you are ready to make a trade I take it?"

Erzel raised his eyes to the Demon, a new bravery growing inside. "First you will release them if you want this?"

Infus looked to the Celestial Knight and then to Kail. It
shook its head and a raspy laugh could be heard from within the
dark hood. "I think not. You will place the crystals on the ground
and step away or I will slaughter every single one of you here in
this field."

Erzel stared back hatefully at the Demon as he slowly
bent at the waist and set the cluster of crystals on the soft grass.
He slowly stood once more and took a step back away from them
as he had been ordered to do. The Demon waited until Erzel had
moved back far enough before stooping and grabbing the top of
the staff from the field. It held the item aloft like a trophy, knowing the power it now held in its hands. Infus nodded and turned
its back to the Elf, walking off towards the forests.

The Demon paused briefly. Just as it moved past the last
Slayer gripping the young Elf the Demon turned back to the two
forces in the field. "Kill them all."

With the last words the Demon drew its sword back and
thrust the sharp blade deep into her stomach. The Elf cried out
and Infus pulled the sword free, kicking her to the ground where
the pain curled her into a ball.

Infus suddenly broke into a sprint and disappeared into
the trees. Everyone in the clearing had heard the Demon clearly
and Erzel had expected what was about to take place. He turned
and slung his sword to the left, watching as it flew end over end
into the chest of the Slayer, knocking it off of Kail and freeing the
fighter.

"Hold on Rhen... please... hold on!" Erzel cried, rushing
towards the Slayers and his fallen love.

Alora acted just as quickly, opening her mouth and firing
a blinding bolt of lighting across the field at the Celestial Knight.
The bolt raked across the two Slayers holding her, sending them
to the ground engulfed in flames. Lavian dove forward to her
crossbow, feeling the sting of one of the blades that had been
pressed against her neck. The deep gash ran across her cheek, but
she ignored the pain, rolling to avoid the Slayer archers.

Alora blanketed the field with surges of lightning, torch-
ing every Slayer in her path. Erzel dove under the swing of an
attacker and watched as a bolt from Lavian's crossbow struck the

creature in the chest, sending it backward to the ground. The Elf grabbed the Slayer's sword from the ground and stabbed it into the creature, the body rupturing and fire leaping from the wound.

"Erzel, get down!" came a thunderous roar from behind.

He turned and fell back as three Slayers rushed towards him, their swords and spear raised to attack. He landed on his back and rolled, attempting to avoid the attack that was seconds from landing. As the Elf rolled to the left Alora released another bolt of lightning, instantly destroying the three Slayers in their steps. The Dragon took another step towards Erzel and the others, her attacks punishing the enemy.

It was from the left that the attack came, a single archer with the perfect angle on the great Blue Dragon. It pulled the bowstring tight and sighted for a brief second, releasing as soon as it had a shot. The arrow streaked through the air and met the softer skin under Alora's jaw. The Dragon clamped its jaw shut and turned, seeing the Slayer that had attacked her. As she turned, another Slayer fired from the right, its arrow hitting the Dragon at the back of the skull.

Erzel watched in horror, knowing all too well the damage that the arrows did to the other Dragons and to his friend Rathe. Alora staggered forward, her left shoulder sagging as she struggled to stay up to protect the others. With a tear in his eye Erzel hefted the enemy sword and charged toward the archer on the right, cleaving its head with one powerful swing. One more arrow found its mark, sinking deep into the Dragon's side directly behind her shoulder. The pain was excruciating and Alora collapsed with a mournful cry.

The Dwarven archers had moved to the front and though they were not nearly as proficient with a bow as other races they began blanketing the remaining Slayers with shot after shot. Soon all that was left of the enemy were pockets of fire and smoldering remains. Erzel tossed the sword aside and ran to the Princess, grabbing her shoulders and looking down at her face. The pain twisted her expressions but it was her eyes. They were different. As he watched the beautiful red hair softened and began to change color. The red became a dull brown and then a blonde.

The Elf's features changed slowly and finally Erzel realized that the Demon had not only set a trap for them but had managed to trick the Elf into handing over the crystals. In dismay he turned away from the body of the Elf and hurried to the Dragon, falling next to her in the grass. He grabbed the arrow in her side and jerked it out, ignoring the burning sensation that surged though his hands.

"Alora? Alora... are you... alive?"

The Dragon did not move. The faint rise of her chest was the only assurance that she still lived. He moved up to her neck and looked at the arrows still jutting from her body. They had been in far too long and their damage was already done. There was nothing the Elf could do for the fallen Dragon.

Alora's jaw opened slightly and a breath escaped, followed by muffled words as she struggled to communicate. "Erzel... are they... all... safe?"

The Elf looked around and then back to the Blue Dragon, another tear leaving his eye. "Yes Alora, they've all been destroyed. Kail... and Lavian are safe."

"That is... good. Now I know..."

Lavian knelt next to Erzel and placed a hand on the Dragon's neck, looking into her eye. "Now you know what Alora?"

"What it... is like... to... die."

Erzel looked up at the Dwarves who had moved in around the Dragon, forming a wall in case there were any more of the enemy hiding in the forests. Everything around him was a fog, like the world no longer mattered. He looked down at the Dragon, running his hand across her head softly.

"Alora, you can't die... not here... not like this. You are the last one... the last Blue Dragon."

"We all die... Erzel, but... not all... of us have... truly lived," the Dragon choked out, struggling to keep her eyes open.

Lavian reached down and placed a hand on Erzel's shoulder, pulling him back away from the Dragon slowly. She took him and looked into his eyes, her expression very serious. "Erzel, we have to let her go. We have to let her know it is ok to let go now. She saved our lives."

Erzel nodded, his heart still torn at the sight of the Dragon sprawled out in the grassy field. He approached slowly and knelt next to her once more, touching her just behind her eye. The eye slowly cracked open, giving proof that the Dragon was still clinging to life.

"Alora... I can never repay you for what you have done.

You've saved our lives, more than once. You will always be remembered for what you have done, I promise."

The Dragon's eye slowly slid closed, the last few breaths so faint that Erzel could not tell if she was still alive. He rubbed her neck as the last breath escaped the Dragon's lungs. She fell deathly still and it was soon apparent that the Dragon was gone. The Dwarves gathered round, everyone getting a good view as the last of the Blue Dragons slipped away forever.

Erzel stood from the side of the Dragon, staring off into the woods where the Demon had disappeared, knowing now that a horrible fate was waiting for them. Even if they managed to repel the siege at Pentegarn, they would soon be forced to face Valsera all over again, this time without the help of Alora and the other Dragons. Both anger and fear ran through him.

"Erzel... it is ok Erzel... we will get even, I promise you that," Lavian whispered, placing a firm hand on the Elf's shoulder.

He shook his head. "The Demon will free the sorcerer. The sorcerer will call for reinforcements. Our lands will be swallowed by his armies. What do we have to rival the power of Valsera? What is left? I gave up the crystals to save a Princess that was not even here. I let my feelings cloud my judgment. How could I be so foolish?"

Lavian tightened her grip. "I don't know Erzel, but I promise you, we will punish them for what they have done here."

Erzel nodded and pulled away, looking back at the force of Dwarves waiting for their orders. He looked to the body of the Dragon and he knew there was one thing that needed to be done before they continued on to Pentegarn. He caught their attention and cleared his throat.

"We will not leave this Dragon out in the open to rot in the sun. She will be given a burial fit for a King. Cut timbers and build them up around her. We can not bury the Dragon here, but we will send her remains skyward one last time."

Lavian watched as the Dwarves spread out with their duties, the realization that they had lost the last of the Blue Dragons beginning to set in. She knew it pained Erzel deeply as he was the one who had formed a bond with the Dragon. She turned and watched the forests as the rest of the army began building the funeral pyre. She kept her back to the rest of the soldiers and for the first time, allowed a tear to wet her cheek. She looked to the sky, watching the sun leave behind streaks of color.

The Siege of Pentegarn

The walls of Pentegarn were covered with Elves who had resorted to locking their shields together, forming a second wall atop the first. The hundreds of Goblin archers blanketed the walls with wave after wave of arrows. The Elves used the wall of shields to protect their own archers, allowing them a chance to return fire in between the attacks from the Goblins. Hours were spent in the exchange and the Goblins were soon the obvious loser in the engagement. They drew back, continuing their assault as they fell back into forces of Goblins and Ogres. Ectle stared down at the fields, watching the forces reforming around the archers.

The wizard looked back at the inner wall and fortress at the center of the city, wondering what changes the King had made to the defenses behind them as an extra two to three hundred Elven archers and spearmen arrived just before the attack from the Goblin archers. The wizard took note of the soldiers around him and of the catapults below. He turned and watched the Goblin archers approaching again, this time accompanied by large structures rolled out into place in front of the lines. They were called mantlets, large wooden shields used to hide between eight or ten of the enemy archers. The enemy was getting smarter.

"Archers to the ready! Catapults, make ready!" the wizard ordered, watching the lines of Goblins fall in behind the mantlets.

The Elves followed their orders to the smallest detail, their bowstrings drawn tight waiting for the order to fire. For the first time in the history of Pentegarn the torches on the barrels of oils were lit, waiting for the order to loose their attack on the enemy. Ectle turned and watched as the enemy set their defensive mantlets, preparing to fire on the city walls again. He could wait no longer.

"Release the catapults!"

The triggers on the catapults were released and the row of siege weapons launched their attacks across the wall out into the fields, the barrels rolling pitching through the air. The archers in the fields that had stepped out from the mantlets drew their bowstrings back but hesitated, seeing the large objects flying toward them. All of the outer walls watched anxiously as the barrels made their descent.

"Here we go, let's see what they think of this."

The barrels met their targets almost in unison, the explosion rocking the fields around the city. The moment the barrels broke, the wave of oil met with the torches on the sides and the liquid was ignited instantly. The explosions were so violent that the bodies of the Goblin archers were slung back into the middle of the formations of enemy forces. As the fires rolled through the mantlets and soldiers manning them the weapons were armed and torches lit again.

The catapults were altered slightly, ensuring their attacks would reach further than the first. With the weapons set they fired again, the barrels streaking through the air towards the enemy. The torches on either side of the barrels glowed brightly as the projectiles dropped down past the areas already burning across the fields. The soldiers watched again, this time not expecting the attack to reach further. When it did, the results were devastating. The barrels began exploding through the front lines of the enemy forces, sending showers of flames, dirt, and the charred remains of Goblins flying through the air.

Elendil stood on the edge of the inner wall, staring out at the flashes of the explosions and the plumes of smoke invading the air across the fields. He smiled, knowing the damage the newer weapons were inflicting. His archers and those citizens who had been armed cheered as they watched the enemy soldiers falling all across the front lines.

Seeing the first of the siege weapons dealing such powerful damage gave the High Elf King more hope that against all odds, against the strongest army they had ever seen, it was possible. They could hold the city. The soldiers in the heart of the city waited impatiently, half hoping for their chance to spill blood but at the same time, knowing that to do so would mean the enemy had been able to break through the outer defenses. For now they waited, listening to the cheers from the Elves on the walls.

Ectle watched as the second wave of explosions crippled the front lines of the Goblin forces. They fell back towards the forests as those behind them pushed forward. They were terrified of the flying fire, but the fear of Infus's wrath was even greater. That fear drove the armies to unthinkable actions. Even seeing their fellow soldiers slaughtered and thrown into disarray, the armies refused to break. After all, there were more of them than of the Elves.

"Sir, they are regrouping. What orders have you?"

Ectle looked out and watched as the army of Goblins and Ogres began filing back into their formations, smothering out the fires that raged across the front lines. Soon, the black smoke died down and as it dissipated a new sight appeared. Towards the rear of the armies Ectle caught sight of the massive siege weapons loaded and ready. He turned and looked at the ones behind him, armed once more with the barrels of oil and torches flickering in the breeze.

"Fire! Fire everything!" the wizard ordered, watching the enemy catapults release their attacks.

The massive boulders streaked through the air towards the castle as the Elves released their own weapons. The barrels flew towards the boulders and in the moment they crossed paths, one struck the enemy boulder in the sky, a cloud of fire suddenly raining down onto the field below. Ectle watched in fear as the boulders approached.

"Brace yourselves!" he shouted.

The first of the boulders met the wall with a force that threatened to bring the stones crumbling to the ground below. Soldiers on the battlements struggled to keep their balance as the thunderous explosion shook them. Seconds behind the first another struck, and then another, the repeated bombardment continuing as they tried to arm their weapons again. One particularly large stone flew higher, raking the top of the battlements and sending Elves flying through the air with the debris of the ravaged wall.

"Archers, make ready. Catapults, load stone! They're coming again!" Ectle shouted, seeing the gaps in the defenses from the massive stones. Another struck just to the wizard's right and continued through, ripping the entire roof off of a house behind the wall. Even the buildings behind the wall were suffering catastrophic damage from the stones raining down on the city.

The barrels ruptured in the front lines of the enemy and fire swept across the field again. As the fires leapt across the soldiers in the fields, the catapults were rearmed with large stones and boulders to match the destructive power of the Goblin's. Ectle turned, seeing the forces in the field starting to advance toward the gate and raised his staff into the air.

"Archers, fire at will!"

Without the mantlets the soldiers were vulnerable targets, desperately trying to use their shields to block the incoming wave of arrows. Goblins and Ogres were blanketed in a wave of arrows, their fellow soldiers falling all around them as many managed to protect themselves. The wave of arrows was followed with another attack from the catapults, the stones flying out a little short of the front lines of Goblins. The shower of dirt and rock covered the lines of soldiers as their own siege weapons were armed again. The wizard looked out at the lack of damage the Elves were inflicting, wondering how much more the wall could take.

Tanis had heard the explosions and the massive waves of attacks of the catapults from the northern reaches of the outer wall. The Wood Elves had showered the Humans from Cisalia with arrows non stop, forcing them to keep their wall of shields intact and keeping them from advancing on the city. At the same time though, the Elves had dealt little damage to the formation of soldiers outside the wall.

Every other volley of arrows, the wall of Human shields would move forward a step or so, trying to get closer to allow the Human archers a chance to bring down the Elven soldiers on the wall above. The King of the Wood Elves held up his hand, stopping the archers briefly as he struggled to think of another way to force their defenses apart.

"My Lord, they've stopped. What orders have you?"

Tanis looked to his soldiers and then to the defenses of the smaller gate on the northern wall. A group of Elves had arrived from the castle and had since begun manning the large cauldron and the two ballista on the right side of the gate. Though they were not soldiers, the villagers were armed and ready to defend their home with whatever means necessary. The fire beneath the cauldron wrapped around the metal, boiling the liquid inside that was waiting to be poured on those foolish enough to rush the gates.

The few thousand men in the fields below waited for the right time to strike, no longer feeling the arrows pelting down on their shields. The sliver of a hole between the shields widened and the archers hiding beneath took their first shots. The arrows streaked out towards the battlements, most either too high or too low and in any case, none met their targets. The Elves responded with another volley that once again fell on the strength of the shield wall.

"Hold your fire! Wait for their shields to separate, wait for their archers to appear again and punish them. They will not reach the walls."

From within the shield wall appeared groups of five or six men, moving back towards the forest from where their soldiers had appeared. Tanis watched them curiously, wondering why they were sending the men back into the trees. He remembered the force in the forest when they had encountered the first and knew there were no siege weapons with the army. The Elf watched as the shields parted once more and this time the Elves were ready, releasing their arrows the moment they saw the gaps.

The arrows struck the shields and skipped off in different directions but some did manage to hit their targets. From within the shield wall they heard the cries of pain as the arrows met their targets. The shields quickly pulled back together and locked the wall together firmly once more. Though the King worried briefly for the gate, his concerns once again turned to the Humans fleeing for the woods.

"What thoughts have you about those Humans in the forest now?" Tanis asked one of the soldiers at his side.

"Yes, I saw them my Lord. I have no idea why they have fallen back into the forest. There were not many of them, a paltry dozen if that many. Perhaps they were going for reinforcements? Maybe there are more soldiers back in Cisalia?"

Tanis shook his head, not quite believing the reasoning but unable to explain it himself. There were no resources that could be used to build any sort of catapult or siege machine. The

Humans locked down their shield wall and held their position, waiting for a break of some sort. From their position the Humans could see the flanks of the Goblin army to the south and it gave a testimony to how large Valsera's forces had become.

The Goblins and their leaders knew Cisalia had marched against the city just as their forces had and watched as the mass of armored Humans formed a wall of shields that appeared unbreakable against the simple attacks from the archers. The Human soldiers were patient, knowing that eventually they would storm the walls. All they had to do was wait.

Tanis watched as the two ballista were set and aimed, the soldier waiting for the order from the Wood Elf King. He held the order, as if wondering whether or not the weapon would be effective against the wall of shields. With the southern reaches of the city being bombarded constantly by the enemy Tanis wanted to be sure to break them before they could manage any sort of successful attack. The Wood Elf looked to the right and raised his hand, catching the attention of those manning the ballista.

"Fire!" he shouted, dropping his arm.

The Elves steadied the war machines and aimed them at the heart of the wall. With one last look to be sure they had their sights set true the Elves threw the triggers, watching the two massive spears shoot forward towards the Humans. The Elves along the wall watched anxiously, eagerly waiting to see the damage the attack would do. As if expecting every move the Elves made the center of the wall split and drew apart, allowing the spears to strike nothing but the earth. As quickly as they had split the Humans shifted and slid back together, reforming the wall once more.

Tanis grit his teeth, seeing the attack useless and the Humans far more intelligent than he had originally anticipated. The Wood Elf turned and looked behind him at the inner wall and the giant fortress even further in. The Elves of Pentegarn were all at war, none able to move to the northern gate to break the Human army that had arrived. This was Tanis's task and he would complete it or die trying. The Wood Elves drew their arrows once more and prepared to fire, waiting for the order from their King.

The catapults in the Goblin armies were relentless, showering the outer wall with stones repeatedly. The damage to the wall was beginning to take its toll and though it was the thickest wall of the city, the battlements were in ruin. The catapults suddenly stopped the assault and the wizard and the soldiers around him watched massive ladders appear through the ranks of the Goblins, carried by heavily armored Ogres.

Ectle turned to the Elves who had taken cover behind their shields and ordered them to arms. The archers drew their arrows back and aimed down into the field, picking their targets as they waited for the order to loose. The wizard curled his fingertips and between them an orange glow appeared, growing into a whirling ball of fire. He waited as the soldiers on the move began their march, growing closer. Sensing the moment was at hand he turned to the Elves on the battlements.

"Prepare to fire! Aim for those Ogres, stop them from setting those ladders! Ready!"

The Elves all held their bowstrings taunt, waiting for the order. Nearly a dozen monstrous ladders, each carried by eight to ten of the Ogres. Ectle raised his hand and drew back, hesitating for a second before hurling the ball of fire like a stone. It flew through the air and curved downward, meeting the ground within the rows of Goblins, exploding instantly

The fireball was the signal for the archers and they began releasing their arrows in waves, dropping countless Goblins in the attack. Ectle drew back again, a second fireball churning and growing in his grasp and a second time he attacked, watching the same destructive effect. The Goblin line, however, was hardly affected and their numbers replenished almost instantly.

"Fire at will! Stop those Ogres now!"

The thick armor on the Ogres allowed them to withstand the onslaught of arrows as they pushed further, looking to set the ladders against the battlements of Pentegarn and allow their armies to swarm the walls. One of the Ogres in the front fell, a cluster of arrows finding a gap between the plates around its neck. Before the Ogre could fall to the ground another grabbed the ladder, replacing its fallen comrade.

The Elves continued firing and in their distraction, another wave of boulders was launched. Boulders fell across the tops of the wall in a thunderous chorus of explosions, sending Elves all across the wall falling back towards the stairs. Ectle ducked a shower of stone and debris and glared back angrily at the Goblins.

The Ogres thrust the massive ladders into the ground at the base of the wall, the pivot slinging the top of the siege ladders up into the air. The Goblins rushed towards the ladders even before they had met the top of the stone wall. The Elven archers leaned over the edge of the wall, firing straight down on the Goblins swarming up the ladders. All across the southern wall the tops of the ladders began landing.

"Make ready the walls! Defend the battlements!" Ectle shouted, moving back and forth across the battlements, rallying the Elves to the wall.

The archers did well for the first few minutes, firing directly down the ladders to stop the Goblins. After the first dozen Goblins fell the Elves found themselves under fire from the Goblin archers in the field. The Elves began falling quickly and were forced back away from the edge of the wall again. The soldiers drew back away from the edge of the wall, giving the enemy the few seconds they needed to climb the ladders. The first few soldiers that made it to the top of the wall were met with the tips of arrows until they began arriving faster than the Elves could rearm themselves.

"Draw swords! Defend the battlements to the last Elf! Here they come!" Ectle shouted, knocking one Goblin from the ladder.

The ladders were covered with enemy soldiers scaling them as fast as they could. The Elves abandoned their bows and drew their swords and spears, preparing to meet the enemy. The first Goblin to meet the battlements was met with a trio of spears, its blood splattering across the wall. The creature fell back and slid down the stone wall atop the battlements, a low gurgle the only sound it made. The battle erupted all across the tops of the wall as Goblins continued flooding up the ladders.

The army in the field spread apart as they had when the Ogres appeared with the siege ladders and from it came another mass of Ogres, a monstrous battering ram carried between them this time. It took more than a dozen of the brutes to carry the siege weapon towards the gate. Ectle knocked another Goblin from the wall, catching sight of the battering ram. A chill ran up his spine.

"Brace the gate! Ready the cauldrons! Here they come!"

The Elves on the battlements did exactly as they were ordered, those at the gate locking long poles under the cauldron as they prepared to pour them down onto the besiegers. The Ogres broke into a frenzied run and Ectle watched in horror as they smashed into the gate. The battlement above the gate shook violently but the gate stood solid, the massive wooden doors resilient to the attack.

Ectle ran towards the top of the gate, ducking a swing from an opponent as an Elf to his left stepped in, slaughtering the Goblin in its steps. The wizard watched the Ogres take a few steps back as they prepared to charge again. The group rushed forward and smashed against the gate again. The moment the battering ram met the gate the Elves above poured both of the cauldrons down the openings in the battlements. The boiling flood of oil rained down on the creatures, searing their flesh and sending the frantic howls of pain into the air.

Ectle stopped at the edge of the wall and reached back, hurling a ball of fire down onto the Ogres and their battering ram. The second the fireball met the ground it erupted in a massive burst of flames, the boiling oil immediately igniting. The pain of the oil was intense but the added torment of the flames sent the Ogres rolling across the ground in peril. In their moment of torture the archers above unleashed on them again, slaughtering the creatures before they could strike the gate again.

With the battering ram in ruin and those carrying it slain and lying in the field the wizard turned his attention back to the wall. Behind him the Goblins were still rushing up the ladders and flooding out onto the top of the wall. Elves had managed to destroy two of the ladders but the enemy kept coming. A massive force of Elves appeared from the stairs behind the wizard and rushed the battlements, slaughtering the Goblins still atop the wall in one quick rush.

Uljic watched from the heart of the army, his temper flaring wildly as he witnessed his forces repelled from the ladders and battlements and the Ogres burning in the field in front of the gate. The creature roared angrily, pacing through the lines of his soldiers. One of the Goblins stepped up to the creature and with one quick swing Uljic cut its head from its shoulders, hardly slowing in his tracks.

"Rearm the catapults! I want those walls in ruin!" Uljic roared at the Ogres manning the siege weapons.

"Sir… but… sir… our soldiers are still on their… walls." one Ogre stammered, fearful of the anger from the creature. The Ogre was nearly twice the size of Uljic but the fear the commander had instilled in the army was impressive.

"What? What did you say?"

The Ogre stepped back, realizing it had brought on punishment from the powerful creature. "Just… uh… our soldiers are still… are still on the wall and on the la…"

Uljic cut off the last word from the Ogre with the head of a spear thrown suddenly, impaling the creature. The Ogre's head snapped back and the brute collapsed to the ground, dead before it met the grassy field below. The Ogres around the catapult watched and immediately began loading the siege weapons to keep from receiving the same gory punishment. Uljic eyed them angrily and then turned back to the city, waiting to see the rain of stones land on the wall.

The Goblins continued up the ladders as Uljic gave the order to open fire. Reluctantly the Ogres threw the switches on the siege weapons and watched as they lurched forward, slinging the massive boulders out towards the city walls. The soldiers on the wall never saw the attacks coming and the stones began falling, sending Goblins and Elves rolling across the battlements. One of the boulders landed short, smashing a Goblin covered ladder into splinters.

A jagged smile formed on Uljic's face, the bloodshed giving him the joy that he had longed for. The screams of pain and confusion filled the air as the Ogres loaded the catapults again and hesitated. The creature turned and glanced back at the Ogres waiting at the catapults.

"You are waiting for?"

A brief nod and they threw the triggers again, sending another wave of large boulders into the sky. The outer wall was beginning to look rough, large cracks running along the top of the battlements and several craters in the middle where the boulders were striking. One of the boulders dipped low and met the arch just above the gate, bringing down a cloud of dust and debris. The creature nodded happily.

Ectle pushed himself up onto his hands and knees, the warm trickle of blood on his forehead the only feeling he knew at the moment. The wizard reached up and ran his fingers through the warmth, remembering the explosion against the battlements from the boulder and the spray of rock that struck him seconds after. He looked at his hand, seeing his blood on his fingertips.

"Sir! Sir are you alright?" a soldier asked, dropping to a knee beside the wizard.

Ectle could hear a faint ringing in his ear and shook his head to rid himself of it. He looked up and nodded, his words coming slowly. "Yes... get the soldiers... back to the wall. We can't lose... the wall."

"It's ok master wizard, the Goblins are retreating back down the ladders and away from the gate. We've pushed them back."

Ectle shook his head and looked over the edge of the battlements. "It will not last."

The Elves filing up the stairs pushed what Goblins were still on the wall back over the edge, slaughtering them without the slightest sign of resistance. In the moment of victory the Elven archers returned to the edge of the wall and continued to fire on the retreating soldiers. The Goblins and Ogres fell back out of range of the archers, their losses piling up all across the front of the city walls.

Ectle looked up into the sky and took a deep breath, seeing the snowflakes crisscrossing in the wind. The air was growing colder, bringing a sting to the gash on his forehead. The Elves took the moment to look around at the destruction that had fallen on the battlements. The defenses of the outer wall were in ruin. Reinforcements had arrived from the inner city as the Elves struggled to strengthen their moral as well as the outer wall.

"Sir, you should let me take a look at that," a soldier said, noting the bloody gash on the wizard's forehead.

Ectle waved his hand to the side and shook his head. "No, it will heal. We have to prepare the defenses again. They will be coming again very soon."

"Yes sir, at once."

Ectle let the soldier take one last look at the wound before turning and helping the other Elves clear the wall of the fallen Goblins and pull their wounded brethren out of danger. Ectle looked out at the armies surrounding Pentegarn and then back to the inner reaches of the city where the King was watching. The Elves had repelled the first attack the Goblins and their soldiers had brought, but the next would definitely be stronger.

In the fields the creatures had fully retreated back away from the castle. They had suffered heavy losses but nothing was going to make them lift the siege. At the same time the Elves were pulling their defenses back together across the battlements. Their losses reflected their superior fighting abilities, having managed to slaughter the waves of opponents that crossed the top of the battlements.

The Elves manning the inner defenses had watched, feeling helpless to help the soldiers fighting to hold the gate. Though they longed for a chance to defend their city as well, thhey stood on the defenses and manned the towers of the inner wall, fulfilling their orders and praying the outer defenses held strong through the constant attacks.

A shadow streaked through the trees, its sole purpose to outrun those now pursuing it. The Demon was unnaturally fast, not tiring from its constant run and not sparing a second to rest. Where a Human or Elf might grow tired from the hours of running through the thick forest the Demon only grew stronger, more determined to reach the cities in the south. Spurred on by revenge, it clutched the cluster of crystals tightly, knowing that in its gauntlets was the power to release the sorcerer. But more important to Infus, it held the power to fulfill the Demon's own dark desires.

The Demon knew the secret of the crystals. They were the only thing that could be used to restore Valsera to his once powerful self and now that Infus had them he would let nothing get in the way. Infus hurtled a fallen tree and kept running, the obstacle not slowing its pace in the least. As the sky began to grow dark the creature gained speed and strength, benefiting from the dark of night that was closing in on the lands.

Infus slowed a step, looking down at the cluster of crystals that could soon set free the mighty Valsera. The stones had a faint glow to them, pulsing softly as they had when the Elf first found it in the chamber of the sorcerer. As soon as the sorcerer was released they would return to the northern lands and exact their revenge on the foolish races that continued to defy his rule. Hidden in the back of its mind though the Demon had a different idea, one that it let no one know of as it continued to pick up the pace once more. The Elves and Dwarves would be punished, no matter which course of action the Demon followed.

Their True Strengths Revealed

*T*he Elves and their soldiers worked through the night to reinforce their numbers and restore their defenses. The task was not an easy one as they had to remain alert to the movements of the enemy. Through the late hours fresh soldiers arrived and blended with the old. They cleared the bodies of the dead and dying from the battlements, throwing the fallen enemies over the edge of the wall. Those Elves no longer able to fight were quickly taken back to the inner city to rest and heal.

Ectle had spent every moment after the initial attack pacing the heart of the battlements and watching intently out into the dark fields. Countless torches and fires dotted the surrounding forests and open plains, assuring that the enemy was still there. Several times throughout the night the Goblin archers launched a wave of arrows over the walls at the Elves to remind them that they could not rest. By the early morning the Elves had managed to consume what little food was available on the outer walls and began preparing for what the day would bring.

Ectle could see the dim glow of the morning sun as it struggled to appear over the distant horizon. In the lingering dark the armies in the fields had begun to mass once more, their intentions for the coming day very clear. The Elves had already prepared for the Goblins and there was no shock this time in the sight of their numbers. The Goblins made up the heart of the army but scattered throughout were large groups of Ogres. The creatures stood much taller than their fellow soldiers. They all stood motionless, watching as the early morning rays of light began to fall on the highest peak of the towers of Pentegarn.

Ectle looked to the enemies waiting in the fields below. "Why did they not attack throughout the night? Why wait until morning light to send their forces?"

"I have not a clue sir," a soldier to the wizard's right answered, watching their numbers begin to stir with the morning light.

"Well no matter what the reason they will be on us again very soon. Send word across the battlements to be ready. We can not afford to be ill prepared. Hurry, go!"

The Elves on the battlements had been locked in place watching the Goblin armies every minute through the night but now they too came to life, racing around the defenses in an attempt to prepare for the inevitable. The Goblins would come again, that much was obvious. Being ready when they did was the only thing the Elves could do at the moment.

"Ectle, are the defenses sound?"

The wizard turned and found King Elendil walking up the stairs to the outer defenses atop the wall. Surprised by the sudden appearance of the King the wizard forgot the bow that normally came with the greeting of royalty.

"Sir... what are you doing out here? It is not safe."

Elendil ignored the question and looked past the wizard at the armies that had been brought north to break the Elven lands. Elendil turned and repeated his question, looking over the Elves as they prepared.

"The defenses are strong my Lord. They have obviously underestimated us and they paid the price heavily the first time. I do not expect we will be so lucky the next time they attack though."

The King nodded. "They will learn and change their tactics. They may be foolish, but they are not without some form of intelligence. Do not underestimate them Ectle."

"I will not my Lord, I assure you."

The King gave another look to the soldiers out in the field waiting for their chance to flood the city walls. With a nod to the wizard the King turned and dropped back down the stairs, headed back towards the inner wall and keep. The walls of Elves were as thick on the inner defenses as they were across the outer. Archers and spearmen made up the force that covered the outer walls with a full regiment of swordsmen stationed behind the outer gate.

The Elves fell silent as the deep sound of Ogre horns filled the air around the fields. The sound coming from the fields below was impossible to make out. No distinct words, no one voice heard over the others. Thousands of Goblins pushed forward at once, their movements covered by the hundreds of arrows that now pierced the sky. The impending attack hesitated in the sky and then curled downward.

"Arrows! Lock shields!" the wizard yelled as he lifted his staff to the sky.

The head of the staff resonated light and from it appeared a light green disk no larger than a saucer. As the arrows grew closer the disk suddenly grew, completely engulfing the air above the battlements for a full fifteen feet on either side of the wizard. The soldiers beneath watched as the arrows hit the glowing shield and glanced off in different directions. Not one penetrated the powerful magic.

The shields of the Elves were as effective as the magic the wizard used to cover himself and those around him. Out of the volley, only a handful of Elves found themselves in the path of the arrows. Those Elves unfortunate enough to fall victim to the volley were immediately cleared off the battlements as the Elves moved back together to fill in the gaps. The glimmering shield grew smaller and then disappeared with a silent flash.

The Goblins continued to march, their siege ladders and ropes very clear in their ranks. They marched fearlessly, all knowing they were expendable to the creature who ordered them but all dying for the chance to spill Elven blood. As they moved further into range of the archers on the wall Ectle gave the order to fire.

Like a swarm of angry insects the arrows of the Elves streaked through the air towards their targets. The Goblins threw up their ratty shields and stopped moving as the arrows fell all around them. With the main army pinned under the Elven archers the creature known as Uljic ordered the catapults to resume firing.

Massive boulders arched through the sky towards the city, descending with blistering speed. The Elves watched the siege weapons release and in the moments following they tried to clear where the boulders would land. Timing was everything but they learned harshly that the stones were as unpredictable as they were deadly. The first to strike met the face of the outer wall, shaking the battlements above violently. The strike left the Elves unstable, their footing compromised in the strong attack.

Directly behind the first came the remaining boulders,

falling across the battlements where the stunned Elves had tried to flee. Sadly, their unstable footing mixed with the confusion left many in the paths of the siege weapons. The Elves were sent flying from the top of the wall. Shouts of pain and confusion sparked across the battlements as the Elves below the wall released their own siege weapons. Barrels of fiery oil as well as boulders soared over the walls and out into the fields in retaliation.

Back and forth the attacks came as the Goblins drew closer and closer to the city walls. Ectle followed one of the boulders as it flipped end over end through the air towards him. He yelled desperately to the soldiers around him, shoving them away from the area. His judgment was sound and when the boulder dropped from the air it landed directly where he had been standing moments earlier.

The area of the battlement struck by the boulder was left in ruin, the damage creating a massive void in the defensive structure that protected the soldiers on the wall. The Elves were hesitant to fill the area after the damage was dealt, finding they no longer had the cover from the thick stone defenses. As the arrows fell around the Elves they realized they had no choice. The gap was filled again by the archers and they immediately began firing once more at the army moving towards them.

"Keep firing! Give them everything you've got."

The archers didn't stop firing, even when the massive boulders from the enemy catapults fell on the walls again. They dropped row after row of Goblin infantry but the creatures kept coming. In the waves of arrows and the exchange from the catapults the Elves never saw the siege weapons the Goblins and Ogres had moved into the field. From the rear of the fields appeared three large towers, wheeled forward by teams of Ogres. It wasn't until the first of the ladders landed against the walls that the wizard caught sight of them.

Ectle stopped in his tracks as he caught sight of the hulking towers being moved towards the city walls. They were tall, stretching higher than the top of the walls and defended across the fronts with thick wooden planks and shields lashed to the beams. It was apparent that soon more enemy soldiers would be flooding the city than in the first attacks. The ladders would let dozens up at once; the towers would allow hundreds a chance at the Elves.

"Sir, are you seeing this?" a soldiers asked, pointing out at the monstrous siege weapons.

Ectle rolled his eyes and glared at the soldier. "Do you really think I would miss something that big?"

The towers moved so slowly that it seemed like it would take hours for them to cross the fields but the fact was that they kept moving. No matter how many arrows were fired out into the army below the towers did not stop. Elves fired straight down the ladders at the Goblins that were now swarming their way up to the top of the battlements. Their spears and shields waited atop the wall for the moment the creatures topped the ladders.

Ectle looked back over his shoulder towards the inner city, wondering what the King had made of the sight now crossing the field. He had told Elendil the defenses were sound and ready for anything that the Goblins threw at them but in that moment he wondered how they would fair against the horde that would flood out of the towers. No matter how many soldiers the Elves pushed to the outer defenses the Goblins were ready to match the number time and time again. The wizard reached out and grabbed a spearman as the Elf hurried by.

"Man the ballista on the walls at once. When they come to range I want them to feel just how strong we really are."

"Yes sir," the soldier replied, running to give the teams at the siege weapons their orders.

Ectle drew in a cold breath and glanced across the field at the towers rumbling closer. A single snowflake danced on the breeze past his face and then disappeared below the edge of the wall. The effects of winter were felt across the city as the wind brought the cold weather further south. The wizard focused past where the snowflake had crossed his vision, his glare falling on the towers once more. No matter what he did he realized that the Goblins were going to make a strong offensive against the top of the wall again.

To his right an armored Goblin crossed the wall, its shield blocking the arrows fired from the archers as it leapt at the Elves. Before the creature's feet touched the stone battlements it was skewered by a wall of spears. The Goblins making it to the top of the ladder and pushing the Elves back gave three more a chance to flood over the wall. The three fought for minutes before they too met the same fate, but the distraction gave more and more Goblins a chance to make it up the ladders.

The wizard whipped his staff around and with it came a blinding light and an amazingly loud crack. The nearest Goblin fell back against the wall and slid over the edge, plummeting to the ground below. The creatures were caught off guard but they did not fall back. Instead they pushed forward, their deaths allowing more and more of their comrades up the ladders and out onto the battlements, turning the space atop the wall into a blood-bath.

Ectle ducked a spear and cracked the Goblin across the face with his staff, whirling to miss another attack and then another. The spears and swords seemed to come from every direction as the Goblins battled madly for control over the outer city walls. The wizard knew the Elves had the upper hand, driving the Goblins back time and time again but finding the creatures fierce when cornered against the top of the battlements. When he looked up he realized the towers were now hovering close to the outer wall.

With the ramps to the towers nearly twelve feet wide they would allow five Goblins out at a time, the creatures rushing shoulder to shoulder down the ramp. At the rate the creatures were flooding up the ladders, it was possible to believe that the soldiers flooding out of the towers would completely overpower and outnumber the Elves. The Ogres struggled with all their might to force the monstrous towers closer and the wizard turned to his left.

"Fire now! Fire the ballista!" Ectle yelled.

The Elves at the ballista to the left threw the switch and the massive bow jumped, slinging the spear forward with unbelievable force. The projectile shot through the air and pierced the closest tower halfway up, continuing out the other side with a bloody gush. The soldiers inside the tower were skewered and killed instantly as the giant spear broke through the wooden defenses of the siege tower. The other ballista fired as well, having very similar effects on the towers and the Goblins inside of them. The only problem was that the towers continued to creep closer, not even hesitating as the spears pierced them.

The wizard's blood ran cold as he realized the attack had done absolutely nothing to slow down the towers. He had hoped that at the very least the ballista would slow their pace. To his right he saw Elves appear with small jars filled with oil and a fiery rag hanging out of the top. After a few more feet they threw the jars, watching as they arched and broke against the front of the towers.

The oil met the fire on the rags and suddenly swept up the side of the tower. The heat pushed the Goblins inside of the tower back a few feet as the flames leapt higher and higher. The idea was great but the intense flames burned through the oil quickly, leaving the wooden structure charred but not destroyed. As it crept closer the Elves followed with a second round of fiery explosions. If nothing else they were managing to prolong the Goblin attack.

Ectle turned around to the archers on the wall. "Archers to the ready, hold your fire until they open their ramps. Make every shot count!"

The first of the towers came to a stop and the ramp hesitated, the tension unnerving the Elves as they waited for the enemies to appear. With a loud creak the massive ramp fell forward, smashing onto the top of the wall and revealing the horde of creatures within. The moment the Goblins took a step foward the Elves loosed their arrows, mowing down the creatures before they had a chance to raise their shields. The Elves that had been throwing the jars of oil attacked once more, the glass breaking against the inside of the tower. Flames leapt across the inside of the siege weapon and across the Goblins, sending them into a panic.

The Elves fired wave after wave into the tower as the second ramp landed against the battlements higher up to the western stretch of the wall. The Elves there used similar methods to fight back the Goblins, mixing their arrows with the jars of flaming liquid. The explosions in the second and third towers had disastrous effects just as the first and for the moment, the creatures had no way of advancing without feeling the stabs of arrows and searing pain of the fire.

From the inner wall Elendil watched the towers advance on his city, knowing there was nothing he could do to stop them. The ballista had damaged the structures but did little if anything to stop their progress. The King ordered a full battalion of swordsmen to the outer defenses to reinforce those now plagued by the swarms of Goblins from the ladders and the ones soon to arrive through the towers. In the time it took for the towers to reach the walls and the ramps to fall open his entire battalion had reached the stairs to the outer defenses.

The sight of the monstrous ramps falling open revealing the creatures inside was a terror all its own for the soldiers on the walls. The numbers flooding into the bottom of the siege weapons was unbelievable and the thought of those forces flooding out onto the battlements was a nightmare. The worst part of it was what was happening in the fields behind the towers. The Elves were focused on the Goblins flooding up the ladders and out of the towers and did not at first notice what was taking place.

"My King, what would you suggest we do sir?" a soldier asked, watching the Goblins and Ogres.

"I don't know… I… we should send word to the northern wall at once to begin with. Get a runner to Tanis and his Wood Elves and reinforce them with our own archers and spearmen."

In the fields behind the towers the Goblins and Ogres began shifting to the north, close to a third of their forces now headed towards the northern gate. At the moment the northern gate was weakly defended, only Tanis and his Elves spread across the battlements. With the Humans and now the might of Valsera's army backing them the northern gate would never stand a chance.

Elendil took a deep breath as he watched the forces march up the length of the field, their forces suddenly more disciplined, marching in to join the wall of Human shields. The only sliver of hope was that the armies of Goblins and Ogres did not bother moving the catapults or ballista north, relying solely on the might of their soldiers to break the northern gate.

The northern gate was not nearly as strongly defended and braced as the southern where the Elves had anticipated the full force of the attacks. With only the Wood Elves ready to defend the gate it would most likely crumble. The archers on the outer wall had been defending well, keeping the Humans at bay with the constant waves of arrows, but now a massive horde of Goblins was moving around the city to the north. Tanis stopped, his bowstring pulled taunt as he watched the army moving in behind the Humans.

"Sir, their armies are on the move. We can not defend

against that."

Tanis watched the soldiers mass in behind the army of Humans, more than doubling the size of the force now waiting for the northern gate to fall. The Goblins and Humans began a rhythmic beating of their swords, clubs, and spears against their shields, perhaps a ploy to instill terror in the Elves on the wall, perhaps to work their own numbers into a frenzy. From the look of things it was having both effects.

Tanis looked back behind him, seeing the High Elves marching from the inner city. "Look, we are not going to have to do this alone."

The reinforcing Elves from the inner walls began arriving at the outer defenses, massing behind the gate and funneling up the stairs with the Wood Elves. They formed up behind the Wood Elves and waited, watching the formations of Goblins building around the Humans. The Wood Elves had no idea what was taking place across the southern walls and at the moment there was no time to find out. The archers pulled their bowstrings tight once more and waited, watching for the signal.

Ectle and the Elves on the battlements had noticed the army moving out towards the north and were powerless to send any sort of warning to the rest of the soldiers. The wizard knew Elendil was watching and hoped the King of Pentegarn would take action to stop them before it was too late. The towers had been burned with oils and assaulted by the ballista but they still stood, allowing swarms of Goblins a chance at the battlements. The Elves not blanketing the creatures in arrows had now locked their shields together, forming a powerful wall of steel. The Goblins that met the wall of shields were immediately stopped in stride and shoved backward. The moment the creatures were knocked back a step the Elves advanced that far themselves, locking the shields together and preparing for the next rush.

"Keep pushing them back! Kill them all!" the wizard shouted over the clash of steel.

Overhead came a shrill shriek and the soldiers on both sides looked up to see the large Warbirds streaking down towards the wall. On their backs were the remains of the Celestial Knight force. From the saddle of the Warbirds the Celestial Knights fired their bows, the blinding flashes of light finding targets across the walls. One of the Warbirds appeared from the north, a large boulder clutched in its talons.

It dropped low across the wall and cut left, releasing its grip on the boulder before shooting up into the sky. The boulder rolled through the air, curling downward and hitting the tower in the center. The boulder met the heart of the tower and ripped through it with catastrophic results. The splinters of wood filled the air as bodies of Goblins fell to the ground below. In the wake of the attack other Celestial Knights dropped their Warbirds down into the city to arm their mounts with whatever they could find. The damage the first had dealt was crippling to the enemy which was finally a break for the Elves.

The tower that had been hit initially creaked and groaned in the wind and the Warbirds dropped again, letting loose the chunks of stone. The first tower teetered dangerously and then the boulders landed again. Two boulders struck the same tower and it crumbled, falling in on the hundred or so Goblins that were still looking to climb out onto the wall. The tower fell violently to the ground below, crushing the forces of Goblins underneath it.

The archers in the fields began filling the air with arrows, hoping that the random firing would find the Warbirds as they streaked through the sky. Fortunately they were lightning fast, darting through the sky away from the waves of arrows. They curled back from the east and prepared to attack again.

The Warbirds dropped low, and as the chunks of rock were released, the Goblins loosed a volley of arrows ahead of the flying enemies. The Warbirds inadvertently flew directly into the volley of arrows, knocking three of the creatures from the air. What remained cut to the east and disappeared, preparing for another attack.

Just as the wave of attacks from the Warbirds ceased a new shadow spread across the fields of soldiers. The army of Goblins looked up and found the shadow belonging to the massive Gold Dragon that had rescued Ectle and the Dwarves from the swamp. The massive beast dropped lower and opened its jaws wide as a powerful heat began to grow.

More than one hundred archers drew back their bowstrings and sighted in the Dragon that suddenly released a massive torrent of flame on the field. Though countless Goblins were swallowed in the flame, dozens of archers released their attack.

The arrows filled the sky and before the Dragon could release a second attack dozens of deadly projectiles struck its head, neck, and chest. The Dragon gave one last flap of its wings and then plummeted into the forests behind the army. Dozens of Goblin soldiers immediately charged into the trees to finish it off.

Ectle watched in utter amazement as the second tower followed the first, imploding on itself as the Warbirds and their handlers pummeled it with boulders and waves of enchanted arrows. The Goblins that had made it to the top of the battlements watched as well as their siege towers fell from the constant attacks and now there was only one still standing. Even though it was intact the swarm of Goblins charging up through it had slackened greatly, Now afraid of the soldiers in the sky they seemed content with swarming the gate, frantically trying to break it down.

The Ogres in the heart of the army brought forth yet another stronger siege weapon, this one with broad walls and a roof over what appeared to be a reinforced battering ram. It rolled slowly, the Ogres beneath protected from the archers by the sturdy roof. Even though the Ogres were well protected the Elves continued firing. Ectle knocked the last of the Goblins near him over the edge of the wall, turning and watching the rest of the Elven soldiers battling fiercely to regain their defenses. No one else seemed to notice the strong battering ram rolling towards the gate and he noted the armored structure surrounding it.

"Make ready the cauldrons! They have a battering ram on the way and it is well armored. Get ready!" the wizard shouted, watching the liquid boil wildly.

In the back of his head Ectle knew that the oil had little chance of reaching the Ogres underneath the roof but they had to try. Giving up was out of the question. The Goblins on the wall had grown sparse and were now retreating as the battering ram was wheeled closer. Even though the Elves had regained control of the top of the walls the gate was now in danger of being breached as the battering ram stopped just feet away, the large head pulled back and released.

A thunderous boom echoed as the steel headed ram struck the gate, shaking it violently. The Ogres went to work, pounding at the gate with their ram as the Elves continued picking off Goblins not covered behind their shields. The soldiers at the top of the gate poured the two cauldrons at the same time, watching the boiling oil slosh down the opening in the battlements and out onto the roof of the ram. As Ectle had expected the oil met the roof and was diverted away from the ram, protecting the Ogres underneath. Ectle flicked his wrist and a small ball of fire streaked down to the top of the roof and it burst into flames.

The structure continued to give the Ogres protective cover, even from the flames rolling across the top. The heat permeated through it, but the Ogres continued bashing away at the sturdy gate. Soon the Goblins in the field below resorted to using their shields and hands to sling sand and dirt up onto the flames. They no longer pushed together and waited for the gates to fall, instead choosing to fight the torrent of fire threatening to destroy the siege weapon.

"Archers, focus on the Goblins. Do not let them put out the fires!" the wizard yelled, watching the creatures working feverishly to extinguish the burning oil spreading across the roof and down the walls of the battering ram.

The fight had changed from trying to stop the Ogres manning the battering ram to killing any creature trying to extinguish the flames that were ravaging the defensive structure surrounding the ram. The soldiers manning the battering ram soon felt the effects of the fire and a few of the Ogres strayed away from it, finding themselves blanketed with arrows the moment they came into view. There was a thunderous boom from the battering ram against the gate which was followed by a soft creaking.

The Elves inside the gate watched as the gate rocked in deeply and then back out in rhythm with the battering ram until the final strike created a large crack at the top of the gate. The Ogres hesitated and then struck again, the right side of the gate now splintering as the cracked section widened. Yells from the soldiers below rang out alerting those on the battlements above, and Ectle wracked his brain as he struggled to find a way to stop the Ogre siege weapon.

"Sir, the gate is cracking! It won't last much longer!" one spearman yelled as he charged up the stairs to the battlements.

The wizard waved the archers and spearmen away from the heart of the battlements above the gate and knelt, sitting on the top of the wall with his legs crossed and his eyes closed. "Keep the Goblins off the wall and away from this spot. While in this spell, I will be vulnerable to their attacks. Form ranks and prepare for their next attack."

The Elves did as they were told as the wizard folded his palms down to the floor of the battlements, chanting in a whisper while remaining deathly still. When his palms met the stone a soft bluish glow was emitted. It seeped across the edge of the wall and then down the face of the gate like a wave in the ocean. The shimmering wave rolled downward until it met the ground, appearing to solidify the moment it made contact with the earth.

Though the Ogres had stopped all attacks as the shimmering wall appeared they now began again, the steel head of the ram punishing the wall of magic as blow after blow struck its translucent surface. When the head of the ram met the wall the surface rippled in the same manner it had when the magic wall had flowed down the surface of the city gate, but it stood firm, not giving an inch. The wizard held the wall intact, continuing his trance like state as the battle looked to erupt around him once more.

The Elves had been watching as the battering ram continued to bash at the gate even with the magic wall between the two and a plan was formed. To their dismay the flames had been extinguished and the Goblin archers began firing once more at the soldiers across the walls. A group of spearmen locked their shields in front of the wizard to protect him while another force hurried down into the outer city to one of the catapults, returning with a barrel of oil and torches, identical to the ones used in the exchange earlier.

"So, we light it and toss it over and hope for the best? That pretty much the plan?" one soldier asked as he secured the torches to the side of the barrel.

"Pretty much indeed. The explosion should drive them away, destroy their battering ram, and maybe that shield the wizard has over the gate will protect it from any further damage. It's all we've got right now," the second replied as he and another Elf rolled the barrel in against the defensive wall atop the battlements.

It was difficult to safely raise the barrel over the edge of the wall through the waves of enemy archer fire but with a lot of luck the Elves managed to find a gap in the attacks, hefting the wooden barrel and tossing it over the edge. The barrel rolled in the air, the two torches on the sides burning bright as it fell to the top of the battering ram. The barrel cracked and there was a moment between the oil spilling out and meeting the torches where nothing happened. Then they met and the explosion of flames and heat rocked the edge of the battlements.

Ectle felt the wall beneath him lurch, throwing him out of his trance and breaking his concentration. The cloud of smoke was the first thing he noticed and he climbed to his feet. Looking over the edge he found himself staring down at the remains of the battering ram that had been on the verge of demolishing the city gate. Just as the Elves had predicted, the magic wall the wizard had conjured protected the weakened gate from the blast and they watched as it slowly began drawing together, disappearing with a silent flash.

"Someone tell me what happened," Ectle demanded angrily, stunned at the sudden destruction that had taken place.

"We've destroyed their siege weapons."

"I can see that soldier, I want to know how."

The Elf looked at the wizard with a worried glance. "We lit one of the barrels of oil the catapults use and threw it over the side. The burst of flames was so intense that there was nothing left when they finally cleared."

Ectle nodded. "Very... intelligent. I am impressed. Back to your stations and get ready. The gate is weak and their army is angry. Send word to Elendil and let him know I do not know how much longer we can hold the outer wall."

"Yes sir, at once."

Ectle stepped back up to the edge of the wall again and took a deep breath. Two of the towers that had been letting swarms of Goblins up onto the Elven walls were now scattered on the ground in heaps with the third leaning drastically to the right, threatening to crumble as the others had. The battering ram that had heavily damaged the gate was scattered around the front of the wall in pieces from the explosion and raging flames that engulfed it. Though they had survived the massive attack, the Elves were exhausted and weary. Ectle worried that if the enemy quickly attacked again they would overpower the forces trying to hold the outer city.

"Soldier, come here."

The archer left his post and stepped in beside the wizard.

"Yes sir?"

"Soldier, what do you make of our situation? What would you advise?"

The archer shook his head. "Sir, I do not understand. I am not fit to advise you in this matter. How could I?"

"I need the views of a soldier, of one who has seen battle time and time again, of one who would stand in the thick of the armies and decide his own fate. I would order soldiers to their deaths and they would obey, but what those soldiers truly feel inside I do not know. Tell me, how would you proceed if it were you standing where I am now?"

The archer stared out at the armies that were still massed in the fields. He had never thought of such a question before. He had never been given a reason to think in such a way. All his life he had served the King and the armies of Pentegarn without question or hesitation. Looking to the ground below he nodded and then turned to the wizard.

"Sir, because you have asked of me... I would have sent for help long ago, I would strengthen the gates and pull back to the inner wall, use its height and defenses to our advantage."

"Thank you for your honesty, for your insight. We can not abandon our outer defenses and fall to the inner walls until we have no choice. The longer we stay here and hold their forces at bay, the longer it takes for them to break our city. The Dwarves will come to help, we need only to outlast our enemy. We will fall back to the inner wall in time. There is no need to do so prematurely."

Tanis and his Elves had watched the armies of Goblins and Ogres march in behind the force of Humans, the army now far larger with the new reinforcements. They hesitated briefly as the reinforcements arrived before the order was given and the new force began to advance on the northern gate. Their approach was slow, the wall of shields carried by the Humans forming the front of the army. The Wood Elves held one second longer and then in one wave they all loosed their arrows.

The cloud of arrows streaked through the sky like mad hornets, dropping down on the wall of shields and those marching behind them. Goblins fell as the archers continued to fire, dropping every possible opponent not hidden behind the Human shield wall. They moved ever closer and for the first time the archers in the fields below began to return fire. On the walls the Wood Elves were well protected, ducking behind the defenses and making every shot count.

Tanis watched curiously, noting that the enemy carried with them no visible signs of siege weaponry, no catapults, no battering rams, nothing. It seemed foolish that they would rely on the sheer strength of their forces to break down the gates. The archers on the wall picked their targets and easily dropped every soldier that did not hide behind a wide shield. The Goblins that did not learn from the deaths of their brethren soon joined them.

The field seemed lopsided as the archers continued to rain down on the forces in the field who seemed to have very little to fight back with. Focused on the Humans, Goblins, and Ogres massed at the gate, the Wood Elves never realized the catapults had been moved and set. The locks were taunt fighting the trigger as the Goblins hesitated, looking at the city walls. With one last glance they pulled the pins and weapons sprung forward, hurling the heavy stones through the air.

"To the right! Their right flank is crumbling! Bring them down!" Tanis yelled, watching the Goblins staggering backwards.

The boulders curved and then came down, landing on the top of the battlements to the left of the force of Wood Elves. Seconds before they hit Tanis caught the sight out of the corner of his eye, turning his head to see a massive explosion of rock and wood fill the air. The cloud of debris showered the Elves who were completely caught off guard. The boulders fell in pairs, most missing the battlements but a lucky few found their marks. Tanis covered his head as a second boulder hit, sending up another shower of debris that fell across the Elves like a wave.

A rogue chunk of stone whirled across the battlements and though Tanis was ducked down with the other Elves, the stone followed an almost perfect path. The chunk of stone struck the King of the Wood Elves on the side of the head and he fell, his body limp and lifeless. The soldiers dropped in next to him, fearing they had lost their King to the attack.

"My King! My King please, wake up!" one soldier yelled, shaking the King by the shoulder.

"Is he… is he?"

"No, he's still alive. This looks bad though. Hurry, we

must get him clear of this at once. Here, help me," the same soldier ordered, grabbing the King under the shoulders.

The two soldiers grabbed the King and carried him away from the battlements, down the stairs, and towards the inner city. A rush of wind filled the air and the two looked up, seeing the end of a boulder curling down into the outer defenses, destroying a small house behind the wall. They moved quickly and just as they drew near the inner gate the King stirred, looking to each of the soldiers carrying him.

"Wha... what are you... doing?"

"My King... my Lord are you all right?" the soldiers asked, gently lowering the King to the ground.

"What... happened?" Tanis asked, raising his hand to his bloody head.

"Sir, their catapults... they... hit the battlements... and you were hit. Are you alright?"

"Yes... I'm... fine. Hurry, back to the wall. Do not... leave the defenses," the King ordered, his head still swimming as the blood soaked his hair and the side of his head.

The two soldiers hesitated briefly as their King held himself up off the ground, his body drained and exhausted from the wound. The sound of stones meeting the walls and the buildings of the outer city filled the air, accompanied by the screams of pain as the archers continued firing on the enemy. Tanis rolled onto an elbow and looked around the city. Even with his vision blurred he struggled up onto his feet, determined to get back to his soldiers. The King wiped the blood off of his face and took a shaky step back towards the outer wall.

The southern gate was up in arms as they watched the forces in the fields below begin to stir and swarm once more. Hundreds of Goblins and Ogres pushed forward towards the wall only to stop before the archers loosed their arrows and withdraw again. They had exhausted much of their resources in their previous battles, their battering rams and all of their towers destroyed and sent crumbling to the ground where they lay still smoldering. No matter how much damage the armies of Qwaz and Nomaria took, they never gave a thought to giving up.

Ectle had seen his share of wars and bloodshed but it was one of the most depressing battles he had ever witnessed. The enemy was indeed an enemy, but watching as they led hundreds of their forces into hopeless slaughter was a sight no one could grow used to. The wizard took a deep breath and shook his head to rid himself of any possible sympathy that might be welling up inside him. These creatures were the enemy.

"Sir, what are they waiting for? What are they doing?"

Ectle shook his head. "I have no clue. Nothing they have done has made any sense. One of our lives is worth a dozen of theirs. They throw their soldiers away without a thought. I have to admit... I have no idea what is in store for us."

The cold wind chilled his face and the wizard turned out of the breeze. A soldier approached and handed him a small bowl of what appeared to be some sort of stew. In the cold air the food let off a thick steam and the wizard took a deep breath, savoring its scent in the cold wintry air. Even though the city was stained with blood and scarred from the numerous battles the Elves were able to create an edible meal.

Ectle picked the bread that was slightly staled out of the stew and bit into it, looking out at the army that seemed to be waiting long enough to give the Elves a chance to eat. The food was bland but it was warm and it gave him a welcome fullness that had been absent for quite some time. Though the food was simple it eventually spread across the battlements to every Elf soldier at arms.

The wizard passed the bowl off and turned around to the edge of the wall again, looking at the enemies that were feasting on whatever they could pull together or find in the forests. They were striving to destroy the city of Pentegarn but in the process they were successfully stripping the lands around it of life. Soon the lands of the Elves would look as drained and dead as those around Qwaz or Nomaria. The thought of the their rich, lush lands being turned into barren wastelands was depressing

The trees of the forests were beginning to fall, showing massive cleared sections where the thickest woods had once been. The clear cutting had created horrible scars in the woods that surrounded the fields and the Elves behind the walls could do nothing to stop it. They were forced to watch as the enemies destroyed the lands they had called home for longer than some could remember.

"Sir, what are your orders?" the head of the spearmen

asked as a full battalion of Elven infantry arrived.

"Fill in where we've lost soldiers and give those no longer able to stand their ground a chance to rest. It will only be a matter of time before their armies come again. I need everyone as well rested and ready for battle as they can be."

"Sir, the walls are strong still and they are being fought off of the walls every time they make it to the battlements."

Ectle shook his head in dissatisfaction. "We've held them thus far, you are right. The gate however has sustained heavy damage and the defenses around it have already begun to crumble. When they come again, the defenses will be tested."

The soldiers looked at the wizard, half expecting to hear him build them up with talk of success and the strengths of their Elven brethren. Instead the wizard had been completely truthful. He did not try to make things appear better that they were, he did not tell them what they wanted to hear. Instead, Ectle told them the truth.

Deep Gaps in the Armor

*E*rzel fell to his knees in the field as the remains of the funeral pyre died down, the realization of their loss setting in. The loss of the Dragon had hurt the Elf significantly more than the others, the Dwarves not understanding the ties that the others had with her. Lavian and Kail both approached the Elf and the Celestial Knight placed a hand on his shoulder. He kept his eyes on the ground as the fire died out completely.

"Erzel… we really need to get the soldiers moving again. Pentegarn is a less than a day away and none of us know what to expect when we get there. We will further mourn Alora after we have driven Valsera's armies back into the southlands," Kail said, trying to comfort the struggling Elf.

Erzel nodded and pushed himself up onto his feet. The Dwarves had assembled in the fields behind them and Erzel knew they were growing restless, ready to move out for Pentegarn again. At the moment though there was very little he was concerned about other than the item the Demon now possessed. It had left the clearing in the blink of an eye and judging from the speed at which Infus had disappeared, it would be far out of their reach.

"What happens when Infus releases Valsera? What happens when the sorcerer is set back on our lands and the horrors start again? I am responsible for it all."

"No Erzel… you did what you had to do. We would be dead if it wasn't for you and you know that. If Valsera is released, we will fight him again. No matter what, we will keep fighting," Lavian said quietly.

Erzel turned and looked at the Dwarves massing in the clearing, waiting for the order to march again. After seeing the Slayers in battle the Dwarves had grown wary of the new opponents. They had faced the Goblins and the Ogres years before but it was the first time they had ever seen these creatures. The sight and the abilities were very intimidating, but the Dwarves were ready to continue on to Pentegarn to face Valsera's armies.

Erzel reached down and took the whip from his belt, remembering the power it possessed and wondering if he had used it, would it have been enough to defeat the Demon. He could not imagine sacrificing Kail and Lavian to do so but in his moment of deep thought, he wondered. If he had killed Infus there, would he have ended the war for good? The thoughts plagued him as he tried to ready himself for the march to the Elven city.

"Erzel, clear your mind. You can not fight Valsera's armies if you are unable to focus. I know you are pained. I know there is much hate in you, but you must clear these emotions to punish those responsible," Lavian said softly, her hand on his shoulder.

The Elf took a deep breath and looked ahead to the forest where the Demon had disappeared earlier. Lavian reached up and gripped the saddle on her Warbird, pulling herself up onto its back. The beast flapped its mighty wings and with one last nod the Celestial Knight disappeared into the sky. Kail stopped next to the horse he had been knocked from, collecting what gear he could before falling in line next to Erzel. The Elf ignored his horse, remaining on foot with the rest of the soldiers.

"Erzel. If Infus releases Valsera there may be no stopping the sorcerer. We have to break the armies at Pentegarn now before they have the chance to regroup and reinforce."

The Elf waved to the Dwarves and the massive force resumed their march to the Elven city. He looked to the side at Kail. "That's what I'm afraid of. What if we fail at Pentegarn? His darkness will swallow the land whole without the Elves to hold his forces back."

Kail looked over his shoulder at the Dwarves and then back to Erzel. "The rest of the Dwarves will be moving south behind us. If these forces are able to simply hold the armies attacking Pentegarn at bay, then the rest of the Dwarven army will be able to break them. We will slaughter these Goblins, I promise."

Erzel and Kail marched the army into the forests, the Dwarves forced into long lines and small groups instead of the massive boxed formations they were accustomed to. They marched long and hard, never stopping to rest after reaching the woods. He knew that marching straight through to Pentegarn would leave the soldiers exhausted but if they did not push as hard as they could, they may not arrive to find the Elven city still standing.

The war had stretched the races thin and their discipline was being tested. Every Elf and Dwarf no longer looked at their enemies with a sort of respect, but now with a tiring hatred. The greatest of soldiers and leaders had always stressed respect for ones adversary but that time had long since passed. Respect was a distant dream, much like freedom. No matter how many battles the Elves won they knew there would likely never be an end to the bloodshed.

"Erzel, I have a thought that has been plaguing me," Kail said as he moved in next to the Elf.

"Go ahead Kail."

"Well, say that we arrive at Pentegarn and find the city overrun, completely lost. What will you do then?"

Erzel thought things over for a minute as they kept marching. "I do not know Kail. Everything I have planned leads me to Pentegarn. We have been moving towards this moment from the first moment the Goblins and their armies spread across the borders. Everything points to this battle. This could be where we break them."

"Or... this could be where they break us Erzel," Kail replied, knowing that there chances of success were slim against the forces Valsera had commanded.

Erzel did not answer. He did not have to. He knew that what Kail said was true. The size of the armies in the south was not to be underestimated no matter how many Dwarves joined the Elves and their allies. Not to mention the Slayers and whatever other dark creatures the evil sorcerer had at his disposal. Even encased in crystal Valsera managed to continue to stretch his dark shadow across his soldiers who still followed his orders without question.

The fear that Valsera instilled in the northern armies was something that could not easily be shaken and it was done without the sorcerer even having to be present. The feat was one that was impressive no matter what army you served. The forces of Dwarves kept marching behind the Elf and his companion, never once questioning what was to be expected of them. The Dwarves had not been involved in the wars in a long time, but they were ready to take the lives of the enemy once more.

The cold wind continued to blow across the walls and through the city as the Elves finished preparing for the next wave of attacks. There was no way of knowing when it would come or how strong the enemies would be this time but they were doing everything they could to prepare. The southern gate had been heavily damaged in the past few attacks and now it was being braced with whatever the soldiers could find. Even with the extra defensive measures the Elves knew it would only be a matter of time before the Goblins and Ogres broke through the gate.

Ectle watched the Elves hurry back and forth through the outer city as they prepared the catapults and siege weapons for the next assault. If the Elves were to lose the outer defenses they had planned to make it an end that the Goblins would never forget. The archers and spearmen were ready, their positions on the battlements filled and ready for the attack. For the past few hours the enemies in the fields had been swarming angrily, dying for the chance to stain the battlements once more in the blood of their Elven enemies.

Ectle looked back at the catapults loaded and ready, and then glared back at the armies in the fields. Every time the armies in the fields attacked they would blanket the walls with a combination of catapults and arrows. Watching them in the field, the wizard knew the attack was coming soon and there was little they could do to stop it. Ectle touched his temple and like a flash of lightning an idea invaded his thoughts.

"Ready the catapults! Prepare to fire!"

One of the archers turned to the wizard, "Sir, you mean to fire on them before they attack?"

"Yes. Until now we have waited until they are battering our gates and walls before we fight back. It is time we take them by surprise. Archers to the ready! Catapults... fire!"

The Elves hesitated only a second before they threw the trigger on every single catapult. The stones and barrels flew through the air and dropped into the fields before the Goblins realized that the Elves had attacked. The lines of Goblins hardly had time to raise their shields which were useless against the siege weapons. The creatures were knocked off their feet in the explosions. Showers of dirt rained down on the rest of the front-lines as the Elves reloaded the siege weapons.

The attack had done exactly what the wizard had wanted. He wanted to break the cycle of their attacks and catch them off guard. The sudden attacks changed the armies in the fields, moving them from determined to panicked as another wave of attacks from the siege weapons was set to be loosed. The archers aimed a little higher and just as the catapults were released they fired, the combination of arrows and large stones sent flying through the air. Ectle gave a slight smile, watching the bodies of enemy soldiers thrown backward as the boulders ripped through the enemy lines.

The Elves refused to let up their attacks, slaughtering countless Goblins before they decided to charge the city once more. Like before, the catapults in the back of the fields began firing on the city, their stones meeting the face of the walls and shaking every inch of the battlements. Through the clouds of arrows and the enormous boulders the enemy revealed a new siege weapon that the Elves had not seen before. The Ogres were wheeling out what appeared to be a massive crossbow, its spear more than twice the size of that used in the Elven ballista.

"What... is... that?" an archer asked, stunned at the sight of the monstrous crossbow being moved towards them.

The armies of Goblins and Ogres stopped close to the wall and used a massive wall of shields and mantlets to protect themselves from the Elven arrows. Through it all the crossbow continued towards the city until it stopped some eighty yards from the gate. The soldiers in front of the weapon moved to the sides, clearing the path and giving it a clear shot at the gate. In the moments before the Ogres fired the weapon Ectle realized what it was going to be used for. The realization came too late.

From behind the wizard came a familiar voice and Ectle turned, seeing Thorgrim coming up the stairs. The Dwarf carried with him the magic weapon, dying for a chance to use it.

"Thorgrim? What are you doing here? Where is Nimir?"

"Nimir is still out. I could wait in the castle no longer. What has happened?"

Ectle turned and looked out into the fields, hearing a

deep Ogre yell followed by a strong jolt of the bow on the siege weapon. The massive spear sliced through the air and hit the gate, penetrating through into view of the soldiers inside the city walls. The shaft slid back out and then locked into place by the large barbs on the head of the spear. From the shaft of the spear were long ropes that stretched back into the masses of Ogres and Goblins.

The hulking brutes grabbed the ropes and heaved with all of their might, tugging the spear back against the battered gate, causing it to bow outward. Thorgrim and Ectle shared a nervous glance before the wizard moved back off of the battlements to the stairs. They stopped at the bottom, seeing the head of the huge spear dug deep into the gate. A stunned feeling spread across the force of Elves as they watched the gate crack again.

"Ectle…" Thorgrim whispered.

The wizard turned and looked at the Dwarf, feeling the shock himself. The gate was going to fall this time, there was no way to stop it. The spear had impaled the gate, and because of its sharp barbs there was no forcing it back out now. The army in the field was banding together, pulling the gate out.

"Ectle, what do we do?" the Dwarf asked, hearing the creaking wood strain against the strength of the creatures on the other side.

Ectle looked up at the battlements as one of the Elves fell off, an arrow jutting from the soldier. The wizard looked back at to the inner wall and then to the gate that was threatening to collapse. A new feeling began to sweep across him, a swell of fear. The wizard turned to Thorgrim and took a deep breath.

"Thorgrim, fall back to the inner walls. Start pulling the archers back and build up at the inner gate. We have to pull our forces back before they are completely overrun by the enemy."

"Fall back… but Ectle, you will give them the outer city?"

"What would you have me do Thorgrim? Once this gate falls it will be a fight of our swords against theirs and it is simple math, they have more. If we give them the outer defenses and fall back to the inner city we will double our numbers there and they will still have to break the inner wall. It is taller and stronger. If we fight for our survival, this would seem the most logical option."

As the wizard finished the last of his words the top of the gate broke violently, allowing bright streams of light to flood in. There was not a lot of time to consider the matter. The gate was minutes from falling, forcing the wizard to act fast.

"Archers, fire on their frontlines! Hold them back! Soldiers, fall back to the inner city gate at once. Withdraw and prepare to fight any that get through us."

The swordsmen and spearmen waited even after the wizard had finished his orders, reluctant to leave the post they had been assigned. Hearing the gate crack again the soldiers began to pull back as they had been instructed. The wizard stepped closer to the gate and waited, seeing the defense that protected the gate now failing. He watched above as the archers began dropping back down the stairs, retreating in groups as the others continued firing on the enemy.

"Why do you stay?" Thorgrim asked, running his palm across the head of the war hammer.

Ectle turned to the left, stunned to see the Dwarf still behind him. "Thorgrim, fall back to the inner wall at once! You were to lead the soldiers back and ready the defenses."

"Sorry lad, this is one fight I am not walking away from."

"Thorgrim…"

"Face it Ectle, I'm not leaving. I don't take orders very well."

The Dwarf tapped the weapon and gave the wizard a smug grin, knowing the aggravation he was causing Ectle. The gate creaked once more as the last of the archers abandoned the walls, retreating back to the inner defenses. With one last heave the Ogres put all their might against the rope. The spear lurched and the entire right side of the gate was ripped off of the wall, creating a gaping hole in the defenses. The left side of the gate hung precariously on what remained of the hinges.

The two soldiers stared out through the gaping hole at the immeasurable number of enemies now charging towards the battered defenses. Thorgrim looked up at the wizard and then back to the broken gate, wondering why he and the wizard had still not fallen back to the inner defenses like the rest of the soldiers. He wanted to ask but the wizard held up a hand, silencing him before he had a chance to ask.

Ectle waited, staring down the Goblins as they charged

ever closer. From behind he could hear soldiers yelling for the two to fall back, begging them to retreat while they could but both the wizard and the Dwarf stood firm against the enemy. Ectle took a deep breath and glanced to the Dwarf out of the corner of his eye.

"Are you ready Thorgrim?"

The Dwarf looked up and then out at the enemy. "Ready... ready for what?"

"You'll see. I will need you. After this, I will likely be quite weak. If you see no other choice, save yourself and leave me."

The wizard turned and raised his staff, a bright ball of fire rolling and glowing above him in the air. With each second the fireball grew larger and though the wave of enemy soldiers could see the magic they did not slow their charge, not for one second. They continued bearing down on the gate, only steps away. As the first Ogre reached the outer wall the wizard thrust his staff towards them, watching as the ball of fire streaked towards the battlements above what was left of the gate.

The second he loosed the spell a second ball of fire took the place of the first and it too grew. The ball of fire hit the stone above where the gate had once been and an explosion filled the air. The cracks stretched across the stone wall beneath the battlements as the second fireball followed the same path as the first. The enemies continued marching in on the city, the soldiers now crossing in under the gate.

Fireball after fireball met the stone wall and with the fifth there came a thunderous roar as the battlements and all the stone that supported them above the gate collapsed on the soldiers starting through into the outer city. Monstrous chunks of stone fell on the creatures now marching in on the Elves, killing them before they ever realized what had happened. The rubble continued to fall, plugging the hole on top of the bodies and momentarily halting the charge from the enemy.

Thorgrim was beside himself in awe, watching the wall collapse in where the gate had once been. He turned and looked at the wizard, watching as Ectle collapsed to one knee from exhaustion. Fearing his condition the Dwarf hurried to his side.

"Ectle, what's wrong? Are you alright, lad?"

"Yes Thorgrim... I am just... drained. Casting so many

spells... has exhausted my strength. Here... help me up," Ectle pleaded, extending his hand while leaning on his staff.

Chunks of rubble and massive pieces of stone continued to fall in on the hole and all who had tried to hurry through it. The Dwarf grabbed the wizard's hand and helped him to his feet, guiding him back towards the inner city. Elves from the inner gate hurried out to the two, taking the wizard from the Dwarf and helping him inside. Thorgrim stopped and stood at the mouth of the inner city, watching as the first of the enemy appeared over the edge of the rubble. It had stopped the charge, but it would not stop their advance. The enemy would keep coming.

"Get inside!" came an order from one of the Elves as the massive inner gates began to close together.

Thorgrim gave one last long look to the outer wall and ducked in behind the gate, listening as the mighty inner gates closed with a thunderous boom. Though the creatures outside the city were beginning to work at clearing the rubble the Elves were unnaturally quiet. The sight of the outer defenses now left in ruin and soon to be flooded by the enemy had silenced the soldiers in the city. On top of that, watching the outer battlements collapse in on the gate was shocking.

Ectle was still weak when King Elendil arrived at the inner gate and struggled to stand in front of the King. Elendil reached out and placed a hand on the wizard's shoulder, assuring him it was alright. Kneeling next to the wizard the King gave a nervous glance into his eyes.

"Ectle... what happened?"

"My King... the defenses were lost. I had... no choice..." the wizard struggled, his eyes blurred and heavy.

"Ectle, you destroyed the outer battlements and the gate. Why? Why did you... what were you thinking?"

"My King, the gate had been destroyed, the walls were being flooded, your soldiers had no chance of holding their armies back. I brought the section of wall down on their front lines... when they were charging through the gate. It will keep them at bay for quite a while."

Elendil tried to understand the reasoning of the wizard but the outer walls had been lost and the outer gate to the south had been destroyed by one of his own soldiers. The King patted the wizard on the shoulder and took a deep breath. No matter the reason, he knew the wizard was right. If the soldiers had flooded into the defenses unchecked and unchallenged they would be battering the inner gate at the moment. Instead, the army in the fields had been stopped.

"Alright Ectle, forgive me. Are you going to be alright?"

Ectle nodded and pushed himself up onto his feet, leaning on his staff as his head continued to swim. "Yes, just quite drained... that took every ounce of my strength. It will be a time before I can cast as strong as before. I must rest."

Thorgrim had not left the wizard's side since the gate had closed and kept a close eye on him as he took his first steps through the inner city. The soldiers around Ectle looked at him in disbelief, having witnessed the destruction of their city defenses by the wizard. Few understood why he had done what he had done in the outer defenses. No matter what they thought though, the King had understood and that was enough to clear the wizard's intentions.

The inner city had fewer catapults to defend with but the wall was thicker and taller and dotted with reinforced towers along its length. In several places on the battlements there were large ballista identical to the ones on the outer wall, only more of them in the place of the catapults. Even the battlements themselves were wider, allowing more archers and defensemen on them in the event of a siege. The outer defenses had been strong but now that the gate had been breached that strength was compromised and the army of Elves had fallen to the inner defenses instead. Everyone that is, except the Wood Elves.

Tanis had finally cleared his head of the ringing and blurred vision and promptly returned to the wall with his soldiers. They had continued without him, firing on the enemy as the creatures maintained their bombardment on the city wall, knocking countless Elves from the battlements. Tanis climbed the stairs and found his bow where he had dropped it in the earlier catapult attack. He bent and retrieved the weapon and looked out at the army now pressing to the gate.

The Humans had created makeshift battering rams from the trunks of trees and though they were primitive and little thought went into their creation, there were several waiting behind the one that was being charged towards the gate. The ram hit the gate and did almost nothing against the sturdy wood and steel which was braced from the inside as well. The soldiers felt the weapon jarred in their hands but drew back and prepared to charge again. Compared to the ram that had been used against the southern gate, the one wielded by the Humans was pathetically puny and looked as if it would deal no damage any time soon to the gate. Though their progress was almost nonexistent, the Humans continued battering away on the gate with determination. Tanis was still feeling the effects of the previous catapult attack as he pulled the string of his bow back, sighting along the arrow and waiting for the target to present itself. Finally it did.

The arrow sank deep into the neckline of one of the Humans still maintaining the shield wall, dropping him and creating a gap in the wall which the other Wood Elves immediately blanketed with arrows. The lack of the shield gave them new targets and as more of the Humans fell, the gap in the wall grew. Soon, Goblins massed in with their shields, trying to offer some protection in the loss of the Human soldiers.

"My King, are you well? You should not be here if you are unwell. The gate is holding strong and..."

"Do not cease firing soldier! I am fine; otherwise I would have died earlier. Keep them held off no matter what!" the King interrupted, his voice booming over the noise of the battle.

The Elves had been picking off every soldier that found themselves not hidden behind a shield for hours and looking at the enemies you never would have been able to tell they had suffered heavy losses. The battering ram continued to pound against the gate and the Elves were starting to see the strain on the defense. The Humans were far weaker than their Ogre comrades but their persistence looked to be paying off. The continuous rattling of the gate was almost mesmerizing to the soldiers. They watched and waited.

The King of the Wood Elves watched another force appear from the southern edge of the walls and his heart sank as he realized there was no end to their reinforcements. No matter how many they slaughtered, three more would take their place. The Elves behind the gate stood their ground but without the unwavering bravery that they had earlier. Knowing the horde that waited on the other side of the wall was taxing on their nerves. The soldiers stood their ground, not knowing what moment might be their last.

No Turning Back

*E*rzel and Kail knelt at the edge of the forest, staring out into the clearing where the overwhelming masses of Goblins and Ogres stood waiting for their chance to rush into the city. Erzel took a deep breath and bit his lip, not even capable of counting the strength of the armies in the field. Kail shifted on his knee and looked further to the south where there seemed to be some activity. He reached up and tapped Erzel on the shoulder, nodding through the brush to the force starting towards the wall.

"See that Erzel?"

The Elf nodded. "I see them. The city is still standing. At least there is a shred of good news, though I can't tell what they are doing. Where is Lavian?"

In the clearing behind them the great Warbird dropped low and landed, letting the Celestial Knight off its back and down to the ground. She stepped silently through the brush, stopping behind Kail and Erzel. Erzel peeked back over his shoulder and nodded to her.

"Lavian, did you get a view of things in the fields?"

She nodded. "Yes Erzel. It does not look good."

"How so? Please, tell us."

The Celestial Knight ran her fingers through her hair and then pinched the bridge of her nose, a dull throbbing in her forehead. "The fields are filled with their armies and their siege weapons. That is the least of the problems though. To the south the gate has been destroyed and the battlements have collapsed in on themselves. The rubble has stopped the advance of their armies but it will not hold them forever."

Erzel held his breath for a moment, the words from the woman slowly washing over him. "Wait, the defenses were…

destroyed?"

"The southern gate. It is in ruins and Valsera's armies are working to clear it, most likely so they can push even further into the city. I am sorry Erzel, I have no idea how your small number of Dwarves are ever going to be able to stand against the force attacking the city."

"It does not matter. I did not march this army of Dwarves from Tvan to Pentegarn to simply fall apart and let my home burn. If Pentegarn is going to fall, I will fight to my death to protect what is left of it. We need to ready the soldiers and prepare to move out at once."

"Erzel... I know you want to save Pentegarn... but..."

"Lavian, I can not command you. You do not serve my army nor fight for my King so if you do not want to follow us now I will not think ill of you. My soldiers and I on the other hand are charging into that field and I intend on fighting Valsera's armies until I am dead or until the rest of the Dwarven armies arrive. I am sorry, I will not wait any longer. Kail, are you coming with me?"

The soldier nodded. "Yes Erzel, I am with you. I will move back and let the forces know we have arrived. We will be ready for battle in no time."

The man moved back through the trees to where the massive Dwarven army had set up to rest, their forces all taking in what might be the last moments not engaged in battle. Meals were handed out like that of previous days, stale bread, water, and whatever fruits were available. They could not risk fires or smoke for fear that the southern armies would learn of their approach and their element of surprise would be ruined.

Kail gave the signal and at once the entire encampment began packing their gear and supplies, preparing to move out. Prepared and ready for battle the entire Dwarven army waited in their formations. Kail rounded the clearing and returned to where he had exited the forest. He stood and waited, running his fingers down the face of his bow. A snap was heard and Lavian appeared, followed shortly thereafter by Erzel.

"The soldiers are ready Erzel. How would you like to proceed?" Kail asked, watching the Elf pass him by, headed for the middle of the clearing behind him.

"Listen up!" Erzel shouted, catching the attention of all

the Dwarves. "Pentegarn is less than a hundred yards through the trees. On the other side of the forest however is a force far larger than we could have imagined. Make no mistake, we are going to be in for the fight of our lives the moment we break the tree line. No matter what comes our way, we will not fall back, we will not run, and we will not give up."

"We are with you master Elf... all of us. Lead the way," the closest Dwarf shouted, rallying the other Dwarves around them.

The Elf turned to Kail, a desperate look on his face. "Kail, there is no telling what we will be faced with. I have no idea what to expect."

"Expect these soldiers to fight for their homes and their lands. Expect them to face the enemy and refuse to run even when Valsera's armies are bearing down on them. Erzel, march this army out into the field and let us retake the city."

Kail made sense and Erzel gained a swell of pride listening to him. The Dwarves had pulled together their gear and weapons and were lined into the formations they had marched south in. Erzel and Kail took lead as Lavian mounted her Warbird once more, disappearing into the sky. The Elf walked through the forest without a word, the army behind him amazingly silent as they moved through the brush. Taking one last deep breath Erzel pushed apart the lower branches and stepped out into the clearing.

Bright sunlight invaded his eyes as he found himself staring at a massive horde of Goblins and Ogres waiting to rush the city. The army of Dwarves started appearing, curling around where the Elf was standing in a massive half moon formation. They locked their shields together tightly with the heads of their spears in between the small gaps of the shields. The wall appeared impenetrable as the archers lined in behind them, their bows drawn tight and ready. Seeing the Dwarves ready and the enemy having just noticed their advance the Elf let out the deep breath he had been holding.

"Archers... release!"

The Dwarven archers were less talented with their bows than the Elves but with the enemy numbers as thick as they were there was hardly a need to aim. The wave of arrows fell on the Goblins in a broad wave, bringing down the entire front line. The

Dwarves grabbed another arrow and drew the strings back again, sighting briefly before releasing them. The Goblins and Ogres had prepared for the second wave but it still had an effect all the same, striking down plenty of the enemy even with their shields raised. Erzel knew more than he let on and though the archers were having some luck, the front wall of the Dwarves were where the enemy would never stand a chance.

The Goblins picked up their pace in between the waves of arrows, soon charging up the hill towards where the Dwarves had set up their lines of heavy shields and deadly spears. The Goblins were halfway up the hill when the Dwarves revealed a measure of their strength that had been well hidden in their smaller stature.

"Soldiers, shift!" Erzel yelled, watching the shields move a bit higher and tilt.

The Dwarves acted together at once, their shield wall changing their angle slight enough to make a difference that had an amazing effect on the enemy. The sunlight breaking through the clouds caught the polished surfaces of the shields and with a small shift it was then sent back down into the fields. The glare was so intense that it stopped the enemy in their steps. The Goblins and Ogres that had moments earlier been charging the Dwarves were now stopped dead in their tracks as they struggled to shield their eyes from the bright glare.

The sudden blast of light disoriented the enemies, creating gaps in their shield wall that was charging up the hill. The gaps were perfect targets for the archers who had yet to stop firing, not giving the Goblins and Ogres a second to adjust to the Dwarves and their unexpected attack. The charge had been halted completely and now the Dwarves moved down the hill a little more, maintaining their shield wall and keeping the blinding glare on the enemy army below them.

"Erzel, they can not blind them forever you know," Kail noted, firing his bow frantically into the armies moving towards them.

The Elf did not respond. He knew the Dwarves would not be able to keep their composure forever against the armies but they were going to do everything they could to hold them off and fight their way to the gate. At the least, they could fight until the rest of the Dwarven army arrived to reinforce them. Even if they lost everything in the process, Erzel would not let the city fall as long as he could still draw his sword.

"Erzel... did you."

"Yes Kail, I heard you," the Elf interrupted, keeping a watchful eye on the armies moving towards them. "Pentegarn will stand against this, I am sure. We will hold their forces at bay here to give the city a chance. The rest of the armies of Tvan will arrive soon. Have faith."

The statement have faith was almost comical to the fighter as he watched another massive force of enemy soldiers appear from the main southern army and begin marching towards them. The Dwarves moved down the hill with their shields still catching the rays of sunlight and sending them back into the eyes of their opponents. The blinding effect was exactly what the soldiers had anticipated and their first moments into the fray of battle were better than they could have ever imagined. Their front lines drew their swords and spears and prepared for battle as the soldiers found themselves yards away from the disoriented Goblin lines.

All at once their strengths were neutralized, much to the dismay of the Dwarves. The bright sunlight that reflected off of their shields was slowly growing dimmer and soon the light disappeared completely behind thick wintry clouds. The Dwarves halted their advance and looked up to the sky, realizing their advantage had just been taken from them and now they were set to fight the Goblin army toe to toe. Though the front lines of Goblins were still dazed and fighting the blindness that had swept over them, those further back pushed forward when they realized the glare had ceased. Erzel and Kail gave one another a nervous glance.

"It was a good idea Erzel. Do you happen to have any more handy?"

Erzel was still swallowing the sight as the Dwarves had lost their advantage over the creatures marching towards them. "I'm thinking Kail... I'm thinking. By all means, I am open to suggestions."

Overhead the Warbird streaked by and from the saddle came a bright bolt of light. It streaked down into the middle of the hordes moving across the field and knocked two of the Goblins off their feet in the attack. It would never be enough. Lavian was doing all she could and it was hardly even apparent that she had attacked the enemy forces. The winged beast circled the battlefield and soon others appeared led by the remaining Celestial Knights. The magic arrows and bolts rained down on the Goblins and Ogres but it all looked to be a waste.

"Erzel…"

"I said I was thinking!" the Elf snapped, his mind racing desperately as the frontlines between the Dwarves and Goblins met at the bottom of the field.

"Erzel… a Dwarven soldier is worth two Goblins. Stretch the front lines further to the left and right and have them hold their positions. Let the Goblins and Ogres come to us. We are stronger."

The Elf looked up. "It would increase the number engaged. I do not want to spread our forces too thin though. One break in the wall and it could all crumble. Start shifting the heart of the force outward but be careful. We have to hold until the Elders arrive."

The fighter nodded and started down the hill into the mass of Dwarves. The forces instantly began shifting outward, flooding the edges of the shield wall and stretching it further and further. The archers continued to fire as the swordsmen and spearmen made their wall of steel stronger. For the moment the battle seemed almost light, the two sides hardly clashing with one another even though the opponents were clearly in range to attack. The lack of bloodshed was both a relief and a puzzle.

Erzel looked up to the walls of Pentegarn, wondering if King Elendil even knew they had arrived to help. The Elves in the city were surely engulfed with battle at the moment but the sight of a Dwarven army marching into the plains outside of Pentegarn would surely capture the attention of both sides of the battle. The wall of Dwarves spread outward and when it had reached its maximum length the Dwarves locked their shields and drew their weapons back ready.

In the moments of watching this Erzel wondered if attacking something the size of the Goblin army was even rational, but in the back of his head he reminded himself that the Elders would be marching towards Pentegarn by now. They had to hold out against anything the enemy threw at them until the Dwarven armies could arrive. The Dwarves had spread their forces across the northern edge of the field and waited.

"Alright, let's get things moving," Erzel whispered to

himself.

The Dwarves in the front of the formations had their shields locked tightly together and were waiting for their orders. They had pushed back the lines of Goblins time and time again, knowing to wait until their time was at hand. The wall of Dwarven shields pushed forward one last time and locked their shields again, the heads of the spears jutting out towards the enemy. The Elf took one last deep breath and raised his sword.

"Push forward! To the city gates!" he shouted, charging down the hill in behind the wall of Dwarves.

The Dwarves hesitated momentarily as the order rang through their ears. It was almost a surprise to finally hear the order to attack but they were happy to comply. The front wall of shields broke apart instantly and from it came a charging wall of Dwarven fighters. The charging wall of Dwarves stunned the Goblins and the first to stand their ground were instantly slaughtered. The first two lines of Goblins were mowed down before they managed to pull their guard back together.

The wall of Goblin shields and armor stood strong even though they were obviously shaken by the sight of the smaller force charging them so bravely. There were countless more Goblins and Ogres on the field of battle than the Dwarves and their allies. Even so, the Dwarves charged, fearless in the face of possible defeat.

Erzel closed his hand tighter on the grip of his sword, focusing on a point between the Dwarven soldiers and charging towards it. The Elf passed between the Dwarven soldiers and onto the front lines, his first sword stroke splitting a Goblin opponent from the top of its head to the center of its chest. Blood splattered the Elf's face as he whirled and struck again, striking down Goblin after Goblin as the Dwarves moved further out into the field.

The forces that had been attacking the gate and its battlements now caught word of the battle to the rear and their attention had turned. They no longer seemed concerned with the gate of the northern wall but now they began marching back away from the city. Confused soldiers on the city walls finally caught sight of the charging Dwarven army. Knowing the Dwarves had started to arrive gave them hope they had not felt for quite some time.

Tanis and his Wood Elves had been trying desperately to stop the Humans and Goblins attacking the gate but it wasn't until word of the massive battle on the northern edge of the field reached their ears that the Humans stopped with the battering ram and turned away from the city. Bowmen in the field continued to fire on the walls as the foot soldiers and Ogres began marching in with the rest of the soldiers moving against the Dwarves. They were so foolish, attacking an army ten times their size. There was nothing to be accomplished in a battle so one sided, or so the enemy soldiers thought.

The Elves in the city were passing word across the walls and into the heart of the castle that the Dwarves had arrived, sending a thrill of excitement through their forces. The Dwarves had forced the Goblins out of the Elven lands before during the Chaos Wars and would do it again.

Soon the Elves realized that what had arrived was not the Dwarven army, but instead a small force that had no chance of ever helping to break the siege. Their thrill was short lived, even as Elendil moved to one of the balconies on the northern side of the castle.

"Is that it? Is that all that the Elders of Tvan would send? I was wrong to believe that the Dwarves would match our own attempts to defend Nalawren. Surely this has to be a mistake."

Ectle appeared beside the King and shared his view, watching the Dwarves maintaining their line as they continued to move forward ever so slowly. Their numbers were almost comical but as they continued to watch, the wizard and the Elf King realized the Dwarves were not losing ground. They were not falling back, they were not breaking their formations, and they were not stopping their advance. At the moment, the Dwarves were winning their battle.

"Correct me if I am wrong my Lord, but the Dwarves do not seem to be fairing poorly. Perhaps there is something afoot we are not aware of. Is that… there… is that Erzel… and Kail?"

The blade of Erzel's sword was clearly distinguishable in the fray of the battle, as were the arrows from Kail's bow. In the thousands upon thousands of weapons, the two stood out from the rest and the two on the balcony were suddenly sure that the two had returned.

"They got through to the Elders and returned... with a very small force."

"At least they have returned. I am sure this is not all that the Dwarves have sent my King. Have faith. They will not abandon us in our time of need."

Elendil cut his eyes to the left side of the field where more of the enemy had begun to mass and march towards the Dwarves. In the field they had no cover, no way to create an advantage over the Goblins and Ogres. The soldiers had spent days in the fields, firing on the walls and the gate with no real chance of battle. Now that there were Dwarves in the fields with them they were eager to spill blood.

The King nodded and placed a hand on the wizard's shoulder, turning him back towards the castle. "Come on, we have our own defenses to look to. Erzel and Kail can take care of themselves. That mountain of rubble you created out of my gate and battlements will not keep them at bay forever."

Ectle looked to the ground as he walked. "I am sorry my King..."

They walked silently the rest of the way through the castle and out through the innermost city buildings before climbing back up the stairs to the inner wall. The King had been right. The mountain of rubble that had earlier sealed off the gaping hole into the city was now being cleared at an alarming rate. Soon the Goblins and Ogres would be climbing across and swarming the undefended buildings and markets of the outer city.

From where their soldiers were on the inner wall the Elves could do nothing to stop it from happening. They were forced to fall back and defend the inner city, hoping their strength on the walls and in the towers would be enough to keep them busy until more of the Dwarven army arrived.

Even if the armies of Tvan arrived they would have to fight their way through the entire southern army to help those in the city. Even if they arrived, they would have to continue to hold out until the Goblin army was broken or retreated from the city.

"It is obvious that we will soon be facing their numbers again. I had not expected it to hold them for long. Just long enough to get the forces back into the inner city safe and sound."

"It worked for a time Ectle. Now we have to start thinking about how we are going to keep them from breaking through this gate in the same manner. Their methods are becoming increasingly more sophisticated and successful. We must keep them out of the inner city no matter what the cost."

Archers notched and fired out onto the outer defenses and into the outer city at the enemy forces that were starting to make their way across the piles of rubble and debris. The Goblins were relentless. They ducked and dodged in between the buildings as the arrows dropped from the inner wall. As more of the creatures penetrated the city the wall of shields began to form again, protecting the southern forces the way it had in the fields.

It was difficult to tell from where the Elves were positioned but after a little time it became apparent that the Goblins and Ogres were now moving the massive catapults towards the outer city wall. The Elves knew that with no force available on the outer wall to fight the advance, the siege weapons would be able to strike the inner wall from the field. The Elves could no longer see the strange ballista the enemy had used to rip the gate down but they knew it had not been destroyed and more than likely it would only be a matter of time before they used it again.

Rubble shifted where the gate once was and more soldiers charged through the hole, some feeling the sting of the Elven arrows while some managed to escape the attack and slide in behind the wall of shields. The soldiers not locked into the wall were now plundering the buildings, setting fire to anything they could not use. The fire swept from building to building, charring the structures before spreading further. With the Goblins and Ogres helping it along the flames were spreading at an alarming rate.

"My King Elendil... they are burning everything! There will be no city left!"

"Quiet yourself... they will not break this gate. They will not touch our inner city. So long as the heart of Pentegarn remains the Elves have a future. We can rebuild what has been lost. Focus on the defenses," Elendil ordered, watching the enemy army in the fields.

The enemy forces seemed less than interested with the Elves and the inner defenses while there was so much to plunder and destroy in the outer city. Blacksmith shops, the outer barracks, tons of armor and weaponry left behind as the soldiers had to flee to the inner defenses. The Goblins and Ogres had raided the buildings, pulling from them anything they felt could be used against the Elves.

The Elves watched helplessly, the sight of the enemy using their resources becoming a sickening thing to watch. Their city was being plundered before their very eyes and they were powerless to stop it. A torch was thrown into a pile of the barrels that was stacked next to one of the catapults and the flames immediately engulfed them. Seconds later the flames reached the contents inside and the oil was ignited. Waves of flame spread through the area as the barrels ruptured and spewed forth a rolling carpet of fire.

Goblins narrowly avoided the fire themselves as they fell back. Elves on the wall began manning the few ballista that were available and the large spears were sent down at the enemy with lightning speed. The moment one would leave the large siege weapon another was loaded and aimed. The idea was simple. Fire enough at the enemy to keep them pinned down and unable to move against the Elves. It would not last forever but it would at least buy them some time.

Elendil stopped at the edge of the fortress balcony and watched as the Elves blanketed the inner city with arrows and ballista fire. Thick smoke blacker than the night rose from the buildings throughout the outer city and though the King knew it could all be rebuilt in time, he allowed a tear to fall across his cheek. Losing even a part of his city was as painful as losing a close friend. Friends could not be replaced.

The cold wind had started to grow once more, pushing the dark smoke out across the battlefield where the Dwarves continued to battle the Goblins and Humans with surprising success. Every one of the enemy the smaller soldiers cut down was another step closer to the city gate and their allies. Erzel had worked his way through the front line of the Dwarves and was now carving a path of carnage through the Goblins. They hardly seemed to put up a fight as the smaller army continued pressing forward.

Kail had at first tried to keep up with Erzel but had lost sight of him in the fray of battle. The Goblins were coming at him from every direction and after one last shot he abandoned his bow and drew the sword at his hip. Rarely did the fighter resort to his sword but the constant flood of enemies compelled him to wield his blade. The first to charge was instantly decapitated and the fighter dodged back to the right, the following sword stroke mirroring the first. The warm blood that splattered across him mixed with the cold air spurred him on.

Dwarves that had been fighting madly across the field were beginning the feel the draining effects of the long battle. With no reinforcements to help freshen their numbers they struggled to stand against the enemies whose armies had reinforcements, countless formations waiting for a chance at the Dwarves and the one leading them.

Suddenly the armies of Goblins and Ogres stopped their advance on the Dwarves and their forces parted into the depths of their ranks. From the heart of the army appeared a taller figure walking towards them, its stride confident and fearless. Kail stopped next to Erzel and took a deep breath, staring down the opponent with a familiar glare.

"Kail... what is that?" Erzel asked.

"That Erzel, is Uljic. Valsera's next in command under the Demon Infus. Infus is the shadow of the sorcerer, Uljic is the might and muscle. He commands the armies while Infus is in charge of other, more tactful tasks the sorcerer might have need of."

"Such as?"

"The Princess's abduction, the attack on the Dragon Isles, the capturing of the crystals. These things would never have been orchestrated by any other than Infus. I guarantee that Uljic was there when the Pass of Merwold fell... and Mihlann."

Uljic stopped and the lines of soldiers behind him pushed back together and waited as the two looked him over. The opponent was much different from the other soldiers around him. He was taller, more muscular, and fiercer looking than the rest of the army. Erzel could see a mixture of races combined in the creature. It definitely had strong Troll blood as well as Goblin and something else. He was not sure, but it was an opponent he had never faced before. Uljic had waited long enough and took another step forward.

"Stop where you are Uljic!" Erzel ordered.

The creature stopped and tilted its head to the side. "I must say Elf, I have no recollection of threatening you before... how would you know of me?"

"Does that really matter? You did not come for simple introductions. Say what you have to say and let us get this over with," the Elf demanded bravely, his patience nonexistent at the moment.

"Straight to the point... I like that. Your bravery could be confused for stupidity. In fact, yes, stupidity... definitely that one."

Erzel leveled the blade of his sword at the creature and locked eyes. He watched the blood running down the length of the sword. Uljic followed the tip of the weapon with his eyes, looking back up at the Elf. "Defend yourself."

Erzel did not bother waiting for the conversation to progress any further. He gripped the sword firmly and drew it back over his head, leaping at the creature. Uljic lifted his sword and blocked the Elf's attack with ease, stepping to the side and returning the attack. The two traded blows back and forth, their fight almost looking more like a dance in the center of the two armies. Every soldier that could see the two stopped to watch.

The Elf ducked a high swing from the creature and quickly brought his sword low across Uljic's hip. The gash spread open and blood flowed freely, followed by a roar of anger. Erzel stepped right and did it again. This time his sword was blocked and the creature lashed out with its empty hand, punching the Elf square in the jaw. A ringing filled Erzel's ears and he stepped back, shaking his head and raising his sword to defend once again. He had greatly misjudged the creature's strength and it cost him a stunning blow.

"How does that feel Elf? Everything you were hoping for? There is much more to come," Uljic taunted, seeming to completely ignore the wound on his hip.

Erzel did not reply. He raised the sword and charged again, fearless even though the creature was far stronger. Uljic knocked the Elf to the side and began raining blows down on him over and over. In the back of his mind Erzel wondered if his sword would withstand the blows, but it had been forged and enchanted by the Celestial Knights and it held. Another mighty swing and Uljic knocked the Elf back a few steps, advancing fast before Erzel had a chance to recover from the blow. Uljic kept a jagged grin on his face as he continued attacking over and over.

Though the Elf lacked the strength of the creature, he

found himself to be much faster. Soon he began avoiding the blows instead of trying to defend against them and his speed gave him an advantage he desperately needed. Erzel ducked left and then right, dodging the swings with ample room and the grin began to fade off of the creature's face. Uljic attacked again and this time the Elf stepped to the right and lashed out, the tip of his sword tearing through Uljic's right ear.

Blood dripped from the gash and the creature appeared stunned for the first time in all of the battles it had fought. The first stab to the hip had been luck but now the Elf had cut him again. This opponent was different. The Elf was fierce with his blade and faster than any other opponent the creature had faced. Uljic lifted his sword again and took another confident step towards the Elf, completely ignoring his wounds as he approached. The Goblins and Dwarves that had stopped to witness the battle were now watching intently, on edge to see who would remain standing as the victor.

"You know death isn't so bad Elf… it could end quick and painless. For you though, I am going to make sure it is slow and filled with unimaginable agony. I'm good at that… are you ready to find out?"

Erzel ignored the taunting from the creature and advanced. Uljic was not intimidated and drew his sword back again, all of his strength welling up in his thick muscles. To his right the Goblins and Dwarves seemed to be skirmishing again and their watching the battle ceased. The soldiers around them had no effect on the focus between Erzel and Uljic. They were locked on one another and again their swords met violently. The Elf was beginning to time the attacks, learning the rhythm of the creature and waiting for the chance to strike.

The blows continued as the soldiers around them erupted into a wild battle as Elves on the wall watched the events. The soldiers had stopped trying to break through the northern gate and were pushing out into the fields to strike down the small army of Dwarves. Their overwhelming numbers were pushing the Dwarves back, but just as quickly the soldiers from the north would charge and break the lines of Goblins and Humans. Things looked to change as the Ogres began arriving in behind their smaller comrades.

Erzel ducked inside the swing and slammed his shoulder

into Uljic's chest, shoving the creature off balance and drawing his sword back to attack. Uljic hardly had time to lean back away from the attack as the tip of the sword cut through the air mere inches from his face. The Elf was getting brazen, more comfortable in the fight and soon he would draw blood again. The creature was on the defensive side of the fight, retreating and dodging the attacks of the Elf as they continued to come in an endless wave.

Erzel could sense his advantage and pressed it even harder, charging in towards the creature with blistering speed. He bluffed an overhead strike which he quickly pulled down and struck under the creature's guard. The tip of his sword sank into Uljic's tough skin just below the ribs. Feeling the creature stiffen Erzel forced the blade even deeper. Blood gushed around the guard of his sword and across his armored hands as the creature brought a weak elbow down to the Elf's temple.

Even cut and stabbed as deeply as it had been, the monster was still putting up an impressive fight. The Elf pulled his sword free as he staggered back from the blow. His vision was blurry but he still charged, his sword leveled off and ready. The two collided in the field and the Elf was knocked back off his feet. Laying flat on his back with his sword out of his reach Erzel watched the creature step across him, fresh blood running down his side from the deep wound.

"You… see. I will… heal but you are… going to die…" Uljic said with heavy breaths.

The creature raised its sword over its head with its free hand, the other clutching the wound where the Elf had stabbed moments earlier. Erzel turned his head and looked up to see where his sword might have landed but unfortunately it was far out of his reach. In the last second he remembered the whip at his hip and grabbed the handle. Before he had time to release the powerful flames hidden inside the handle the creature attacked.

The moment Uljic flexed his muscles to send the sword down on the Elf a brilliantly bright flash blinded them both. Uljic staggered back away from the Elf, howling in pain and covering his face. From the commotion behind the Elf appeared Kail, his bow still level from the shot that had hit Uljic in the face. His skin was charred and blackened from the heat the magic arrow had given off in its impact.

Even that was not enough to stop the creature. It did however give Erzel enough time to get back to his feet and activate the whip, the magic flames spurting forth and coiling on the ground until the Elf snapped it back. Now Uljic stopped, never knowing that the Elf possessed a weapon of such strength. The Elf snapped the whip and advanced, amazed to see the creature still bravely standing its ground. Uljic clutched the deep stab wound with its right hand and raised the sword to defend.

Erzel snapped his arm and the whip shot forth towards the enemy. The flames met the sword and coiled around it, snapping the blade as the Elf jerked back on the weapon. Uljic took a step back and then another as the Elf advanced. The creature looked at what remained of the sword in its hand and then to the ruined blade on the ground. For the first time ever Uljic was retreating and the moment he turned his back on the Elf, Goblins formed a wall of shields and spears between the two. The Elf grinned triumphantly as he watched the leader of the southern armies retreating for the safety of the heart of the army.

Kail was awestruck. No soldier had ever fought with Uljic and beaten him, let alone forced him into retreating. Erzel willed the weapon back into its dormant state and stepped back away from the wall of Goblins. He turned and started back towards Kail and the heart of the Dwarven army when disaster struck.

Erzel took another step and watched as Kail drew his bow taunt and the magic arrow appeared. His eyes dropped to his enchanted sword on the ground and he stopped to reach for it when an unimaginable pain tore through the entire right side of his body. The Elf fell to one knee on the ground, a scream of terror and agony filling his ears. It was moments later when he realized it was coming from him.

When he collapsed the Dwarves realized there was an arrow jutting up from under his shoulder blade. The arrow pierced the chain armor on his back and lodged deep between his ribs. His breaths came short as he crawled towards the Dwarves, struggling to use his right arm. Dwarves rushed forward and formed a massive wall around the Elf as Kail grabbed him and pulled his left arm up over the fighter's shoulder. The two stumbled back under the cover of the Dwarves as the two armies parted for the first time.

"Erzel... are you alright? Keep your eyes open, do you hear me?"

"Yes... Kail... I... ugh... hear you," the Elf replied through gritted teeth.

Erzel lost his footing and all of his weight was on the fighter who continued to drag him toward the tree line. "We're almost there. No one has ever beaten Uljic in battle. You made him flee. I can't believe..."

"Kail... save it... please," Erzel grunted as he took another heavy step.

Just inside the trees the Elf collapsed to the ground and laid face down, breathing in the smell of the dried leaves and dirt. Every breath was a challenge wracked with pain as he fought to keep himself calm. He had turned his back on the enemy in his moment of triumph, letting his pride leave him vulnerable. He was angry at himself for such an act of stupidity.

Kail reached to the shaft of the arrow and then pulled his hand away, unsure of what exactly to do. Blood soaked the back of Erzel's tunic and chain armor and the fighter knew that something had to be done soon. A Dwarf appeared beside the two carrying the Elf's sword and laid it on the ground next to Erzel before hurrying back to the line of soldiers that had drawn back to the forests. The armies had withdrawn from one another and a brief period of inactivity occurred, each looking at the other and waiting.

As some of the soldiers crowded around Kail and Erzel to see how bad the wound was, a deep rumble filled the air. Kail raised his head and turned toward the clearing, remembering the sound of the Ogre horns giving the signals to attack. He could see the Goblins and their allies in the fields around the city and they were neither attacking the city nor charging the army of Dwarves. They seemed just as confused as Kail.

The only ones who did not seem the least surprised were the Dwarves; they were cheering and beating their weapons against their shields in a wild frenzy. It was in this moment that Kail realized the sounds were not coming from the horns of Ogres. They were Dwarven horns. Kail grabbed Erzel's left shoulder and roused him gently.

"Do you hear that, Erzel? Do you hear the horns?"

"Yes... Kail... I hear... them."

Three more blasts and the sound permeated through the forest and into the clearing, reaching the Elves in the city as well. Instantly they all knew exactly what the deep blaring of the horns meant. The armies of Tvan had arrived. The rest of the Dwarven forces would soon be flooding the fields and the enemies from the south would be driven out. Erzel turned his head and reached up beside him, grabbing his sword and holding it tightly. All was not lost after all.

The Dwarven horns echoed across the fields and up into the city, completely halting the advance of the Goblins and Ogres. The creatures knew instantly that the horns were not from them nor their allies and their forces turned to the north where the sound seemed to be coming. Goblins, Ogres, and the Humans all knew that with the Dwarves in the northern edge of the field, the horns would be signaling the arrival of their main army. This posed a problem for the southern armies.

Uljic had retreated back into the heart of the army and then continued south, disappearing into the forests to hide his shame. He had never been beaten in combat and having the Elf wound him so was a shame he no longer wanted to bear. He trudged through the forest even as he heard the Dwarven horns bellow from the north. There was no reason to turn and go back now. The Dwarves would push Valsera's army south. It was only a matter of time.

Walking with his head down Uljic could feel his body weakening slowly. His strength was draining and he stumbled. The creature reached out and gripped a small sapling, lowering himself down against the tree next to it. He slid to the ground and pulled his hand away from the deep wound. Blood continued to seep from the wound even with the pressure that had been applied and a shocking realization came to the creature. It had always been able to regenerate a wound, but with the rate Uljic was losing blood there was little chance he would be able to heal this time.

"That... bastard... Elf..."

Uljic felt his head slump forward and then things were blurry. His senses were no longer sharp, but had now grown weak and foggy. He could only see in blurs of color and a soft hum filled his ears. The creature could taste blood and a thin stream of drool escaped his scarred lips. He heard one last long blast from the Dwarven horns before darkness swallowed him and the last ounce of life slipped from his war torn body. The mighty warlord Uljic had fallen.

The North Fights Back

Elendil stood on the balcony anxiously peering out to where the Dwarves had retreated as the sounds of the Dwarven horns filled the air. Deep inside the King had wondered if he would see the reinforcements from Tvan before his city fell but now, hearing the sound of their approach, faith was restored.

Though the Dwarven army was moving towards the city, the armies that had breached the southern gate had not stopped their attack. In fact, the sound of the enemy army closing in only seemed to strengthen their desperation to break through the inner gate.

Elves cheerful for the reinforcements were now faced with the task of holding the inner wall until the Dwarves were able to get to the city. The task was shaping up to be a very challenging one. The Goblin catapults were now locked and ready and though Uljic was no longer there to give the orders, the Ogres carried on with their duties. Dozens of stones suddenly flew through the air in a massive wave, striking the face of the wall and the battlements as they had on the outer wall. Elves moved about trying to clear themselves of the massive boulders but in the thick of the chaos some never had a chance to get clear.

"Ectle, help us hold these walls at all costs. The armies of Tvan are coming!" the Elf King ordered, rushing from the balcony of the keep towards the inner wall defenses.

Ectle grabbed Thorgrim by the shoulder and jerked him along, the three hurrying for the inner wall to lead the soldiers still standing their ground atop the battlements. A rogue boulder from a catapult struck inside the inner city, flattening a building to their right. The moment they reached the stairs leading to the top of the wall a boulder struck one of the towers on the wall above them, demolishing it.

The thunderous boom filled the air and a cloud of dust and debris rained down on the inner city as the tower collapsed. Ectle grabbed the King and shoved him up the stairs where he was safe from the falling rubble. Where the tower had been was now a cloud of dust and a mass of ruins. Any Elf that had been inside was surely no longer alive.

"Come on, we're there! Stand your ground! Don't back down!" the King yelled as he charged up the stairs.

Ectle and Thorgrim were on his heels and as they crossed the top of the stairs all three stopped and stared out at what was left of their inner city in total shock. There was no longer a building standing outside of the inner wall to the south. Skeletons of structures still engulfed in fire collapsed in on themselves, sending showers of sparks up into the air. Goblins and Ogres filled every gap and crevice of the inner city, waiting as catapults and arrows smothered the Elves on the upper battlements.

They did not move until a clearing appeared in the front row and stretched back, allowing the massive ballista that had broken through the outer gate to roll slowly forward into the city. It was already armed and the bow had been drawn back tightly and locked into place. The massive Ogres pushing it forward strained under the weight of the siege weapon but did not dare stop. When the weapon was completely in view the creatures stopped and took a long look at the gate standing tall before them. Elendil looked to the right at the wizard with concern spreading across his face.

"Ectle, stop that weapon. It will tear down another of our gates."

Ectle took a glance over the edge and realized the massive spear was aimed dead into the center of their gate once more. He reached back to fire off a spell when the Ogres fired it suddenly, far sooner than Ectle had anticipated. The spear hit the stronger gate with a loud bang that shook the battlement above as well. Just like the first time the two ropes were drawn tight and the Ogres and Goblins began pulling with all their might against the projectile.

Ectle wracked his brain about what to do now that the gate had been penetrated by the spear and the enemies were threatening to pull this gate down as well. He heard the gate under him groan under the strain and a crazy idea formed in his head. He leaned far out across the battlements, looking down at where the spear had pierced the gate. Reaching back Ectle felt the ball of fire growing in his fingers.

His target was the iron loop that the ropes stretched through. Missing would mean the ball of fire hitting the gate and the damage it would cause could possibly destroy the gate instead of save it. He concentrated and then as if he were throwing a rock he released the swirling ball of flame. It rolled as it flew through the air and Ectle watched as it missed the iron ring but instead erupted on the ropes themselves.

The fire burned quickly and to his relief he watched the two ropes snap, sending the Ogres and Goblins lurching back against the ground. Though the gate was heavily damaged the ropes no longer threatened to rip the gate off its hinges. The soldiers below looked at the remains of their ropes and then at the gate that they were now to break through without the added help of their handy siege ballista. From deep in the ranks of their army came Ogres carrying the barrels the Elves had used earlier in their catapults.

"Elendil, what are they doing with those?" Thorgrim asked, pointing to the four or five Ogres carrying the large barrels of oil.

Elendil did not answer. He was afraid to guess, though in the back of his head he already knew the answer. The enemies knew what the barrels had been used for in the attacks and now they could dish out some sort of punishment with the Elves' own weapons. The Elves began firing down on the enemies as the Ogres moved closer. The Ogres stopped at the edge of the front lines and stared up at the battlements of the inner wall.

Things grew quiet and then all at once the Goblins began firing on the battlements to cover the charge of their Ogre comrades. The Ogres moved surprisingly fast and in a flash they were out of sight of the archers and hidden against the gate. They piled the barrels against the gate under the spear and then retreated back into the safety of their own army. As they retreated back one of the oversized brutes took an arrow to the neck and fell, trying to crawl to safety.

"My Lord, the barrels of oil... they've piled them against the gate! If they ignite them..."

"I know what will happen Ectle. What will you have me

do?"

Ectle stared out into the ranks of the Goblins and watched as torches were being lit. There were several bright flashes and out of the center of the army appeared an oversized Ogre, a glowing torch in each hand as it rushed toward the gate. Archers began firing on the creature and though it soon had several arrows jutting from its body it continued lumbering forward. Ectle reached back and the moment the creature took the last step he threw forth a massive bolt of lightning.

The gleaming streak of energy hit the Ogre and wrapped around it in bright coils, scorching the creature and knocking it to the ground. The Ogre raised its head and looked up at the pile of barrels and felt its energy sapped and gone. With one last ounce of strength the dying creature reached back and hurled one of the torches at the gate.

"Ectle…" Thorgrim whispered.

The wizard watched the flare of fire streak through the air and strike the gate, falling in amongst the barrels. He felt his breath catch in his chest and waited, knowing what to expect next. A small spurt of smoke appeared from the heart of the pile and then a massive wave of flame rolled up the front of the gate. The barrels ruptured and the flames stretched skyward, licking the bottom of the battlements where the Elves watched disheartened. Though the gate was mostly steel it would be weakened greatly by the intense flames.

Ectle and Thorgrim turned, locking stares as they both realized the wizard had failed to stop the creature. Now there was a torrent of fire swallowing the gate, wrapping around the structure and raging wildly. He fought to think of a way to extinguish the flames before they ruined the gate. Goblins began blanketing the wall with arrows to keep the Elves and wizard from smothering the flames. Ectle ducked and then fell back away from the edge of the battlements.

"Where are you going Ectle?" Elendil asked, watching the wizard retreating back down the stairs.

"To pull your Knights to the gate. It will not stand forever like this. We have to hold them out until the Dwarves get here, should the gate fall."

Elendil was in a swirl of disbelief, fear, and concern, knowing that it would be some time before the Dwarves managed to reach the heart of the city and push back the Goblin army. Until then the Elves would have to do everything in their power to hold off the attacks.

Tanis had watched the Dwarves battle their way through the Goblin ranks to the north of city and then stared as they began to retreat back to the forest. The Dwarves falling back only gave the Goblins and Humans the chance to refocus their attention on the battered gate of the northern wall. His archers had already begun falling back through the gate into the inner city as the King of the Wood Elves took one last look across the field. He knew they had failed to hold the outer defenses and were retreating to the inner wall.

"My King, we need to move. There is no time left," an archer said, stopping next to him to stare out at the field.

"I thought they had come to break the armies but they've already fallen back to the forests. What good were the Dwarves in the end?"

"My King, surely you can see that was not the entire Dwarven army. Perhaps it was a scouting force for the main army. You heard the horns signaling the main army is on the move. They will not desert us."

Another loud blare of a horn filled the air and Tanis took a wary step back towards the stairs. He felt as though he was betraying the High Elves by abandoning the outer defenses but there was nothing left there to defend. The sound of the battering ram on the gate below kept him moving and soon the King was crossing through the inner gate. It slammed behind him and the Wood Elves were already starting up the stairs to defend the inner wall. Tanis hesitated, wondering if the Humans manning the battering ram would ever make it through the gate. He heard the soldiers above him on the wall shouting.

"They're breaking through! Archers, be ready!"

The Elf took a deep breath and looked to the sky, His body was wracked with exhaustion and sore from the attack that had left him wounded earlier. All the Wood Elves were low on strength and morale and the Goblins had what seemed to be an endless supply of soldiers. What would the Dwarves be able to do against such masses? All seemed hopeless to the Elf as he wearily climbed the stairs once more.

Atop the battlements both High and Wood Elves were already aiming down on the gate, waiting for it to break open and the flood of soldiers to rush in. They had no surprise up their sleeves, no great army at their backs. Only the overwhelming drive to protect their people and their homes. The gate below cracked loudly and another series of shouts filled the air. As Tanis listened he realized they were less panicked than before, almost cheerful. Looking up the King's heart lept. At the edge of the forests all around the clearing appeared the massive Dwarven army. The sight was a flush of relief that almost brought a tear to Tanis's eye. The army of Dwarves stretched from the northern edge of the forest to west and east, surrounding one hundred and eighty degrees of the clearing. The Goblin and Ogre army stopped everything, turning and looking on the full might of the Dwarves of Tvan.

Tanis looked up to the right and to the left, a smile appearing on his face for the first time in a week. The Dwarves continued marching from the forests in towards the armies of Goblins. For the first time in close to forty years the two armies squared off. They had not faced one another since the end of the Chaos Wars. It was the first time the Goblin army had seen a force that matched their own numbers and they were noticeably shaken by the sight of their opponent.

"The Dwarves came after all," an archer exclaimed, seeing the numbers continuing to stream from the trees.

All across the army came the blaring of the horns again, letting the world know the army had arrived at Pentegarn. Even the mass of soldiers that had pushed through into the outer city had now stopped and listened, realizing the Dwarves were preparing to attack.

Ardis and Odar stood on the crest of the hill overlooking the field as their massive army waited for the order to advance on the Goblins. Beside them appeared Kail who had left Erzel's side only after the Dwarven physicians had arrived. He knew there was nothing he could do for the Elf and decided instead to return to the battlefield to continue fighting. The two Elders stared out at the massive army facing them and the pillars of smoke stretching into the sky from within the walls. They could see the outer gate to the north breached and could only assume the southern gate had suffered the same fate.

"Quite an army they have managed to pull together. The outer wall is in ruin, smoke rising from inside the walls," Odar noted, resting his hand on the head of his axe.

"Valsera has near endless reaches and fear as his methods of recruiting. Races know not to defy his wishes or face the same fate as those who stood against him. Not until he is dead will these great armies disband and leave his grasp," Kail added.

"Very true. Well Ardis, we've marched all this way. Why don't we remind them what it felt like to be beaten. They've no idea what is in store for them," Odar said with a smile.

The Dwarves pushed together in large blocked formations, watching as the Goblins mimicked their moves. The enemy army lacked any real sort of discipline which the Dwarves knew would cost them in the long run. No discipline meant they would not stand well against the full force of the Dwarven army. Without discipline they would break and run when the Dwarves charged.

Kail stepped in beside the Elders again. "My Lords, might I ask where are the other two Elders?"

Ardis glanced at the fighter and then back at the fields. "Divos stayed in Tvan to continue the mining and general duties of our people."

Kail waited a second before pressing the matter further. "Alright... and the other is?"

"Velex took one third of our forces and marched on Cisalia not a day and a half ago. They will meet us here after the Human city has been dealt with," Odar answered gruffly.

The answer was not exactly what Kail had expected. In fact, it made almost no sense. "Perhaps I do not understand your warring methods, but the armies of Cisalia are here, mingled in amongst the Goblins and Ogres. What need is there to attack the city when everything they have is here? There is no one there to... fight."

Odar smiled. "Then Velex should have no trouble with the Humans. Sound the charge. Let us drive the monsters back to their cities again."

Kail knew he had heard the Elder correctly but still he did not truly believe the words. The Dwarven army was going to descend on the people in Cisalia, not all of which were evil. They would be killing innocent people, women, children, old folks, all because of the mistake of the soldiers. They were not all responsible for the crimes of their King. He felt his face growing hot and reached out, grabbing Odar by the shoulder and turning him.

"You can not destroy all of Cisalia. There are innocent people there, people who had nothing to do with what Calyn and his army plotted against us. This is madness."

Odar's glare was stern and cold, reflecting his mood at the given moment. He looked to the hand on his shoulder and then back up. "Remove your hand from me at once."

Kail drew back but his gaze on the Dwarf intensified.

"The Humans are our enemies lad, and all will be dealt with in the same harsh manner. Once a traitor, always a traitor. One day you will understand the price of war. Some will suffer, but all will learn the lesson."

Odar and Ardis turned back around and started in behind their soldiers as the horns blared and the entire Dwarven army marched out from their positions. Kail stood rooted to the spot, unwilling to follow the Elders but not sure what he was supposed to do. It was likely already too late for the people in Cisalia. Hundreds of families slaughtered without warning, without reason. He hung his head, knowing that the Elders had just committed an evil similar to that of Valsera.

He turned and hurried back through the trees to where the Dwarves were tending to Erzel. The Elf was barely conscious as the Dwarves carefully removed the armor and tunic from around the shaft of the arrow. The bleeding had nearly stopped but judging from how pale Erzel had become there was likely little left in his body. The Elf could make out the form of his comrade but in the blurred vision he was not sure of who it was.

"How is he?" Kail asked, kneeling next to the Elf and the three Dwarves.

"Very weak. We have to get this arrow out of him right now. Alright master Elf, this is going to hurt, a lot."

"Fine… just get it… over with," Erzel muttered, taking a deep breath to prepare for the pain.

Two of the Dwarves braced the Elf, one holding his shoulders while the other held pressure on his lower back. The third reached down with one hand to spread the wound and with the other he gripped the shaft of the arrow. The Dwarf pulled firmly, twisting the shaft a little as the head started to slide back out. Erzel's face was twisted and flushed as pain spread from the wound all through his back. The head of the arrow slid again and then tore free from the flesh, causing the Elf to cry out loudly.

"Give me... the uh, give me bandages," the Dwarf ordered, taking them and applying pressure as the flow of blood started again.

"Here, gonna have to sew him up."

Kail remembered what the two Elders had said and wanted to tell Erzel of it but not with the three Dwarves around. For the time being he kept quiet and watched, waiting in case there was anything he could do to help.

"Kail... how many... came?" Erzel asked between heavy breaths.

"Enough. Valsera's armies will not be able to win this battle, I am sure. They will be driven back across the Pass of Merwold if not completely broken here and now."

"Ah... good. I am sorry..."

"Erzel, you shouldn't speak. You need to rest and save your strength. They will have you stitched back up and ready to fight soon. Just rest."

"By the time... I'm better... the war... will have ended."

"Just get better Erzel. There will always be another war."

The sound of battle suddenly erupted all across the fields as the entire Dwarven army charged the Goblins. Wave after wave of Dwarven infantry smashed against the front wall of Goblin shields. Soon the two front lines became more of a shoving match, neither side giving an inch. More and more Dwarves pushed in behind the front wall. The Goblins and Ogres stood their ground even though it was obvious that they were terrified at the sheer size of the Dwarven army. The waves of Dwarves continued pushing forward, their broad shields and long spears keeping the Goblins from dealing any damage to the superior opponents. Rampaging through the lines of Goblins came the Ogres, trampling their own as they charged at the Dwarves.

The monstrous creatures ripped through the front line of Goblins and into the wall of Dwarven shields, sending the small soldiers flying through the air. Swinging wildly with their massive clubs and maces they created holes in the Dwarven army front line, which were rapidly filled with Goblins. A group of Dwarves pushed together and with the combination of their six spears managed to bring down one of the Ogres. Once on its knees every soldier around it took a shot at the beast, killing it in seconds.

Scenes like this occurred all across the battlefield as Dwarves used their numbers to bring down the Ogres, an effort that required no fewer than five to one. Having found a way to nullify the strength and size of the Ogres the Dwarves once again reclaimed the advantage and pressed it firmly on their enemies. The Goblins did not dare flee the battle, but were doing nothing more than giving their numbers to the slaughter.

At the heart of the Goblin armies the Ogres were loading the catapults with whatever they could find and were now aiming them towards the northern clearing. The Dwarves were still pressing forward when the siege weapons were released and the boulders and rubble filled the sky. The Dwarves further back from the front lines noticed the attack and tried clearing the soldiers to minimize their losses. Sadly, they were too late to avoid the inevitable.

Dwarves were crushed under the rain of rock the catapults had slung into the air. The boulders sent up showers of dirt and grass as the massive stones met the earth. Even though the Dwarves had realized what was about to take place they were helpless to prevent it. In the aftermath they witnessed the Ogres rearming the catapults to attack once more. The Dwarven army continued to press forward, knowing there was nothing else they could do.

At the city gate Ectle watched helplessly as the forces outside had begun to pummel the charred structure with all of their might. They knew their armies were under attack in the field yet they continued to fight their way into the city where the Elven soldiers had been forced to retreat. At the front of the gate several large Ogres had appeared, their bodies covered in plated armor and their heavy maces battering the weakened defense. The gate would soon crumble under the fury of the monsters.

Every blow against the gate sent small splinters flying as the wood gave way, leaving only the steel standing. Even the steel was not strong enough though, and soon the left side of the gate suffered a massive crack stretching its entire length. Two more blows buckled the hinges and the massive door fell in towards the soldiers. Ectle gripped his staff and watched as the right followed only moments afterwards.

The three massive Ogres hefted their steel maces and charged in, the sight of the Elven Knights driving them into a sort of bloodlust. Ectle stepped to the front, his staff leveled at the creature in the front. With a quick thrust the head of the staff flashed bright yellow and the Ogre in the front stopped in the middle of its charge as if it had met a stone wall.

"Fire at will!" Ectle yelled as soon as the Ogre had been stunned.

The Elves in the rear of the formations had been holding their bows ready and the moment they saw the creature hit the invisible wall they released. The creature was swallowed in a cloud of arrows. The other two Ogres raised their arms to protect their faces as the Elven Knights charged. With their spears leveled the Elves skewered the two Ogres and dropped them. They then raised their shields and prepared for the Goblins that followed.

In the mouth of the gate the Elven soldiers created a solid wall of steel shields and spears, forming a sort of bottleneck and preventing the massive numbers of Goblins and Ogres from all getting into the fight. In this position the Elves could limit the number of soldiers they were forced to fight, giving their superior discipline and war tactics the chance to shine. The wall of Goblins met the Elves with a thunderous crash but the Elven wall stood firm.

The Elves on the top of the wall fired down on the enemies below, focusing on the soldiers four to five rows back from the Elves which created a large gap between the reinforcing Goblins and those now battling the Elves at the mouth of the gate. As more Goblins surged forward, more archers fired down on them. It was one of the worst slaughters of the battle, but the enemy refused to stop no matter how many they lost.

"Let me up there Ectle, get me to the front!" Thorgrim cried out anxiously, watching the bodies of Goblins piling up.

The wizard grabbed the Dwarf by the shoulder and pulled him back a ways. He did not want the soldier on the front lines while the Elves were fighting with such success. He looked down. "Calm down Thorgrim, you'll get your chance. Do not break that line for any reason. They can not get through so long as our shields remain locked together and the archers keep their reinforcements pinned down. Patience my friend, you must have patience."

Thorgrim shook his head with a disgusted expression on his face. "I didn't come here to watched others fight. This is my war too Ectle."

"I know. I assure you, you will get your chance. I can not be sure how long the Elves will be able to hold back their forces. I have an idea though, come on."

The wizard almost had to drag the Dwarf with him as they moved to the north around the keep and up to the northern gate. When they got there they climbed the stairs, finding Tanis and his Wood Elves ready to defend the battlements from the inner wall. They looked around, realizing that the outer gate had not been broken.

"Why are you and your forces here on the inner defenses?" Ectle asked, confronting the Wood Elf.

"The gate was minutes from being breached. We fell back here so we would have the chance to defend when the Goblins and Humans break through. That was before we saw the Dwarves and their armies arriving. It is a welcome sight at last."

"We are going back out to the outer city and we need your archers and soldiers to come with us."

Tanis looked at the wizard with a flare of disbelief. "Why would you want to leave the inner defenses? The outer wall has been breached to the south and the northern gate is not far behind. You and whoever goes with you will be slaughtered."

Ectle looked back at the Wood Elf with a hollow stare. "So is that your way of saying you will not come with us?"

The pressure the wizard was putting on the King was smothering and Tanis took a step back, looking over the edge of the wall at the massive battle that was stretching the entire length of the northern field. In his mind the thought of moving back to the outer city was insanity.

"What are you looking to accomplish Ectle? If their forces break through that gate you will be facing the entire northern Goblin force, the Humans of Cisalia, and the Ogres. How are you going to fight that?" the King asked, still not imagining any form of victory in what the wizard was wanting to do.

"The southern gates have been breached but the Knights of Pentegarn are holding the Goblins back at the inner gate. They've massed their forces in the small passage of the inner gate and are denying the enemy entrance into the heart of the city. If we move through the outer city around to the southern edge we can use the archers to add even more of their numbers to the piles of dead."

"It seems risky Ectle," the Wood Elf noted. "I suppose it will hold off their numbers long enough for the Dwarves to break the armies around the city"

"That is exactly my thinking, my Lord."

Tanis pondered what the wizard had suggested and turned to his soldiers. They all stopped and gathered to hear what the King had to say. "Alright then, fall back off of the wall and prepare to move on the southern gate. My archers will make short work of their forces so long as you and the footmen can guarantee that you will be able to hold them back."

"They will not reach your archers Tanis, I promise. Make ready!"

The wizard and Dwarf turned and hurried down the stairs; the force of Wood Elves right behind them. They stopped briefly at the gate to allow the soldiers to open it. They could see the weakened and battered outer gate and were grateful that it had withstood the abuse from the enemy outside. Ectle led the way, his eyes scanning every building to ensure their presence had gone unnoticed.

Their advance was slow but they eventually rounded the western wall and caught their first glimpse of the soldiers trying desperately to break through the Elven Knights. All the buildings around them had been torched and what was left standing were only skeletons. Ectle and Thorgrim took the lead with the footmen behind them and the archers bringing up the rear. Once close enough they formed a stout line and the archers fell into lines behind the infantry.

Their force had not been seen and the archers drew back their bows, aiming for the mass of Goblins near the mouth of the gate. Just when they released their bowstrings one of the Goblins caught sight of them out of the corner of its eye. It turned just in time to receive an arrow in the chest. Confusion spread as the soldiers realized they were being attacked by a new force. A second volley cut down more of the creatures and finally a large number of Goblins turned their attention to the archers and small force of infantry.

"Alright, here they come. Do not break your line of shields. Tanis, do not stop firing, no matter what happens."

A nod assured the wizard that the force was ready and he turned, he and Thorgrim in front of the wall of shields. They stood ready, waiting for the enemy to advance further and knowing it was their duty to hold back the force as long as they could. The wizard raised his staff and prepared as Thorgrim brought the war hammer up level with his shoulder. The Goblins had formed a wall of shields and were slowly marching forward, the arrows no longer bringing them to the ground.

The Wood Elves saw the wall and aimed higher, sending their waves of arrows further behind it to those not expecting the attack. With the shields in front of the Goblins, the numbers in the back had not expected an attack to make it through. Their assumption proved fatal as a cloud of arrows skirted over the top of the shields and began slaughtering the unsuspecting forces.

"It's working! Keep it up!" Tanis shouted, releasing another arrow.

The Elves at the gate watched as the enemy further back began falling to the waves of arrows and morale began to grow. They found themselves pushing the Goblins back out of the inner gate, fighting further out into the outer city for the first time since its fall. It was the first sign of offensive life from the Elves and the Goblins and Ogres were caught off guard.

They fell back towards the inner gate but did not fully retreat, letting their reinforcements from outside of the gate flood in behind them. No matter how many of them the Elves killed there were plenty more to face. Like a never ending swarm of ants the enemy forces pressed towards the city and Dwarves at the same time. The Wood Elves moved in tighter behind the infantry and continued to fire.

The front line of Goblins came in against the Dwarf and wizard but soon regretted their actions as they spread from behind the shield wall to attack the two soldiers directly in front of them. From the head of the wizard's staff burst a thin bolt of blue lightning. The bolt hit the nearest Goblin and then split, jumping from enemy to enemy until it finally fizzled. In all, more than twenty of the Goblins had felt the power from the bolt and now lay smoldering on the ground.

The sight frightened the other Goblins and they immediately fell back. Seeing the nearly two dozen soldiers charred and dead the Goblins no longer pressed toward the Elves and their wizard leader. It gave the archers plenty of time to fire on the enemy as they were no longer under threat of the Goblins charging at them. Joined by the archers on the walls above, the Elves began driving the horde back out of the gate.

Ectle looked back at Tanis and then to the footmen with their shields locked together. They all watched the Goblins retreating and a wave of bravery spread through the Elven soldiers. The wizard raised his staff and turned back to the creatures, charging at them with a yell that would have been enough to scare the Goblins by itself. Behind him the Dwarf and the Elven footmen broke from their positions and charged with the wizard, the roar of their attack heard all across the walls.

Their Bittersweet Victory

The Dwarves pushing from the north had completely cleared the entire northern curve outside of the city and were now marching their entire army down the western edge of the city walls. Even though this was where the enemy forces were the thickest the Dwarves were not stopped for long. Locking their shields together they marched through the Goblin forces. Even the threatening forms of Ogres could not hold back the Dwarves as they pressed on, slaughtering anything that decided to stand against them.

As the Goblins fell back to the southern forests they pulled with them the Ogres and what remained of the Human armies. They fought as they retreated, the fight inside of them not fully extinguished as the Dwarves managed to break the Goblin hold on the fields. The Dwarves never wavered in their attacks, never once finding their forces pinned down by the Goblin army.

Out front the soldiers kept their spears lowered and their shields locked tightly, moving forward with an impenetrable wall that could do far more than defend the Dwarves behind it. The spears kept the Goblins and Ogres far enough back that they were not able to strike the wall itself. With the wall never ending in its march the enemy had no choice but to retreat, and even though their enemies appeared to be in retreat, the Dwarves did not stop. They continued their charge, killing their opponents whether they stood to fight or ran for their lives.

Ardis and Odar had worked their way through the heart of the Dwarven army and found themselves near the front lines. They had been marching across the dead bodies of their opponents the entire time, showing the superiority of the Dwarves. The Goblins, now battered and beaten fell into full retreat.

On the edge of the western forest an impressive force of Ogres massed, watching as the Goblins fled wildly. The Goblins were not a brave species, relying on their massive numbers to overpower their opponents. Now that the heart of the army was in retreat, the rest of their forces followed, not willing to stay and fight on their own. The Ogres ignored their smaller comrades, starting a slow march towards the far larger force of Dwarves. They were much braver, their sheer size giving them the drive to keep fighting.

With the last of the Goblins falling back into the forests and turning to watch, the Ogres made their charge. A few hundred remained. They stretched across the width of the field as a single file line. Their feet on the ground created a rumble as the creatures reached a full speed charge. They wielded large reinforced clubs, axes, and spears.

The Dwarves watched the massive wall of Ogres charging at them and stopped their advance, setting their line of shields and bracing for the impact that looked to destroy their front wall. Even the Dwarves behind the front wall locked their shields and pressed them against the backs of the Dwarves in front of them, creating reinforced sections of walls. There was no doubt that the Ogres would break through the front line, maybe even the second, but the Dwarves would not fall back.

Ardis took a step towards the front lines. "Hold your lines! Fight for Tvan! Fight for Pentegarn! Fight to the very last!"

One solid cheer sounded through the Dwarven ranks as they dug down and prepared to receive the charging Ogres. The rumble intensified as the Ogres grew closer and the Dwarves could soon feel it under their feet. Their courage was intact but they realized how destructive the force was going to be when the Ogres met the wall.

Ardis looked over his shoulder at Odar. "This is going to be messy Odar."

The Dwarf nodded and a slight grin appeared on his face. "What kind of war would it be if we didn't get our hands dirty?"

Ardis gave a hearty laugh and turned back to the enemy as they were now only steps away. He held in his hand a broad sword and in the other a wide shield much like one that his Dwarven soldiers carried. Odar appeared beside him with his axe over his shoulder, watching intently as the enemy made contact with the Dwarven lines.

Dwarven soldiers on the front line were sent flying through the air violently, the oversized brutes demolishing the wall of shields with ease. The Ogres charged deep into the Dwarven formations, wide swings of their weapons beating back the small Dwarves. Even facing brutes more than twice their size was not enough to break the courage of the Dwarves. They pushed towards the creatures even as their comrades were knocked through the air by massive blows from the Ogre weapons.

Ardis and Odar pushed forward with the surge of Dwarves, moving closer to the nearest Ogre as one to the far right was finally brought down by a collection of spears and arrows. Even as it collapsed to the ground the Dwarves continued pummeling it with blows. The soldiers directly in front of Ardis were knocked back over the Elder's head and into the formation of Dwarves from a powerful blow of the creature's club.

The Elder stepped forward and quickly attacked, slashing the creature across its lower back and then ducking as it turned, its club streaking overhead. He watched as another Dwarf struck it from behind and the creature whirled back around, soon finding itself completely surrounded by a mass of Dwarves. They attacked at different spots, keeping the creature from dialing in on just one of them until Ardis drew back and threw his sword at the creature.

The blade sank deep in between its shoulders and the Ogre dropped down on one knee, desperately trying to reach the sword in its back. As the creature struggled Odar approached and raised his axe. With one quick glance down at the creature he attacked, severing the Ogre's head and sending it rolling across the ground in amongst the feet of his soldiers. He wiped a splatter of blood off of his cheek and looked out at the Dwarves still battling the Ogres.

The Ogres had destroyed the entire front line of the Dwarven army but with their massive numbers the Dwarves quickly replaced their comrades that had been killed in the initial charge. Now they were fighting madly, battling the brutes with everything they had. In the battle against the Ogres the Dwarves lost more than they had in every fight against the Goblin and Human armies. Every so often one of the Ogres would land a massive blow, killing several Dwarves with one strike, but it was apparent that the number of Ogres was thinning.

The Goblins that moved out of the forest to watch the Ogres charge had momentarily gained a swell of bravery. Some almost had the urge to charge back in until they saw the Ogres falling all across the field. Without the massive fighters the Goblins knew there was virtually no chance to win. What forces had been in the fields had fallen back, taking with them those that had at one time broken through the gate.

The Humans retreated with them, no way to fall back to Cisalia. They were trapped now, serving the ranks of Valsera's army far away from their homes. What was left of the Ogre force continued to fight the Dwarves, surrounded and desperate, knowing they would die in the field. They would take as many of the Dwarves with them as they could.

Ardis and Odar moved forward together as three of the brutes had pulled into a single area. The trio was racking up piles of Dwarven bodies and though the Ogres were outnumbered a hundred to one, the Dwarves around them were not too eager to be the first to lead the charge in on them.

"Odar, on the left. I will take the right. Come on, let's bring these bastards down," Ardis said, blood dripping from the blade of his sword.

The two Elders separated and circled through their forces, the Dwarves rallying in behind them as they stared at the three Ogres and the carnage they had caused. Both Dwarves had a massive group of soldiers backing them and they paused briefly as the Ogres ceased their attacks. With a loud battle cry Odar charged at the creatures, his axe hefted up over his shoulder.

The Dwarves around them did the same and like a massive tidal wave the soldiers flooded towards the three brutes. The Ogres tensed and prepared to attack even though the odds were beyond calculation. Odar reached the Ogres first and left the ground, leaping through the air at the beast's chest with his axe ready. The Ogre leaned back with its club drawn back to strike, the two weapons closing ground on their targets.

Odar released his axe, sending it end over end through the air. It flew straight and true as the Ogre's club came around and met the Dwarf in the air. Odar crashed against the steel headed club and was instantly sent flying back through the air. About the time the Dwarf felt the crash of the club against his chest his axe sank deep into the creature just below its chin.

The wave of Dwarves converged onto the Ogres from every direction and an ear shattering crash filled the air. Dwarves were thrown through the air as more converged on the remaining Ogres. Ardis had led the charge, ducking a massive axe and plunging his sword deep into the gut of the beast. He ripped it free and spun away, letting the Dwarf behind him sling his spear at the creature.

A few minutes of loud clashes and horrid screams of pain filled the air and then silence. The Dwarves drew back from the bodies on the ground, leaving the Ogres an unrecognizable mess of blood and gore. Ardis pushed through the formations of Dwarves until he found a group huddled around the body of Odar lying on the ground.

"Odar! Tell me you are..."

Ardis stopped in the middle of his sentence, looking down at the twisted form of the Elder. It was evident that the blow had broken the Dwarf's back on impact and the landing had only worsened the damage. His face was contorted with the last remnants of pain just before he passed and Ardis gave a tough nod to the body of his fallen friend.

"Wrap the body... send it back to Tvan. Soldiers, keep your guard up in case they decide to make another attack. The city is safe!"

Triumphant cheers rang out across the fields as the Dwarves began moving their dead and dying off of the field. The Elves that had been pushing Goblins back out of the city were now moving through the outer gate and out into the Dwarven army. The two races greeted one another warmly as they set up their defenses against any force that might dare attack them.

Ardis moved through the forces towards the city until he caught sight of Ectle coming towards him. He stopped and waited a moment, taking in the cold winter air.

"Glad to see ya pulled through Ectle."

"Yes, and you as well. What has become of Erzel and Kail? I saw them with the first force of Dwarves that arrived."

"Ah, the Elf. We found him struck down when we arrived earlier. It didn't look good lad."

Ectle stared at the Dwarf for a moment, the words sinking

in. "Erzel is… dead?"

Ardis shook his head. "No, he looked mighty rough though. They were tending him when we arrived. Excuse me, I will speak with the King."

The Elder moved off towards the gates of Pentegarn alone, leaving Ectle rooted to the spot where he stood. He pictured the Elf lying dead with the thousands of others in the fields somewhere and prayed he had time to be of help. The wizard forced his feet to work, taking a step out toward the northern forests where he had last seen the force. He passed mounds of dead and soldiers moving out to the new shield wall that surrounded the western and southern edges of the city.

The walk was long, stepping over bodies and pushing through soldiers. He finally found the hill where the Dwarves had first made their stand. He looked up and stopped short. Coming down the hill towards him he saw Kail and though he looked a shade shy of death, Erzel. The Elf leaned against the man, bracing himself as he took each step with a heavy breath. They stopped in front of the wizard and stood silent for a moment.

"Erzel… I thought you were dead," the wizard said quietly, reaching out and taking his other arm over his shoulder.

"Truth is… I feel like it… Ectle."

"Take it easy Erzel, we'll get you to the city and tend your wound. What happened Kail?"

The fighter looked from Erzel to Ectle. "He fought their commander Uljic and won. Right afterward one of their archers attacked. The arrow hit just under his right shoulder blade between his ribs. We managed to extract the arrow but the blood loss has been substantial."

"Well no matter, we are going to help you. Here, take him through the northern gate," the wizard said, leading them towards the open gate. "We have driven them out of the city and back into the southern forests. I had my doubts early on, but we are victorious!"

Erzel did not bother responding, choosing instead to save what little bit of strength he had left. Everywhere he looked he saw the bodies of Elves and Dwarves and the death surrounding him was bringing a shiver of fear to his body. He knew he was near death himself, and seeing the lifeless bodies all around him made it all too real. He took another weak breath as they reached the stairs to the keep.

"Erzel! Kail! I had no idea you were even still…"

Thorgrim stopped when he saw Erzel. He moved ahead of them, clearing the hall and opening the doors to the large great hall. Soldiers with wounds filled the room waiting to be examined. They laid Erzel down on his side on one of the large tables and the wizard quickly examined the wound.

"This is a serious injury. The arrow penetrated very deep. I will do what I can Erzel."

The Elf gave a weak nod. "All… in your own… time, Ectle."

An Elven physician appeared as the wizard was preparing and he too examined the wound. "Shall I help, sir?"

Ectle looked up and realized the man was better equipped to handle the wound. The stitches the Dwarves had put into the wound in the field had been the only thing keeping the Elf from bleeding to death right away. The physician touched the wound around the edges and reached into a pouch on the front of his robes. He presented a jar of cream colored salve and opened the lid. It was odorless and when it met his skin Erzel felt a wave of cold spread over the wound and the skin around it.

"This will get rid of any infection and make sure that the wound stays closed. Hopefully after that you will begin to regain some of your strength. Very slowly now, you will have to rest for a few days."

From the arch on the far wall appeared the small form of a Dwarf. He walked towards them on noticeably shaky legs and stopped a few tables away. Ectle, Kail, and Thorgrim looked away from Erzel to find Nimir leaning against the table, stunned by the room filled with heavily injured soldiers.

"Nimir! You pulled through after all!" Ectle exclaimed excitedly.

The wizard hurried over to where the Dwarf was standing, finding Nimir's color had returned and though he still appeared weak, he was at least up and moving around. The Dwarf looked to the injured Elf to his right and then back at the wizard.

"I take it that I missed something," he replied, rubbing his head.

A chuckle escaped Ectle's lips as he reflected on everything the Dwarf had slept through in the last few days. "Yes

Nimir, you definitely have missed a little. Not to worry though, the city is still standing."

"Oh, well that's good," the Dwarf mumbled, still very confused as to how he ever got back to Pentegarn in the first place. "Erzel... are you ok?"

The Elf nodded and looked around the room, keeping a grip on the side of the table as he tested his shaky legs. He could tell the blood loss had weakened him greatly and he had to take each step carefully. "Still alive, Nimir."

The endless lines of injured were brought into the great hall as those able to heal them worked feverishly to get to every soldier. Every wound imaginable was seen and soon the great hall of the keep was as bloody and gory as the fields outside. Erzel moved aside with the rest of the group as an Elf was laid on the table behind them, his left arm severed just below the elbow. The Elf was in shock and stared off into space as the physicians did what they could to help him.

The scene continued for hours and with evening approaching Erzel and the group made their way through the castle to the upper levels where they would finally be allowed to rest. Nimir headed back to the room where he had slept before and sprawled back out on the bed to rest. The other four made their way into the throne room where Elendil, Tanis, and Ardis sat around the long table. The door closed loudly behind them and the three looked up.

"Erzel, Ectle, Thorgrim, Kail, you've all managed to survive. A blessing indeed," Elendil said, standing from the table and holding his arms out to greet them.

"Some of us a little worse for wear I am afraid, but all present and accounted for, my King," Ectle replied as he led them into a bow.

Erzel struggled to bow as the wound still gave him plenty of pain and Elendil reached out, stopping him before he hurt himself. "It is fine Erzel, please, come and sit. We were discussing what is to take place now that Valsera's armies have been driven from our lands."

The group joined them at the table. After sitting Erzel realized they were still missing members of their group. He looked around at the Kings and Elder and raised an eyebrow. "Where is Lavian? Where are the rest of the Celestial Knights?"

Tanis and Elendil shared a concerned look and the High Elf King turned back to Erzel. "We have not seen anything of them since the last attack they and their Warbirds made on the Goblin siege towers. Shortly after the second one fell, we lost sight of the Celestial Knights. I think it is safe to say..."

"Safe to say what?" Erzel asked, his tone dangerously close to disrespect.

"I can only hope they are not mixed in amongst the fallen, Erzel. Perhaps they will be found safe very soon. I am sorry I do not have the answer to your question."

The Elf looked down at the table, unhappy that he did not know anything for sure on the condition of the remaining Celestial Knights. Elendil gave the Elf a few minutes to collect his thoughts before continuing the conversation with Tanis and Ardis.

"I am sorry for the loss of Odar... he was a brave Dwarf to the very end. What is to be done with the soldiers that follow him?" Elendil asked Ardis.

"I will see that they are moved into the other ranks of the army and that he is honored. A more pressing matter is upon us though," Ardis replied as he changed the conversation topic. "Valsera's armies have done this before and we drove them back to the southlands. This time, we can not stop here. We have to pursue them and finish them once and for all."

The table was silent for a few minutes as what the Dwarf suggested sank in. The task could not be considered lightly as it would require all the armies moving together into the lands of the south. Elendil raised his hand to slow down the talks.

"Give us a moment away from the fray to consider our options Ardis. We have all lost brothers and comrades today. We should make sure our next declaration of war is well thought out."

Ardis nodded to himself, even though he did not fully believe that they should hesitate in their attacks. The Dwarves were more set on attacking over and over, never allowing their opponent a moment of rest while the Elves were more tactful, looking for the best place and time to engage the enemy forces. It was a difference between the two races that looked to bring about many confrontations in the future.

From the balcony the group heard a loud thud and they

left the table to investigate. Standing in the middle of the balcony was one of the large Warbirds and beside it was Lavian. She looked from face to face and approached, taking a knee in front of the Kings.

"My Lords, Elder of Tvan, I have returned."

"Where were you Lavian? I thought that perhaps, something had happened…" Erzel asked, happy to see the Knight alive.

"Once their forces began to withdraw from the field I took to the sky and followed the movement. Their numbers are still very dangerous and they have begun massing at the area your people call the Pass of Merwold. Where… are the rest of my Knights?"

"The Celestial Knights? We've not heard word from them for some time. You are the first to return," Elendil said, looking down at the table.

Lavian stood in silence, wondering what had happened to the rest of the Knights under her command. Being the only one remaining was a terrifying thought. She had known how the Dragon felt all those years, but now she understood on a more personal level. She turned and pretended to examine the balcony, hiding a tear.

"I am sorry Lavian, Odimous was a good Knight. I must stress though that there is very little time to mourn now. We must keep our guard up and prepare to strike back as soon as we can," Elendil said solemnly.

"They are setting back up at the pass? What good would they do to try and hold our forces there?" Tanis asked out loud, knowing that if they were driven back before they would surely retreat again if the Dwarves and Elves marched together on the southlands.

The Goblin army was still sizable even after their humiliating defeat in the fields around Pentegarn. The damage they had dealt to the city and to the Elves was near catastrophic. Virtually nothing remained of the outer city. The Elves would rebuild their city in time. Right now though, they had to deal with the Goblin army.

"Alright, we've a lot to consider. The armies of Goblins and Humans have stopped at the Pass of Merwold and evidently wait for us there. Because the pass is relatively easy to defend with a sizable force, their numbers still pose a threat. This behavior would dictate that they are either protecting something or buying time until reinforcements can arrive. Wait… where is Alora?" Elendil asked the group, looking from Kail to Lavian and finally to Erzel.

The Elf looked down at the table and recalled the events that took place above the fields. He looked up and breathed a ragged breath. "The Dragon Alora died a day before we arrived in the fields of Pentegarn. We were attacked by the Demon Infus and a force of Slayers. She is the only reason the three of us survived to be here now. Even though she died, we…"

Erzel stopped himself, realizing for the first time in a while that they no longer possessed the crystals that imprisoned the sorcerer. He had given them to save who he thought at the time was Rhen. Had his judgment not been clouded with emotion he would have known there was no way the Princess had been taken captive by the Demon and its soldiers.

"You what? What is it Erzel?" the High Elf asked.

"We um…" he started, looking from Kail to Lavian. "I uh… lost the crystals. The ones that Yanosh used… to imprison Valsera"

"You what!?" Elendil yelled, rising from the table.

"My Lord, I had no choice. The Demon had Lavian and Kail held captive and was threatening to kill them both. I refused and he produced the Princess Rhen and threatened the same against her unless I gave up the crystals."

Tanis was right behind the High Elf, his face red as he heard what had become of his daughter. "What did you say? How… what happened… to her!?"

Kail stepped in as Erzel's expression was one of self loathing. "It was not the Princess, my Lord. The Demon disguised a young Elf to resemble Princess Rhen but we could not tell the difference. Erzel was doing everything he could to protect her. We all were. We had no idea that it was in fact an imposter."

"What happened to the Elf? How was it not her? You said she was identical to my daughter!"

"She is dead Tanis. The Elf died after the Demon stabbed her through the stomach. After the battle died down the Elf's hair changed from red to blonde and her face shifted to one of a younger Elf. It was an illusion placed on her to take the crystals from Erzel," Lavian answered, trying to dispel the tension that was growing in the room.

Even though the Wood Elf had heard a reassurance that his daughter was not in fact the one killed in the forests above the city, he still held onto his fear that something had happened to her. The loss of the Dragons meant they were now back to fighting Valsera the old-fashioned way. With sheer force and smothering numbers of Elves and Dwarves.

Ardis sat silent in the midst of the conversations, knowing inside that his Dwarves had broken the armies of Goblins once before and they had the strength to do it again. What was more, they still had the army led by Velex to add to their force, knowing that Cisalia would never be able to stand up to their might. They would have a massive force moving south against Valsera, assuming the Elves ever agreed to march.

Lavian's voice cut through the idle chatter and everyone listened as her words brought with them a frightening reality. "That is not the worst of what is to come though. Releasing Valsera is not what the Demon is after."

Everyone turned and looked at her, confused as to how she knew the intentions of the creature. Tanis rubbed his chin and waved his hand off in no specific direction. "I wonder, how is it you know what the Demon intends to do."

Lavian took the seat at the head of the table alternate Elendil and prepared to reveal what the creature had planned. "The Demon will use the near endless energies stored in the crystals to open a portal to its dark lands where the Slayers inhabit a vast wasteland. With the portal opened, it will no longer need the Goblins, Humans, or Ogres. An army of Slayers is ten times as deadly as any of those creatures."

"That does not answer my question," Tanis said bluntly. "How is it you know all of this?"

Lavian lowered her eyes. "I have seen it, when we still had our homelands. Infus captured one of our more powerful wizards and harnessed his energy. After it was done, thousands of the Slayers were swarming through our cities. There was nothing left of our world, nothing at all."

Everyone in the room fell silent as they realized what the Celestial Knight had been forced to endure. It was obvious that she knew what was at stake. She had seen it happen before. Erzel reached over and laid a hand on her shoulder to offer comfort. He raised an eyebrow and coaxed more information out of the Celestial Knight.

"Then why has Infus not done it here? Why do the Goblins and Ogres reign supreme over our lands? Why are the Slayers hardly evident except when Infus is carrying out some sort of secret attack?"

"When it happened the first time Infus grew confident and sought to overthrow Valsera with the massive army of Slayers. Valsera destroyed the portal and ordered the Demon to disband the Slayers. Out of fear of retaliation, Infus followed the commands. Valsera would never allow Infus to bring the army back onto the lands again for fear that the Demon would try to overthrow him again."

"… and now there is nothing stopping the Demon from raising its army and swarming across these lands like locusts. What sort of hope is there now?" Elendil asked, realizing that an army of Slayers would smother the Elves and Dwarves with their darkly tainted nature.

"We are still alive Elendil. So long as we live, there is someone to stand against Infus and the Slayers," Erzel said bravely.

"Lavian, how long exactly will it take for the Demon to prepare and then to open the portal?"

Lavian stared off into space for a minute and then looked back at the group. "That depends on where Infus plans to open the portal. If at Qwaz or at that other city you mentioned."

"Nomaria?"

"Yes Erzel. If Qwaz, it is likely he is less than a day away on foot. It would then take another three, maybe four days to complete the ritual and then summon the portal between the two lands. So realistically, judging from the distances on this map, it could be anywhere between five and eight days. Of course, I can not guarantee anything with this creature. I hope we have longer."

The Kings and Elder Dwarf sat in silence, listening as their odds dwindled as more and more details of their situation were given. The Celestial Knight had been there. She had seen the horrors that the creature was able to unleash on her lands.

Now the creature was set to do it again, on a new land. If there was something she could do to stop it, Lavian was set on making that happen. She pushed her chair back and stood from the table, walking through the room slowly as she started weighing every option they had.

"How long would it take to get to Qwaz from here?" the Celestial Knight asked.

Elendil and Tanis looked at one another, confused with the nature of the question they were being asked. "Well, without an army between us and Qwaz, it would usually take no more than four days. That is, under favorable circumstances."

"If we were to move on Qwaz or Nomaria, we would first have to make it through the army that has massed at the Pass of Merwold. That will not be a simple or quick skirmish. The armies there will undoubtedly fight with everything they have to keep us from making it through to the southlands."

"There has to be a way!" she yelled, remembering what her people had gone through.

"What if… there is?" Ectle asked quietly, looking up at the group.

Everyone looked at the wizard. What did he know that they didn't? Elendil turned to Ectle and raised an eyebrow.

"Well Ectle, why don't you share with us your grand plan to get past what is left of Valsera's armies."

The wizard pressed his elbows onto the table and tapped his fingers together as he played the idea through in his head. "If you would like to make it through Valsera's armies and into the southlands in time to battle Infus, I think I just might know a way. When I was in the swamps searching for Thorgrim and Nimir, we witnessed the Goblin soldiers battling with the Lizardmen. Valsera's armies are fighting amongst themselves now."

"So… how is that our key to getting to the Demon?"

"We share a common enemy with Valsera. If we were to make that enemy an ally for a period of time, we could use the swamps to move around the pass and then attack the city directly. If things go well, we might even have those Lizardmen marching out against Qwaz with us."

The two Elven Kings stared at the wizard in disbelief. Tanis rubbed his temple and then pointed at the wizard. "You would mean to seek an alliance with those Lizardmen? The ones we've been fighting since before Valsera ever descended on our lands?"

"Yes…" Elendil noted with a slow nod.

"What are you talking about?" Tanis asked the King in disbelief.

"It makes since. As much as I hate them, if we are going to make it to Qwaz before the Demon's armies are marching through the portal, we are going to have to bypass the army waiting at the pass. If those creatures are fighting Valsera on their own, perhaps they will fight him with our armies."

"I can not believe you are even considering this Elendil. An enemy we have been fighting for nearly a century is being sought for an alliance? This is an insult and an outrage," Tanis said, standing from the table.

"Sit down King!" Ardis ordered angrily. "I am not about to lead my armies to battle if there is no chance of victory. If the wizard has a plan, then I suggest we hear it."

Tanis stood in the middle of the room looking at everyone else. Everyone was siding with the plans of Ectle and the Wood Elf knew his opinion was not going to matter at the moment. Realistically they had to get to the city and stop the Demon at all costs. It was time they took a chance.

"Fine. We'll do what we must. I refuse to trust those reptiles though."

The group all sat together, realizing that against all odds, against the worst possible conditions, the Elves and Dwarves had a chance. They had not lost, not yet.

One More Moon Over Pentegarn

Erzel sat in the evening sun, staring out over the fields as the soldiers worked to clear the countless numbers of bodies. The mountains of dead Goblins were piled at the edges of the forest as the Elven and Dwarven fallen were brought back towards the city to be buried among their own kind. They would likely work all through the night and into the morning hours to finish the task. The Elf sat in silence, the events that had unfolded throughout the battle still rolling through his head. They had lost so many soldiers in the fields and across the city walls. So many more than the other battles before.

The Elf was trying to imagine making an alliance with the forces that called the swamps home. The Elves and the Lizardmen had warred for a century and to the day no measure of peace had ever existed between them. Now, after years and years of bloodshed they were to seek a treaty with the creatures. Whether they shared an enemy or not, the reptiles could not be trusted. They would surely turn on the Elves the moment they had the chance.

"Erzel? Are you alright?" Ectle asked, stepping out onto the balcony.

The Elf turned and nodded. "I am fine Ectle. I only wonder what we are about to attempt. To make an alliance with our oldest nemesis, to make war against the Demon and its Slayer army. Does this not seem like suicide to you?"

"Perhaps... but only if we were forced to face the army of Slayers. If our armies arrive on the battlefield before those of Infus we stand a fighting chance. If the Lizardmen charge against Valsera's armies with us, we will likely find ourselves the victors. The odds no longer matter at this point, we must try."

"Yes, very true my friend. Yet I wonder what it will take

to truly drive the evils from our lands. If Valsera and Infus are defeated, will the armies simply disperse? Will the Goblins and Ogres just pick up and leave Nalawren? What will happen to the forces under the sorcerer?"

Ectle shook his head and gave a weak shrug. "There is no way for us to know that yet Erzel. One thing is for sure though, if we do not stop them, they will continue to sweep back upon us time after time until there is nothing left of our people but bone and ash. Erzel, every fight in the past has led to this."

The setting sun cast strange shadows across the fields and the wintry wind brought a chill to the two on the balcony. Even the Elf who had been hardened by battle could not ignore the cold. He stood from his seat and leaned against the railing. Ectle joined him and together they looked out at the overwhelming numbers of fallen. Though the field was covered with the dead, it was not the piles of bodies that captured the attention of the Elf.

"Ectle, look there, at the forest edge," Erzel said, pointing to the trees.

The wizard followed the Elf's gaze but at first did not see anything. Then, as if appearing instantly, Ectle caught sight of a large carriage moving towards the city. It had around it a large contingent of Knights riding in front and behind. Erzel reached out and placed a hand on the wizard's shoulder, realizing just what was happening.

"Ectle, send for Tanis at once. I will meet the two of you at the lower gate to the north."

The wizard nodded and turned in to the city to find the King of the Wood Elves. He was not entirely sure why the Elf wanted the King summoned but he had an idea. Erzel stood rigid on the balcony, watching as soldiers in the field stopped the carriage and just as quickly let it continue. He could not see the details of the carriage or the Knights around it but inside he felt a swell of excitement.

Erzel dropped down the stairs inside the keep and started through the inner halls and tunnels. He did not acknowledge the other Elves that he passed, focusing on making it down through the keep. As he made it out into the large courtyards outside he saw the first of the Knights appearing through the northern gate. He stopped and watched, seeing more and more soldiers arriving until he caught sight of the carriage. The banners on the carriage were familiar, the banners of Swanhaven.

The Knights came to a stop and dismounted, lining from the side of the carriage doors to the mouth of the keep. Erzel stood at the end of the Knights and waited, knowing inside the carriage was a royal of Swanhaven. Though he could not imagine why she would have come back to the lower lands, he was excited inside.

The door to the carriage opened and he watched as the Queen of Swanhaven appeared, looking around the city before she continued out through the line of soldiers. Erzel immediately dropped to one knee as she approached, lowering his gaze to the ground at her feet.

"Forgive me Queen Narissa, I have sent for your husband Tanis but he has yet to arrive. I had no knowledge of your arrival prior to seeing your carriage in the field."

"Do not worry Erzel. If you will please excuse me, I will retire to the keep and find Tanis."

Erzel gave another nod and waited to stand until the Queen had passed him. The Elf turned and watched the Queen until she disappeared inside. As he turned back to the soldiers around the carriage he watched another figure emerge. The Princess stepped down off the edge of the carriage and out through the lines of soldiers. She stopped ten feet away and stared at Erzel, as if seeing him for the first time all over again.

The two Elves stared for a few moments before they were able to move again. Erzel remained rooted where he stood but Rhen approached quickly, throwing her arms around his shoulders. He grit his teeth silently as her arm put pressure on the wound from the battle earlier but he did not stop her. They stood embraced in the cold wind together for what felt like an eternity. When they finally broke Erzel felt mostly confusion.

"Why... wh... what are you doing here? Why are you not still in Tvan where it is safe?"

"We couldn't stay there, underground, shut away from the light and the world outside. I don't care about the risks anymore. I don't care about Valsera, the Demon, their armies... I just want to be a part of the real world."

"What about... the..."

"The baby? Erzel, the baby is fine. I am fine. Valsera's armies aren't anywhere to be seen. Is it wrong to want to be with you through this?" she asked timidly, hoping he did not resent her decision.

Erzel sighed, remembering the surprise he felt when he had found the Princess aboard the ship when they were searching for the Dragon Isles. He did not mean to seem disappointed but she had been safe in Tvan. The Elf shook his head and reached up, touching her cheek.

"Erzel... you look pale... and... is something wrong?" she asked, seeing how he carried himself.

"No, things are fine. I just can not guarantee any form of safety out here. Yes, the Dwarven armies are here, mixed with the High Elves and Wood Elves. That does not mean things are as they should be. There is more happening here than you know my dear."

Rhen took his hand and turned to the keep. "Can we just go inside? That was a very draining trip and I just want to relax for a little while."

"Ok... after you Princess."

The soldiers that had arrived with the carriage quickly dispersed and moved throughout the city. They were quickly re-united with the other Wood Elves that had fought to keep the city safe and at last the army was whole again. The forces moved throughout the field, collecting the weapons and supplies that had belonged to the Elves while discarding everything the Goblins had brought.

Inside the keep Erzel and Rhen made their way up into the higher levels, finally finding themselves at the throne room. The doors were pushed open and they walked in, catching the attention of everyone inside. At the table sat Elendil, Tanis, Narissa, and Ardis. Scattered throughout the room he noticed Ectle, Kail, and Thorgrim. They all turned as the two doors closed loudly.

"Erzel... Rhen, thank you for joining us," Elendil said, waving to the available seats at the table. The two crossed the room and Erzel pulled out the chair, letting Rhen take the seat. He stood in behind her as Ectle and the rest of his group moved in around the table with the rest of them.

"We have a problem," the High Elf noted, looking to the Dwarf next to him.

Erzel looked at the Dwarf and then to the King. "What

happened Elendil?"

"It seems that a part of the Dwarven army is not present at the moment. The force under the command of Velex has laid waste to Cisalia. The Queen brought news of their intentions but by now there would be nothing left," Elendil said as he turned to the Dwarf. "Ardis, how can you attack a city with no way of defending itself? They were not soldiers."

The Dwarf looked at the King with a measure of surprise. "Elendil, we had no knowledge of Velex's intentions. Odar and I left the city with the main army a day ahead of him. I assure you, this was not something we meant to have happen."

Just as the words left the Dwarf's mouth, Kail turned, remembering what the Elder had said when they arrived in the field.

"The Humans are our enemies, lad, and all will be dealt with in the same harsh manner. Once a traitor, always a traitor. One day you will understand the price of war. Some will suffer, but all will learn the lesson."

Kail turned to the King but as he did he caught the glare from the Dwarf and stopped. Something in Ardis's eyes made him rethink speaking. Kail had caught the Dwarf in a lie but could not understand why. Why was he speaking as if he had no knowledge of the attack on Cisalia? He had admitted early in the battle that this was a punishment for an enemy being an enemy. Kail turned and looked out the large archway that led to the balcony. For now, he decided to keep what he knew to himself.

"They've turned a war into a slaughter. The people at Cisalia were not soldiers. They were women, and children, and the elderly. This was not a battle. It was a massacre," Tanis said angrily.

"I told you master Elf, this was not what our forces had intended on doing here. We marched to free Pentegarn of Valsera's stranglehold and I think we accomplished that. Now, the focus turns to the Pass of Merwold and to Qwaz and Nomaria... or should I take my armies back to Tvan?"

Elendil raised a hand to calm Tanis and looked at the Dwarf. "No Ardis, nothing like that will be necessary. I only ask that your forces maintain a little more discipline. Granted, we are at war, but killing innocent people makes them no better than those serving under Valsera."

Ardis jumped from the table angrily, staring at the two Elven Kings. "They were no innocents! They murdered countless Elves and Gnomes at the pass! They plotted to kill you here, in your own throne room! What measure of innocence are you speaking of?"

Tanis's temper flared even further. "Those left in Cisalia were not enemies! They did not come to war with us, they did not try to harm our people, they did not…"

"They stayed behind to support the army while it waged its war with you! They supported their King as he killed your people!"

"Tanis, Ardis, sit down!" Ectle yelled, his voice like thunder in the room. "I suggest you both get a grip on yourselves, now!"

The Dwarf did not sit as the wizard had ordered. Instead he walked around the table towards the large doors leading into the halls. He had been singled out of the group and no longer was there any form of gratitude for the actions of the Dwarven forces.

"Why do you go, Ardis?" Kail asked, approaching from the corner of the room where he had waited earlier. "I think you have more to tell the Kings. More they deserve to know."

Everyone looked from Kail to Ardis as the two forms faced one another. There had been tension between the people in the room before, but now that Kail had stepped forward it thickened. Ardis knew what the Dwarf had admitted to in the fields and knew that he had lied to the Kings. He would keep that knowledge a secret no longer.

"Ardis knew Velex took an army against the Humans remaining at Cisalia. He admitted it early on when the Dwarves first arrived in the fields. They sent Velex to destroy what remained of the Humans at Cisalia."

"That is a very strong accusation, Kail," Elendil chastised, not sure if he should believe what he was hearing.

"Yet he does not deny it. What sort of ally destroys the innocent, kills the helpless, chooses cruelty over mercy? There is no honor in what has been done. The shame is truly your own, Ardis," Kail said menacingly, his anger pushing past the boiling point.

"Kail, back down. Ardis, you may answer to these charges," the High Elf ordered.

The Dwarf stood in the center of the room away from the everyone else. No one in the room could quite understand how things had gotten so out of hand so fast. The armies of Dwarves had freed the Elves from the Goblin armies but in their brief moment of foolish stupidity, they had greatly damaged their status in the alliance. Ardis looked from each of the faces in the room, unwilling to back down from his actions.

"I did what was expected Elendil. An enemy was punished at the heads of our spears and the blades of our swords. Their betrayal earned them every punishment they received. If only your weaker race would open its eyes and look around, you would realize there is no time for blind compassion. You are going to have to learn that not everyone is worth saving. Do not make an enemy out of me, Elendil."

The final statement was all it took to cross the line. Erzel, Kail, Thorgrim, and Ectle turned on the Dwarf, forming a wall between the Elven royals and the Dwarven Elder. Elendil stood from the table and came around in front of his loyal soldiers. He did not want to make an enemy of the Dwarves, but he refused to allow an ally of the Elves to reek such havoc on innocent people.

"You are not my enemy Ardis, nor are Velex or Divos. Sadly, I can not allow one of my allies to ravage the defenseless as you have done at Cisalia. I am grateful for your efforts here at Pentegarn to drive out the Goblins and their armies, but I do not wish for you to remain here," the High Elf said reluctantly.

"Elendil... this is foolish. You will never break the force at the Pass of Merwold and never reach the city in time to stop that Demon and we both know it. Is this the way you want things to happen Elendil?"

The Elf turned and looked over his shoulder at the others in the room to make sure they were all in agreement. A collection of silent nods reassured the King and he turned back to the Dwarf.

"Take your armies back to Tvan. I can not have a force by my side that I can not trust."

Ardis took his eyes off of the King and walked away, cursing as he went. Before he made it to the doors he turned back to everyone in the room.

"When they are done with your armies, it will be my Dwarves that once again come to the rescue. This time Elendil...

and Tanis… my services go without price but if we are forced to come back to save the midlands again, there will be a cost. I am not going to protect those who take our strength for granted. Remember that as you march south. Remember what it will cost with this alliance in ruins."

The room sat in silence for a few minutes after the doors closed, wondering if they had made the right choice. It was Tanis that finally broke the quiet.

"Rhen, Narissa, what are you two doing here?" he asked, his tone bordering on anger.

The Queen held up a hand to quiet her husband. "Partly, we were coming to warn of the Dwarves and their intentions to destroy the people of Cisalia. I see though that this information is not currently needed. Unfortunately we were unable to move as swiftly as their armies. The Humans have been devastated."

"Still, had you been faster than their forces, word still would never have reached us with the siege in place. It was a foolish move to try and warn us of what they were plotting."

"Well you can be mad about it or you can get over it Tanis. I am not here to quarrel with you," the Queen replied hastily. She stood from the table and quickly hurried out onto the balcony.

"Narissa, wait."

The Wood Elf chased after her, leaving Elendil with his daughter and the rest of the group. They remained silent as the magnitude of what had happened sank in. They had just lost their most powerful ally and there was little if anything they could do to fix the alliance. The Dwarves would return to Tvan, leaving what remained of the High and Wood Elf armies to deal with the Goblins and Humans at the Pass of Merwold and the potential Slayer army if Infus was able to raise it.

"This changes things quite a bit, wouldn't you say, Elendil?" Ectle asked, realizing that now they would be forced to face the Goblins without the promise of reinforcements as before.

"Quite a bit. We are going to have to rethink things a little before we march out against those armies again."

Erzel looked up from the table quickly. "With all due respect my King, I am not sure if we have time to rethink the plan completely. We should stick to as much of it as we can. Even without the Dwarves, we can still attempt to enlist the Lizardmen and strike at either Qwaz or Nomaria."

"While the combined armies of Elves try to break through the armies holding the Pass of Merwold?"

"Yes my King, that would be the plan," Erzel nodded, realizing how insane the idea seemed to sound now.

Ectle leaned on the table, looking at the two. "Erzel is right my Lord. If we hesitate, we could end up losing far more. With or without the Dwarves, we have to do something. This is no time to hesitate. This is our moment to go on the offensive. If nothing else, let us enhance our current plan."

"What do you have in mind Ectle? The King asked, taking his seat at the head of the table.

Ectle looked to the balcony where Tanis and Narissa had disappeared. "Send the Wood Elves through the swamps with Erzel and our group. That way, if the Lizardmen do not turn against Infus with us, there will still be a sizable force moving out against the Demon. If they do turn, our numbers will have doubled with the added reptilian soldiers."

Elendil shook his head. "Tanis will not approve of that. His hatred for the Lizardmen will without a doubt be a problem."

"Convince him, order him if you have to," Ectle started, knowing that their tiny group would never be a match if the Lizardmen did not join their cause. "Tanis can be persuaded. With the Wood Elves moving around the Pass of Merwold through the swamps, we will definitely have an element of surprise. We need that my Lord Elendil."

"He's right my King," Erzel agreed. "Infus has every card in hand. Now is the time to throw something at the southern armies that they are not expecting. Catch them off guard and punish them dearly."

"Very well then," Elendil said with a nod. "I will do my best to convince him. The rest of you, get everything you need ready. The moment the Wood Elves are ready and willing, all of you will be headed south... and stay clear of the Pass of Merwold."

Elendil turned and slowly walked out onto the balcony where the two Wood Elves had disappeared before the conversation began. The tension in the room had eased slightly but the realization that the Dwarves were no longer willing to back the Elves was putting a great strain on everyone. Erzel crossed the room and stopped next to the window overlooking the fields outside of the city.

The armies of Dwarves could be clearly seen marching north out of the field towards their homelands. The lines of Dwarves seemed as confused as the people in the throne room, but they did not hesitate to march back to Tvan the moment they were ordered. It meant breaking the alliance, something the Humans had been twice punished for and were still suffering the consequences of, those who remained alive anyway.

Soon the fields and walls of Pentegarn would only house the Elves as they had in the past and though the army at Pentegarn had survived to fight another day, their losses were felt heavily across the city defenses. Even as their former allies marched away, the Elves were allowed a moment of hope. Word had spread as the Dwarves were leaving and that the Elven armies were going to march after those from Qwaz and Nomaria. What did they have to lose?

Erzel and Rhen left the room together, hand in hand as they looked to retire to a room to rest for what time they were going to have together. She knew that he was going to leave her behind again and had come to the realization that there was nothing she could do to stop that from happening. They walked in silence as they both were afraid to say what they were feeling inside.

He stopped her at the door and pushed it open, allowing her to walk in first before pulling it closed behind him. He stopped, his attention focused on her dress in her midsection. He knew inside was a growing life, a child that was partly him and partly the Princess. He did not mean to stare but he could not help it.

"What are you looking at Erzel?" she asked, catching his blank stare as she approached him.

The Elf blinked and fought for an answer. "I uh... I was just thinking about the... little one."

"Oh... yes I know. I was quite caught off guard myself. You should have seen my mother..."

"Your parents... Tanis..." Erzel interrupted, realizing it was the first time he had seen the Wood Elf King since their explosive shouting match in the fields outside of Eglarest.

"What's wrong with them Erzel?"

"Nothing… this was just the first time I have been face to face with your father since we left you at Eglarest. As I recall, things did not go very well that day."

"Do not worry about my father. When this all ends, we will be together and happy. No more wars to wage, no more Demons to fight, no more armies to keep you looking over your shoulder. Things will be different."

Erzel sat down on the edge of the bed and ran his hands through his hair, hiding the expression of discomfort as he felt stiffness in his back where he had been wounded. He had to sleep, to rest for what was about to take place but at the moment he was so far from sleep that it was out of the question. Rhen saw his discomfort and exhaustion and crossed the room, stopping in front of him only inches away.

Erzel looked up and ran his hand across the front of her stomach where he felt the smooth skin behind the dress. Behind it was a baby, a child growing inside of the young Princess. She reached down and pulled his head against her stomach, gently stroking his head as he breathed slowly. It was calming, to find himself in her arms again after the bloody battles that continued to plague the countryside.

"You need to rest Erzel," she whispered, gently running the tips of her fingernails back and forth across his scalp.

"Yes…"

"Do you need me to leave you alone?"

"No…"

Erzel was almost in a hypnotic state as the tips of her nails kept a rhythm of small circular motions. It was the first moment of true relaxation he had felt in quite some time. The last month had been spent on edge, knowing any moment could very well spell a disastrous end to him and the rest of his soldiers. Now he was safe and allowed a brief time to rest before being thrust back into the thick of battle once more.

Rhen stopped long enough for the Elf to turn and lie back on the bed, his body finally giving in to the exhaustion. He stretched back out and Rhen reached up, unfastening the clip holding her dress in place and letting it drop to the floor. She smoothed the silky white fabric of her slip and lay down next to the Elf. She snuggled up against him and draped her left arm across his chest. He was already asleep by the time she kissed his cheek.

Erzel woke even before the sun came up, feeling the sleeping form next to him. He struggled to climb out of the bed without waking her but as he stepped onto the floor the Princess stirred briefly. She rolled onto her right side and her eyes cracked open, focusing on the Elf standing in the middle of the room. She slid her elbow up under her and pushed herself into a sitting position.

"Is it time... already?" Rhen asked softly, fighting off a yawn.

"Go back to sleep my dear. I just needed to stretch for a moment. I do not think it is time for our forces to leave the city. Just get some rest."

Erzel stretched, being sure not to strain the injury that was beginning to plague him. He did not want to let on that he was injured to the Princess and managed a smile. Erzel crossed the room to where she still lay on the bed and leaned down, kissing her gently on the lips. Rhen savored the moment and after what seemed like only a second she felt his lips leave hers.

The Elf pulled himself together and stopped at the door, looking back at the Princess who watched his every move.

"I will be back as soon as I check on things around the castle. I have to make sure they are not ready to leave. I promise to come back to see you very soon my dear Princess."

Erzel slipped into the hallway and closed the door behind him, moving through the dimly lit corridors as the effects of sleep slowly began to wear off. He stopped outside of the throne room and pushed the door open, finding the room completely deserted. He scanned it a second time and then headed further down the hall to the stairs. The castle was lifeless with the exception of the occasional soldier passing by, keeping their rounds.

Erzel followed the staircases down through the heart of the keep until he walked out into the courtyards around the castle. There he caught his first glimpse of life from the group. Ectle was standing near the edge of the city wall looking up into the dark sky. The snowflakes that had at one time dotted the breeze were now replaced with a much heavier snowfall. The winter air was colder now that the night had fallen and Erzel rubbed his shoulders.

"Quite a bit cooler now isn't it?" Ectle asked without turning to see the Elf approaching.

"Yes, a lot cooler. What are you doing out here so early in the morning?"

"Just looking at the sky. This is probably the most peaceful things have been around here in quite some time. It is almost strange, knowing the battles that have been waged over the last few weeks here in the fields and south of Pentegarn."

"What about the others? How soon will they have us ready to leave? Has Tanis agreed with Elendil's plan?"

"Yes, though it took a lot of convincing, the Wood Elf did finally see the benefit of allying ourselves with the Lizardmen in the swamps. After all, this could be the only way to match Infus swing for swing."

Erzel rubbed his arms again and looked out across the dark fields as the snowflakes dotted his face. He felt the cold flecks of snow hitting his skin and stepped up next to the wizard.

"So, how soon are we supposed to leave?"

"At first light. The rest know already. I was waiting to tell you until you were awake. I did not want to... interrupt," Ectle said, turning to look at the Elf for the first time.

"Well, that will allow for another few hours then. I think I will return to the castle until the sun rises. I told Rhen I would come back to say my goodbyes. If you will excuse me."

"Of course..."

Erzel turned and left the wizard standing alone in the snowy wind. He was quick to get back inside where the air wasn't as cold as it was out in the open. He climbed the stairs slowly, taking one at a time until he finally reached the top.

Erzel stopped and peeked into the throne room one last time before heading on to the room he had left earlier. He pushed the door open silently, peering in to find the young Elf sound asleep on the bed. He closed the door without a sound and crossed the room to the foot of the bed. With the effects of sleep worn off he wasn't nearly as tired as he had been. He slid down onto the bed behind the Princess and draped an arm across her side. He had a few hours left before the sun came up and wanted to spend them resting with the Princess. He leaned close and kissed her neck, taking in her scent one more time.

The Enemy of My Enemy

*T*he sunlight had just started to break over the horizon when Erzel rose. Rhen was already awake and dressed, sitting on the edge of the bed. He quickly swung his legs over the edge and sat next to her, rubbing his eyes to clear them once again. Rhen leaned over and wrapped her arm around his shoulder.

"I guess this means it is time?" she asked quietly, dreading his answer.

"Yes. We were lucky to have this much time together, Rhen, but the sooner we get moving, the sooner we can put our plans into work. I am sorry, Rhen, I have to get to the throne room."

"I'm coming with you."

The two left the room and started down the hall, walking side by side until they reached the doors. Pushing them open they found the majority of the group that had agreed to head into the swamps. The only ones missing were Nimir who was not going, and Ectle.

"Erzel, as always you arrive just as I thought to send for you. It is just about time to get moving," said Elendil as he crossed the room.

"I think I am just about as ready as I will ever be. Have your forces been told of what to expect in the swamps, Tanis?"

"Yes..." the Wood Elf replied, keeping his conversation with the Elf as short as possible. He still had not forgiven Erzel for the shape his daughter was now in.

A servant brought a large package wrapped in brown cloth and handed it to Elendil, giving a quick bow and then disappearing back out of the doors. Elendil opened the corner and smiled, handing the item to Erzel. The Elf looked at it and then up to the King.

"What is this my King?"

"Open it..."

Erzel pulled the corners open and then unfolded the brown cloth. He tossed it to the floor beside him and looked at the cloth in his hand. It was crisp and deep blue with a tuft of white in the corner. He unfolded the fabric and as it spread he realized what he was holding. It was the tunic of his order, the Order of the White Eagle. He looked up at the King who was now holding the shield that matched the tunic.

"Elendil, I had nearly forgotten all about these. The... Order was destroyed at the Pass of Merwold. Well, I never thought there was anything left of my Order."

"This is basically all that remains. I want you to wear it into battle. You've hidden your identity through the trek to Tvan, through your voyage to and across the Dragon Isles, and all the way back across Nalawren. If this is the last time these armies march against our enemies in the south, I want you to do it as yourself."

Erzel nodded and took the shield from the King. He walked to the table and leaned the shield against his chair, waiting for the meeting of their forces to get started. Elendil took his place at the head of the table and waited for everyone to be seated. He set a rolled parchment on the table and rolled it across the table. The parchment held a long map and everyone leaned forward to get a look at it.

"Alright, everyone pay close attention as time is now of the essence. Our forces are about to be divided even further with the loss of the Dwarves. Erzel, Ectle, Kail, Lavian, and Thorgrim will be joined by Tanis and his forces of Wood Elves. I will lead the remaining army of High Elves myself."

"Agreed..." Tanis said with a nod.

"Your force will head for the swamps and by whatever means necessary, recruit whatever remains of the Lizardmen to fight alongside you. It will take everything you have to break whatever is left at Qwaz... or Nomaria for that matter. At the same time, I will lead the High Elves into the Pass of Merwold once more and we will fight there to keep their armies busy, and their attention off of your movements."

As Elendil laid out the events and plans for what they

were about to attempt the doors opened and Ectle entered. He took his seat beside Erzel without a word and whirled his thumbs across one another, waiting for the king to continue.

"Thank you for joining us Ectle."

The wizard gave a slow nod and the King continued with his speech.

"There is little chance that my armies will break those at the pass so it appears that your forces will be on your own once you leave the swamps. We may not be able to break the armies at the pass, but I do know we can keep them occupied. That is all I have set at the moment. Suggestions are welcome."

The group was silent as the information sank in. Knowing they would be set against the armies still at the cities in the south without any form of available reinforcements was a stressful thought. They did not have time to try and make amends with the Dwarves. This was their only hope and they were going to have to take it.

"I don't think there are any objections my King. The sooner we get on the move, the sooner we can put this plan to action. I will meet everyone in the courtyards below when you are ready," Ectle said, standing from the table.

Everyone in the room began moving around, leaving their seats and continuing with their tasks and duties. Elendil and Tanis continued looking over the map to see if there was anything they had forgotten or missed. Erzel gathered his shield and tunic and headed for the room to change before they left. He closed the door behind him and stripped down to the chain armor covering his torso. He heard the door close behind him and turned his head.

"Kail? What are you doing?" the Elf asked, trying to refasten the armor on his shoulder.

"It looks like you could use a hand. I take it that wound is still giving you some trouble."

Erzel did not answer. He did not want to think of his wound slowing him down when he needed to be his strongest.

"Just help me with the clasp, there, at the back of the neck. I don't care about the wound. I don't have time to worry about it."

Kail reached to the clasp of the armor and took a look down at the area where the arrow had pierced the skin and bit his lower lip. The wound was seriously inflamed and swollen, surely causing the Elf great discomfort. Kail pulled the clasp tight and fastened it to the hook. As Erzel turned, Kail looked him directly in the eyes, his face very concerned.

"Erzel, the wound is not healing. It looks rough. You should let one of the healers take another look at it soon."

"We don't have time, Kail. The forces are getting ready to move as we speak. There is nothing they can do for it now..."

"You'll not live through the journey, Erzel. The travel could put so much strain on the wound that the infection will spread. You will surely..."

"Kail, I said stop and I mean it! The wound is a wound, I have had them before and will surely get them again. I am not going to sit here and watch the armies head out to war. Keep this quiet Kail. I will join you and the rest of our group shortly in the courtyards below the keep."

The conversation was over. There was no way he was going to admit to being injured when there was so much at stake. He was moving out with the armies no matter what condition he was in. The Elf had lost countless soldiers and several close friends because of the armies in the south. He was out for revenge.

Kail nodded and left the room, leaving Erzel alone for a while. The Elf knew Kail was right and that his wound was getting worse as time progressed. He could not see the wound on his back but he could feel it. The skin felt hot and tight, a sure sign that an infection and swelling was occurring. He picked up the shield and tested the weight, remembering the feel even though it had been some time since he had held the shield in his hands.

There was a knock at the door and it opened slowly. Rhen peeked in and then slipped through the crack, closing the door behind her. She pressed her back against the door and stared at the Elf.

"Something is wrong with you, Erzel. I could tell when we arrived, I could see it in the way you walked out of the throne room. Are you going to tell me what is happening or not?"

Erzel did not want to lie to the Princess but at the moment, giving her another reason to worry seemed even worse. He looked around the room, stalling as he searched for a believable excuse to his condition. In the end, only one thing came to mind that would suffice as an answer.

"Rhen... Alora died."

The Elf Princess looked at the Elf and cocked her head to the side. "What do you mean? Where is she?"

"Dead... we burned her body in the lands above the fields of Pentegarn. The Slayers, they killed her just before we got here."

Rhen stared at him with obvious shock.

"Why didn't you tell me sooner, Erzel?"

"We've been a little busy. Between nearly losing Pentegarn and now the plans to attack the Pass of Merwold, Qwaz, and possibly even Nomaria. I guess it slipped my mind momentarily. My apologies."

"Did she... go quick?"

Erzel looked at the ground for a moment, recalling the events of the battle where she had been killed. He could remember the pain the Dragon was in after the three arrows had met their targets. She was in agony and there was nothing they could do to help her.

"Fairly quick Rhen. The Slayers are a brutal and savage race and sadly we paid the price on the Dragon Isles and in the fields above Pentegarn. There will only be more bloodshed in the days to come Rhen. We have to march my dear."

"Just wait a minute Erzel. I want to... I just want to see you for just a minute longer... before you go. Please, sit down."

The Elf leaned his shield against the wall and followed her to the bed where he joined her. She rubbed the back of his hand and kissed him on the cheek. She wanted to spend every second she could with him. A thought came to mind and she turned his face to hers.

"If it is a boy... what shall we name him?"

Erzel didn't have any idea. He had never really thought it through and being put on the spot did not make the answer come any easier. "I uh... I have no idea. How about you?"

"I want it to be a girl, Erzel. I want to name her Eryn."

Erzel nodded. "I like that name, for a girl. So what if it is a boy though? You don't have any names coming to mind in that case?"

Rhen shook her head. There had not been any time to sit with him and talk about names, or about their future. Every time they saw one another after the battle on the Dragon Isles was met with a rush to mobilize and prepare for war. They'd not had any sort of time together in quite a while.

"No, not yet. I really want it to be a little girl though. I can see her running up the stairs back home, combing her hair just before sending her off to bed, picking flowers with her just after a brief summer rain. I dream about her."

Erzel had the overwhelming stress of what was about to take place looming over him and that alone was enough to make it nearly impossible to focus on anything else. He knew how much it meant to the Princess but he had never really thought about names or whether he preferred a boy or a girl. It was difficult to concentrate on anything other than the war they were about to wage once more.

"I assure you Rhen, once this is all over and done with, we will sit down and decide on our names for either a boy or girl. Right now though, I am having trouble concentrating on anything other than what our forces are set to face. I apologize."

"It's ok Erzel, I understand. I suppose that means you will be leaving now?" Rhen asked, rising from the bed and standing in front of him.

Erzel reached up and took her by the hand, pulling the Princess down into his lap. She wrapped her arm around his back across his shoulders and waited, wondering what the Elf would say this time before leaving her behind.

"Listen, Rhen. There is no reason for us to be naïve, we both know how this could turn out. This is our moment, our time to cherish before all hell breaks loose again. Right now, there is only you and me. Lets make the most of it."

Rhen sat for a few moments, wondering what she should do in such a brief amount of time. She stood up from his lap and then turned, changing her position so that she could sit in his lap, a knee draped over either side of his legs. She had to lift her dress up to her hips to slide down onto his lap. The hesitation came from Erzel this time but the Princess was quick to fill the moment. She leaned down and locked her lips firmly against his, her hands raking down his back. The sudden aggression caught Erzel off guard, though he welcomed the attention.

Erzel ran his fingers up her legs to her thighs and then eventually across her butt. He could feel her firm skin underneath the dress and the touch of his hands on her only seemed to intensify her passion. Rhen's eyes were closed tight as she reached up and unfastened the dress behind her head. The straps of the dress fell forward revealing her chest to the Elf again.

Erzel instinctively kissed down her neck to her chest, his lips caressing her soft skin. He brought his hands up to her firm breasts, kissing her again and again as the fire inside of him was soon taking over. She pulled his head tightly against her, running her fingers through his hair as his lips continued to probe across her body.

"Erzel... do we... have time to..."

The two Elves stared at one another for a brief second, wondering if what they were both desiring was a possibility. Just as Erzel nodded and traced his lips down her neck to her chest there was a strong knock at the door.

Erzel and Rhen pulled away and looked at one another, realizing that their moment was coming to an abrupt halt. They stared at each other for a moment before another knock was heard.

"Erzel, everyone is moving to the courtyards. You should join us."

The voice was Kail's. Erzel looked at his love briefly and a frown appeared on his face. They had been locked in the middle of passion so intense that he had completely forgotten about meeting with the soldiers and the two Kings. In those few minutes, all that mattered to him was the Princess. His eyes dropped down her body and he closed them, shaking his head.

"I'm sorry Rhen, I do have to go. I uh... I... I'm just sorry," he stuttered as she stood from his lap, covering her chest with the front of her dress.

Rhen fastened the clasp back behind her neck and smoothed the front of her dress as Erzel retrieved his shield. They were silent, each aching for the touch of the other yet knowing they had no choice but to head to the courtyards at once. She felt her stomach flutter and bit her lower lip to control the desire attempting to overpower her.

"Ok Erzel, I'm coming with you."

Together they left the room, finding Kail just down the hall waiting on them. He didn't say a word as they fell in behind him and the three moved down to the courtyards outside of the castle. Rhen slid her hand in against his and their fingers inter-twined. As they moved out into the open they could see both King Tanis and Elendil standing with Narissa, Ectle, Thorgrim, Lavian, and Nimir. Erzel stopped and gave a bow to the Kings and Queen.

"Thank you for joining us, Erzel. I had briefly wondered if you had forgotten," Elendil greeted, turning to the rest of the group.

"Of course, my King. Are the forces ready to move out?"

"The Wood Elves are gathered outside of the city waiting for orders to move out. As you can see, your group is ready to move as well. Alright, line up!"

The soldiers moved in around the King of the High Elves and stood at attention awaiting their orders. The King walked down the short line of soldiers followed by the King of the Wood Elves. Nimir stepped back out of the line in beside Rhen and watched, knowing there was nothing he could do to help the oth-ers in their attack on the armies in the southlands. He elected to stay behind in Pentegarn with the Princess, offering what little protection he could.

"This is how things are about to unfold. King Tanis will be leading his Wood Elves into the heart of the swamps with the help of Erzel and his group. They will infiltrate the Lizardmen, rally their allegiance, and continue on into the fields outside of either Qwaz or Nomaria. You can expect heavy resistance from Goblins, Ogres, even Slayers, but in the end, it is up to you to fin-ish this."

The group listened intently to everything the King had to say, knowing there was going to be one shot at defeating the forces on their own land. There was no retreat and failure was not an option.

"I will lead the remaining High Elven army into the Pass of Merwold and keep their army busy. With them set on fighting up here on our lands your forces will be free to engage without the threat of their main army coming back on you. This is the mission you have accepted. With any amount of luck, this will be the last push we ever have to make into the southlands. We'll rid our lands of this plague."

The group nodded in agreement and with one last fare-well from King Elendil they started through the city towards the plains. Rhen walked between Erzel and her father and upon exiting into the fields outside of the city she turned and hugged her father one last time. The exchange was brief but the emotions were definitely on edge. After parting with her father, the Queen Narissa took her place, wrapping her arms around her husband, kissing him passionately.

As the group gave their goodbyes, Lavian mounted her Warbird and took to the sky, planning to offer a keen eye on their movements and warn of any enemy that might manage a surprise ambush on the force. She had no need for the farewells of the others, knowing her people were all dead and gone.

Rhen turned to Erzel and reached up, running her hand across his chin. "You know that I love you, right?"

"Of course, Rhen, and I love you as well. This will not be the end. I will come back to hold you again, I promise. We'll be happy after all of this ends."

The Wood Elf wrapped her arms around his waist and looked up into his eyes. Their exchange earlier had left her dreaming of having him alone again yet knowing that in minutes she would have to watch him ride away with the rest of the soldiers. She was miserably in love, hoping she would have the chance to hold him again one day.

"Stop worrying, Rhen. We will come back to Pentegarn, I promise. I never plan on breaking a promise to you. No matter what, I will do everything in my power to make it back here alive."

Rhen pushed herself a little higher on her toes, kissing Erzel on the lips and then on the cheek. She finally pulled away and slid past her parents with a slight blush on her face. Their horses were brought to them and they all took their mounts, even Thorgrim. The Dwarf perched precariously in the saddle of the animal as Tanis and Erzel led out towards the trees to the south. Riding next to the King, Erzel could feel the tension between them, knowing he had witnessed the Elf kiss his daughter goodbye.

"Do you love her, Erzel?" the King asked finally, cutting through the silence.

"Yes my Lord, very much. I worry that I may never see her again and if that were the case, I will never see the child either."

Tanis stared straight ahead as the Elf's words sank in.

"She loves you dearly as well. Never before has she ever stood up to us in the way she did after you left Tvan. It was very surprising indeed."

"My apologies, my Lord, I never meant to cause trouble for you and your family."

The brief conversation was over and though he still felt odd riding in next to the King, he felt somewhat better knowing there had been some sort of exchange between them that did not involve hostility. The Wood Elves behind them formed a long line leaving the city, all knowing what their duties would be once they reached the swamps in the south.

The hatreds the Elves had carried for the Lizardmen guaranteed there would be hostilities but there was no alternative. They had to try or there would be no way of breaking Infus's army and the forces that might soon be flooding out of some otherworldly portal.

Back in Pentegarn the army of High Elves was beginning to mass in the fields as the Wood Elves had done an hour or so earlier. They massed every available soldier that was still battle ready: archers, footmen, spearmen, and what remained of the Knights. Elendil had retired to the throne room to dress for the march to the south. His armor was brought from the armory and strapped onto him and with it came his sword. The High Elf walked proudly down the stairs to the courtyard where he found Narissa, Rhen, and Nimir waiting to see him off.

"This is goodbye my friends. Narissa, I will do everything in my power to see that your husband is returned to you. Likewise, I will do the same for you Rhen with Erzel. I know you both love them deeply and once this has ended you can all live peacefully. Farewell."

The King turned and reached up to his horse, pulling himself up into the saddle and taking the reins from the soldier at the front of the animal. He pulled them and gave a quick snap, urging the horse forward. The King rode out in front of the army alone, keeping an eye on the trees and thick shrubbery that covered the southern edge of the fields. The soldiers behind him had hardly even had time to rest after the massive siege at Pentegarn and now were marching into another battle.

Though the soldiers were tired, hungry, and many suffering from the wounds they had received in earlier battles, they marched on. Even with the worst of conditions the Elves were not willing to show weakness or allow their enemies to believe they were beaten. They would meet the forces believed to be holding at the Pass of Merwold and they would fight until there was no one left to fight.

Elendil rode with his head held high, ignoring the thoughts of defeat and death that were swimming through his head. If he was going to ride into the fray of battle, his mind had to be clear of anything that might damage his chances of victory. He had to keep his head up, for the sake of his soldiers. Seeing the King in a state of defeat before the first swing would ultimately lead them down a path of destruction.

A Knight moved in beside the King with a nod of respect.

"My King, if I may, what is your plan of action once we arrive at the Pass of Merwold?"

"Charge their forces, overwhelm their front lines, and crush their defensive positions before they have a chance to regroup and reinforce."

He said it all in one breath, as if he had rehearsed it for this occasion. The plan of course sounded very simple at first but when it was thought over there were numerous flaws. Charging them would be very simple, overwhelming their front lines was a very real possibility, but breaking their front lines and cutting through their reinforcements was something that had yet to be achieved.

Even in the battles for the fields and walls of Pentegarn, the Elves hardly managed to push the Goblins and Ogres back out of their cities. When the Elves finally did break them and push them back out of the outer city it took a desperate charge from the High Elven Knights and footmen combined with the Wood Elf archers and the wizard. They were now without the Wood Elves and without the strength of Erzel's group. The wizard made a huge difference through the course of the siege, possibly even averting the fall of Pentegarn with his spells.

"Is there another plan, in case the first does not have the desired effects?"

Elendil reached down and rubbed the neck of his horse, thinking things over for a decent explanation. "We do what we have to do. We fight to keep their armies busy and their attention away from the force moving on the cities. So long as we keep them occupied, Erzel and Tanis have a chance."

The King's horse kept its lead over the army but after a few hours of riding through the forest he sent scouts out ahead of him. The light cavalry moved swiftly even though the brush and trees would normally slow down other soldiers. The main army kept moving until King Elendil began seeing signs of the initial camps of first force at the pass. The scouts all three returned from over the hill and the word was passed confirming their beliefs.

"It is true, my King. The Goblins and Ogres have massed on the other side of the Pass of Merwold, waiting for us to come out into the open. It seems clear on the northern side of the pass but we did not spread through the trees to be sure though."

"That is fine. We will not waste time setting up camps or preparing our own defenses. We are here to drive them back out of our lands. We hit them hard, we drive them back, we make them run!"

The Knights and soldiers gave a loud cheer of agreement, echoing through the trees all across the pass. There was no need to remain quiet now. They had no intention of trying to mask their approach. They wanted the armies to know they were there and that they were coming for them. Elves began banging their weapons against their shields, the loud steel against steel echo spreading through the forest.

Elendil drew his sword and urged his horse forward slowly, the footmen and spearmen moving past him to form the front lines. The army moved through the trees past the ruins that were at one time the main barracks for the Elven forces at the pass. They did not give the charred remains a second glance, focusing on the incline and the pass that would soon open to the river.

They could now hear the war chants from the opposite side of the river, the Goblins trying to whip their forces into a frenzy to face the Elves once more. The bloodthirsty creatures gave whoops and yells, daring the Elves to approach even though they had recently been driven from the lands around Pentegarn. They were brazen, fearless, but most of all, reckless. They were so sure that they would hold the pass that they hardly seemed concerned with holding formations or preparing at all. Even so, would it be enough to give the Elves the upper hand?

Erzel and Tanis had dropped back a bit, allowing Ectle to take the lead as they crossed into the swamps. They were forced to abandon their horses just outside the swamps, continuing on foot through the marsh. The wizard had been there before and would possibly know his way around though every scraggly tree and pool of muck all looked the same. Thorgrim had also been through the worst of the swamp but hardly took a step past Erzel and Tanis, letting their Elven ears and sharp eyes keep a close watch on the surrounding swamplands.

They had been marching through the swamps for over an hour and there had been no sign of life. No random animals crossing their paths, no tracks or trails of any sort. Ectle held up his hand to signal them all to stop and the gesture was carried through the soldiers. The wizard waited, his nose twitched as he stabbed through the thick fogs trying to catch the slightest hint of their targets, the Lizardmen. At the moment, the area was as still as death.

Erzel trudged forward a few steps through the mud and stopped just behind the wizard. "What is it, Ectle? Do you feel them?"

"No Erzel, and there lies the problem. I do not feel anything. No sign of life, no evidence that anything has moved about the swamps in some time. Something is amiss here, I just can not place it. I think it wise to be on our guard."

"Yes, lead the way when you are ready," Erzel said as he turned back to the King behind him.

"What did he say?" Tanis asked, watching as the wizard took a few steps further into the fog.

"He believes we should have seen a sign of something by now, of anything. Keep your guard up and your eyes open."

Ectle moved ahead, with Erzel following and Tanis behind him. Kail and Thorgrim remained directly in front of the army which wound back through the trees and muddy waters. They walked on through the area, stopping briefly for Ectle to get his bearings. When he came to a stop again Erzel could see why.

Ahead was a stretch of drier land and all over it were signs of a major battle. Deep gashes and gouges in the earth accompanied by the festering carcasses left after the skirmish.

The dead bodies filled the swamp air with an even more pungent odor. Blood filled the swampy water and covered the ground all around the area. Elves crowded in around to see what had halted their progress. It was the first time many of the Elves had ever ventured into the swamps of the Lizardmen.

The fog was setting in again and thickening, making Ectle strike the butt of his staff against the ground, making the cluster of stones atop the staff glow brightly. The beams of light cut through the fog, revealing a similar scene deeper in the swamp. The forces of Elves spread a little and continued deeper through the heart of the marshes. Festering bodies filled the areas no matter which direction they looked and soon there were more questions than answers. No matter where they looked there were the remnants of a massive and gory battle and through all of it, no survivors.

Ectle moved in between Erzel and Tanis, scanning through the endless masses of corpses. No life was visible, no sign of any who had managed to survive. From the looks of things though, the battles had taken place weeks earlier. From the smell and deterioration of the bodies, the heat and humidity of the swamps had accelerated the rot of the flesh.

Tanis reached up and covered his mouth and nose briefly as a gust of wind blew the strong odor into his face. The swamps remained warm and moist year round though the lands around them managed to grow cold and snow fell freely throughout the northern lands. In the south, it was rare to see the frigid temperatures and the ice and snow that accompanied it.

Erzel unfastened his cloak and tossed it to the side in the swamp as his temperature was climbing higher and higher the longer they stayed in the marshlands. Ectle looked to the right at the discarded clothing with a raised eyebrow.

"Erzel?"

"It's too hot for the extra layers. I don't have the time to worry about neatly folding it and leaving it somewhere I can pick it back up. Come on, keep moving."

They continued on deeper through the swamps and the sight was the same no matter where they moved. Ectle recalled the encampment of the Lizardmen somewhere close by and pressed on, determined to manage what King Elendil had ordered. He would find out why the swamps were filled with the bodies of

Lizardmen as well as Goblins and Ogres.

Just as Ectle had expected the thick swamps opened up into a more stable ground and the large encampment of the Lizardmen came into view. It was just as he remembered it with one exception. It was completely in ruins.

What was left of the huts and crude buildings were charred black while others were piles of ruins. The bodies of the dead covered almost every square inch of the ground and the Elves moved in and about them carefully in case one was not as dead as it seemed. From the smell, they were all dead. The army stopped as Erzel and Ectle evaluated the situation.

"What are your thoughts, Erzel?" the wizard asked, looking around at the countless dead.

"I... have none. This is definitely not something I ever expected. This is... horrible."

"Horrible? They were just another enemy in the end. Better they've been dealt with now to save us the problems later," Tanis added without the slightest hint of remorse.

Erzel glanced over his shoulder at the Elf but bit his lip as the urge to snap back at Tanis became too tempting. The Wood Elf was right, the creatures were an enemy but they had sought to make them allies, even if only temporarily. Now it appeared there was no chance for such an alliance. They were too late.

"So what happened here?" Tanis asked nonchalantly.

Ectle looked around the area and shrugged. "The forces of Valsera had been seen battling with them in the swamps when Nimir and Thorgrim were trapped here. It appears that Valsera's forces finally finished off all that was left of them."

"So what now? We don't have to worry about the Lizardmen so on to the fields outside of Qwaz?" Tanis asked as he nudged one of the dead bodies at his feet.

Erzel finally turned, his mind made up. "As much as you seem to think this is a good thing, this only means more of your Wood Elves are going to die when we get there. The Lizardmen were something we could use against Valsera's armies to keep our own casualties at a minimum. I personally care about those I am leading, so this is a moment of sorrow for me. Perhaps not for someone without a heart though."

"What did you just say to me?" Tanis growled as he took a step toward the angry Elf. "I'd be careful, Erzel, there is no

Dragon here to save you this time."

Erzel reacted without thinking, his anger pushed far past the boiling point. He didn't reach for his sword or dagger but instead lashed out quickly, striking the Wood Elf across the face with his armored fist. Tanis stumbled back and the Wood Elves in the clearing suddenly pressed forward, their spears and swords prepared to defend their King. Tanis raised his hand to stop the soldiers, staring back at the Elf with an amusing smirk.

"Well that's more like it. You're lucky this group needs you and that King Elendil believes you able to lead us to victory or I would kill you right here. Instead, if you are still standing after this is over, I'll personally see to it that you are punished."

Ectle grabbed Erzel by the back of his armor as he took another step toward the King, jerking him back away from the mass of soldiers watching. "What are you thinking you fool? This is no time for you to drive a wedge in what is left of this alliance. The Dwarves are gone and you want to split the races of Elves as well?"

"Get off of me, Ectle!" Erzel ordered, jerking free and wheeling around to look at the wizard.

The wizard pushed him back another step and pointed back to the soldiers and their King. "You'll destroy the only chance we have. You'll send only Thorgrim, Kail, Lavian, you, and myself in against the forces at Qwaz if you are not careful. What chance do you think we will have?"

"I'd rather die in the fields alone than cower under someone who openly insults me and laughs about it. I do not serve him," Erzel replied coldly, making sure to stress his words.

Tanis approached and Ectle took a deep breath, praying he could suppress their tempers long enough to find a measure of peace between them. There was only one thing now that they shared.

"This has to stop. Tanis, you want to make it home to your wife and your daughter, right?"

"Right."

"Erzel, you promised Rhen that you would return for her before you left correct?"

"Yes..."

Ectle stepped in between them and looked from side to side. "Then put this disagreement behind you and open your eyes. We've already lost every ally in our alliance. The Humans betrayed us, the Dwarves abandoned us, the Gnomes were completely killed off. If this continues you two will successfully split the races of Elves and kill any shred of alliance that remains between us. Is that what you want?"

"No," they replied simultaneously.

"You had no right..." Erzel started, remembering Alora's horrible death in the forests above Pentegarn.

"I apologize, for the sake of the Dragon that is. Not to you. Just be grateful you are still standing after what you just did."

"As close to an apology as I would ever have expected from someone like you," Erzel snapped back, trying to keep what he really wanted to say hidden inside.

"See there, the best of friends once again. Come on, we have to keep moving. I will think of something before we get to the plains where Infus awaits us."

The formations had changed somewhat with Ectle remaining in lead, Erzel directly behind him, with Kail and Thorgrim between the Elf and the King of the Wood Elves. They moved slowly, taking in the sight of the countless dead that covered every inch of the surrounding swamplands. The worst of it was the smell, a never wavering odor of rotting carcasses and festering flesh. It was enough to make the hardest stomach turn.

The fog spread apart with a strong wind and the group watched as the Warbird dropped lower to the ground, scanning the land to see if it was firm enough to land. After a moment the Warbird carefully stretched out its legs and gripped the ground, pulling its wings in to its body. Lavian looked across the scene and dropped onto the soft ground.

"What have you seen Lavian?" Ectle asked as they approached.

"This is what the swamps look like everywhere. Where I could see the ground through the fogs there is nothing but death and carnage. I have not seen a sign of life the entire time I've been above."

The Warbird behind her flapped its wings and jumped into the air, disappearing quickly. Ectle watched and then turned to the Celestial Knight.

"The smell. It will not stay here with the rotting odor in

the air," she answered even before the wizard asked the question.

"How near is the edge of the swamp?" Erzel asked her, looking off to what he believed was the west.

"Not far now. I could see the towers of Qwaz in the distance to the west. Another twenty minutes. I take it there is no alliance with the races here in the swamps then."

The wizard shook his head. "There is nothing in the swamps left to ally ourselves with. We will do what we must when we arrive without them."

Lavian fell in line next to Kail and the march continued through the defiled swamplands. The army of Wood Elves behind them did not make a sound, marching in complete silence as the thoughts of what would happen once they pushed out into the plains raced through their heads. There had almost been a touch of hope that the Lizardmen would join their forces, even if just to give them larger numbers. Now their hope had withered and died.

Erzel felt his boots sink in the mud and he pulled loose once more, looking for a little firmer land. No matter where he looked though, there was nothing available. They would have to trudge through the softening mud, hopefully not exhausting themselves before they broke the tree lines and charged the city.

Twenty minutes turned into forty and still there was no sign of the end of the swamp. As the army closed in on an hour of marching Erzel almost felt as if they had wandered off course and were now even further away from where they should be. When he looked up he noticed the fog clearing and the trees becoming less and less grotesque. They were getting closer to the lands around Qwaz, which meant that much closer to yet another massive bloodbath.

Erzel raised his hand and the army stopped. He and Ectle crept forward further and stopped in the thickest part of the trees, peering out at the plains. Further away was Qwaz. With it came the first shred of good news they had received in a long time. Around the city there was no great army waiting for them. Not even a presentable force to challenge their Wood Elves.

Just as the wizard and Elf allowed a smile of relief cross their faces their happiness was stripped away instantly. From around the southern side of the city came a fairly large force of Goblins followed by what was unmistakably a full battalion of

Slayers. They marched in solid formations and they numbered no more than a hundred, that was more than enough to cause disastrous problems for the Wood Elves.

Ectle looked to the side at the Elf and bit his lip momentarily. "Well, this is where a genius plan would really come in handy."

"So you have one?"

The wizard sighed. "No... nothing even close to genius."

The Fury of Evil

*I*nfus stood on the lower balcony of the northern tower, looking out across plains where what was left of the Goblins and the Slayers were mobilizing. They would be the only defense for the city should the Elves manage to break the forces at the Pass of Merwold. It would never happen of course but the Demon knew to take precautions while it planned its next move. The creature lifted the cluster of crystals it had secured in the attack above Pentegarn and stared closely at them, watching as they gave off a slight pulse.

The door to the room closed and Infus turned back inside, looking to see who or what had entered. In the center of the room was a sole Slayer standing at attention. It waited until the Demon had stopped in front of it before speaking.

"The forces are ready, my master."

Infus nodded. "Good. Soon the rest of them will be joining us. I need time to open the portal. The Slayers are not to leave the field until I have opened it, understood?"

"Of course, my master," the Slayer replied with a half bow.

It turned and strolled out of the room, the door slamming closed behind it. Infus was alone again and turned its attention to the crystals once more. They were almost mesmerizing, their soft glow pulsing every few seconds. Infus headed for the door and moved up the tower to the room where Valsera was still imprisoned in the crystal. Stopping in front of the statue, Infus looked hollowly at the figure behind the sheet of crystal.

"With this... I could free you. I wonder if you can even see it in there," the Demon started, looking to the cluster of crystals. "I would hope so. You see, I am not here to free you. I like your armies. I like having control. I think I will take command,

and you will just cease to be."

If it had been possible to see the Demon's face, there would have been a very evil smile cross it. Long ago the Demon had pressed for control and pulled back when challenged. This time, there was no one there to stop Infus. The creature reached up and traced the tip of one of its clawed fingers across the crystal opposite Valsera's face. The sorcerer was still a prisoner and would remain that way.

Infus had planned for this ever since the sorcerer had been rendered incapacitated. Finally there was a chance to take over. The Demon applied more pressure and a scratch appeared on the face of the crystal, carving an emblem across the smooth edges. The angles and turns formed a strange cluster of diamonds that intersected one another and then continued.

It was the same emblem he had carved into the chest of the wizard a long time ago when he drained the power from the Celestial Knight to open the portal the first time. The moment the Demon completed the symbol the lines flooded with a deep red and throbbed in unison with the cluster of crystals.

"That's right Valsera," the Demon taunted even though it was not clear if the sorcerer could even hear. "Your power will become mine and with it, I will reopen the gateway and bring my armies here to finish what you started. Your life... to strengthen mine."

The Demon gave an inhuman laugh and touched the crystals to the emblem on the face of the crystal statue. The red, pulsing light intensified and then began to draw into the crystals. As the power was drained the crystal holding the sorcerer grew dimmer and dimmer. The Demon stood rigid, feeling the power growing in its hands, minutes away from completely rendering the sorcerer powerless.

"Yes... it draws nearer. Thank you Valsera, for your contribution to my rise to power. I only regret I was not more supportive of yours," the Demon whispered sarcastically.

After ten long minutes of waiting, the crystal holding Valsera grew dimmer and its power was drained. The stone was finally silent. At the bottom of the stand small cracks began to form. They stretched up to where the emblem had been carved and the entire formation crumbled. Infus watched intently as the crystal fell away from the figure encased inside.

As the last of the crystal fell away the figure of the sorcerer collapsed to the ground in a lifeless heap. The form did not stir and after a few minutes Infus reached out and nudged the body with its foot. It remained lifeless while the crystals in his hand now glowed continuously, a powerful light filled the room.

"It is done. Thank you, my Lord," the Demon hissed sarcastically with a bow.

Almost on cue the door behind the Demon opened and a trio of Slayers entered, grabbing the dead body up and preparing to carry it out of the city. Just as they stopped at the door the Demon raised its hand.

"No... do not waste the energy. Toss him over the edge of the balcony. We do not have the time to waste on him. We have to prepare!" Infus said proudly, holding the cluster of crystals aloft.

The Slayers carried the body of Valsera to the edge of the balcony and with one last glance at the Demon they tossed it over the edge. Infus did not bother watching the body fall. Together with the Slayers he walked down the winding staircase and out into the courtyard at the bottom of the castle. Slayers covered the area, with the Goblins further out in the fields between the woods and the city.

Infus walked further out into the clearing and examined the ground, the sky, and the defenses they had managed to set up. The position was perfect for the portal, guaranteed to have an army to protect it and plenty of room for an army to flood out of it. The sooner the Demon began the ritual the sooner the army of Slayers would be unleashed on the lands of Nalawren.

Infus knelt in the rough clay and pulled a long dagger from its scabbard. Reaching out the Demon began cutting lines deep in the ground, soon forming a large five pointed star. At the point of each star Infus carved a glyph, five different symbols, one for each realm of the world that the Slayers called home. Each glyph opened a different doorway and eventually they all pooled to the portal that the Demon was working to finish. Everywhere the dagger had cut was now a soft glowing yellow. Soon the symbol on the ground was alive with energy and Infus prepared to unleash the Slayers.

Elendil had broken the tree line and found the opposite

side of the river so heavily defended that even he had to take a second look at the odds. His Knights moved in behind him and his army stared across the river at the sight. They would not allow their bravery to waver, but like the siege at Pentegarn, they began to wonder how they would ever manage against a force that large. Even here the cold of winter touched them and all across the shores the soldiers could see their breath. The hundred yards of water separating them was hardly an obstacle now as both sides looked eager to charge.

The Goblins on the opposite side of the river caught sight of the Elves and their bows were instantly raised, the arrows trained on the front lines of the Elven Knights. Elendil waved to his own archers and then to the Knights who raised their broad shields against the wave of arrows only moments from being sent at them.

"We do not falter, we do not back down, we do not run! If we fail here then our lands, our families, and our way of life will be lost. This is it, our chance to make one last stand! Who's ready?"

The Elves that covered the northern shore and continued filing out of the trees gave a chorus of cheers and together the force turned to the Goblins. The front lines of Elves locked their shields together and urged their horses forward into the rushing current of the river. The horses pushed together as the Goblins released their first wave of arrows into the sky. The wall of shields did plenty to protect the Knights but out of the wall of soldiers two horses were hit, lurching forward and throwing their riders into the water.

The Goblins reloaded and fired again with the same outcome and soon the Knights were crossing through the middle of the river. Before the third volley could be released the Elves fired their own. Without a wall of shields to protect them the front wall of Goblins was met with waves of arrows. Rows of Goblins fell as the Elves continued to fire their bows, refusing to relent their attack.

From the heart of the forces on the southern shores came what was left of the Ogres, their number charging into the icy river at full speed, sending up a spray of frigid water. The Ogres charged madly at the Knights, their weapons raised above their heads ready to strike. Less than a minute separated the two forces as both sides charged forward.

Elendil raised his sword up over his head and hid behind his shield as the first Ogre crashed against the line of Knights. "As one!"

The Ogres broke through the first wall of Knights and started battling wildly, swinging in every direction against the wall of steel and horse. The footmen charged in behind them, struggling against the current of the river but pushing forward. The battle in the middle of the river was close quartered and tight, leaving little room to move and even less to avoid the blows from the opposition.

Elendil raised his shield across his body as the club of an Ogre met the steel, sending him flying back off of his horse into the water. The King felt the frigid water invading his mouth and nose, threatening to flood his lungs. A strong pair of hands jerked him up out of the water, coughing and sputtering as air was once again available. Elendil reached into the water, searching for his sword for a few minutes before finally finding the hilt and jerking it from the muddy water. He looked back up through the fray of battle as arrows streaked through the sky from either side of the river. Terror gripped the Elf when he realized his soldiers lacked the mobility of the larger, more muscular creatures. The spasm from his muscles soon showed his body was threatening to collapse from the intense cold.

Spearmen and swordsmen were pushing in behind the Knights even as they watched them being slaughtered by the Ogres. Their armor counted for nothing against the sheer strength behind the swing of an Ogre's axe. Horses without riders appeared from the fray of battle and disappeared into the forests away from the commotion of battle.

Elendil found his feet and stood, the water dripping from his armor. He waited a moment as the swordsmen and spearmen moved in beside him. The infantry locked their shields in the middle of the river and waited, what was left of their Knights reluctantly falling back into the main force. Behind them archers continued to fire but the Goblins had learned from the Elves and were forming their own crude wall of shields.

Elendil steadied his shield and ducked his head low, feeling the head of an arrow strike the sturdy metal. The arrowhead pierced through the shield and appeared just above his wrist.

Taking a deap breath, the King pushed his way forward. The wall followed his move and together they advanced a step.

The massacre in the middle of the river left the water blood red and the current carried bodies downstream away from the battle. Soon the area in the middle of the river had been cleared by the swift flow of water, leaving no immediate sign of the battle that had just taken place. The remaining Ogres, many of them injured from their battle with the Knights, were slowly moving towards the wall of shields.

Elendil looked up fearfully, knowing that if the Knights had not fared well in close combat, his Elven footmen would stand even less of a chance. Things were starting to look bad as the Ogres stretched their numbers and created a small concave, the head of their line only steps away.

"Stand fast Elves! No matter what they bring, we will not run this day!"

Ectle and Erzel watched the movements around the city. The armies were starting to move around. There was life to their forces, and knowing that the Slayers and Goblins were restless gave the wizard an idea.

"I wonder.."

Erzel turned to the wizard. "What is it, Ectle?"

"They are restless, almost like… fearful. It is possible to prey on their fears now, to make them break and flee. All but the Slayers that is. We are going to have to face them whether the Goblins run of not."

Tanis crouched down next to the two. "How do you suggest that be accomplished?

"With an army of Dwarves," Ectle replied nonchalantly.

Erzel and Tanis looked at the wizard as if he were crazy. The Dwarves had pulled their armies from the lands and returned to Tvan. What did the wizard mean? Did he really believe the Dwarves were going to come to the rescue after what happened in the throne room of Pentegarn?

"Ectle, are you mad? What makes you think Ardis would send the Dwarven armies after what happened? Where are these Dwarves?" Erzel asked, shocked and amazed at the thought.

"I am a wizard, Erzel, the possibilities are endless."

Erzel raised an eyebrow and wondered what the possibilities were that the wizard spoke of. "I take it you mean magic?"

"Of course Erzel, and I think I have just the spell to give us a powerful advantage, though it will not be a permanent fix to our predicament. We will not truly have the Dwarven armies with us, but the armies of Qwaz will not know the difference. I am going to need a volunteer though, a Dwarven volunteer," Ectle said, turning to look at Thorgrim.

"Ugh... why me, Ectle, why always me?" the Dwarf grumbled.

"Simple, Thorgrim, you are the only Dwarf here," Ectle replied, stressing the fact that the he was the only one that would fit what he needed to work the spell.

"So what is the idea you have, Ectle?" Erzel asked, ignoring Thorgrim's unwillingness.

"The spell may require every ounce of my strength to complete and to manage for longer than a few minutes. I will create mirrored images of Thorgrim, enough to form an entire Dwarven army. They will mimic his moves and his attacks, giving the impression that the Dwarven army has arrived after all."

"It will not work as you think, Ectle."

The wizard looked up at the Elf. "Why is that, Erzel?"

"The Goblins may lack the intelligence to make out the fact that every soldier out there will be mirroring Thorgrim exactly but the Slayers do. They will know it is a bluff. It would be better if you had several soldiers all armed and dressed differently, giving the impression of a diverse army."

Ectle nodded. Erzel was right about the Slayers. Though they seemed capable of only one thing, they were intelligent enough to pick up on a trick like that. If they had fifty Dwarves each with twenty mirrored copies, it would be possible to fool even the Slayers. As it was though, they only had one.

"We could use the Wood Elves!" The wizard was once again excited with the idea.

Everyone turned to Tanis who realized what was being implied. "Just how are you suggesting to use my soldiers?"

"We mix a force of them with Thorgrim and multiply their images to form an army. The enemy will see Elves and Dwarves, archers and swordsmen and perhaps they will not dive too deep into sorting out the details."

"Another problem with that idea," Erzel said, pulling the

attention back to himself. At this point Ectle was beginning to grow tired of someone picking his plans apart.

"Yes?"

"These copies will not be any use if they are engaged in battle, correct?"

Ectle looked at the Elf for another minute or so and realized that even if an army of a thousand appeared, only a fraction of them would actually be capable of battling with the Goblins and Slayers. He held his hands up as if to show defeat.

"Well, they could just be used to get the attention of the army and keep them occupied while we strike from another angle. A diversion of sorts and by the time they realize that it is not a real army we will already be fully engaged with them. By then it will not matter so much if they charge in with the real forces."

"You know that is not that bad of an idea," Lavian said, stepping into the conversation. "I think if it managed to distract half of their forces then we have that many less to fight. We marched down here on the belief that we would be able to break their forces and fight our way to the Demon. Perhaps trying something as crazy as this sounds will give results."

Everyone looked around the group and silently agreed with nods. Even if they did not fully believe in the plan, none of them felt like trying to find problems with it. Ectle looked across the fields to the north and pointed at the tree line that seemed the thinnest.

"That's where the force should appear, out of the thinnest parts of their forests. It will seem believable for a large army to move out through there instead of the thicker areas. We will wait while the force gets in place."

"How many of my Elves do you require?"

"For the best results, ten or so of each. Ten swordsmen, ten archers, ten spearmen, and of course, the Dwarf. That should be a believable number I think."

"Fine, your heard him. Ten volunteers of each head up around the edge of the forest and wait for our signal," Tanis ordered, watching the soldiers moving off away from the main force.

Thorgrim stood in the trees for a few minutes as if he had planned to argue the plan but in the end he just nodded and started off through the trees behind the Wood Elves.

"Thorgrim!" Erzel called out to the Dwarf.

He turned and looked back at the group.

"Be careful…"

He did not bother answering, only giving a slow nod and then turning to continue on around the clearing. Erzel watched him disappear in the thicker part of the trees and then turned back to the wizard with a concerned glance.

"You're sure of this, right, Ectle?" he asked nervously. "I don't want to send him in to meet his death when the spell does not give the desired results."

"It will work, Erzel, I promise," the wizard replied without turning to meet his gaze.

The army that remained around the King and the others sat and waited for the other force to move into position. It would take a little while for them to travel to the northern edge of the clearing if they did not run into any opposition in the forests. That did not seem likely considering all forces of Qwaz were now pulled back to the city to protect the Demon and its plans.

"I have another thought. Lavian, your Warbird is the only surviving one, isn't it?"

"Sadly yes, Erzel, all the others were killed during the siege of Pentegarn. Odimous was the last to fall. Why?"

"I need to get close to Infus with this whip. If I could fly, that would make it quite a bit easier. Do you know where I am going with this?"

"No, Erzel," Ectle interrupted. "You would not last long against the Demon with your injury. It will take more than one of us to bring down the creature."

"How, Ectle? You are going to be busy holding that spell and I am the only one with the ability to damage the Demon. This whip and the Dragon Alora are all that Infus seems to fear. With you busy, I am the only one capable of the task."

"I hate to agree with the Elf, but he is right," Tanis chimed in, surprisingly taking Erzel's side.

"I have to get to the creature first though and fighting through the Goblins and Slayers will take too much time. By then the portal will have opened and the Slayer army will be flooding out across our lands. We have to act fast. Hopefully I will be able to keep Infus from completing the ritual."

Ectle continued to shake his head in defiance at the Elf's

plan, knowing how foolish it was to send him in alone against the Demon with his wound plaguing him so. He could tell by the way Erzel stood that it was no better healed than when they had been at the city. Kail had confirmed his concerns just before they left.

"Ectle, show me another way."

The wizard struggled with the statement for a few moments before he realized that there really was no alternative. Letting Erzel face the Demon once more was the best plan they had at the moment. With little time to plan, it was the best they could come up with. The wizard knew in the back of his mind that more often than not, plans made in that kind of haste never went according to plan. Every feeling in his body was against the plan, knowing there was little room for error now.

"Do whatever it is you are planning but know that if you find yourself up against the Demon in the way you suggest, there will be no one there at your back. This is your decision, I leave it to you."

Erzel could not hear any support in his voice but all he wanted was the words. He took Lavian by the arm and together they moved back into the forest further, waiting for the Warbird to land. Somehow she had a connection with the bird and didn't have to speak a word to bring it down to her. It landed and stretched its wings out wide, plucking a random feather from under its wing.

"Remember, it has the choice. Approach it slowly, reach out to its neck, and place your hand just above the shoulder. If it lowers its head and body then it will allow you to ride it. If not..."

"If not?"

"Well, let's just start and take things one step at a time."

Erzel looked at the large creature and slowly reached out to its body, his gloved fingers raking across the soft feathers. As his hand came to rest on its shoulder he waited, watching the animal to see how it reacted. It did not bow its head but instead it turned to face the Elf, locking its gaze with his.

"Erzel, step back slowly."

The Elf kept his stare with the animal, not entirely hearing the Knight's order. He raised his hand off of the feathers and the bird turned, looking at the spot where his hand had been. The Warbird plucked a feather from the spot and then its head dropped lower, giving him the sign that he was welcome to come closer.

"Well, I had not expected that. Go ahead Erzel, get acquainted with her. There is not the time to wait."

Erzel looked back at Ectle who had knelt in the leaves, apparently beginning to weave his magic and soon the spell would reveal its true power. He reached up to the back of the Warbird's head, finding the feathers there far softer. As he gently stroked the animal he reached to the saddle, pulling himself up on top of the Warbird. The creature scratched the ground and looked up through the trees, preparing to take flight.

Erzel looked down to Lavian and nodded. "Thank you. Take care of yourself out there."

Lavian reached up and touched him on his leg. "Goodbye, Erzel."

The Warbird kicked up off the ground and streaked up through the air, its wings never missing a beat as it tore through the clouds. Erzel could not see clearly through the wind and the tears that streamed out of the corners of his eyes. With one last beat of its wings the Warbird shot out of the clouds, hesitating in the sky as the Elf took a moment to scan the scene below. He could see the emblem glowing yellow and focused on the spot, knowing any minute he would be diving towards it.

The Elves and Dwarf stood at the edge of the trees staring out into the fields where the Goblins and Slayers waited for them. It felt like the enemy knew Thorgrim and the Elves were there, watching and waiting for the chance to spill their blood. The Dwarf looked back at the Elves behind him and nodded, watching them spread into a loosely scattered formation.

"Alright, I guess this is it. Remember, we're an army," Thorgrim urged, hoping his words gave some sort of encouragement.

The Dwarf took the first few steps bravely, his war hammer leaned back over his shoulder. From the trees they began appearing and just as the wizard had promised, their numbers began changing. One Dwarf now appeared as twenty with the same happening to the rest of the Elves. Thirty Elven soldiers now became somewhere close to two hundred and the scene caught the attention of the armies outside of the city of Qwaz. The Elves and Dwarves stopped as their entire force came into view.

Thorgrim watched as the Goblins formed a long line several soldiers deep as they moved north away from the city. The Slayers on the other hand drew back closer to Qwaz, tightly pulling their army in closer to the Demon. They were very obviously looking only to protect the Demon and the portal it was trying desperately to summon.

"What now?" one of the Elves asked, his spear lowered at his waist.

"Now we wait. The rest of the army will reveal itself and then all hell will break loose," Thorgrim said quietly, tightly wringing the handle of his weapon.

Things were quiet as the two armies squared off against one another. The worst part was knowing that only a fraction of their forces were actually able to fight in this battle. The only up side was that the Goblins and Slayers did not know that. Too many things could go wrong and in the back of Thorgrim's mind he began trying to think of another plan for when this one fell to pieces.

In the moments between the Ogres charging and them actually meeting the wall of shields there was time to think things through. Elendil pictured the lands around Pentegarn if the armies of Valsera were to break through the Pass of Merwold. He imagined those still in the city, its main army now fully engaged at the pass. There would be no one available to help protect them if they failed here. There was no regroup and attack again at a later date. This was it. In the end, the future of the High Elves all came to rest on this one battle.

The crash of the large Ogres against the shield wall cut his thoughts from him and immediately he found himself ready again. The cold water numbed his feet and legs. He staggered forward through the water as his legs seemed to fail him. As sensation returned he set his sights on the handful of Ogres battling with the desperate Elves in the water.

The Ogre nearest the King had its back turned as it continued to rain down attacks on the soldiers around it. Elendil took a step through the current and leveled the blade of his sword with the middle of the brute's back. He could not understand why it seemed he was moving in slow motion but he pushed on, driving the top of the blade into the center of the Ogre's lower back. The creature howled painfully and tossed its shoulders back as the sword slid deeply through its muscle into the organs that gave it life.

The creature toppled forward into the water face first with Elendil pulled in behind it. He gave his sword a hard jerk and it gave a little, sliding free after two more jerks. An Ogre to his right threw a powerful attack in the King's direction but he managed to dodge behind the body of the fallen Ogre in time to avoid the blow. The axe met the flesh of the dying Ogre and sent a splash of red across the surface of the water. The carnage was once again being carried downstream while some of the bodies clustered on the bottom of the river, their heavy armor weighing them down.

"My King Elendil! Fall back away from the front lines!" a Knight to his right said, appearing without his horse.

"No... I will not leave..."

"I must protest, my King! Let us hold the front wall. You must conserve your strength!"

Elendil sought to argue but the Knight had already charged into the line of shields that was struggling to recover from the holes the Ogres had pushed through. The bodies of Elves that had not sunk to the bottom or floated away were cleared back out of the way as fresh soldiers were moved in. Archers had not once let up from their volleys of arrows but now they waited, watching the enemy wall of shields pushing its way down into the river as well. The Goblins would meet the Elves in the middle, where the battle for the pass would pick up once more.

Elendil stood on the land at the northern end of the pass, watching the two armies square off the way they had at the ruined gates in the end of the siege of Pentegarn, neither force ready to charge the other. Both forces of infantry waited in the water as the archers from both armies drew their bows back and waited for the single match that would ignite a firestorm.

The Elves in the water watched as the forces of Goblins waded through the water towards them. Any other time the Elves would have already broken the lines and charged the enemy down but there was a reason for their waiting. They wanted the enemy to spend as much time as possible engaged here at the pass and never have a second thought of retreating back to Qwaz. Waiting was torture, but it was worth it in the end.

Elendil now stood on the edge of the northern shore, his desires to charge back in pushing him steps closer to the front while the Knight's words replayed in his head. He had to stay alive. The King could feel a sting in his lower arm where the Ogre's club had struck his shield and he wondered if it was broken but after a quick test he decided that was not the case.

"Are you alright, my King?" a soldier to his right asked as he watched Elendil testing the wounded arm.

"Yes… it's nothing… just sore."

"Here, you need a shield."

The footman handed the shield to the King but Elendil waved it off, knowing his wounded arm would never be able to support the heavy shield. It was not broken, but there was definitely damage done.

"No, keep your shield. I can not wield it at the moment."

"You are hurt. Please, come back with me, let us get you some sort of med…"

"I said I was fine soldier now get back in line!" Elendil ordered forcefully. His tone bordered on anger but he caught himself just before it was carried too far.

The soldier nodded and secured his shield once more, moving back to the edge of the water as he waited for an area where he could move in and fight. Minutes before the Goblins and Elves met in the water a swarm of movement on the far shore caught Elendil's attention. He watched as teams of Goblins pulled forth siege weapons that very closely resembled the goliaths that the Gnomes had designed. The three siege weapons stopped on the shore and were now being loaded.

"Oh no… archers, fire at will!" he cried out, knowing what would happen once the trigger had been released on the siege weapons.

The Elves fired in one massive wave, their arrows crossing the river and striking targets before the Goblins had a chance to comprehend what was taking place. Their forces around the siege weapons took heavy losses but the archers that remained standing immediately returned fire. The exchanges continued back and forth as the first of the siege weapons on the southern shore was loaded and armed..

The King watched as the weapons were adjusted for a higher shot and then the lone Goblin in the back threw the first switch. Spears shot through the air, mixing with the Goblin arrows and falling all across the Elven infantry. The shields were the perfect deterrent for the arrows but the spears managed to pierce through from the sheer force behind them. Elves in the line of fire were soon defenseless and out of rage King Elendil raised his sword and charged into the water.

He trudged through the waves and over dead bodies as the Elves behind him on the shore eagerly charged in behind him. The entire front line of the Elven infantry and Knights was collapsing from the spearfire of the siege weapons. Finally their ammunition was spent and the seige weapons were useless as the Goblins rearmed them. It was a small window of opportunity for the Elves.

"Forward! To the beach!" Elendil shouted, knowing how far out of their reach the other side of the river was at the moment. He wanted them to see his unwavering bravery, to see him unwilling to be frightened by the Goblins and their superior numbers. He charged out to the front lines, his orders still ringing out above the deafening sounds of metal against metal.

The first to face him was met with a powerful overhead strike that split the Goblin's head in two. Blood sprayed through the air as Elendil planted his foot against the creature's chest and kicked the body back into the water to free his sword. The moment he freed his sword it found another victim and then repeated the process, whirling and stabbing anything that was not an Elf.

"My King, to the right!" a Knight yelled, stepping between Elendil and a charging Goblin.

The King watched the spear pierce through the Elf's breastplate and emerge out the back with a splatter of blood. He shoved the Knight to the side and stabbed the Goblin in retaliation, his sword now dark crimson from the bloodshed. He turned but had lost sight of the Knight in the scuffle, hating himself for abandoning him for dead in his haste to kill the creature.

He had only seconds to mourn the death of the Knight as he was forced to dodge a low attack from an axe and then return with the stroke of his sword. He grabbed the axe from the dying creature with his wounded arm and turned to the numbers of Goblins charging towards him, two weapons wielded and ready to shed blood again.

The pain rising up his arm into his shoulder was briefly ignored as he used the axe to knock aside the thrust of a spear. He cleaved the Goblin's head and tossed the axe aside, realizing that in his condition there was no way he could wield both weapons at once. The soldiers were now swarming in around him and the real battle began, the furious Elves pushing back against the swarms of Goblins.

The High Elf continued his attacks, killing Goblin after Goblin as he pushed further into the enemy lines. His energy inspired the Elves behind him and their smaller army kept pushing forward into the Goblins. The front wall of the Goblins finally seemed to fall back, their forces not hardly as brave as they seemed. The Goblins were losing momentum with their attack, their formations no longer working together. Now it was every soldier fighting for himself.

Elendil knocked a dying Goblin to the side into the water and stepped forward, the battle around him spreading and thinning through the river. It wasn't until the King looked up and found the weapons on the shore armed and ready that he slowed down. For a moment he couldn't process what was happening but then it all hit him at once. The Goblins had fallen back out of the middle of the river just as the weapons were armed and now only the Elves were left in the path of the siege weapons. Elendil stopped and locked eyes with the creature at the trigger and for one second he thought he saw a smile.

"Get back! Get out of the water!" Elendil yelled, turning to run as soon as he realized what was coming.

The King turned to run back out of the water. The Goblins at the triggers of the seige weapons watched happily as the Elves retreated back in a panic. In the seconds between the Goblins throwing the triggers and the spears leaving the siege weapons, the Elves had only managed a few steps. The two siege machines lurched violently and close to thirty spears streaked through the air.

Elendil saw the first spear strike to his right and then one to his left sank deep into the back of a fleeing Elf. Elves began falling to the left and right and he turned his head to the side, glancing back at the shore behind him. Then he felt it, a searing pain in his shoulder that spread down his arm. He fell forward, staring down at the head of a spear shoved more than a foot through his left arm. He collapsed into the water, a spray of blood filling the current in front of him.

Screams of pain filled the air all around him and Elendil realized that the loudest was coming from him. Elves skewered by the wave of spears fell into the water, their bodies filling the water all through the river. He leaned up but the spear sent blinding pains through his body, making him struggle to keep his face out of the water. The waves of water hit his face and he sank a little lower, no longer feeling the strength to keep himself up,

Just as King Elendil's head slid under the water he felt a strong pair of hands on the back of his armor, pulling him up out of the frigid water. A second set of hands grabbed his uninjured arm and together they pulled him up into the air once more. Gasping for air, the pain wrecking his body, Elendil found himself looking at a sight he would have never expected. His rescuers, the two strong sets of hands that had pulled him to the surface again, both belonged to Dwarves.

The Fiery Portal Opens

The Wood Elves appeared from the western forests slowly, catching the attention of the Goblins and Slayers immediately. They turned, realizing they were now facing two separate armies, one from the northern woods and another from the western forests. The two armies stood silent, staring at the creatures. Soon they would be fighting the armies again, this time against more of the strongest enemies of the lands. They had never faced so many Slayers at once but Tanis had been warned of their strengths and had an idea of what he was about to face.

Kail stepped in beside the King of the Wood Elves and followed his stare across the fields to the spread of Slayers that stood, waiting for the Elves. He remembered facing them on the Dragon Isles and then again in the forests above Pentegarn and he knew just how strong they were. Facing them now in full force was something no one was prepared for.

"So this is it? This is what it comes down to?" Tanis whispered, the sight of the Slayer army truly frightening him inside.

"What do you mean, my Lord?" Kail asked as he finally pulled his gaze off of the Slayers.

"This is where we will meet our end? Fighting their armies on their lands, dying against the strongest enemies the Demon has to throw at us? This just doesn't feel… right."

Kail gripped the handle of his bow a little firmer and shook his head defiantly to the King's words. "No, this isn't it. It doesn't have to end here, my Lord. This battle could be the very beginning. We can not give up before it begins."

Kail held his bow and drew back the bowstring, watching as the glowing blue arrow appeared. He could feel the power of the weapon in his hands and raised it up across his body. He brought the bowstring to his eye and sighted, releasing the arrow and watching as it curved down and met the ground in front of the Goblins, a bright blast of light filling the area. The Goblins pulled back away from the flash of light, shielding their eyes.

The blast of light was the signal for the Elves and both forces began to move down towards the city. Tanis let the front lines of Wood Elves pass by, their ranks moving into their formations and moving down on the Goblins. Lavian stepped in beside Kail and Tanis and slid her crossbow in against her shoulder, marching in with the rest of the group. A quick glance across the field assured that Ectle's spell was still as strong as when he had first cast it.

The Goblins bunched together in front of the Slayers, their attention switching from the northern force of Elves to the one pushing in on them from the west. The two would converge on the Goblins together, pushing back into the ranks of the Slayers. No matter what the Elves did, they would be forced to face the Slayers in the end. If they were to get in against the Demon, they would have to fight their way through the most ferocious soldiers to ever plague Nalawren.

"Fine, Kail, this isn't the end. I can only hope that I will not be leaving this field on my shield."

"Just keep your head down and don't miss with your bow my King, and you'll walk out of here with the rest of us," Kail replied, drawing the bow back again,

The front line of the Goblins was now yards away and the arrows between the two forces began flying. The limited infantry of the Wood Elves formed a sturdy wall of shields as the archers behind it began picking their targets one by one. Ten feet separated the two walls of shields when the Goblin army finally broke formation and charged at the Wood Elves.

The lack of space between the two forces did not allow for the Goblins to develop enough momentum to break through the shield wall. The small wall of Wood Elf infantry locked together and pushed back, giving their archers time to pick off the enemy. The archers then turned their attention further back, their shots arching and falling down onto the mass of Slayers.

Some of the soldiers shielded the attacks but several were not quick enough and showers of sparks and flames leapt into the air. In all, only four of the Slayers fell but numerous were still standing with arrows piercing their bodies. Tanis shook his head and drew his bowstring taunt again, focusing on a target, witnessing first hand the strength of the Slayers. They were able to remain standing and battle ready with arrows marring their bodies.

"They do not die..." Tanis whispered as he watched his arrow glance off the edge of a shield in the ranks of the Slayers.

The volleys of arrows sent the Slayers into a frenzy and their forces suddenly began to pull away from the heart of Qwaz. Though the Goblins were hardly capable of dealing with the Wood Elves, the Slayers were a threat on the move. Kail and Lavian moved around to the left side of the Elven wall and raised their weapons as the Slayers rounded the edge of the Goblin army.

Just as the Slayers fell into position, the northern force led by Thorgrim closed in on what was left of the Goblin force that had not been caught in the initial volleys of arrows. Though only a handful of the soldiers were real, the entire force charged into the shattered lines of the Goblin wall. For a moment there was silence and then, a thunderous clash of steel.

Thorgrim led the charge, his war hammer knocking a pair of Goblins back and creating a hole for the rest of the Elves to fill. Seconds behind him the rest of the force crashed against the crumbling wall of Goblin shields. The mirrored images were revealed as they passed through their opponents with no damage being dealt. The Goblins did not grasp what was happening initially but as the false soldiers continued through the enemy lines they became wise to the attack. What came with that was a new issue, not knowing which enemy was real and which was false until the sword met its target.

Knowing the spell had run its course, Ectle appeared from the trees and walked out in behind the force of Elves. The mirrored images of the soldiers to the north began fading and soon fizzled out completely. With the loss of the conjured army, Ectle was free to unleash the fury of what magic remained that he had been keeping inside. The battle was starting to thin out as the Goblins were pulling back away from the lines of Elves and the Slayers began to take their places. The Slayers had seemingly abandoned the Demon further back as they pressed out to face the Elves. Alone, but still very dangerous.

The dark storm clouds were rolling across the fields around Qwaz, hiding the battle from the spot where Erzel and the Warbird hovered. The Elf pulled the restraint and the Warbird tucked its right wing, gliding far to the edge of the storm. The Warbird dropped under the thick canopy of dark clouds and skirted the tallest tower of Qwaz, giving Erzel a view of the field below.

The Elves had formed a strong shifting wall that moved and flowed into the weakest points of the enemy forces. As he watched the Goblins draw back and the Slayers move forward to strengthen their own forces, Erzel saw what it meant. Near the gate of the city he could make out the Dark form of the Demon Infus. In front of the dark creature he saw a strange collection of symbols glowing a fierce yellow. Infus stood alone.

The Elf ran his free hand across the feathers at the base of the creature's neck and gave one last glance to the battlefield below. He was ready to sink his sword into the enemy and lash out with the whip. He wanted to face the Demon with its own weapon at last, to hand it a hint of pain that it had long deserved. He felt the handle lashed to his belt and with a glance down he pulled it free, ready to use it the moment he landed.

Erzel snapped his wrist and dug his heels into the restraints to prepare for the dive. The Warbird lowered its head and tucked its wings, the wind cutting past the Elf fiercely. Figures and sights that he once could make out were now blurred as he hurtled down towards the earth. The Warbird tucked tighter and shot through the air above the Elves, Goblins, and Slayers. Once clear it threw its wings out and drastically slowed its approach, making Erzel grip the reins as tightly as he possibly could.

Infus caught sight of the Warbird but by the time the Demon drew its sword Erzel had his in hand as well. The Elf shifted in the saddle and threw a leg over the side, dropping the ten feet between him and the ground without the mount even coming to a stop. He rolled and stood, locking his eyes on the Demon. The two stood motionless, the large, glowing glyph the only thing between them now.

Infus gave a very slow nod. "I will give you this Elf, you are very persistent. No matter where I go you just happen to show up. How do you do it?"

The Demon started a slow approach around the edge of

the glyph and Erzel mirrored it, keeping the glowing yellow carvings between him and the Demon as he fumbled with the whip behind his back. Arming it would reveal that he was well capable of besting Infus at last.

"Yet I wonder, do you have the slightest idea of how to fight me? I can not remember the last time I actually had a challenge. I suppose this time shall be no different. I shall kill you," Infus hissed, pointing the blade of the sword at the Elf. "I will kill you and then I will raise this portal. I shall call forth my army and burn all of your precious Nalawren to the ground."

Again Erzel did not respond. He did not want to show any emotion to the Demon, to give it anything to feed off. He was struggling to manage the weapon but a third failed attempt frustrated him. He knew the whip would make a difference but failing to wield it was like not having it. A crack of lightning sent shivers down Erzel's spine but he did not dare take his eyes off of the creature. Infus on the other hand turned and looked up into the sky, scanning the dark storm clouds growing more ominous by the minute. The Elf was stalling the attack to give himself time to activate the whip. Infus was stalling in the hopes that the Elf would live just long enough to watch the birth of the portal. As Erzel finally found the etching everything happened at once.

The clouds stirred above them and both Erzel and Infus glanced upward. They could feel the charge in the air and as it grew Infus knew exactly what to expect. The Demon raised its arms wide and looked into the sky, welcoming the storm. A bright bolt of lightning cut through the sky and curved downward, hitting the cluster of crystals in the middle of the glyph. The bolt sent a powerful surge of energy into the crystals and then the field was rocked as the glyph exploded.

The power of the blast knocked the Elf off his feet and sent him rolling across the ground. He came to a stop at last and looked up to where he had been a few moments earlier. The ground all around the glyph was charred black and the cluster of crystals was no longer visible. The largest change was the glyph itself. It had changed from a bright yellow to a deep red that seemed to pulse.

Erzel climbed to his feet and took a cautious step forward, realizing that the bulk of both armies was now silent, watching the area behind the Slayers where the powerful bolt of lightning had struck. Infus was still standing and now walked around to the front of the glyph, knowing any minute the portal would rise. Every minute of preparing and planning had been building for this one moment.

"You may have brought more soldiers Elf, but soon I will have destroyed all of your armies down to the last Dwarf hiding in the mountains. Is there anything you want to say before it all ends?"

Erzel felt the glyph and then the weapon activated behind his back. The whip curled behind him and the Elf snapped his wrist, bringing the weapon around in front of him. The Demon cocked its head to the side, finding the Elf wielding its weapon. "This is not over."

"Well that is astounding. The Elf grew a backbone. So where did you learn to wield a weapon I designed?"

Erzel snapped the whip again and smiled for the first time. He took another step towards the Demon when a rumble shook under his feet. He stopped and scanned the ground. The glyph had grown quiet and the pulsing red light had now disappeared into the depths of the ground. The rumble was now constant and Erzel looked up at the Demon with the whip ready to strike.

"It does not matter now, the portal lives. Stand your ground or run, you're going to die either way."

The clay ground where the etchings had been carved now broke into two small spots, the dark earth piling and crumbling away from the center. From the crumbling earth appeared two thin spines of sharp, black stone. As they stretched higher out of the ground they grew thicker, the edges were as sharp as the blade of a sword. As they stretched higher the tips curled downward and sharp points formed off of the edges. The black stone finally reached its peak around fifteen feet and the tips of the two pillars curled back down like the tips of claws.

The Demon stepped in closer and raked its clawed gauntlet down the face of the closest pillar. Almost instantly the tip of both pillars flashed red and from them bright streaks appeared. The two formed a curve that met the ground and then red flames began surrounding the outer edges. The flames rolling across the mouth of the portal licked the edges of the pillars as the Demon seemed frozen in the front where its army would arrive.

The flames were so intense that they cast light all across the backs of the Slayers in the field as well as the walls and battlements of the city behind it. It was also enough to bring Erzel to a complete halt as he hesitated in shock. The Demon had been right, the portal had been opened, and soon a new army would march on Nalawren.

"It will not end, not like this!" Erzel yelled, flinging the whip above his head and leaping for the Demon.

The flaming whip snapped in the air not a foot away from the creature and Infus retreated back a step, brandishing the sword in its hand. Erzel knew that he was causing some sort of fear in the Demon and refused to relinquish his attack. Again and again he struck though never quite close enough.

Behind them the two forces had resumed combat. The Elven forces had made a mockery of the Goblins but now they faced an army composed entirely of Slayers. Before either side could make a move to attack, the first of the reinforcing Slayers stepped out of the portal. The red flames wrapped around its dark armor as it stepped forward, bow in hand and arrow ready.

Erzel ignored what was behind him, all of his energies focused on the Demon as he finally managed a blow. The flaming whip curled and snapped at the edge of the Demon's head, cutting a small piece of its hood free. The Elf watched as the piece of tattered black cloth fell to the ground and lay still like a leaf without the wind to guide it. It was true, the Demon was not as invincible as it claimed to be.

Elendil felt the sandy earth under him as the two Dwarves drug him up across the beach. Though the Goblins had brought down the King of the Elves, he was not dead and his soldiers still fought valiantly in the face of annihilation. The sight of the Dwarves came as a surprise to both armies. The Goblins were reeling in fear, remembering what had happened the last time they faced the Dwarves. The Elves pressed forward anxiously, the reinforcements giving them renewed life and energy.

The Dwarves had arrived in full force in one large wave from the northern forest, their numbers not giving a second thought to the situation as they charged through the Elves to the weakening wall of Goblins. The pass became a scene of chaos as the Dwarves and High Elves charged the river once more. The water surged higher on the Dwarves than on their taller comrades but it did not deter them as they continued a strong march, their shields locked together as they pushed in on the enemy.

"King Elendil, you must keep your eyes open! You must stay awake!" one Dwarf ordered as they finally laid him down in the sand, far away from the fury of the battle.

The King could not speak. The responses were coming through his head but he could not form the words with his lips. His entire body was in a state of shock, the pain from the horrid wound leaving him unable to communicate. The Dwarves rolled his head to the side and laid him face down on the sandbar to assess his wounds.

"This is so far beyond us. What do we do?"

"Quiet! King Elendil... can you hear me? Can you understand me?" the Dwarf asked looking into a face of total shock. There was no expression, no response of any kind.

The King could hear them, but was unable to manage any form of response. He lay in the sand, the smell of his blood mixed with the many scents of the earth. The shaft of the spear stood erect in the air and one of the Dwarves gripped it, holding it straight to minimize the pain and pressure the King felt. The other two Dwarves carefully examined the wound and the spear, their concerns now in keeping the King from bleeding to death.

"We have to do something fast or he will bleed to death right here. To remove the spear... looks impossible. It has pierced him so deeply."

"Clean through. What must we do?"

The conversations between the Dwarves continued, their words reaching the King's ears even though there was no way for him to respond. He wanted to scream out in pain, to cry for them to just pull the spear free. In the end he could not form the words. The pain smothered out every attempt to communicate with the Dwarven physicians.

"There is no time," the first replied, opening a sack sitting in the sand. "We must remove it now. We must cut the shaft of the spear and then pull it free. We must hurry!"

From the sack he produced a long saw used originally to remove a limb when it was beyond repair. Now he was going to use it to cut through the wooden shaft of the spear in hope that he could stop the flow of blood before the King died.

337

"Alright, one of you hold the shaft steady and the other hold the King. May he forgive us for what we are about to put him through."

The wall of Dwarves had taken the front lines from the Elves and now pushed the Goblins back to the southern shore without swinging a weapon once. The solid wall of shields and spears was enough to force the Goblins into a slow retreat, their armies now creating one solid mass across the southern shore from tree line to tree line. Shortly after King Elendil was struck down, the archers began targeting the siege weapons much more heavily, their arrows slaughtering the unsuspecting Goblins. Their volleys had finally put an end to the siege weapons.

"Forward!" came the cry from a Dwarf on the front line.

The Dwarves all moved forward in one massive push, the line locked tightly together. The Goblins did not bother to charge down the shore to meet the Dwarves as they knew the soldiers would be upon them very soon. Goblins in the front tried to mimic the wall of shields that the Dwarves had created but they hardly had the discipline to do so. The Dwarves reached the edge of the river and set foot on the sands in front of the Goblins.

The two races squared off again just as they had in the fields of Pentegarn, this time the Goblins knowing all too well what the Dwarves were capable of. They had felt the strengths of the northern army and had been punished horribly for underestimating the smaller warriors. The Goblins still felt the rage and desire to break the Elves and Dwarves but now there was also uncertainty as the Dwarves had pushed them back before.

The timing of the Dwarves was near perfect, their heavy infantry closing in on the front lines fast as a sudden attack on both the left and the right flanks of the Goblin force took place. Further up the river and downstream a large portion of the Dwarven army crossed the river and moved in on the sides of the enemy. With the Goblins and Humans fixed on the front lines of Dwarves closing in on them from the river, they hardly noticed the soldiers charging through the forests.

The moment the arrows and axes found their marks from the flanks, the front line of Dwarves charged in full force. Three different forces of Dwarves converged on the spot where the Goblins and Humans had dug in, prepared to fend off the northern army, but now they found themselves battling enemies from three sides. In the confusion and hysteria that was now sweeping the Goblin army, their forces began to retreat back away from the river.

Pentegarn had seen hours of fighting but in no more than fifteen minutes the Goblin army had almost fully retreated away from the pass. They pulled back to the edge of the forests but the Dwarves did not let up on their attacks. Dwarves pressed forward with their shields across their bodies and their spears keeping the enemies at a distance. They alternated the thrust of their spears with the powerful swings of their axes and swords, covering the sandy beach thick with Goblin blood. The Dwarves slipped and marched through it all, their sights set on their enemies.

Back behind the battle the Dwarf made the cuts through the spear as quickly as he could, the blade catching twice on the heavy, wooden pole as he struggled to get through. The vibrations of the saw on the pole had seemed to jolt the King back from his numbing shock. When the blade of the saw broke through the shaft of the spear Elendil let out a horrendous howl of pain. The Dwarves pushed him onto his side and readied him for what was about to take place. Two of the Dwarves tore away a section of the armor at the front and back of the wound and nodded.

"My most sincere apologies, King Elendil, I must continue. Here, bite down on this and it will be over quickly," the Dwarf said, reaching down and putting a small hunk of wood wrapped in leather at King Elendil's mouth.

Elendil relaxed his jaw long enough to let the wood slip into his mouth before clenching his teeth tightly, sinking them past the leather. He could see the Dwarf kneel in front of him while another held him from the front and another from the back. He stared straight ahead, knowing the pain was coming as the Dwarf wrapped his fingers around the spearhead sticking out of the Elf's shoulder.

"Ok, hold him tight. I'll make this quick."

With the two holding the King firmly the Dwarven physician held the shaft and spearhead tightly and gave a slow pull. He felt it slide a little and intensified the force, the shaft sliding through the meat of arm. With one last hard pull the shaft came through and the Dwarf tossed it aside. Elendil's mournful cry of agony sent chills through everyone around the scene.

It was what would have to be done next that had the Dwarf hesitating for a few moments before continuing. He looked to his right at the Dwarf and Elf who had started a small fire. They brought a handle with a flat, wide head on the top out of the flames and held it up in the air. The head was glowing bright and Elendil stared at it intently, knowing that the pain he had felt was only a touch compared to what was coming. With his teeth locked on the object in his mouth he gave a weak nod.

"This is going to hurt... a lot. We have to cauterize to stop the bleeding now. The back first, and then the front."

The Dwarves positioned the King and helped hold him as the Dwarf brought the glowing piece of metal closer to the torn skin and free bleeding. With a last breath and a prayer for forgiveness the Dwarf quickly pressed the metal against the skin. The smell of burning flesh invaded the air and Elendil clawed the ground with his free hand, his jaw locked down tightly. The skin seared and blistered and the Dwarf pulled the metal away, trading it for another identical tool.

They rolled the King and the Dwarf immediately pressed it against the other side of the puncture wound, glancing from the King's tortured face to the wound. With a wince he finally pulled the metal away and handed it off, holding the King to help with the pain. The Dwarves checked the wounds where the burns had closed the puncture, finding the flesh charred and blackened but no longer bleeding.

"This will do. This is a very serious wound though. We will have to watch for signs of infection and it is entirely possible that the amount of damage he sustained may result in it needing to be amputated. This was one of the worst wounds I have seen in many years," the Dwarf whispered to the one beside him.

"We have to get him back to Pentegarn. Fashion a stretcher and let us get moving now. Time is going to be an issue. The soldiers will take the pass back from the Goblins. Hurry, we have to move now!"

"Why... did you... come back?" Elendil asked, his body shaking from the intense pain.

"Sir, you must not speak. I must warn you that you are far from ok. We have to get you back to the city where we can heal you properly. Please, try to relax."

Relax. He had been skewered with a spear, had it pulled from his body, and had two separate wounds cauterized with searing hot metal. How could anyone in his situation relax?

"… but… who told you… to come…"

The Dwarf put a firm hand on the King's forehead and tried to keep him calm even though the pain he was feeling had to be excruciating. There were no words he could think of to comfort the Elf.

"Sir, all of your answers will come in time I assure you, but please, conserve what strength you have left for the journey back to Pentegarn."

It was obvious that he would not be hearing the answers to his questions and Elendil laid his head back in the sand, the pain still unbearable. Somehow he had managed to find a spot between agony and shock and that is where he hovered, fully aware of the torment but understanding there was nothing he could do to stop it. He could still hear the sounds of battle further off on the other side of the pass but around him there was only discussion.

No more than ten minutes had gone by but to Elendil it was an eternity when the Dwarves returned with the makeshift stretcher to lift the King into the back of a wagon. They were as gentle as they could be but with every second as precious as the next they had to be speedy. With a crack of the reins the wagon lurched and the horses pulled it out of the pass, followed closely by the remaining Elven Knights.

Elendil stared straight ahead as tree branches and patches of sky flew by. The pain was no less but he refused to give in and let it break him. He was aware that the wagon was moving and he knew the Dwarf had mentioned he was headed for Pentegarn but at the moment he could not remember what had happened at the pass. He was wounded, that much was certain, but how had it happened?

The King looked to his left, watching as the Elven Knight on the horse rose and fell with the pace of the galloping animal. They were moving swiftly, the wagon that he lay in occasionally caught a low spot in their path and rattled the King as it lurched violently. All around him were Knights and soldiers riding as the defenses for the fallen King. He was alive, but the chance that the wound could bring further harm was still a very real possibility. As the Dwarf had warned, the King was still in danger of infection. They had to hurry now, putting behind them the battle at the pass and trust the Dwarves would finish the fight.

The Slayers welcomed the sight of their own kind as their reinforcements began to flow from the portal one by one. Though the Elves attacked the moment they saw the portal rise from the ground, they had not moved the enemy back an inch. The Slayers were far more disciplined than their Goblin allies and their strength against physical damages greatly exceeded any other race. With the tide of the battle now turning, the Slayers would soon outnumber the Elves.

Ectle and Tanis found themselves shoulder to shoulder as the Slayers made a charge towards them. The Wood Elf loosed another arrow and watched as it pierced the shoulder of a charging Slayer but the projectile hardly slowed the creature down. In one swift move it ripped the arrow from its body and tossed it aside, its hollow helmet fixed on the King who had fired it. With the lines of Elves beginning to break down Tanis now found himself face to face with the Slayer with no one there to help.

The Elf raised the bow again and sighted in the creature's head as it charged, but before he loosed the arrow the wizard stepped in, knocking the Slayer back across the ground with a wave of his staff. In his right hand he held a long sword and in his left the staff and Ectle whirled from skirmish to skirmish in the lines, doing everything in his power to give the Elves a chance.

"Ectle! What do we do, Ectle? Our weapons are worthless against their armor and strengths. What do we do?" Tanis asked in a frantic yell, firing another arrow with no results.

"Outnumber them. Three Elves to one Slayer. Four even! Cut their heads from their bodies!"

All those who had heard the order hurried to follow it. Tanis turned to his left and found two Elven swordsmen fighting one Slayer and raised his bow. The arrow shot straight and hit in the center of the creature's back just above its beltline. The attack stunned it and one of the Elves managed a killing blow that sent flames into the air from the area where the head had been severed.

"The wizard's plan works! Come on! Fight in groups and spread their forces out!" Tanis shouted, looking for another target.

Elves spread out in groups numbering between three and five and began facing the Slayers as forces instead of one on one combat. Even though they had devised a plan to use against the Slayers, the creatures continued to swarm out of the portal freely. At the rate the Elves were losing soldiers there would soon be no one alive to face them. They would take Qwaz for their own and the wars would sweep all of the lands into darkness. Another arrow brought a Slayer's attention away from the sword it faced and more flames covered the body as it collapsed.

Thorgrim had moved through the weaker resistance to the north and now had the Demon in sight. He had no idea what he was going to do but the portal, the Demon, and Erzel were all right there. A Slayer rushed towards him and the Dwarf side-stepped the first two attacks with ease, returning with an attack of his own that sent the armored creature rolling across the ground.

The Dwarf ducked another attack from the right and then one from the left, moving faster than it seemed possible for a soldier his size. He swung back as he dodged to the side, the war hammer crushing the helmet of the closest Slayer in a shower of sparks. He was moving like water now, his dodges and attacks flowing so smoothly that it seemed impossible to disrupt him.

To the southern edge of the battle Tanis and his Elves had disappeared in the horde of Slayers and Ectle began to worry for the fate of everyone else. After the battle had begun he had lost sight of everyone in the group: Erzel near the portal, Thorgrim to the north, Lavian, Kail, and now Tanis all to the south. He ducked the thrust of a spear and cut the arm off of the attacker. He didn't even bother finishing off the attacker as he searched through the mayhem for the rest of the group.

A blue flash to his left reassured him that either Kail or Lavian was still alive but it was not enough to rid him of the worry. Elves scrambled around the battlefield in large groups as the Slayers were soon spread wider and thinner than the northern armies believed they would be able to manage. With Slayers now breaking their lines and formations the wizard caught his first uninhibited view of the portal. It stood high in the air and the flames gave it a red glow. He also witnessed the Slayers arriving from its depths and a new worry took the place of the first. How would they ever close the portal now that it was opened.

"Get down!" came a cry from the left.

Ectle instinctively dove forward to the ground as he heard the blade of a sword cut through the air where he had been seconds earlier. The attack was followed by a bright blue flash and he rolled to find Kail standing to his left. An Elf finished the Slayer off and the wizard quickly climbed to his feet.

"I lost Tanis in the battle. Have you seen him anywhere?" Ectle asked desperately as Kail approached.

Kail shook his head, a deep gash in his right cheek. To the south they both saw another blast of blue light and Kail nodded towards it. "Apparently they've yet to best the last of the Celestial Knights though."

Kail raised his bow and fired again, this time knocking one of the creatures down and allowing a trio of Elves to converge on it with spears and swords. Just like before the soldiers were fairing pretty well with their groups of attackers but overpowering a few Slayers here and there was not making a significant enough hole in their forces. If things continued on the path they were headed, the Elves would all be slaughtered. Kail nodded to the wizard and drew the bowstring tight, heading off into the battle once more.

Erzel found himself being pushed back towards the portal. Slayers soon began to get between him and the Demon, only to crumble under the strength of the whip. Even with a weapon as powerful as the one the Elf now wielded, the Demon had begun to advance with its sword drawn and ready. Erzel blocked an attack from a Slayer with his sword and wrapped the length of the whip around its helmet. He watched as it collapsed in on itself and a gush of flame escaped.

He was growing desperate with his attacks, hoping one would land but none ever did. Behind him a Slayer raised its sword to attack the Elf and for a moment things looked grim. From the right of the two came a whirling object and before the Slayer could deliver its thrust, the war hammer of Thorgrim crashed into its chest. The creature stumbled backward and fell back into the portal with a shriek of pain.

The attack left Thorgrim unarmed and the creatures were quick to take advantage. A lone Elven swordsman tried to step in and protect the Dwarf but an arrow cut across the field, catching the Elf in the temple. He was dead before he hit the ground. Thorgrim quickly scrambled to retrieve the fallen Elf's sword but before he could reach it he felt a strong force collide with him.

The Slayer had brought its knee up into the path of the Dwarf and caught him in the ribs, sending him tumbling across the ground. The Slayers converged on the downed Dwarf as Kail appeared from the thinning battlefield, his bow ready. He just caught sight of the Dwarf as a Slayer crossed into his view. He released the arrow and hit one of the Slayers from behind though it was only one of the six charging down on the Dwarf.

Kail continued firing but he felt in his heart that he was too late. The Slayers fell back away from the powerful blast from the bow and as the last took the glowing arrow to the chest Kail got a look at the Dwarf. Or what was left of him.

The Dwarf never stood a chance once the first sword stroke fell, followed by more than a dozen more. His body was covered with deep stabs and a thick pool of blood had already formed around the body. Kail fell to his knees beside the Dwarf and stared in disbelief at the body. That bloody body had been his friend, his comrade. Now there was no life left in him.

Kail felt tremendous anger growing inside. He stood, drawing the bowstring back and sighting down the glowing arrow. He waited until a Slayer stepped out of the portal and then fired, knocking the creature back into the fiery portal. He kept firing, keeping their reinforcements from exiting the portal. It would work, but for how long?

The Elf and the Demon

E rzel had not seen the attack but out of the corner of his eye he saw the Dwarf on his back in the pool of blood. His attacks ceased as he stared at the Dwarf. Infus approached, looking past the Elf at the scene. The Demon did not bother attacking and killing Erzel but instead found enjoyment in the pain the Elf was now feeling.

"How sweet this sight is. Now you see how pathetic your soldiers are. Weak, undisciplined, this is what you and your kind bring to face my armies? This is going to be a lot easier than I thought. Look at them die! Watch your precious Elves bleed!" the Demon cried out happily, digging at the Elf.

Erzel could hardly tear his eyes off of the remains of Thorgrim even as the Demon slung insults at him. He felt his hands tighten on his sword and on the handle of the whip. He felt his knuckles crack as he tightened further and he turned on the spot, cutting his eyes at the Demon. The blood of his friend was still warm and the Demon insulted him as if it were a joke. Erzel clenched his jaw tightly and prepared to strike.

"Come on then, let's finish this."

The Demon opened its arms wide, its sword brandished and ready. "I am going to enjoy this."

Erzel stepped to the right and cut down a Slayer that was momentarily distracted before turning and swinging at the Demon. The creature ducked and the whip lashed across the edge of the pillar behind Infus. Where the whip had struck was a distinct gash and as Erzel caught a glimpse of it, an idea formed in the back of his head. Now he knew how to destroy the portal.

Seeing the Elf deep in thought gave the Demon a chance to go on the offensive and it did just that, immediately crossing the distance between them in one long bound. Before Erzel had a chance to react the creature delivered a powerful swing of its closed fist, smashing Erzel across the jaw. The Elf stumbled back with his sword raised, not sure why he had let himself become distracted.

He didn't understand why the Demon had not struck a deadly blow, more just playing with him than trying to kill him. The thought sent a shiver through his back. The Demon did not want to kill him, it wanted to torture him in every imaginable way and only after breaking the Elf completely would it allow him death.

Kail fired just behind the Elf and caught another Slayer emerging from the portal in the middle of its chest, sending it stumbling back into the portal like the others before it. To the right a Slayer charged at the archer, its sword raised and ready. Kail caught sight of the attack and rolled away from the swing. He landed on a knee and drew the sword from his hip. As the Slayer charged again Kail stood and held the blade ready. The creature swung but Kail's agility took hold.

The fighter dodged right and gave a quick swing to the creature's shoulder. Before the Slayer could turn he struck again and the creature collapsed. Kail turned and walked towards the battle where Erzel and Infus were now locked on one another. He had rarely abandoned his bow but now he had to. The battle was too thick for ranged weapons and relying on his sword was possibly the only thing that would keep him alive.

Two Elves fell in behind him and the trio fought through the last few Slayers near the portal as another appeared. Kail dodged a sword stroke and looked up to see the Demon closing on the Elf. They were fighting back and forth and though Erzel had the whip, he was no closer to killing Infus than before. The creature was fast, much faster than the Elf had expected. His swings of the whip missed above and to the side while his sword had the same results as before, passing through the Demon with no damage being dealt.

"Come on Elf," Infus teased in a delightful hiss. "Elves are dying as we speak. I thought you were going to fight me. You are going to let their deaths all go without revenge."

"Shut up!" Erzel shouted, the whip snapping no more than an inch away from the Demon's head.

He could hear the Demon's hiss of laughter as he missed

again. To the right an Elf approached but Infus was watching and made a quick spin, cutting the Elf swordsman's head from his shoulders. The body of the Elf fell to the ground in a crumpled pile and Infus whirled back around in time to dodge yet another attack from Erzel.

Not only was the creature near impossible to hit, it was managing to kill other soldiers while avoiding the attacks. The Demon stepped in under one of the lashes with the whip and avoided the sword as well, opening its clawed gauntlet and striking out with it. The sharp tips on each of the fingers of the gauntlet raked down the left side of Erzel's face, leaving deep gashes that immediately gushed forth a spurt of blood. Erzel dropped his sword and staggered back with his glove pressed against the horrible wound that had marred his face.

"A taste of your own blood. How does that feel Elf?"

Erzel gripped the whip but kept his gloved hand pressed against the wound on his face. The pain was excruciating but he refused to take his eye off of the creature. Blood dripped freely down the side of his face and down the inside of his arm. After a few minutes he pulled his hand away, revealing the wound to the Demon.

"Ah... a beautiful sight, one of your kind suffering. I'm glad to know it does not end here. All of your kind will suffer, your little Princess the most."

Erzel knew the Demon meant to enslave all of Nalawren but hearing that the Demon wanted to torture his own love was only adding more fury. He stepped in and then faked an attack with the whip, catching the Demon off guard and whirling around with the weapon. By the time the Demon realized it had been caught in the open it was seconds from feeling the power of the whip.

Just before it did though a Slayer appeared from the left and stepped into the path of the weapon, the flames ripping through its body and leaving only a flaming pile of remains on the ground. Erzel drew back again and waited a moment, feeling the effects of the wounds and of exhaustion. He did not know how much longer he would be able to keep up his attacks, but the creature he faced seemed to never tire.

Lavian finally appeared from the heart of a massive battle

with her crossbow still leveled and ready to fire. The Slayers seemed to have fallen back to the center of the field and were fighting what was left of the Elves as their reinforcements continued to appear from the portal. She looked around the area and realized that the Elves were almost done in, leaving only a handful that had fallen back to where the wizard was standing.

"Ectle… what do we… do?" she asked, out of breath.

"Their armies just keep coming. Where… is King Tanis?" one of the archers asked as he joined the group as well.

Ectle and Lavian looked through the numbers around them but they did not see the King anywhere. Dread swept over the wizard as he realized that he saw neither King Tanis nor Thorgrim. It was entirely possible that they had lost the two in the masses of others and for the moment he tried to keep from thinking the worst.

"Have you seen Thorgrim, Kail, or Erzel since the battle started?" the wizard asked, looking at the Celestial Knight.

"No. I last saw the flash from Kail's bow a short time ago but nothing since. Their numbers just keep growing Ectle. Tell me you've an idea."

The wizard shook his head. He had spells that could wipe out a large number of their opponents but with the rate they were being replaced, he would quickly tire and be left vulnerable. Judging from the number of fallen Elves there would soon be more dead than alive. The wizard saw soldiers starting to clash again on the outer edges of the formations and now the centers charged again. Ectle hesitated for only a minute and then bolted as well, leading in with a whirling ball of fire.

In the midst of the battle the wizard continuously glanced around, wondering about the others. In the chaos of bodies he hardly had time to avoid the attacks coming his way, let alone pinpoint the King or the others. One creature charged but just before it could land its blow the wizard raised a hand and the creature stopped as if meeting a brick wall. In its stunned state, it was instantly finished off by one of the many Elves surrounding the wizard.

Ectle became a flurry of spells, sending fireballs, energy blasts, and bolts of lightning in every direction. The Slayers soon became wary of the wizard, but one of the creatures that did venture close enough was instantly leveled with a powerful ball of fire. He could feel the energies lessening as his waves of spells continued to fly from his hands and staff.

To his right he caught sight of Lavian and another Elf dragging a soldier back away from the battle. He stepped in behind the path of the three to cover their retreat, falling back with them. He watched the front lines of the Slayers falling but in the rear were more lines. He took another step back and turned, seeing the Elf and Celestial Knight at the edge of the battle.

"Ectle! Come here now!" Lavian yelled, discarding her crossbow and kneeling next to the body.

Ectle hurried back to them and fell to a knee beside her and the body. After all he had witnessed on the battlefield the wizard would have thought himself seasoned and strong against the horrors that accompanied the war but the body lying on the ground next to him caught him completely off guard. It was Tanis.

The Elf stared straight ahead, still alive but pale and growing lighter by the minute. He had an arrow in the right side of his chest and several stabs in his left side. Blood covered his chest and sides and Ectle fought to figure out what he needed to do to help him. Tanis slumped and looked to the side at the wizard.

"Ectle... I don't know... what happened."

"Quiet my Lord, save your strength. We're going to..."

"Save it Ectle... I know... this is beyond... you."

"Tanis, lie back. At least let me see the wounds. Perhaps I can do something to help. Lavian, you have to put pressure to the wounds in the side. I have to try and..."

Tanis pushed the wizard back with what little strength he had, trying the get Ectle to leave him. The battle around them was no place to attempt to heal the wounded and Tanis knew it. "You can't save... me."

Ectle looked down at the King and then glanced over at Lavian. He gave her a nod and the Celestial Knight stood, leaving the King and wizard alone. Ectle leaned down next to the King's ear and whispered softly so only he could hear.

"Have you anything for me to tell the Queen?"

Tanis looked past the wizard into the sky as if blinded by a light. His face brightened and he nodded very slowly. "Only that I... am sorry. I promised to come home. Tell Narissa... tell her that I love her."

"Of course my King," Ectle replied with a nod, feeling the King's hand tighten on his own.

"Ectle… and tell Rhen… let her know that I… that I approve of him. Erzel is a…"

The King stopped in the middle of his thought. His jaw continued to move ever so slightly as if he were only mouthing the words. Ectle reached down and touched his cheek which immediately seemed to bring him back to reality.

"Erzel will be a… fine husband. They have my blessing. Take… care of them Ectle…"

The wizard gave him a hollow stare and then nodded. Before he had time to respond Tanis reached up and grabbed him by the collar, pulling the wizard down closer to him.

"…and the boy… her son. Tell her to name him…"

"Yes? To name him what, my King? Tanis?"

Tanis coughed and his head rolled to the side. With one last effort he pulled it up straight and looked the wizard in the eyes, his whisper barely audible. "Naben…"

A trickle of blood appeared in the corner of his mouth and quickly fell out across his cheek, disappearing somewhere below his chin. Ectle stared at him for a minute but soon realized that the Elf had no life left in his body. The King had died. Ectle gently laid the King back on the ground and closed his eyes, remembering his last words.

"Yes my King, I will honor your wishes."

For the last ten minutes he had completely ignored the battle that continued to rage around him but now the sound of steel against steel pulled him back to the fight that was starting to surge towards him. Elves were still fighting valiantly, refusing to give up, but the Slayers were much stronger. They continued to surge through the portal in droves and the wizard wondered in his mind about retreating. Soon there would be none of them left alive to fight against the creatures. If they fell back now, there was a chance they could meet up with the Elves marching from Pentegarn and attack again afterwards. That of course would allow an even greater force of Slayers to swarm the lands around Qwaz. Desperation was pulling him one direction while duty was pushing him in the opposite.

From the south he was suddenly surprised to find an answer to his dilemma. They had apparently marched in and locked in their formations without either the Slayers or the Elves realizing they had arrived. To the southern edge of the fields around Qwaz came large formations of Dwarves marching in from the forests. Ectle grabbed an Elf as he moved past and turned him to the sight to the south.

"Are those…"

"Yes, the Dwarves. They were headed back for Tvan before we left for Qwaz. What a beautiful sight… reinforcements. Push back against the Slayers with everything you have! We have to contain their armies!" the wizard ordered loudly.

He continued to watch the Dwarves march slowly up the fields towards the massacre to the west of the city. The Elves were almost completely wiped out by now and the strongest of their leaders had fallen or were unaccounted for. The Dwarves would add strength to the resistance, but there was still one problem. How were they to destroy the portal?

Erzel did not know of the Dwarves. He had no idea that there were reinforcements on the way. All he could see were the countless Elven bodies covering the ground and the Slayers that continued to appear from the flaming red portal. Sweat covered his face and the wound on his back was sucking all of the strength from his body. The infection had taken hold and was slowly poisoning his body. He had no choice but to keep fighting.

For the most part the Slayers ignored the Elf engaged in battle with the Demon but occasionally one would foolishly step in between the two. Erzel found the whip a powerful weapon against the slower moving Slayers, but he had yet to hit the Demon. The Slayer caught in the path of the whip stood no chance and fell to the ground in flames. The cycle repeated with Erzel attacking, Infus avoiding, and Slayers foolishly stepping in to die.

Erzel had been on the offensive almost from the moment he had revealed the whip so it was understandable that he was caught off guard when the Demon suddenly dodged right and came in swinging. His agility served him instantly and Erzel knocked the strokes of the sword to the side as they continued to rain down. With the Demon this close Erzel found that he could no longer effectively use the whip. He ducked and rolled away, rising onto a knee and lashing out.

The whip arched through the air and met the sword in the Demon's hand. It wrapped around the blade of the weapon several times and Erzel gave a firm jerk. Just as many times before the power of the whip reigned supreme and the strong flames cut through the sword. With a snap of his wrist the blade separated from the handle and fell to the ground beside Infus. The Demon stepped back.

"Not so confidant now it seems," Erzel taunted, snapping the whip in front of him as he prepared to strike again.

Erzel watched as the Demon retrieved an Elven sword from the ground and the thought of the creature using a weapon from one of his Elven brothers made Erzel feel sick at his stomach. He saw the Demon then draw a long, thin dagger from inside its robes and it advanced again. They squared off once more and just like before the Demon made a fast advance on the Elf.

The Elf drew back a ways before lashing out to the right of the creature's head. Again he attacked and this time the whip found the blade of the Elven sword, rendering it useless just as before. The Demon discarded the ruined sword in stride and pushed inside the reach of the whip. Erzel struck with his sword but in his desperation he had forgotten that the sword would deal no damage to the Demon.

Just as it always had, the blade of the sword slid into the chest and out the back without a hint of resistance. This had been what Infus had expected. Missing with the whip and then stabbing with his sword had left the Elf overextended and vulnerable. The Demon reached in under the Elf's sword arm and thrust the dagger in through the chain mail armor. Erzel felt the sharp point penetrate his skin and then plunge deep in between his upper ribs on the right side of his body.

"How does that feel?" the Demon hissed, watching the sword fall out of the Elf's hand.

Erzel could not answer. The pain was worse than the claws that had marred his face, worse than the arrow that had lodged in his back. He felt his knees start to give and Infus twisted the dagger, snapping the blade off inside the Elf. Erzel collapsed to the ground.

"Look what we do to those who oppose us! Look how they suffer! Look how they die!" the Demon cried out to the Slayers around it.

Erzel glanced to the left at the portal now only feet away from him and then back at the Demon. He had been so close. He could have destroyed them both had he known how to use the whip properly. The whip was all powerful. No metal nor stone resisted it once it landed against them. No armor protected a wearer from its searing flames. The portal seemed to pull at him, sucking him in. Then the Elf realized that the Demon had left itself open to something it would never expect.

The Elf looked to the side and caught sight of the war hammer that had been carried by Thorgrim and stretched out to the handle. He wrapped his fingers around the leather handle and pulled it down to him, the pain racing through his side more ex-cruciating than anything else he had ever known. The Elf glanced up one last time at the Demon and then with all of his strength he struck with the whip.

The green flames shot out and struck the Demon from behind. The long whip wrapped over its shoulder and then down around its body twice, creating a firm hold on the creature. The moment he felt tension against the whip the Elf rolled and swung the mighty war hammer. He did not aim for the Demon nor the Slayers around it. His target was the pillar next to his head.

The steel head of the war hammer hit the black stone with a deafening crack and was instantly knocked from the Elf's hands. Where it met the stone was a deep crack that was now growing up the length of the pillar and branching, creating a bright spider web effect across the face of the stone. Red light shone out of the cracks and then the pull from the portal grew stronger, sliding the Elf in closer. Infus reached to the flaming whip but the sudden tug pulled it over and then onto the ground. It looked up at the Elf who gave another strong pull.

"I'll die... but I'm taking you... with me..." Erzel choked out, blood dripping over the edge of his bottom lip.

The crack continued to spread, reaching the top of the pillar. The portal was growing more and more unstable by the minute and in its fury the force jerked Erzel up off of the ground. Infus felt the pull and reached out, clawing the ground as the Elf pulled it in as well. It left deep gashes in the earth as it slid closer. The Elf clung desperately to the handle of the whip as his feet touched the red flames of the portal. An intense burning surged up his legs as he slid deeper into the portal, but he refused to release the whip.

The Demon gave one more desperate swing with its clawed gauntlet but missed any sort of hold and fell back from the force of the portal pulling the Elf and whip. Erzel was suddenly engulfed with flames and disappeared into the portal, the whip sliding in like a snake. At the very end came the Demon, its shrill hiss of anger filling the air as it too met the red flames and found itself burning just like the Elf. Seconds passed between the Demon hitting the portal and disappearing but the scream of anger still filled the air.

Kail stood no more than twenty yards away with his sword frozen above his head. In shock he watched the Elf fall to the ground and then lash out with the whip. The sound of the Demon shrieking in anger filled the air and every soldier there stopped and stood rigid. The fighter watched Erzel disappear into the flames, and then seconds later the Demon followed, its terrifying scream still echoing in the air.

The pillar on the left had cracked fully and was now crumbling in on itself, the movement bringing down the pillar to the right. They folded down onto the flames of the portal and as the last of the blackened stone crumbled onto the flames an earth-shaking explosion rocked the fields. The force of the explosion sent debris flying through the air, accompanied by a thick cloud of ash. Even in the sickeningly thick cloud Kail did not move from the spot.

To his right he saw Slayers bursting into flames and collapsing. Every Slayer in the fields outside of Qwaz was now a flaming wreck, their armor collapsing to the ground where they remained lifeless. As the ash began to settle the fighter realized what had happened. With the portal closing on the Demon, its grip on the Slayers had been broken. They were now all lifeless and fallen. The handful of Goblins that remained immediately broke for the forests, trying to get as much distance between them and the Elves as they possibly could.

Cheers now filled the clearings but Kail remained silent, falling to his knees beside the body of the Dwarf. He could not find happiness in the moment even though the armies of Slayers had been vanquished and the Demon defeated. All of his friends were lost. Guilt gripped him as he remembered he had once served Valsera. He dropped his eyes to the ground and a tear formed in the corner of his eye when a hand gently touched his shoulder.

"Kail, are you hurt?"

The fighter turned and found Ectle now kneeling in beside him.

"Yes... I mean no, I am fine. They're all dead Ectle."

The wizard looked to the side at the Dwarf and nodded solemnly, realizing that the fighter was wracked with grief. "Tanis has fallen as well. The King of the Wood Elves, dead. What of Erzel?"

Kail looked up to the area where the portal had been. The smoldering remains wrenched his guts as he thought now about the Princess who would never see her love again, her child who would never see its father. He raised a shaking hand and pointed to the crumbled remains, uttering only one word.

"There..."

"In the ruins? Come on, we have to dig him out!"

Kail remained where he was and shook his head sadly. "No, not the ruins, the portal. He pulled the Demon in with him just as it collapsed. He... sacrificed himself."

Ectle stood from the spot where Kail was and walked slowly through the burning masses of Slayers to where the portal had been. The black stone was now in ruins with smoldering, shards of it slung across the fields. To the right side of the pile a glimmer caught his eye and he stooped to retrieve the item. As he pulled it from the dust and rubble he realized he held Erzel's sword, the gift from the Celestial Knights.

He carried the sword back to the fighter kneeling next to the fallen Dwarf and laid it in his lap, catching the look in Kail's eye as he did so.

"Erzel would have wanted this to be delivered to Rhen in the event of his death. I feel you will be well trusted to deliver it. Consider it an honor."

Lavian arrived moments later with a Dwarf by her side. She stopped when she saw Thorgrim on the ground covered in blood and Kail and Ectle on their knees next to him. She walked in behind them and cleared her throat to catch their attention.

"The Dwarves have arrived, Ectle. May I present Velex, Elder of Tvan."

The wizard and fighter stood together and Ectle stepped in between the two to prevent any hostilities that might flare up with Kail's pained losses. He stared down at the Elder and bit his own lip, wondered what was appropriate in this sort of situation. The Dwarves had deserted them in Pentegarn and now they arrive just as the battle ended, after the Elves had nearly lost every soldier they had brought. Instead of speaking, Ectle gave a respectful nod.

"I see one of my kind has been killed in this battle. He will be honored greatly of course. Forgive my tardiness, our ships were a touch slower than we had originally anticipated."

"What honor will you give to the rest of those here who have lost their lives protecting the north?" Kail snapped quickly, stepping around the wizard.

Ectle shook off the man's anger and took a step towards Velex. "What ships? What are you talking about?"

"Well, after Cisalia fell, Ardis sent word that we were to make for Qwaz immediately. He said with the army at the Pass of Merwold we'd do well to find another way into the southlands. So it was with ships. You made quite a mess of things, don't you think?"

Kail saw red and raised Erzel's sword as he took a quick step towards the rude Dwarf. "We managed quite well considering we were forced to fight on our own while Elder Ardis sought to pull his armies out of the alliance. He made a mess of things."

Ectle grabbed Kail by the shoulder and pulled him away as the anger was clearly escalating. He pushed the man back a few steps and raised a finger. "Calm yourself Kail before you start another war."

"That's right, reel your dog in. I think he should have a bit more civilized tongue considering we came all this way to help your Elves."

Now it was Ectle who was enraged as he turned on the Dwarf. "Came to help? You managed to get here just as it ended! What help were you? So far you've done nothing but insult those who died here trying to protect their homes. Perhaps you should heed your own words, Elder."

Velex cocked his head to the side and took a step towards the wizard with a mischievous smile crossing his face. "I would be offended but I think I will just walk away and let you clean up your mess. You'll all get what you deserve soon enough."

The Elder turned and his army moved to the west with him, avoiding the mass carnage in the middle of the field. They marched away from the Elves once more, abandoning their alliance for the second time. Ectle decided he could care less. Their soldiers were not needed now that the battle had ended. They had become rude and ungrateful, neither of which the wizard was willing to tolerate.

Lavian and Kail approached and stopped beside the wizard, staring out across the field as the Dwarves reached the trees to the north of the city. Kail still held Erzel's sword in his hand, a searing urge to use it on the disrespectful Dwarf for his words. It was lucky that the Dwarf had turned and left. Ectle reached over and placed a firm hand on the fighter's shoulder.

"Let it go, Kail. They will be punished for what they have done to their alliance. I am sure of it."

"What do you think the Dwarf meant when he said we will all get what we deserve soon enough?" Lavian asked curiously, a hint of worry in her voice.

"I am not sure," Ectle replied. "I hope it was only Velex's empty threats. The Dwarves are becoming more and more unpredictable with every move they make. I do not know what to expect now. Let them go."

The three watched as a group of Elves walked by, carrying the body of Tanis with them. The Elf was now pale white, the color of death. Ectle, Lavian, and Kail all gave one last respectful bow to the King as the Elves carried him off to be sent back to Pentegarn with what was left of the army.

One thing the Ectle noticed was that there were hardly any wounded Elves on the battlefield. They were either dead or alive. The Slayers did not look to wound their opponents and instead chose to kill them as fast as they possibly could. The rows of fallen Elves became depressing to witness and the wizard turned away, leaving the soldiers to their tasks. Lavian and Kail had moved to the far edge of the field and Ectle made his way over to them.

Kail looked up and nodded to the city. "Qwaz and Nomaria are probably still crawling with Goblins and Ogres even though Infus has been defeated. What do you think we should do?"

"Forget about the cities. Without Infus or Valsera leading them the Ogres and Goblins will break apart and no longer be a threat. We need to get back to Pentegarn and report to Elendil. I only hope he managed well at the pass."

"Elendil had more than twice our forces behind him when he marched for the pass, I am sure the High Elves faired well. Add to that the Goblins and Ogres were on the run."

"Perhaps," Ectle began. "Elendil was also facing far more soldiers at the pass. His numbers did not count for as much with the enemy armies so strong."

"He didn't fight Slayers…"

Ectle stared at the fighter and breathed in a deep sigh of frustration as he tried not to argue with Kail. He knew the fighter was suffering after watching Erzel disappear into the Demon's portal and knew he had to try to show some sort of compassion. The wizard reached out and patted the fighter's shoulder twice as if to reassure him that things would get better.

"You're right, Kail, the Slayers were far stronger and in the end, outnumbered us greatly. We just have to hope that the King was able to make it out of the pass unharmed now that the King of the Wood Elves has fallen. The Elves have to have a King."

Ectle stood and Kail followed him as they looked to the north. They would be returning home soon, back to the families that had survived, back to the soldiers who had lived through the battles, back to tell them all that the wars and terrors had finally ended.

The Lives of Those Lost

*T*he Elves in the fields outside of Qwaz had managed to pull their fallen together and though they did not have the resources to carry all of them back to their homelands, they honored them in the best way that they could. Monstrous funeral pyres were built and all of those who had given their lives were honored the way the Kings of old had been. Flames stretched into the sky all through the night and by morning of the next day the coals were just beginning to die down. The bodies of Tanis and Thorgrim were loaded onto a wagon and taken north with the rest of the army.

Knowing the Dwarves had moved north through the pass gave Ectle some reassurance that the battles there had died down. He rode ahead of the remainder of the forces, scouting and keeping his eyes peeled for any sign of opposing forces. As he closed on the river he realized the army that had retreated from Pentegarn had been destroyed.

Soon he began finding bodies in the woods as he drew nearer to the Pass of Merwold and as he got closer, the piles of dead grew taller. The stench of death continued to grow and the wizard soon found himself standing on the southern shore of the Pass of Merwold. All over the pass were the Dwarves, now working feverishly to clean up the dead and finish the dying. The Dwarves paid no attention to the Elves as they tossed the dead Goblins into piles and shoved the rest into the current of the river.

"This is sickening. They contaminate the water," one Elf whispered as he watched the mangled body of a Goblin float by.

Ectle did not bother offering any sort of response to the soldier. He too found the sight grotesque and disturbing to see the bodies of the dead filling the water and lining the shores of a once beautiful area. He walked down the slope of the shore to the edge of the water and stared across to where the largest mass of Dwarven soldiers remained. He turned to Kail and the other soldiers, nodding to the far shore.

"We have to cross. Put aside your angers and your dissatisfaction with the Dwarves until we are all home. For now, let them believe they have done a great service in destroying the forces here at the pass."

It was obvious that the Elves still loyal to the fallen King were unhappy with the thought of allowing the Dwarves to continue defiling the land around the pass and its resources but with their army left in shambles and their King dead they were in no position to make their concerns heard. The Elves followed the wizard through the river with the wagon and their fallen in tow. As Ectle crossed and arrived on the other side he received mixed looks and glares from the Dwarven soldiers.

Hushed whispers crossed the lips of the Dwarves as the Elves continued up across the shores on their way to the northern lands. They did not bother making eye contact with the Dwarves, knowing the disrespect they tended to show as of late, picking up every detail of their whispers with their Elven ears.

"Is that all that is left of their army?"

"You see, I told you they were weaker, they've nothing left of their soldiers."

"It's a good thing Velex went south to help them or there really would be nothing left."

Ectle dropped his eyes to the ground as the whispers continued, their ungrateful nature filling the air with disrespect. He wanted to turn to the Dwarves, to yell at them and let them know just how pathetic their presence in the south was. That the Elves had given their lives and beaten the Slayers on their own. The Dwarves had arrived just in time to claim the glory, but not to fight for it.

Instead he stared straight ahead, leading the broken Wood Elves out of the pass on their way to the Elven lands. By the time the Elves had cleared the Pass of Merwold, every soldier was fuming with anger at their smaller allies. Ectle maintained his lead out front, trying to keep the rage that was swelling inside of him from bursting forth. Halfway through the upper field above the Pass of Merwold Kail moved up next to the wizard and examined his mood.

"Ectle? Are you alright?"

"What is going on? Those Dwarves owe everything to these Elves and what they did at Qwaz. If the Elves had not given their lives there, the Slayers would be swarming north right now."

"The Dwarves have never shown gratitude. The Elves could have saved the lives of a million Dwarves and they would still be ungrateful. I fear that when Elendil learns of their nature it will likely destroy what is left of the alliances. This is going to create a lot of tension between the races."

Ectle nodded. "Possibly worse than just tension. There is no telling what Elendil will do. Perhaps nothing now that Valsera and Infus have both been defeated. Though I know Elendil and the way he views things. This will not sit well."

Kail draped his bow across his right shoulder and Erzel's sword on his left. He marched next to the wizard, the events of the pass still rolling through his head. It was one thing for the Elder Velex to show the disrespect that he had but for the armies of Dwarves to do the same was unforgivable. Deep inside he hoped there would be consequences but he was smart enough to know that what remained of the Elven armies would never manage against the Dwarves. They would keep their real feelings hidden.

"Ectle, what do you think happened to Erzel? I mean, when the portal closed on him and the Demon."

The wizard allowed himself to think for a moment, not knowing for sure what exactly had happened when the Elf pulled the Demon in. He saw the devastation the explosion left as the portal collapsed in on itself but he could not begin to speculate what waited on the other side.

"We can only hope that whatever his fate was, it was quick. I like to imagine that the portal closing on him was the end and the same for the Demon but I can not say. What exactly did it look like from where you stood?"

"Like torture," Kail recalled, remembering the Elf's face as his body was pulled through the flames of the portal. "Erzel was in so much pain but he refused to release his grip on the whip. It was clear though that the Demon felt the same pain. I can still hear its shrill screams as it too was drug back into the portal."

Ectle nodded to himself as the information rolled through

his head and he turned to Kail, his face very stern and serious. "Listen carefully Kail. We can not tell Rhen of that. If she must know, there was no pain, there was no agony, and that he died to save us all. In her current state she likely could not handle knowing the torment he was put through."

"I agree fully. In the end, his life was what saved us all. Had he not pulled the Demon in with him, we would never have left the fields alive. If the Dwarves will not honor him for what he has done, we shall."

"Absolutely," Ectle whispered as they caught the first sight of the city in the distance. "I believe the time is upon us."

Kail and Ectle continued out ahead of the rest of the soldiers as Pentegarn grew nearer. The whole time Ectle worried about how he was going to manage telling the Queen she had lost her husband while at the same time telling Rhen she had lost her father, her lover, and the father of her unborn child. The Princess would likely take the news far worse than the Queen and to the wizard that was the problem. How she reacted could possibly put her unborn child in danger.

"Have you any ideas on how to break this sort of news to someone?" the wizard asked, feeling uneasy in the pit of his stomach.

"I would expect as gently as possible, but in the end, being compassionate and offering whatever you can to help them through their difficult times to come... or something like that."

Ectle gave a weak smile, "That isn't half bad, Kail, thank you. I find I sometimes come across with less compassion than might be expected. I guess through the years I have found the direct approach the most efficient."

"That is needed at times. Are you ready for this?" Kail asked as they were now approaching the ruined gate to the south.

Ectle shook his head, scanning the walls and the faces of the Elves on them. "Not hardly. Good news to King Elendil while painfully bad news to the Queen and Princess of Swanhaven. Come, let us find the King first."

The wizard continued through the massive gap in the wall where the gate had once been and continued on through the blackened and crumbling buildings of the outer city. Elves had already begun cleaning up the worst of the damages, salvaging anything they could out of the ruins. They stopped to watch the two pass, followed shortly by the Wood Elves and the cart carrying the King and the Dwarf. Elves seeing the wagon and the bodies that were covered inside it immediately feared the worst, their whispers spreading through the numbers like wildfire.

As they moved through what was left of the outer city Ectle took a moment to notice that the bodies of the fallen, both Elven and Goblin, had been completely cleared from the city. The Elves that had been left behind to protect and repair the city had been quite busy.

Ectle now found himself at the inner gate which had received catastrophic damage similar to the outer. It had yet to buckle though and with some bracing the Elves seemed to have managed to strengthen it enough to make it stable. Only one of the large doors to the gate remained intact while the other had splintered and collapsed. The one thing that the Elves had been unable to change was the bloodstained ground that stretched from the outer fields to the inner gate. Ectle shook his head and raised his stare back to the inner city as he and Kail crossed under the weakened inner battlements.

Ahead a large group of High Elves appeared from the heart of the castle and waited as Ectle and Kail approached.

The wizard nodded to them. "We are here to speak with Elendil. Allow us to pass soldier."

The Elf looked to the wizard and then to Kail as if weighing his decisions, but after a moment he waved his arm and the soldiers cleared a path to the castle. The soldier stepped in beside the wizard and matched his pace, speaking briskly as they entered the castle.

"You must know master wizard, even though your business is likely of great importance, the King is in no condition to entertain guests at the moment. He will tire easily and must not be excited in his current state."

"What state is that? Has something happened?"

"He was injured in the battle at the pass. Physicians have deemed his condition stable but he is very weak and needs his rest more than anything else at the moment. I was ordered to see that he was not disturbed, but I do know he will want to hear of the outcome of the southern offensive."

Ectle looked at Kail and raised an eyebrow at the news that the King had been injured in the battle at the pass. If he was stable there was less reason for concern, but the fact that he had been hurt was still unsettling. The soldier led Ectle and Kail past the throne room and further down the hall to the King's bed chambers. Outside there were three armed guards who stopped their approach.

"The King is not receiving visitors at this time," the one in front said, raising his hand to stop them.

"We have urgent news from the battlefields around Qwaz that the King will be awaiting. I am aware of his condition but this can not wait. Please allow us in."

The guard looked to the side at the soldier who had escorted them to the room and then back to the wizard. He took a deep breath and nodded.

"Alright, but try to make this as quick as possible. Let them pass."

The other two guards moved to the side and the first soldier who had addressed them pulled the door open. Ectle led the way through the door and stopped just inside as Kail joined him and waited as the door slowly closed. Inside the room were three more soldiers, waiting around the perimeter of the room and another on the balcony.

Ectle crossed the room slowly and stopped next to the bed. The King was breathing deeply and appeared asleep until Ectle reached down and touched him on the shoulder. Elendil stirred briefly and turned his head to the side. The King was pale white and Ectle could tell it was a struggle to manage even small movements. The wizard gave a false smile as his eyes dropped down the King's body.

The wizard's eyes stopped on the bandages that wrapped the left arm. The only problem was that the left arm was missing. The bandages wrapped around a short stump just below the shoulder. Elendil looked down to where the wizard's gaze had stopped and then raised his eyes back up.

"It only looks bad... old friend," the King whispered, his body exhausted.

"Elendil, you're missing an arm. That seems bad."

The King chuckled and looked down. He was in incredibly good humor considering what he had been through. Ectle was curious as to how the King had lost his arm, but he knew that there were more important things that needed to be dealt with.

Elendil looked from Ectle to Kail and then back to the wizard, his gaze very clear. Ectle shook his head sadly.

"No my King, Erzel did not survive. He battled the Demon bravely but in the end he sacrificed himself to pull Infus into the portal as it collapsed in on itself. The explosion was catastrophic and in the end, all of the Slayers fell. We are victorious, my King."

Elendil nodded very slowly, his eyes foggy and weak from the damage he had suffered. The news was understandably upsetting but he managed to keep his composure. Erzel had always been close to the King through all of the war, taking his orders and carrying them out unconditionally. Losing his best Knight felt more like losing a close friend, a son even.

"He will be... honored. Have you... told Rhen? She's fond of him you know."

"Yes my King, I know. I will find her at once. Take your rest and I will come back shortly."

"Yes... and I will wait here."

Ectle and Kail gave quick bows and turned to leave, both still reeling from the sight of the deathly weak King. Hearing he had been wounded and seeing the extent of those wounds were two different things. Seeing the King made them realize that healing was going to be a long, arduous process.

Ectle and Kail waited as the door closed behind them and turned, knowing their next stop would be to deliver the news of their lost loved ones to the Princess and the Queen. Ectle gave Kail a nod and led the way out through the hall. He walked in silence, rolling over in his thoughts how he would say what needed to be said. Together they stopped at the throne room and entered, finding it nearly empty.

A single soldier approached them and gave a nod to the wizard. "How can I help you, sir?"

"We are looking for the Queen and Princess of Swanhaven. Do you know where we can find them, soldier?"

"Yes sir. Both the Queen and Princess left for the gardens about an hour ago. The Princess has spent a lot of time out there after the armies left. Shall I escort you sir?"

"That will not be necessary, continue with your duties."

The wizard continued on down through the castle to where the hall opened up into the massive gardens. He stopped just inside the entrance and looked around the area, seeing only guards and flowers. He and Kail made their way slowly through the paths of the gardens until they rounded a corner and came upon the fountain. Sitting on the other side of the fountain he saw both Narissa and Rhen.

All he had thought on the walk down through the castle now disappeared, leaving him standing in the open without a clue of how to tell the Princess what he had come to say. The Queen looked up from the bench where they sat and for a moment their eyes met. In that pause she knew that the wizard was there with bad news but she only gave the simplest of nods and rubbed her daughter's shoulders, whispering to her. Rhen looked up next and came to the same conclusion as her mother. She on the other hand was not able to hold her emotions together.

Ectle started across the clearing between them, watching as Rhen's eyes became teary and red, knowing that Erzel would have come himself had he come back at all. Narissa tried to comfort her daughter but there was little she could do.

Ectle and Kail both dropped to a knee in front of the two, the Princess still trying to get her emotions under control. "Queen Narissa, Princess Rhen, we bring news from the fields of battle."

"Please... stand..." Narissa choked, trying to remain strong.

"Queen Narissa, it pains me to tell you that your husband, the King of Swanhaven has fallen in battle. We have brought his body back, but there was no saving him. He died bravely, as was his way."

Ectle stopped long enough to catch the emotion on her face, seeing her strong features weaken slightly. She nodded and clenched her jaw, keeping her tears back long enough to let the wizard continue.

"He had last words I was to deliver to the both of you..."

Narissa nodded and Rhen managed to straighten enough to hear what the wizard had to say.

"To the Queen, he expressed how sorry he was that he would not return as he had promised. He also wanted to me to tell you... that he... loves you very much. No matter what, he loves you. He also made me promise to take care of you two in his absence."

Narissa bit her bottom lip and nodded for him to continue, the first of the tears now dropping down across her cheek. Rhen was still shaking with fear as to what news the wizard was about to give her as Ectle turned to the Princess.

"Princess Rhen. Your father was sure that Erzel would make a fine husband and he... gave you his blessing. He wanted the two of you to be happy and safe. My apologies my dear Princess, I was not able to save him."

Rhen started to reply but out of her only came a choked cry. Inside of her was a mixture of emotions that were all trying to burst forward at the same time. She felt pain for the loss of her father, relief that he had given his blessing to her and Erzel, and now fear for what the wizard still had to say. Ectle nodded and continued.

"He did say one other thing for you Princess. His last words were for your unborn child. I understand you had the name for a daughter and as your father slipped away, he gave a name for a son. In his dying breath he asked for your son to be named Naben.."

"Naben?"

Ectle nodded. "Yes, I understood him very clearly. Does that name have a significance for you Princess?"

Rhen shook her head but Narissa spoke up quickly.

"Naben, it was the name we had chosen for our child had Rhen been born a Prince. He held to that name for so many years."

The atmosphere in the garden was cold. Kail stood a few steps behind the wizard watching with a heavy heart as the Queen and Princess were told of everything that had happened, their worlds crumbling. He still held Erzel's sword in his left hand and it felt heavier as the time to tell of the Elf's death drew near. Ectle reached out and placed a hand on the Princess's shoulder, trying to offer her some stability.

"There is more Rhen."

"Ectle... I don't think I can..."

The wizard gave an understanding nod and drew in a deep breath. "Should I wait until later to give you time to collect yourself?"

After a brief moment of silence the Princess bit her lip and shook her head. "No, please, go ahead."

"Princess Rhen, we are alive and here today only because

of the sacrifice that Erzel made. He single-handedly killed the Demon Infus and destroyed the portal between our lands and those of the Slayers. My dear Princess, he died to ensure your child would never know the pain and suffering the Slayers can inflict."

Rhen knew in her heart the whole time that she had lost Erzel, but it wasn't until she actually heard the words that the shock set in. Her hands were shaking uncontrollably even with the wizard and her mother holding her upright. With her face smothered in tears she stood from the bench and hurried off into the castle, ignoring them as they called after her.

"Ectle… where are their bodies?" the Queen asked as she straightened herself from the emotional moments.

"The body of your husband was brought back with us, my Queen. Erzel's body will sadly never be seen again. He pulled the Demon into the portal as it collapsed, forever sealing him on the other side."

"Was it painful?"

Ectle looked to the ground as he started to wonder how much of what had happened should be told. He looked to the castle to be sure the Princess was not in range of the conversation before continuing.

"Yes my Queen… unfortunately they suffered. Erzel possibly the worst of all. Your husband was mortally wounded and near death when I came upon him. I assure you, if there had been something I could have done to help him, I would have."

Narissa nodded and stood from the bench. "Please excuse me, I must attend to my daughter."

Ectle and Kail gave bows as she passed and then stood in the heart of the garden with their emotions still swimming. Kail still held Erzel's sword in his hands and reached out to hand it to the wizard who took it with a quick glance at the fighter.

"I am sorry, Ectle, I can not be the one to hand this to Rhen. You knew Erzel far better and the Princess as well. If it is truly an honor, I believe it is one that you deserve."

"Very well, Kail. I know this has been an ordeal for you my friend. Please, find a room and rest. You have earned it."

Kail nodded and left the gardens. Only Ectle remained now, taking a seat in the middle of the bench where the Queen and Princess had been earlier. He leaned back and closed his eyes with only the sound of the water in the fountain reaching his ears. In the darkness behind his eyelids he suddenly caught a flash of red light followed by the sight of Erzel's tormented face as he was drawn into the portal.

The wizard sat straight up and his eyes shot open, the sight of the Elf's face tortured from pain shocking him. He stared straight ahead into the shimmering pool of water as the effects faded, but the beads of sweat on his forehead were still very real. He could not understand why the picture of the Elf had climbed into his mind, but it had shaken him.

The wizard ran a hand through his hair and took a deep breath. He had not even seen Erzel's death but now it haunted him somehow. Their group had suffered heavy losses since the beginning of the war and now, with it finally ending, only a few of them remained to retell the story. To his right the wizard heard the clearing of a throat and turned.

"Nimir?"

"You made it back! When I saw how few were returning I feared the worst. Where... is... everyone?"

"Kail just left the gardens minutes before you arrived. Thorgrim, Tanis, and Erzel all fell in battle at Qwaz. The armies of Qwaz managed to kill almost all of the army we arrived with. The losses were unbelievable and on top of that, King Elendil has been horribly wounded as well."

"I have not been to see Elendil. The Elves and Dwarves brought him in and immediately made for the privacy of the royal bedchambers. How bad is it?" Nimir asked as he took a seat next to the wizard.

"I understand it was a spear. They tried to save the arm but in the end it had to be taken. His left arm was amputated just below the shoulder."

Nimir did not speak. He heard what the wizard had said but it did not seem to register right away. As he pieced together what information had been handed to him he suddenly realized the situation they found themselves in.

"So... what happens to Pentegarn and Swanhaven now? Elendil is no longer able to rule in his current state and the death of Tanis has left the Queen and Princess. How do the races carry on?"

This was in fact a question that the wizard had been struggling with since he had learned that Elendil had been gravely wounded. The Elves had to have some sort of leadership. The Wood Elves now turned to a distraught Princess and a grieving Queen after the loss of Tanis. Elendil had no Queen nor heirs to his throne, leaving no one to take the responsibility while he recovered. Ectle shook his head as no answer seemed to present itself, unsure of how to answer the concerns.

"That was not reassuring," Nimir muttered, standing from the bench.

"Where are you going?" Ectle asked sternly.

Nimir tossed his hands into the air and shrugged. "I don't know. Just somewhere else for now."

Ectle could tell the Dwarf was worried. The Demon and the Goblin army had been defeated, but with heavy losses of Elves and the death of the Wood Elf King. On top of that the High Elf was now unable to lead his people, leaving only the Dwarves who had developed an apparent grudge against the Elves that remained. The disrespect of the Dwarves in the fields of Qwaz and at the Pass of Merwold had left the wizard concerned with what was happening.

He raised the sword and looked at the blade, rubbing the length of it along the edge of his robe to remove the dried blood. The etchings seemed to cling to the dark red more than the rest of the blade and the wizard had to work harder to clean them. After a while he restored the sword to its original beauty, admiring the craftsmanship. It was the first time he had really looked at the weapon. It had been Erzel's. Now it was to be Rhen's. He stood, determined to deliver it to her before he allowed himself to rest.

The walk through the castle was a little easier for him this time, now that his bad news had been delivered. He walked with his head held a little higher. He was still concerned about seeing Rhen again after such painful news. He arrived at the door where he believed the Princess to be staying and knocked softly. There was only silence and he waited a moment before knocking again.

"Who is it?" came a weak answer from within.

"Princess, it's Ectle. I... have something that now belongs to you. May I come in?"

There was no answer. The wizard waited for another few minutes before turning to leave when the door to the room cracked open. He could see the swollen eyes of the Princess, her expression one of pain mixed with curiosity. She opened the door the rest of the way and moved to the side, letting the wizard enter. She closed the door quietly and walked slowly to the edge of the bed where she sat, her hands folded in her lap.

"What do you have that you think is mine?" she asked as her voice cracked.

Ectle brought the sword up from his side and held it out horizontally in front of him within the Princess's reach. Her eyes followed the length of the blade before falling back down to the hilt and guard. She recognized it immediately.

"That's… is that Erzel's sword?"

"Yes it is. Though I was not able to recover his body for you, his sword remained on the field of battle after the portal collapsed. You were the closest one to him and it only seems fitting that the weapon now pass to you."

Rhen took the sword in her hands and let the tip of the blade rest against the floor, her delicate fingers wrapping around the leather handle. She traced the etchings and then looked up to the wizard.

"What about Lavian? This weapon belonged to the Celestial Knights. Should it not go back to her now that…"

She was not able to finish her thought as she realized she was about to admit that Erzel was gone. She swallowed and looked to the wizard, hoping he knew what she had intended to say. Ectle nodded, showing that he did indeed know why she had cut herself off.

"Lavian is still in the skies to my knowledge. She was there when I discovered the blade and did not show an interest in having it returned to her. With that no longer an issue, this sword should pass to you and your son… or daughter."

Rhen had never held a weapon with the intention of harming another in her life but holding Erzel's sword now brought forth the emotions and the ferocity that came with fighting for your life. The blade she now held had spilled its share of blood but in her hands she did not feel that urge. It was more of a symbol, a gift she would pass to her child when it was old enough.

"Thank you Ectle. I am sorry for how I acted in the gardens earlier. I know you too are surely hurting with the losses and I acted like… a child."

"No Princess," he said quickly. "I know there was no child in what I saw earlier. You acted out of love and out of heartbreak. You are no longer a child. If it brings you any comfort know that I will always be here to help you through the painful times. It was a promise I made your father, and a promise is something I will not break."

Rhen gave a weak smile and reached out, wrapping her arms around the wizard. She felt a tear on her cheek but she smiled anyway. "Thank you, Ectle, for everything."

After they broke she looked at him and he nodded to her, turning to the door to leave. He stopped and looked back at her, the sword still clenched in her small hands.

"Things will be alright, I promise. Rest now and I will check on you later. I have to see Elendil again."

"Ectle…"

The wizard turned back to her with his eyebrow raised. "Yes?"

"I lost Erzel, my father, my people. How am I supposed to make it through this?"

"Princess, this is not the end. Only the start of a new beginning. I promise you, the sun will rise tomorrow and with it, your future will continue. There is much to look to in the future and I will be there by your side to help you, I swear it."

Two days after arriving in Pentegarn arrangements were made for the burial of Tanis and Thorgrim in the city. Though it seemed fitting that the Wood Elf be buried back in Swanhaven the Queen chose to have him buried in Pentegarn at the base of a statue to be erected in his honor for the bravery shown in the fields outside of Qwaz. It would also serve as a permanent reminder of the alliance between the two races of Elves.

The same was said for Thorgrim who was buried not fifty yards away with his own statue to honor his deeds. The group had turned out in full, even Elendil who stood at attention with some help from a cane and a servant. His condition remained questionable although he gave weak smiles to all those who passed by.

As everyone gathered around Tanis's grave, Ectle walked to the spot where the statue would be erected. He had not rehearsed a speech nor planned to give one at all but in the moment he felt compelled to honor the Elf King. Ectle placed a hand on the top of the beautiful wooden casket and looked up to everyone who had gathered.

"A great King of Swanhaven has fallen, yet never shall he be forgotten. He is survived by the his wife, Queen Narissa, as well as his daughter and Princess of Swanhaven, Rhen. Though it is unknown at this time the gender of her unborn child, there is a line that continues even in his absence. We will all remember the sacrifice the King made on the battlefield the day the Demon was beaten and never again will there ever be a question about the alliance of our races. All Elves as one, no matter from where they hail."

Though the response from the gathered crowd was not loud, it was unified. They mourned his passing but celebrated his life. The soldiers on the sides of the casket lifted the ornately worked wood into the air and shifted, lowering it slowly down into the hole. With ropes they lowered it into position and as it came to rest the Queen and Princess came to the edge of the hole where the casket now rested.

Rhen raised her arm over the edge of the hole and opened her hand, letting a small bouquet of red and white flowers fall down onto the lid of the casket. They bounced and came to rest near the left edge, the feather of a swan just visible at the side of the strand of silk that bound them. She held herself together and stepped back to let her mother have the last few moments alone with her fallen King.

Narissa looked around and then her attention fell back down to the casket, her stare falling on the bouquet of flowers her daughter had dropped in. A few petals had been dislodged from the main bouquet and now danced along the edge of the casket, not yet ready to tumble over the side. She cleared her throat and forced a troubled smile.

"After all this time I can not believe you held onto that name. I had no idea then how much it meant to you. He will be a strong boy, and Naben will be his name. I just... how am I supposed to go on without you to lean on? How am I supposed to pull our people back from the wars that have done so much harm? How do I live without you, Tanis?"

But there was no answer, only silence to greet her. Narissa nodded and looked to the flattened stone pedestal where the statue would be placed to remember the King.

"We are burying you here in Pentegarn, an honor for one of our Elven background to be buried amongst High Elves. Then right here," she said, motioning to the pedestal. "Elendil has declared a statue be erected in your honor for the sacrifice you made to save our lands. Rhen and I will miss you horribly, but we are proud of what you have done for our people."

Further down to the right the Princess had stopped in beside Ectle as the group lowered Thorgrim into the ground. There were still a great many around to pay their respects as the Elves began to fill the graves. With the holes now filled with the cold earth, a group of masons began covering the fresh earth with an ornate pattern of bricks that led up to the base of the statues. Through the slow process Ectle and Rhen refused to leave the graves, waiting for the Elves to finish.

When they finished they left the Elf and wizard standing alone. They were quiet, the reality of what had happened in the past few days sinking in. The Elves had lost a King, nearly lost a second, and were now almost without any form of standing army. Their losses had left both Elven races in a frightening position.

"Ectle, what happens now? You and I both know there is hardly anything left of the Elves. What kind of future are we facing?"

"I can not predict the future, Princess, only make assumptions just like anyone else. The future will be what we make it."

Rhen took a step around the grave opposite the wizard and rubbed her arms as the chill in the air caught her by surprise. "Please, make an assumption."

Ectle nodded. "Very well. If I had to speculate I would think that both races of Elves will crawl back out of this and over time regain the strength they once possessed. For now though, there are troubling and harsh times ahead, rebuilding and rearming the soldiers and in the mean time the Dwarves will be around to help ensure we are all protected."

"Does that disturb you at all?"

"Perhaps a little. I do not enjoy putting my life in the hands of anyone, so to me it does create an unsettling feeling.

The wizard gave a bow to the Princess. "If you will please excuse me, Princess, I have much I need to attend to."

Rhen nodded and the wizard turned, heading into the castle. She stood alone now, thinking differently about the future.

The wizard had been right, the Dwarves would always be around to help protect them but as she thought about the lands before they were ravaged by war she knew that it would take a great deal longer to rebuild than Ectle had implied.

It was then that she realized that from the time they had all left Swanhaven, no Wood Elf had been back. Many of their people still remained in Eglarest to the north while what was left of the army was still there in Pentegarn. She wondered if the city had been hit during the many other battles across the lands. If so, what if anything remained of the home of the Wood Elves.

The wind brought with it new flakes of snow and the cold air drove her inside to find warmth. She felt horrible for leaving the grave of her father but the falling temperature and random winds were soon too much for her. Walking up the stairs of the castle she let her mind wander again until Erzel's face flashed through her mind. It was enough to make her stop in her tracks and she shook a little, not from the cold, but from knowing she would never see him again.

The Dawning of a New Age

Over the next two weeks Ectle remained close to King Elendil, watching every minute of his slow recovery. Compared to the condition he was in when the wizard first saw Elendil, the Elf was making amazing progress. Elendil finally managed to get out of the bed on his own power one cold morning as Ectle remained close by to help him if he were to have difficulties. After a brief walk out onto the balcony and then back into the room Elendil found his strength exhausted. He sat back on the edge of the bed and reached up with his right hand, tracing his fingers over the shoulder.

"Is everything alright, Elendil?" Ectle asked as he watched the King's expression.

The King gave a deep sigh. "This was my sword arm Ectle. What good is a King that can not even defend himself, let alone his people?"

"Your people will follow you no matter what. You missing an arm from a battle to protect them is not going to change the loyalties of the High Elves I assure you."

"Still, I no longer feel whole. I feel like a… like a cripple."

Ectle stepped to the edge of the bed and placed a firm, reassuring hand on the King's shoulder. "Elendil, raising your sword will not lead your people. You are a just, honest, and fair King, and that is what your Elves follow. You do not need to wield a sword when you have an army that will loyally stand with you."

Elendil knew the wizard was right but it was hard to find the light to reach for at the moment. His life had been altered in an unbelievable way and now he had to learn things all over again. Without his arm even simple tasks were now challenges.

His duties as King were now shadowed with relearning the other parts of his life that had been changed like simply eating and dressing.

There was a knock at the door and the guards opened it, allowing a messenger to enter. He bowed and turned to the King. "My Lord Elendil, there is news that the Dwarven forces who secured the Pass of Merwold have at last cleansed Qwaz and are now moving towards Nomaria under the command of the Elder Velex."

Ectle rolled his eyes. "They arrive in time to claim all the glory. Where were they while the Elves attacking Qwaz were being slaughtered?"

The messenger continued. "The Dwarves are also requesting assistance in clearing the mounds of dead that have been piled from the battles at the Pass of Merwold and at Qwaz. Soldiers as well as citizens of Pentegarn are urged to lend a hand."

The last sentences spurred anger in the King and he stood quickly from the bed, his head growing dizzy as he still had quite a recovery in front of him. Ectle put a hand on his back and steadied him as he too grew angry.

"You mean to tell us that the Dwarves, who were absent through nearly all of this war are now telling us what to do? They want us to clean up their messes?" Elendil snapped angrily, using the wizard's hand to brace himself.

"It appears their insults know no limits, Elendil. Please, sit back down."

He nodded weakly and strained as he lowered himself back down to the bed with Ectle's help. Through the pain and stress of what he was enduring, Elendil began to wonder how the Dwarves had grown so confident and become as insolent as they now seemed.

"Leave us," the King ordered, rubbing the sweat from his brow.

Everyone in the room turned and filed out, leaving only Ectle and the King of the High Elves behind. Elendil had regained some of his strength but it was apparent that the news was upsetting him. The King took a deep breath and wracked his brain for a moment.

"Alright Ectle, this is how it looks from my perspective. The Dwarves know they are stronger and they have the only standing army left in Nalawren. Having that on their side, it will not be long before Ardis tries to use that to his advantage. It is only a matter of time."

"Elendil, you look ill. Please, sit down."

The King waved off the wizard's comment and continued to rant and rave about the Dwarves and what he believed they were capable of. It seemed to only infuriate him more the longer he talked and the wizard stood, taking him by the shoulder. The moment his hand met the King he realized how hot his body was, coupled with the pale skin and relentless stammering. Ectle raised his hand to the King's forehead and realized that he was burning up with fever.

"Elendil, sit down at once. You are in no condition to be this upset. Come, sit down."

Elendil leaned against the wizard as he helped the Elf towards the bed, the temperature of his body now a big concern. Before Ectle could manage to get him to the bed Elendil's feet seemed to give way and he collapsed to the floor. His head rolled to the side and he murmured random syllables. Ectle knelt next to the King and turned to the door.

"Guards! Guards get in here! Physician!"

The door burst open and the soldiers moved into the room, confusion showing on their faces. The wizard was yelling at them but for a few moments they could not discern what was being said. Finally, after a particularly loud shout from the wizard the Elves seemed to snap out of the shock and scrambled to do as Ectle had ordered.

Ectle and another Elf grabbed the King carefully and helped him up onto the bed. He still seemed unconscious and every second they waited seemed like an hour. After a solid ten minutes a figure rounded the corner and hurried through the door, rushing straight to the side of the bed.

"What happened? How did this happen?" the Elf asked, checking for a pulse and then feeling the King's skin and its raised temperature.

"He was upset with a message he had received and then went pale. Shortly after that he started murmuring gibberish and collapsed on the floor. We moved him to the bed. Who are you?"

"I am the physician who was watching his condition through the amputation and shortly after. I had no idea his condition was worsening. I need my supplies. Keep him covered and keep him in this bed. I will be back in minutes."

The physician hurried out of the room without offering the wizard or the Elves any answers. They waited as they were instructed but the King did not regain consciousness. The heat radiating off of his body was incredible when at last the Physician returned.

"What is going on? What is wrong with the King?" Ectle asked in a harsh tone.

"He is suffering greatly. The fast rise in his temperature and him losing consciousness in the manner you described point to one thing…"

"Which is?"

"… infection."

The healer checked different things and then reached to the shoulder where the arm had been amputated. After pulling the end of the bandage loose he slowly unraveled the white cloth. The further down the wrap he got, the more stained the bandages appeared. At the end there was only a large cloth doubled and secured across the shoulder and under the remains of the arm. The cloth was dark from the blood loss as well as a dingy yellow in places.

The physician untied the strap holding it and slowly peeled it back away from the Elf's body. Underneath was a sight that made his breath catch in his chest. "Oh… my…"

"What is it? What is wrong?"

The physician laid the cloth back across the wound and turned to the wizard. His face was grim. "The amputation is severely infected. I can not understand it. Something as frightening as this looks would have been causing him intense pain. How could he have gone without saying a word?"

"I have no idea. What can you do for him? What will it take to clear up this infection?"

The physician seemed to ignore the wizard as he pulled the bandage away again, taking a second look at the wound. Ectle stepped to the side and looked past the Elf to the damage. He could see the stitches that held the wound closed and around them there was a great deal of oozing but it was not blood. The physician lifted the shoulder slightly and laid a crisp white towel underneath between the Elf and the bed.

All around the amputation and the stitches the skin was inflamed and swollen, the meat of the arm an angry red color. Elendil had never mentioned pain or discomfort, never once let on that he was suffering. A testament to his true strength, he did not want others to worry about him while there were so many other things that needed to be dealt with.

Ectle raised his voice harshly, making the Elf jump. "I asked you a question! What can you do for him?"

"I will do everything I can but at this point I will not say one over the other. Now please, leave me to my duties. If you've nothing else to do, see if there is another healer or physician available in the city. We are going to need everyone we can get to pull him through this one I am afraid."

"Fine, I will be back shortly to check on his condition. The King's guards will remain in this room and at the door at all times."

Ectle left the room with a bitter attitude growing on him. He had been demoted to finding someone to assist the physician instead of staying beside the King which is where he felt he should be. In the long scheme of things though he would do whatever he needed to do to see that the King was healed and well again.

"Ectle? What is wrong Ectle?"

The wizard turned and found Kail and Lavian behind him in the hall. For a moment he struggled with whether or not he should tell them everything but as he realized they had been through everything with him since it all started he gave in.

"King Elendil has fallen ill once more. There is an infection that has left his body drained and sickened and the physicians rushing to try to clean it up. He never said a word to me, to anyone. Why is that?"

Lavian and Kail exchanged glances and then she spoke. "Perhaps his honor is wounded at the loss of his arm and he felt he had to keep the pain inside to regain some of what he had lost. Relying on someone else is a hard endeavor but to do it just after losing part of yourself is particularly troubling. Is he awake?"

"No," Ectle murmured, remembering how the King had turned into a limp mass as he tried to help him to the bed. "He just went out and has not woken since. I suppose that is maybe for the better if he is no longer feeling the pain that the physician spoke of."

"He will pull through this," Kail said confidently. "Elendil is strong, maybe one of the strongest Elves in this city. He will pull through and be back to running this realm before we know it."

"Possibly, but I worry he will never be the same. Losing his arm caused more than just physical pains. To top it off, the Dwarves sent word that they expect our soldiers and citizens to help with clearing the battlefields while they march off to Nomaria."

"What!" the fighter shouted suddenly.

Ectle simply gave a nod as the Celestial Knight looked from the wizard to the fighter.

"They don't even bother coming to help fight when we need them and now they think they have the authority to command soldiers other than their own. Ardis has gone mad. These victories have gone to his head"

"Elendil felt the same way. He was in a torrent of rage about that very matter just before he collapsed."

"This is very disturbing. Where are you going, Ectle?" Kail asked, falling in line next to the wizard as he continued down the halls.

The wizard did not answer. The truth was that he had no idea where he was going at the moment. He was keeping an eye out for another physician or healer but at the same time he felt like he was just wandering aimlessly. Kail and Lavian followed the wizard through the halls and then out into the grounds of the city. The area was filled with both Wood Elves and High Elves, all working to repait the damages that the walls and buildings had sustained.

The wizard scanned through the masses of Elves with every intention of finding someone to assist the physician in the castle but he had other things plaguing his mind. At the moment the sight of the swollen infection that had taken over what was left of Elendil's arm crept into his head and he closed his eyes, trying to shake the image from his head. He struggled to replace the image with another, the King in full armor charging into battle, wrapped in an ornate cloak in the throne room of the city. As the Elves crossed through the city Ectle grabbed one of them by the sleeve.

"Excuse me sir…"

"I am looking for a healer or physician. Have you any knowledge of where to find one?" the wizard asked.

"A healer… I think there was one near the outer gates tending to the wounded who are still coming in. Now if you will excuse me," the Elf replied, pulling the sleeve of his robe free from the wizard's grasp.

Ectle nodded to the outer wall for Kail and Lavian to follow and wove through the Elves trying to clean the center of town. He passed the ruined buildings and then out through the gate that he had destroyed in the battle for the city. At the mouth of the gate were numbers of Elves helping those who asked for assistance. The wizard stopped and looked through the groups of Elves.

"I need a healer. Who here can assist me?"

A few of the Elves turned as they heard him but then continued their tasks at hand. When the nearest finished she turned back to Ectle and the two standing behind him. She waved to a bench with bloodstains across the top and sides from the numerous injured who had been helped.

"Where is your injury, sir?" the Elf asked as she pulled out a long stretch of clean cloth as well as a needle and thread to stitch a wound closed.

"I am in no need of healing but I…"

"Then move along please, there are plenty of others who do need help," she interrupted.

"I need you to collect your things and accompany me into the castle immediately. I may have no need of your services but I have been instructed to find another healer to assist the one tending to the King. You will follow me inside."

"The… King? I don't… no, I don't know if I should…"

"Listen, I am done negotiating with you on this. Collect your things and follow me. You can argue with yourself later as to whether or not you are willing to help your King. Hurry."

The wizard did not wait for the Elf to collect her things before turning and heading for the castle. Kail and Lavian hesitated as the Elf fell in with them and the group followed Ectle back through the city. He hardly bothered thinking about the task now, feeling it was something a servant could have accomplished, leaving him in the room by the King's side. With a deep breath he stopped and pointed to the door where the guards were keeping watch.

"Through there," he said, pointing to the door.

"Ectle, you seem a little irritable. Is there something we can do to make things easier for you?" Lavian asked, placing a gentle hand on the wizard's shoulder.

Ectle shook his head. "No Lavian, and I apologize for my temper. Things have been so hectic. I had hoped that after the fall of Infus and Valsera things would be simpler, but every day seems to add a new stress."

"I take it that the Dwarves have crossed a line with you?" Kail asked as he pondered the things the wizard had said earlier.

"I just don't understand it. What makes Ardis think it is remotely clever to give orders to other races when he and his Dwarves were not around to lend a hand while we fought and died all across the borderlands and then the pass. What, now the Dwarf believes that the size of his army gives him the right to command us?"

"What is going to happen then?" Kail asked, seeing the picture the wizard was trying to paint.

"Now we will wait and hope that the Dwarves do not push things too far. If Ardis thinks he is going to run over all the other races without someone to stand up to him he is wrong. Excuse me, I need a little time to think things through."

Kail and Lavian stood together, watching the wizard disappear around the corner. Even they felt the tension rising through the city as news of the Dwarven offensive against Qwaz and Nomaria spread. The majority had no idea that the Dwarves expected the Elves to assist after their heavy losses but it did not matter, morale was lower than ever before.

The Celestial Knight let out a deep breath and rubbed the back of her neck. She turned to the fighter and gave a forced smile.

"I think I will return to the air with my Warbird. It would benefit everyone to have a little time to themselves to pull their emotions together and straighten out their feelings. I will return later this evening."

With that Kail was left standing alone in the hall, knowing there was dissatisfaction spreading all throughout the city and not having the slightest clue of how to change it. Everyone was thankful that the Elves had been victorious, but they were still left with deep scars and open wounds.

At some point in the early morning hours there was a loud knock at the door, waking Ectle from a shallow sleep. He sat upright in a heartbeat, his eyes landing on the door where a sliver of light had appeared.

"Sir Ectle, the King has ordered your presence in his chambers at once."

The wizard was out of the bed and at the door in one swift move, following the guard up the hall to the King's chambers. A hundred things were going through his mind as he tried to decide why the King had summoned him. The guard stopped at the door and nodded to the wizard.

"I am not permitted in. You must continue alone."

The guard's words were even more confusing and the wizard pushed the door open. Inside he found the room bathed in the light of hundreds of candles, the flames dancing back and forth at the top of the wicks. His stare landed on the King at the edge of the bed, dressed in his royal attire. On one side of the King was an Elf dressed in plated armor and on the other another in crisp blue robes. In his arms was a roll of parchment.

The three looked up as the wizard entered, the looks on their faces bringing a twist of worry to Ectle's chest. "King Elendil, you summoned me?"

"Yes Ectle... please... come in... and have a... seat."

The wizard did as he was asked and the Elf with the parchment joined him at the table. The armored Elf remained by the King's side as the Elf and wizard took a seat opposite him.

"The time... has come... my friend," Elendil said through heavy breaths.

"A time for what, sir? Are you alright? What is going on?"

"Please... Ectle, let me finish. I no longer... know if I will wake... in the morning. I have no heir... no Queen... no one to... carry out my line. Ectle... I wish to... appoint you as my successor. Just until... I have healed enough and regained... my strength."

Ectle did not initially respond after hearing the King's request. He looked to the right at the soldier and then to the

Elf writing out the King's words onto the parchment. At last he looked back at the King and raised an eyebrow.

"King Elendil, with all due respect, I do not think I am worthy of such an honor. The responsibility of governing your lands and your people is yours alone sir. I could not…"

"Ectle! I can not run this city… or my people… in this condition. You know this. They have to have someone… they can turn to. You… are strong. You… are intelligent. You will stand for me… won't you?"

Ectle still did not want to answer the King but he knew that the Elf was torturing himself with pain the longer he stayed upright and pleaded. To be considered was an honor and to reject the offer would be foolish. He knew he would be faced with tough decisions but with the King urging him he felt as if he had no choice. Before he could give an answer the King continued.

"The people will follow your… decisions. Your orders will be as… if I gave them… myself. I promise."

The Elf slid the parchment to the wizard and the quill to sign it with. He saw the gap where he was to sign and hesitated once more. He looked up and gave a slow nod to the King.

"Alright Elendil, I will do it, but only until you have recovered. I want you to know that I am not comfortable with this though, and that I do so only out of the deepest respect for your wishes."

He fought through the urge to hesitate one last time and scribbled his signature to the bottom of what the Elf had written out. The Elf pulled the parchment to him and examined it closely before passing it to the King for his signature. King Elendil took the parchment and read it over before setting it down and signing it under the wizard. With the Elven soldier as a witness the King was satisfied.

"Thank you… Ectle. The ring."

The Elf with the parchment pulled a small golden ring out of his pocket and set it on the table in front of the wizard. Ectle reached out and picked it up, closely examining the piece of jewelry. The band was smooth until it reached the a small pair of overlapping leaves. He looked at the King who gave him a nod. With the assurance of the King he slid the ring onto his finger.

"You will rule with… mercy. Always remember the people… must have a voice. You will be their voice… and an ear for them. I... thank... you."

The King was finally beyond exhaustion. He could no longer support himself and slid back into the bed. The soldier in the room went to the door and opened it, summoning the servants to help the King. Ectle had not moved from the table, his finger tracing over the ring as he replayed the conversation he had just had. There was little in him that helped him believe he was capable of standing in for the King but he forced the negative thoughts out of his mind.

He watched the servants help the King into a more comfortable position and let him sink back into the blankets. The physician and healer reentered the room and went straight to Elendil's side to check his condition. One ran a towel across his forehead while the other checked the wounds under the bandages.

Ectle gave a nod to the King who was now asleep and turned from the room. He walked in a daze, unsure of what responsibilities he would now be faced with. The Dwarves were calling for the Elves to help them with the demeaning tasks of the battles they were waging including clearing and burying the dead. He did not want to steer them wrong in his first moments in charge of the city by defying the wishes of the Dwarven Elder.

The wizard walked to the throne room and stopped at the foot of the large Elven throne. He stepped up the first two stairs and ran his hand over the arm of the ornate chair. The wizard turned and looked across the room, hesitating as the thought of sitting in the King's throne gave him an unsettling chill. He did not belong there, sitting in the throne of the leader of the High Elves. He finally pushed the thought free and took the seat, taking his first breath as the head of Pentegarn.

Two days had passed since Ectle's charge to govern the city and the Elves. There had been very little that required his attention as the city was still struggling to repair and heal those wounded. He had not sent any soldiers nor workers to help in the cleaning of the battlefields as the Dwarves had instructed, feeling there was plenty that the Elves had to accomplish as it was. He soon learned that his choice had not gone over well with Ardis and Velex.

Everyone knew that the two Elders, Ardis and Velex, had

grown to power, taking over Odar's duties after his death. His forces now fell under command of Velex. Command had shifted and now Velex was the Elder of the Dwarven armies. Ardis was the Elder of any diplomatic affairs as well as the entire city of Tvan and its surrounding lands. Divos had not been heard from in some time but it was still believed that he remained the Elder of the mining community deep in the mountains of Tvan.

It was a particularly cold morning and Ectle had arrived in the throne room shortly after waking. King Elendil had shown no signs of recovery and it was feared that his condition was worsening, news the wizard had deeply hoped he would not receive. He had accepted taking charge of the affairs for a brief period but if the King were to pass from the sickness and infection he could not see himself ruling for an extended amount of time.

"Ectle, are you alright?"

The wizard glanced up to find Princess Rhen standing a few feet away. He brought his chin up off of the palm of his hand and blinked.

"I am sorry, Princess, what did you say?"

"I said my mother and I are prepared to leave. Is something wrong?"

Ectle shook his head and stood from the throne, dropping down the steps and offering his arm to the Princess. He walked her through the halls and then out into the common areas outside the castle. The majority of the Wood Elves in the city had gathered and pulled their resources together to prepare for their trip back to Swanhaven. They had been planning on returning and hoped the city had not been destroyed by war. Ectle had ordered a full battalion of swordsmen of High Elves to accompany them back to the city of the Wood Elves in case the Goblins had moved north without the Elves knowledge.

The Queen stepped up to the wizard and Rhen nodded to him, stepping in beside her mother. They stood a few moments in silence before the Queen finally broke it. Ectle had initially been against the Princess returning to the city without knowing for sure that it was safe, but finally offered the soldiers as a compromise.

"You needn't worry, Ectle, the King would never have put you in charge if he did not believe you were capable of the task. Soon Elendil will regain his strength and take the throne to restore the balance to the lands. We will keep in touch."

Ectle gave a bow to the Queen. "I thank you for your belief in my abilities, Queen Narissa. I will do all that I can to serve the people of Nalawren the way Elendil would. If there is any risk at all, please return to Pentegarn immediately."

"You have my word. If there is danger in our homelands we will turn and come straight back until it can be dealt with."

Narissa gave another nod to the wizard and turned to her horse which was being held ready for her. Rhen approached Ectle and wrapped her arms around him, a sniffle showing she was trying to hold back the emotions that were tearing at her. She had at her side the sword that Erzel had carried, choosing to not let it leave her possession for any reason.

"You need not be sad Princess. Things will work out in time. As well, I have given orders that the masons complete a statue in honor of Erzel and the sacrifice he made at the portal. It will be erected here in the gardens, a place he frequented and loved in the time he spent away from war. I think it would honor him greatly to have it here."

Rhen nodded gratefully. "Please send for me when it is finished. I want to be there when they set the statue."

Ectle gave a nod and held the door to the carriage for the Princess. In her condition the Princess would not be allowed on a horse. Just before the Princess could climb the steps into the carriage a soldier rushed around the edge of the group in search of the wizard.

"Ectle! Where is Ectle! Has anyone... there you are!"

"What is it? What is wrong?" the wizard asked as the Elf stopped before him.

"Sir, soldiers on the outer wall reported large forces moving into the fields. All reported as Dwarves but they are still in formation. We wanted to inform you as soon as we could."

Ectle looked up at the Queen and the Princess. He waved off the messenger and waited as Rhen dropped back down the stairs. Narissa turned her horse and stopped next to the wizard, not entirely sure what the Elf had said.

"What is the matter, Ectle?"

"I am not sure, Queen Narissa. It seems the Dwarves have arrived at Pentegarn in full formation. Please, remain here until I can get to the heart of this."

Ectle turned from the Elves to pursue the messenger to the outer wall but a voice stopped him in his tracks.

"That will not be necessary, Ectle, I can answer your questions."

To the right he found Ardis and Velex standing just inside the gate with a host of their soldiers behind them. They had sent no word of their arrival or news of any victories or losses in the south. The Dwarves arriving in the fields was a complete surprise to everyone in the city.

"Elders, I had no knowledge of your coming to Pentegarn. Please, forgive the nature of the city," Ectle said, hoping to put aside the appearance of the crumbling buildings and ruined wall.

"Well there are a few matters that are in need of discussion, sir wizard. I think it best if we make use of a little privacy. Perhaps Elendil will be so kind as to join us in the throne room?" Ardis replied without the slightest hint of concern for the repair of the city around him.

"He um... he can't... join us that is. Elendil has taken ill and is in no condition to leave his chambers."

"So you're telling me, that the greatest Elven city in all the lands now finds itself without any form of leadership? No one to see that things are kept in check? No one to rule these people?" Velex asked brazenly, waving to the Elves on the walls and throughout the courtyard.

Ardis shook his head at the Elder and nodded to the castle. "Come, to the throne room. We will discuss this a bit further once when we are inside."

Narissa left her horse and joined Ectle and her daughter as they reentered the castle and trudged through the hallways. Ectle had been plagued with issues about his ability to lead but now he was feeling them in full force. The Elders would question his abilities to keep the Elves moving in the right direction and it made him feel inferior.

Servants had already readied the throne room with chalices on the tables as well as pitchers of wine, water, and assorted ales. The wizard waited as Velex and Ardis entered, followed by Narissa and Rhen. Once inside he walked to the head of the table and took the seat below the throne.

"So... we've a slight dilemma here it seems," Ardis started, taking a chalice of ale and draining it in one long swallow. "Pentegarn without a King has about as much future as Qwaz after we purged the city and left it smoldering."

"It is not without a King! Elendil lives and until he has recovered from his wounds he has placed me in charge of the matters that involve Pentegarn and its people. I will speak for Elendil as he is not able to do so at the moment."

"Has he now? Well, that is a very interesting move by the old Elf. He has no heir, he has no Queen, and now a common wizard has been able to ascend to control over the city. Isn't the power just so exciting? So, seductive?" Ardis asked, refilling his chalice.

Ectle grit his teeth. "Not in the least."

Ardis could sense the wizard's hostile attitude and smirked briefly. He set the chalice down on the table, spilling some of the ale over the rim. "Alright then Ectle, seeing as how you are in control of the future of the Elves, I am going to help you with your duties. Steer you in the right direction, so to speak."

Velex laughed to himself as he finished off his fourth drink and reached for another. The Dwarves were abusing every hospitality the Elves had to offer and the complete lack of respect for the Queen, Princess, and himself was leaving Ectle somewhat scorned. After a minute of silence from the wizard the Elder leaned forward and pushed the chalice to the side, his eyes narrowed on Ectle's

"Alright then, I guess I will just tell you how this is shaping up. Swanhaven has no King, Pentegarn has a wizard as a steward, and the lands south of here are still teeming with Goblin forces. There has to be leadership and seeing as how my soldiers continue to fight against the tribes of Goblins that escaped the cities, I feel that I should offer myself to that cause."

Ectle looked to the Princess and Queen before turning back to the Elder. "What are you talking about Ardis?"

A smile crept across the Dwarf's face. "I nominate myself to rule Nalawren until the Elves have regained control of their people. Until Elendil has healed and until the Wood Elves have an acceptable King. This would be the least I could offer."

Ectle stood from the table, glaring at the Dwarf with an unbelievable look on his face. "Have you gone mad? Nothing gives you the right to rule the Elves, the High Elves or the Wood

Elves. You think just because your Dwarves are still fighting means you are entitled to own the rest of the races? You are a..."

"Careful wizard," Velex snapped, standing from the table.

"Calm down Velex, Ectle just hasn't quite caught sight of the good this will do for the Elves. After all, they will need help rebuilding the city defenses as well as its economy. They will need help in protecting themselves against whatever Goblin forces remain out there. Without us, the Elves are weak and vulnerable."

Ectle was still fuming at what the Dwarf was trying to accomplish but the more Ardis talked, the more the wizard realized that the Dwarves were needed. If Ardis and Velex were to pull their forces and strength back to Tvan they would leave the crippled Elven army and weakened cities open to other dangers. That was still not enough though to make Ectle agree.

"This is not something I could ever agree to. I will not turn the Elves into servants to another race. What difference would there be in being conquered by Valsera and being ruled by you and the Dwarves? No... "

Ardis did not seem the least bit surprised that the wizard was unwilling to agree to what the Dwarf had suggested. He tapped his right temple and smiled to himself, knowing he had already planned for resistance.

"Very well, your lack of cooperation will signify the end of the alliance between the Elves and Dwarves. Think of that for just a moment. Think of everything we Dwarves supply to the Elves. Aside from protecting what is left of your races, an end of the alliance would only further cripple your economic recovery."

Ectle was reeling inside. It was like the Dwarf had studied and rehearsed everything he would say to make sure it had the most painful effect on the Elves. Each sentence was almost strategic in the way it made Ectle second guess himself. Ectle pondered what the King himself would say in this situation. Would Elendil be lenient towards the aggression the Dwarves were showing or would he show them the same aggression?

"Ardis... what you suggest is an insult to the Elves and to any other race you look to rule. How do I know that you only intend to rule the lands of Nalawren while Elendil is ill and the Wood Elves are without a King? Suppose you decide the power is too seductive and you refuse to return rule to the Elven King?"

Ardis scoffed. "You worry too much wizard. I will rule Nalawren with an iron fist but a loose grip. My Dwarven soldiers will offer protection to all of the cities in Nalawren and if the Elves are able to take control of their lands themselves, we will sit down and renegotiate the terms of my ruling Nalawren. Of course, I could just leave."

Ardis started to stand from the table but hesitated briefly as the wizard looked to Rhen and Narissa. The two Wood Elves were watching anxiously to see what decision the wizard would make now that the choice came down to him.

"What do you think of all this Narissa? You've been quite silent."

The Queen looked at the wizard and bit her lip. "Ectle, you know as well as anyone else that I will never kneel to another ruler, foreign or domestic. Tanis ruled with me as an equal. He considered my opinion before he made a decision that would effect everyone else. I don't suppose my opinion will matter much with you ruling all of Nalawren, will it Ardis?"

"Of course it will. I will value the opinions of my subjects..."

"I will not be your subject." Rhen snarled, standing from the table and heading for the door.

"Rhen!" Narissa shouted to no avail.

"Ah, let her go. She's just a child and wouldn't understand what I am attempting to offer. So once again I turn my offer to you Ectle. What is it going to be?"

Ectle waved to the servant waiting near the door who immediately hurried to the wizard. "Go directly to the King's chambers and see if he is awake or conscious. If so, I will want to have his opinion on this matter. Go now."

The servant hurried out of the room and left the group to wait as he sped to carry out his orders. Ardis impatiently tapped his fingers on the table surface while Velex assaulted the remnants of the ale and wine. He had consumed more than three times as much alcohol as anyone else in the room and it was evident by his red cheeks and wandering eyes.

"So I take it we have more waiting ahead of us? I thought you were put in charge by Elendil? If you are in charge of the city and the Elves, why are you running to him for an answer?"

Ectle ignored the Dwarf and waited, his eyes continuously darting to the door as he expected the servant back any minute. When the door finally opened he nearly jumped out of his seat as the Elf approached.

"Forgive me sir, Elendil was not in a state where he could see me. The physician said that he has yet to wake today but his condition has not worsened. If you would like I could…"

"No, thank you. That will not be necessary," Ectle interrupted.

"So this is yet again, your decision. It should not be that hard. Either you trust in my offer or think me an enemy of the Elves and decide to go at this alone. What will it be?"

Ectle glanced to the right at the Queen of Swanhaven who only bit her lip and inhaled, waiting for him to answer the Dwarf. With a solemn nod the wizard turned his stare back to Ardis. "I will only agree to such a thing on two terms."

"Very well… name them."

"First, you will return power to the Kings and the Elven people when Pentegarn and Swanhaven have rebuilt and are no longer in need of protection. Second, you will release the captives from Cisalia. The Humans were not capable of defending themselves when Velex and his forces attacked them and their evil King has been punished for his betrayal as well as that of their armies."

Velex slammed the chalice down on the table, making the Elf and wizard jump in surprise. "I ain't gonna let them go nowhere. Those Humans fought my soldiers… they were the enemies…"

"They fought your Dwarves because you attacked them. Even a dog has the courage to defend itself if it is attacked. They were doing what they could to protect their people," Ectle interrupted, his voice even louder than Velex's.

"No… not happening… can't have them… forget it… they are mine…"

Ardis leaned over and grabbed the Dwarf by the front of his breastplate and shook him as if to sober him up some. "Velex… shut up and release the Humans. If the wizard wants them, he can have them."

Ectle nodded. "Those are my terms."

"I accept them. See, it wasn't hard to make the choice. Who needs Elendil when we have such a clever wizard around.

Come, let us drink to our future! Tonight, we will make this official!" Ardis said, picking up the chalice. He realized it was empty and looked around the table.

Ectle looked to the Queen who still had a concerned look on her face. She was supportive of his decision, even though it would put the Elves in service to another race, something they had never been forced to endure in their history. She finally gave him a reassuring nod and stood from the table, leaving only the two Dwarves and the wizard in the room. The wizard dug through his thoughts and remembered what the King had said just before falling unconscious. "The people will follow your decisions. Your orders will be as if I gave them myself. I promise."

The sun had disappeared and the wintry night reclaimed the lands. Just as the Dwarf had said, there would be a large ceremony to commemorate his new title as King of Nalawren. The Dwarves had spent the majority of the day drinking and celebrating in the fields and through the city while the Elves continued their tasks. The battlements above the inner wall had been changed from a bloodstained mess to a clean, crisp area where they planned to hold the ceremony for the Elder. From there, Elves and Dwarves across the city and fields would bear witness.

Ectle had spent a great deal of his time that day in Elendil's bedchamber, hoping that he would wake and the wizard would be able to tell him of the events that had transpired. Unfortunately the King never woke and the wizard was forced to leave to find something to calm his mind. Outside of the castle he found the Elves still busy.

Most of the buildings of the inner wall that had been damaged in the siege were now repaired and the rubble cleared. Food had been limited to stews and whatever the Elves still had available that could be rationed out to the people but as the buildings were repaired, merchants were able to reopen their shops and peddle their goods.

To the right was a small stand and though it was pieced back together somewhat lazily, the racks and stands had a selection of fish that had begun arriving the night before. With the sight Ectle began to wonder if the Dwarves were really going to make that much of a difference in restoring the economic strength to the Elven cities. He walked by the fish market, finding that bakers had also restored their businesses.

The smell of fresh bread was a spirit lifter for not only the wizard but for everyone else who had spent long days working to restore the city. To the Dwarves, it was just another source of nourishment. Ectle wound his way through the areas that were in the best repair, a small group of guards following him everywhere he went.

With the sun now gone the Dwarves in the fields and the Elves within the city moved in close to Pentegarn to hear the announcement the Elders had spread word of. The cold wind kept them all chilled as torches and fires gave off a wild flicker of light. Unfortunately they provided no warmth for those around them.

Ectle was standing at the edge of the inner wall when Narissa approached from the right side near the castle. She stopped and looked out across the mass of torches and people waiting to hear the announcements.

"Have I done the right thing, Narissa? I can't help but wonder if what I have done will lead us into a uncontrollable downward spiral. Have I doomed us all?"

Narissa shook her head and placed a hand on the wizard's shoulder. "No, I don't think so. The Dwarves may be bold and offensive toward us Elves, but they do have something to offer. I think only time will tell."

Ectle turned and stared out across a sea of soldiers, women, children, men, and elderly. Their eyes all trained up to the battlements where the Dwarves had constructed a special pedestal for the ceremony that would put Ardis high above everyone else. Everyone in the city waited and watched, not knowing when the Elder would appear. Another cold wind rolled across the city and the Queen of Swanhaven wrapped her cloak tighter around her shoulders.

To the right side of the battlements appeared Velex in his ceremonial armor, carrying an object in his hands covered in a red satin cloth. He stopped to the side of Ectle and turned, watching as Ardis slowly made his way across the battlements. He stopped a few feet away and looked out across the sea of people waiting to see what the Dwarf had to say.

"Ectle, you will join me at the top of the pedestal for the announcement. Wait until I have reached the top before you start up the stairs."

Ardis gave his orders clear and detailed, turning and taking hold of the rail and then ascending the stairs one at a time. When he reached the top he stopped and looked out even further, the thousands of flickering torches dancing with the breeze. He turned and nodded to Ectle who did as he had been instructed. He stopped beside the Elder and together they waited for Velex to do the same.

"Greetings Elves of Pentegarn, of Swanhaven, and Dwarves of Tvan. The wars have finally come to a close but what is left of our lands... of our people? Mere shadows of what they once were. I offer a solution.!"

The Elves and Dwarves crowded in a little tighter and waited, listening intently as the Elder from Tvan continued.

"After deliberation with the Queen of Swanhaven who so tragically lost her King in the battle at Qwaz and Ectle, the wizard who has been appointed steward of Pentegarn until Elendil has recovered from his injuries, it has been agreed that a new form of leadership take charge until the Elves have recovered from their losses in the wars. I have nominated myself for the position of High King of Nalawren, seconded by my fellow Elder Velex."

There was a mixture of murmurs and cheers that filled the air as the Elder revealed the extent of his plans. The Dwarves were happy with the news while both races of Elves remained somewhat reluctant to agree to such ruling. Not hearing the response he had expected pushed the Elder to revise his speech and continue.

"Obviously it has escaped many of your minds what will become of the cities of Swanhaven and Pentegarn if we Dwarves do not offer some sort of assistance. Your economy is almost nonexistent, your armies have nearly exhausted their strength, and the city of Pentegarn is in no condition to hold off another attack, when it again comes. We offer more than service to a new ruler. The Dwarves will provide protection to the lands while your Elves recover from the wars."

The Elves still did not seem too happy about what was being suggested but they were not able to deny that their races had suffered heavy losses. Acceptance was slow but it seemed that more and more of the Elves were beginning to see the good in what the Dwarf spoke of.

"Have I any opposed to what has been proposed?" Ardis

asked, looking out across the races that had gathered.

Ectle looked around as well, his eyes landing first on Rhen and then Kail and Lavian. In the back of his mind he knew that they were probably opposed to everything the Dwarf was saying but he hoped they would say nothing against Ardis. Rhen locked her stare with the wizard and Ectle gave a slow shake of his head, hoping to convince her that this was not the time for such an argument. Rhen simply turned her head and inside the wizard felt as if he had won a small victory.

"Very well, a resounding show of support from all of my loyal subjects. I will not forget you all and in time, everyone will be rewarded for their loyalties. Now, I will treat everyone to the first of my gracious gifts to come. Wood Elves, my army will accompany your forces to Swanhaven and ensure your people are well protected."

There was now a cheer from the Elves who were obviously concerned about returning to their homeland to find it under attack. Now there would be another army to help protect them. Their cheers continued until Ardis raised his hand, trying to quiet the crowds. As the noise died down he smiled.

"For the High Elves here in Pentegarn, every Dwarf with knowledge of masonry, carpentry, and ironworks will immediately be sent from Tvan to help in the rebuilding of the city. We will make Pentegarn bigger and better than before. With our help, the Elves will rise again!"

Now all of the Elves were in cheers, realizing that by allowing the Dwarf to rise to power they would possibly get their lives back. Dwarves and Elves watched together as Velex handed the wizard the item covered by the velvet cloth. Ectle turned and pulled the cloth off, revealing a magnificent crown adorned with a collection of rubies, emeralds, and a cluster of four diamonds, one meant for each of the races ruled under the Dwarf.

The beautiful gold crown glimmered brightly in the torchlight, the stones across the front and sides sparkling just as bright. Ectle raised the crown high and then slowly lowered it to the brow of the Dwarf. As the crown touched the top of Ardis's head, he closed his eyes and inhaled deeply as though a swell of power surged through him. He reached up with both hands and ran the tips of his fingers over the ornately designed crown.

As the Dwarf's gaze fell back onto the crowds they began

kneeling before the newly crowned High King of Nalawren. The Dwarves and Elves alike fell to a knee in a wave that spread from the edge of the wall out through the city and into the fields. Ardis turned and Ectle gave a short bow. He stepped to the edge of the pedestal and waited for the Dwarves and Elves to rise.

"A new King has been crowned... long live the King!"

The last four words were repeated and echoed across the field as an icy wind cut through the wizard. He stepped back and let Ardis have the front of the pedestal once more, his waves gaining more cheers and applause from his new subjects. The wizard turned and descended to the wall below where he was immediately joined by Rhen, Kail, and Lavian. He had not seen Nimir in days and Queen Narissa had watched the events from the upper balcony of the castle.

As he walked the top of the wall on his way to the castle Wood Elves and High Elves alike were patting him on the back and cheering for him. Now there was good coming to all those who followed the crown, relief that the Elves had been in need of since the fall of the Pass of Merwold. Now they could rebuild and restart their lives.

In the week following King Ardis's speech he held true to his word, sending his soldiers to the lands of the Wood Elves and pulling every able bodied Dwarf with a needed skill to the city of Pentegarn. The buildings that were starting to replace the old ruined ones now bore a touch of Dwarven design but the Elves were grateful all the same. With their city starting to heal from the horrible scars of the siege the Elves had slowly begun to trust the Dwarves further.

Even though the wizard had allowed the Dwarf to rise to the title of High King of Nalawren he still had constant concerns for the strength that the Dwarf now held. Deep inside he knew that one day Ardis would stray from his word. He was not sure how he knew, but something inside haunted him. When Elendil finally broke from his unconscious sleep Ectle was compelled to take full responsibility for the mess he felt he had created.

"Please Elendil, forgive me. I had no other choice in the matter. If I had not entertained the wishes of Ardis, they would have made us an enemy. I only tried to do as I thought you would if you had been able."

"Calm yourself, Ectle. Please, do not overwhelm your-self. In my absence you have acted admirably. We will see the true intentions of the Dwarves in time but for now we shall en-dure. You still have command over the city and its people. See that things continue as they have in the past."

"I will do as you wish until you are well again Elendil. Have you anything you need sir?"

"No Ectle, you have done well. Just keep your eyes on the city as you have promised.

The wizard left the room and sat out on the balcony for a while wondering about the condition of Swanhaven and the Elves who had left with the Dwarves. Rhen and her mother had been gone several days and he only hoped that their people had re-turned safely. He expected word from one of the messengers any day.

Below the castle he could hear the sounds of construc-tion and repairs all through the day and night. The sight of so many new buildings replacing the old and crumbling ones gave him a hint of hope, but he was still faced with the worry that the Dwarves would not be as accommodating and helpful after time passed.

"You've been quite distant for some time now Ectle. How can we help you?"

The wizard turned and found Kail and Lavian standing just inside the archway leading into the room. Ectle welcomed them out onto the balcony with a wave of his hand and they all looked out across the western edges of the city.

"I am fine, Kail. It just seems like I have handed the Dwarves all of Nalawren and now we are bound by that crown. I've taken Queen Narissa and turned her into a servant to another. I've done the same to Elendil. Not a week into taking charge of the city and I have created a mess out of things."

"That is not true, Ectle. You have insured that the alliance is still strong and will remain that way. The races may now look to another as their leader, but they will live on. They owe you that," Lavian replied as she tried to bring the wizard some sort of peace.

"Thank you Lavian..."

"The city would still be in ruins and in desperate need had the Dwarves not stepped in and helped. You may be worried about the future my friend, but what you have done here in the present will help everyone."

"... and thank you, Kail," Ectle said without emotion, trying not to insult the two.

"Ectle, if you are worried for the Wood Elves I will gladly fly out and see what I can find out. Perhaps I can bring back news that the city is without damage."

Ectle nodded and let out the deep breath he had been holding. "Yes Lavian, I would appreciate that very much. Please excuse me though, I have something I need to look into."

The wizard left them again and Lavian stood at the edge of the balcony looking out across the land. Smoke no longer rose from the charred buildings and blood no longer pooled on the battlements, another sign that the Elves were beginning to reclaim their city. She turned to Kail and nodded briefly before turning towards the room. As she passed the fighter caught her hand and stopped her.

"Come back Lavian. We will need you again before this has ended. Please, be careful out there."

They shared a moment, their eyes locked on one another as they waited for the other to speak. After some time she nodded and smiled, knowing inside what he meant.

'I will come back Kail, and you be here when I do."

A Strange New Nalawren

With Ardis now the High King of Nalawren the rest of the races began to look to him for what was expected of them. As he had claimed, the Human prisoners had been released and found safety once more under the protective watch of the Elves. With the massive repairs to the city of Pentegarn the High Elves were not available anywhere else in the lands, and the task of clearing the Goblins now fell solely on the Dwarves. With their fresh battles in the south the Dwarves also began claiming the fallen cities for their own, renaming them and stationing their soldiers there for future skirmishes.

In the south the cities of Nomaria and Qwaz were finally broken and the Goblins driven into the swamplands. The city of Qwaz was completely destroyed and Nomaria was taken over and renamed Mobye by the Dwarves.

On top of their victories in the south the remains of Cisalia were also taken by the Dwarves, and under command of Velex, it was slowly being rebuilt and named after a courageous young Dwarf who died in the battle but single-handedly killed an entire tower of archers and spearmen. It would forever be known as Brayr.

Lastly was the city of Mihlann which had been lost early in the war. The Goblins had laid waste to the city and after Qwaz fell, they had abandoned what was left of it. What remained was in no better shape than the former Human city, but the Dwarves claimed it for their own all the same. Their sudden interest in cities above ground was concerning, but with the good they had done, there was little the Elves or what was left of the Humans could say against them. Once cleared of the enemy Mihlann was renamed Voralla, in memory of another Dwarf who had died in the service of the new High King.

The wars had nearly emptied the city of Tvan as the Dwarves now made their stand across the lands of Nalawren, their soldiers claiming new lands for the Dwarven empire. If the claiming of the fallen and abandoned cities was not enough, the new High King pulled his Dwarves from the city of Pentegarn after the majority of the repairs and construction had been completed. With his people now back at Tvan the High King Ardis unveiled plans to build a massive structure to the north of Mobye in the attempt to bring all of Nalawren closer together. He called it the Arena.

The Arena looked to be larger than most cities in the lands with a single unspecified purpose. The Dwarf sought to use it as a way of entertainment for those loyal to him, and punishment for those who defied him. It brought with it mixed emotions and concerns from the Elves but the majority were still supportive of Ardis's plans. They worked nonstop through the days and nights as the Arena began to take on a life of its own.

With the Dwarves now focused on building the Arena and rebuilding Voralla and Brayr, the Elves helped move what remained of the Human race to the south of where Mihlann had once stood. The people of Cisalia broke ground on a new city that they could call their own. This time there was no King to rule them, no tyrant to sway their choices. They would start over fresh and new, their allegiance and faith renewed. Out of all the names the heads of the Humans settled on one that had no ties with Cisalia nor Qwaz. They decided to name their new city Rhiz.

In the summer after Ardis became the High King of Nalawren, Rhen found herself in the embrace of motherhood. She had been ordered to bed as the healer watching her condition soon found her exhausted without any real exertion. It was late one night when she found herself in a position she could not understand. Pain wracked her body and she could feel her skin burning hot and sweaty. The healer and physician were called and immediately they realized why.

The Princess's room was changed and the servants continued bringing clean towels and cool water for the young Elf. She knew now that her pain and struggle would yield results she had waited many months for and she kept that feeling in her mind through the ordeal.

Twelve hours passed and as the sun reached high into the sky Rhen gave birth. The sight of her child brought a tear to her eye, partly happiness for the life that was healthy and partly sad for the father who would never see his child.

"Princess, you have a boy. You have a son," the Elven physician said, wrapping the crying boy in a soft blanket.

The healer touched the Princess's forehead and then ran his hand across the crest of her stomach, his brow furrowed as he pressed the palm of his hand firmer against her. Rhen looked to the right at the healer and started to ask when he answered without waiting for her question.

"Princess Rhen, you must push again. You are not finished yet. Come now, push."

Rhen felt herself thrown back through the spiral of pain again. Inside she felt as if it were impossible, but shortly after her son entered the world, a second shrill cry followed his. The Princess fell back onto the pillow on the bed, her breathing finally beginning to return to normal. She waited a moment and then the Elf looked up to her.

"A girl. Dear Princess you have a son and a daughter."

Rhen still did not believe she had carried and birthed twins without even knowing, but now she was beyond exhausted. Her mother patted the back of her hand gently, a happy smile spreading across her face. The Wood Elves had another Princess and a Prince as well. She looked down as the Elves brought her two children up to her for the first time and again she felt mixed tears streaming down her cheeks.

She looked to the right and then to the left, her children twins, both with soft reddish hair. She forgot the pain and then there was only happiness. Remembering her father she turned to her son.

"You will be my Naben. The Prince of Swanhaven..." she whispered, kissing him on the forehead and turning to her daughter. "... and you, will be my Eryn, another Princess of Swanhaven."

She kissed her daughter as well and the Elves took the two away. Rhen watched as long as she could before lying back in the bed and feeling the tug of sleep coming for her. She could feel her mother's fingertips gently running through her hair and she closed her eyes, letting the world of dreams take her at last.

Narissa turned from the bed and headed out of the room to where the two children had been taken. Guards were already stationed where the Elves were cleaning and wrapping the two in blankets. The Queen looked down at her grandchildren, watching as Naben was already fighting with the servant who was trying to wrap him tightly while Eryn was sound asleep. They were two completely different little people though nearly identical while resting.

She reached down and touched Naben's cheek, causing him to open his eyes. The small, squinty eyes raked across the Queen and then around the room, everything appearing a blur. Narissa smiled and ran her finger down to his little hand, remembering her own daughter when she too was this size. As the newborn yawned she smiled and turned away to allow the Elves and servants to complete their tasks.

She walked out onto the balcony of her daughter's room, staring out across the trees and flowers that covered the ground in so many places. Splashes of color spread through the forests and as one bloom died and lost its radiant glow, another opened to take its place. Narissa leaned against the railing and wrapped her arms around herself. The thought of Tanis not being there to see the birth of Rhen's children pained her deeply. He would not see their faces or watch them grow up.

"We will miss you deeply my love. She has two children, a son and a daughter. Just as you had asked, she named him Naben. Her daughter she has decided to name Eryn. I wish you could see them, just like their mother. Red haired and so tiny. I will miss you Tanis."

With the last of the tears falling across her cheeks she turned and walked back through the door. Rhen was still asleep on the bed and she stopped long enough to bend and kiss her on the forehead, careful not to wake her. As the Queen continued on out of the room her thoughts turned to Erzel for the first time and she smiled, knowing the sacrifice he had made to ensure his two children were able to grow up in a safe land with their family.

The days after the birth of the two Elves flew by and so did the time that Ardis pledged to help the Elves. The city of Pentegarn had been nearly abandoned by the Dwarves who had been sent to help rebuild, their talents now turned to the new cities under the control of the Dwarves. The Great Arena required an unimaginable amount of rescurces and manpower as it was seen of utmost importance by Ardis.

His Dwarves soon ignored the Elves completely and though rebuilding and repairing were tasks that drained their energy and resources, the Elves were happy to still have a home to repair. In the winter following the complete pull of Dwarven assistance, Elendil finally regained his strength and was able to take back his throne. For Ectle, it was none too soon.

A full year under the wizard's control had left the Elves reeling and hoping their true King would return, even though Ectle had the full support of Elendil and the other High Elves. It was time to take back the lands that had been lost in the wars. It was in the first few snows though that Elendil soon learned Ardis had no intentions of returning power to the Elf King. In what turned out to be a swift and clever move, the Dwarf had smooth talked his way into the throne of all of Nalawren and now, when the cities could once again stand on their own, he refused to hold up his end of the bargain. Instead, the Dwarf sent back a message for the King of Pentegarn that the duties of his people now revolved around the lands surrounding the Elven city.

The rich lands were perfect for farming and the High Elves were now expected to supply food to the Dwarves and their soldiers while they constructed and repaired their new cities. A demeaning task made worse by the fact that more of the food grown in the Elven lands was to be sent out than was to be kept. For a time the good King kept silent about the matter but inside him was brewing resentment.

The High Elves had never served anyone and now that they were viewed as citizens of the Dwarven Empire, the Elves were seeing the shining light the Dwarf had promised changing to a dull glare. Ardis had brought them together and helped them all only to blind them to his thirst for power and control, a trait he had managed to keep hidden for a long time. Now, with the Dwarven army more than triple the size of any other, strongholds and cities all across Nalawren under his control, and immeasurable wealth to back him, the High King of Nalawren played his hand.

He would spread his armies to a point where they could march to any city that showed a hint of rebellion in less time than it would take to prepare the defenses. Having soldiers in every region and city gave him an advantage the Elves had not considered. It gave him power, fear, and the assurance that his rule would not be rivaled or rejected upon pain of death.

Now Nalawren was a shadow of its once glorious self. The Dwarves that had at one time hid themselves in the mountains were now the widest spread race in all the lands. Their numbers were impossible to judge and they continued to grow. In the years following the fall of the Goblin armies and the Demon leading them, the resentment toward the Dwarves grew throughout the lands, though no race had the power to change things. They sat in the dark, remembering the times of old and whispering plans for a future free of rule.

Every day they plotted brought The Great Arena that much closer to completion. Its purpose was clear, even though the Dwarves had never revealed it to the public. It would be a place for any suspected of treason and lesser crimes to bear their punishment. Rumors of similar arenas in other lands had sparked a fear in the Elves and Humans as one such story told of strange and wild monsters being brought from distant lands to fight those found guilty. For some, it would be entertainment but for others, it would just be an alternative to the gallows.

Rebellion was the word, and though just catching wind of such plans would spell death for all involved, the Humans and Elves spread word back and forth by means of secret messages and hidden meeting places. Getting caught meant their necks, but every new voice that agreed with the idea was a step in the right direction. The bravest would continue their secret meetings no matter what threats came their way, choosing to be the voice for those too afraid to step forward, those not willing to risk what little they had for a chance of freedom. In the end though it would all come down to who was willing to stand up and fight no matter what the cost. If the Elves and Humans were to ever be freed of oppressive rule, they would have to rise from the ruins once more.

Character Glossary

Elves

Erzel: High Elf who continues to lead the Elves and their allies into battle against Infus, the Demon who has taken command of Valsera's armies. He is charged with trying to rally the Dwarves and bring them to the south to help break the southern armies and protect the midlands.

Rhen: Princess of Swanhaven, left in Eglarest as Erzel and the others head to Qwaz to battle the sorcerer and his armies. She recently learned that she is carrying Erzel's child. This does not stop her from traveling across Nalawren to find him.

Elendil: King of the High Elves and ruler over Pentegarn and all of the Elven lands that stretch across the center of Nalawren. He is now tasked with preparing all of Pentegarn against the massive army that is moving north, in the hopes the Elves can hold off the siege until the Dwarves arrive.

Tanis: King of the Wood Elves and ruler over Swanhaven and the northern fortress of Eglarest as well as the forests that surround the middle lands. Pulls his forces back to Eglarest but soon decides to return to the midlands to help the High Elves and serve the alliance.

Narissa: Queen of the Wood Elves and mother of Rhen.

Kail: Returns with the group from the Dragon Isles and now remains exclusively by Erzel's side after it was revealed that he at one time served Valsera. The ranger now feels indebted to the Elf and makes every effort to help finish the Demon and the Goblin armies.

Dwarves

Thorgrim: Adventurer who remains with Erzel's group. He and Nimir find themselves lost in the swamps around Qwaz after the battle and fight to find a way back to the alliance in the north. He later finds himself in the middle of the siege of Pentegarn.

Nimir: Originally a miner in Tvan, he is stuck in the swamps with Thorgrim and is gravely wounded while trying to fight their way free of the Lizardmen. He survives and awakes much later as the siege of Pentegarn is coming to an end.

Velex: Elder Dwarf of Tvan in charge of all diplomatic affairs. He secretly brings part of the Dwarven army south to war against Cisalia.

Ardis: Elder Dwarf of Tvan in charge of the defenses on the surface and all soldiers that defend them. He leads the main army to Pentegarn with Odar, but he has a desire other than helping the Elves. His intentions are motivated by his thirst for power.

Odar: Elder Dwarf of Tvan in charge of the defenses underground and all the soldiers that defend them as well as ruler of the main fortress within the Tvan Mountains. He joins Ardis with the main army headed to Pentegarn.

Divos: Elder Dwarf of Tvan in charge of the massive mining community and the mines. He also handles all trade with other races and sees that the funds for their city never drop too low. Remains in Tvan to run the city.

Humans

Calyn: King of Cisalia. He reveals that he is no longer serving with the alliance and has fallen to serving with Valsera. He leads the rebellion at the Pass of Merwold and completely destroys the entire force of Elves there to protect it. He plots to kill Elendil to throw the north into disarray.

Dragons

Alora: Remains in Nalawren with the others, but after the battle at Qwaz she is one of only two surviving Dragons. She continues to offer her services to the alliance and after the battle of Qwaz, the deaths of all the other Dragons only intensifies her hatred for the sorcerer and his Demon.

Wizards / Sorcerers

Valsera: Battled with Erzel's forces and Yanosh in the throne room of Qwaz and is rendered immobile, frozen in a stand of crystals by the last spell Yanosh managed to cast. Now that he has been taken out of the action of the war, his next in command takes over the armies in his place. Only the head of Yanosh's staff could free him at this point.

Ectle: Leaves the group to try to find Thorgrim and Nimir after they are abandoned in the swamps as the battle at Qwaz is coming to an end. Later he returns to Pentegarn and does everything in his power to help hold off the armies of Goblins, Ogres, and Humans until reinforcements can arrive. Eventually helps lead the Elven armies to the south to end the war.

Valsera's Generals

Infus: Demon now takes command of Valsera's armies and sets out to reclaim the key to the crystals that imprison the sorcerer. The Demon has also lost the whip which it wielded on the balcony against Erzel, an item it actually fears. The Demon also has a very sinister plan for Valsera's armies and the weakening races of Nalawren.

Uljic: With Infus now taking Valsera's place as the head of the armies, Uljic moves up as well, leading the massive armies north to Pentegarn to start the siege. The creature shows complete disregard for his own soldiers, willing to let them all die to take the city.

Slayers: Insanely strong soldiers serving under Infus. Extremely strong and more resistant to damage than most soldiers. Their weapons are poisoned, inflicting intense pain and upon their death the body of a Slayer cracks and bursts into flames.

Celestial Knights

Lavian: The newly appointed leader of the Celestial Knights after the fall of Yanosh and Galador. She continues to offer her skills to Erzel and the rest of the alliance. The loss of her fellow Celestial Knights has put a renewed hatred in her heart for the Demon and its Slayers.

Odimous: One of the last few Celestial Knights. He briefly takes command of the Celestial Knights when Lavian leaves for Tvan with Erzel and the others.

City Glossary

Pentegarn: The center of the lands of the High Elves, ruled by Elendil. Of all the cities in the lands, it is the largest, second only to Tvan. From a distance it could be confused with a mountain. To everyone inhabiting the city, it is impenetrable.

Swanhaven: Home of the Wood Elves nestled deep in the forests. It is ruled by Tanis and Narissa and has very little in the form of defenses, as the Wood Elves prefer a more peaceful nature. Most Wood Elves have abandoned the city.

Tvan: Home of the Dwarves and hidden beneath the Tvan Mountains. The city never sees the light of day but houses an army so vast it would match that of all the other races. The Dwarves prefer to remain hidden in their mountains and dig for their riches. The defenses of Tvan stretch from the lands above ground to the heart of the mountains.

Cisalia: Last home of the Humans after they were forced to flee the southlands during Valsera's invasion. Ruled my Calyn, the Humans have taken their alliance for granted, their new sights set on backing Valsera and his seemingly unstoppable armies.

Qwaz: Originally the city of the Humans, Valsera swept over the lands and pushed them north, taking the city for himself and smothering it in the Goblins that served him. Once a beautiful and proud castle, it is now dark and falling into ruin. A staging point for Valsera's invasions. Qwaz has now become a tomb for Valsera, the crystals imprisoning him and forcing his armies to now serve the Demon Infus.

Nomaria: Fortress city constructed by Valsera after the Chaos Wars ended. It serves as his permanent castle and from it he plunges himself into the dark magic from an ancient time. His darkest soldiers were created in Nomaria. The Slayers that had inhabited Nomaria are now moving north to Qwaz.

Eglarest: Large fortress to the east of Tvan, ruled by Tanis of Swanhaven. Since the Wood Elves at Swanhaven have very little as far as defenses, in times of war they tend to move north to the fortress of Eglarest to protect their people. The fortress has never seen a crippling battle.

Murm: Large trade city west of Tvan. It is a center for almost all trade and goods in Nalawren. Also, it is also the largest port city in all of Nalawren. The city remains neutral with a diverse number of races inhabiting the city.

Brayr: After the Dwarves purged the city of Cisalia, the Elder Velex ordered the city be renamed after a Dwarf who was killed in the battle. The Dwarves then take control of the city for their own, using it as another city for their vast armies.

Mobye: Nomaria is cleansed and cleared and shortly thereafter the Dwarves move their forces into the southlands, securing a foothold in the southern edges of Nalawren. The Dwarves begin their tight hold on the lands here.

Rhiz: After the Humans are released from captivity by the Dwarves, the High Elves of Pentegarn help them reestablish a city to the south of Mihlann. The Humans are able to start over, with their tainted pasts behind them. Rhiz becomes a breeding ground for trade and invention.

The Arena: With Qwaz now smoldering and fallen to waste, Ardis chooses to build a new structure in its place. The Great Arena becomes a beacon for the Dwarves in the future, creating entertainment for the Dwarves and a form of punishment for any who defy the new High King of Nalawren. It is larger than most cities with a central field of sand where combatants are pitted against others in games that test their strengths, their wits, and their lives.

Voralla: The last of the cities to be cleared of the Goblin soldiers is Mihlann and though the Elves at one time considered it one of the heaviest defended cities in their realm, they are hardly concerned when the Dwarves claim it for their own. The city is rebuilt and becomes another fortress in the Dwarven empire.

www.ingramcontent.com/pod-product-compliance
Lightning Source LLC
Chambersburg PA
CBHW070350260626
47161CB00001B/92